true calling series - book two

LOVE'S TRUE
Home

Blessings
Prov. 16:3

LORI DEJONG

Scrivenings
PRESS
Quench your thirst for story.
www.ScriveningsPress.com

For Daddy.

CHAPTER ONE

*T*he bouquet sailed through the air, like a guided missile zeroed in on its target.

Hemmed in all sides, Ally had no choice but to catch the thing. That, or let it hit her smack in the face, which would be even more humiliating than being out here to begin with.

Why, oh why, hadn't she gone to the ladies' room when they announced the tossing of the bouquet? Or pled a stomach bug and skipped the wedding altogether?

Because she didn't want to look like a heartsick sore loser, that's why.

So the man she'd once considered the love of her life had just married the love of his. She was over it. She was.

Mostly.

Squeals split the air as her friends, including the gorgeous bride, enveloped her in a group hug.

Ally's gaze traveled past the women surrounding her. Wyatt, *aka* The Groom, stood across the ballroom amidst a crowd of kids from ConnectUP, the student ministry he'd founded and with which she still volunteered. He leaned back and laughed, and thankfully, her pulse didn't do that skippy thing it had the first moment she laid eyes on him in their

1

college library almost four years ago. A welcome sign much progress had been made in her Year of Getting Over Wyatt.

After posing for the obligatory photo with the bride, Ally returned Harper's tight hug. If anybody understood how weird this was for her, it was Harper.

Ally pulled back and looked at her radiant friend. "I'm so sorry if I've made this at all awkward for you."

Harper put her hands on Ally's shoulders, her green eyes sparkling. "I'm happy you caught it. God has something wonderful planned for you, beyond your wildest dreams. And I can't wait to see what that is." She leaned in close. "Or who."

Ally chuckled, buoyed by her friend's sincerity ... and humor. "Me, either. But please know how happy I am for you. For both of you."

After another hug, she returned to her table while Harper joined Wyatt at their four-tier cake festooned with strings of pearls and fresh, blush-pink roses. When the newlyweds fed each other, the wedding guests' *ahhs* floated through the room while the ConnectUP kids egged them on to not be so neat about it.

The teens' antics made her grin, until her breath snagged in her throat when Wyatt and Harper shared another tender kiss. They truly were beautiful together, in every way. A match made in heaven. Or in kindergarten, according to Wyatt's toast to his bride, for that's when he said he first fell for her.

Her friend Shannon, a striking, petite blonde in an emerald-hued bridesmaid's dress, set a glass of punch on the table before taking her seat. "Who is that tall, scrumptious-looking drink of water? With the flower girl."

Ally followed Shannon's line of sight to a dark-haired man with a little slip of a girl in a frilly, white dress perched on his back, his elbows hooked around her legs. He jostled her up and down, and her giggles rang out across the room. His suit coat and tie were no doubt hanging on a chair in deference to the mid-July Dallas heat, and he'd rolled the sleeves of his white dress shirt to just below his elbows. His wide smile never left his face, and Shannon was right. He *was* tall—at least as tall as Wyatt, who at six-foot-two had been the perfect height for Ally's five-nine. Back when it mattered.

"Considering the girl is Harper's niece, my guess would be a family member. Maybe a cousin?" Her hand found the pendants hanging from a thin, silver chain around her neck, her index finger running across the surface of the little house that hung there with four others. One in the shape of Texas, another of a small dog, a bouquet of flowers, and the last one a cross, reminding her to keep Jesus in the middle of it all. Her dream charms, she called them. Like her own personal vision board worn above her heart.

"Maybe. No wedding ring." Shannon picked up her glass. "I saw him earlier and looked."

Ally let go of the small charm and laughed at her friend, another CU ministry leader, and one of her favorite people. "You're impossible."

Shannon finished off her punch and looked back across the room at the handsome stranger. "Cute-guy-with-no-wedding-ring doesn't look like he has a plus one. You should ask him to dance when they start."

"Not happening. He's all yours."

"No, ma'am. I'm taking a break from dating after things went south with Joel." Her always bright countenance clouded. "I wish he hadn't left ConnectUP just because we broke up. The kids loved him, and he enjoyed working with them so much. I feel like I ruined that for him."

Ally reached over and rubbed Shannon's shoulder. "His reaction is not your fault. You couldn't stay in a relationship you didn't believe was right for you. And if it wasn't right for you, then it wasn't right for him. He'll see that someday."

Just as she had. Finally. Coming back from a year-long, self-imposed sabbatical in Central America to find Wyatt had moved on squashed any hope he might have reconsidered in her absence. But seeing him with Harper over the last several months, well, it was impossible *not* to know he was with exactly who he should be.

The lights dimmed as Harper walked onto the dance floor with her father, followed by Wyatt's dance with his mom. Harper then joined him in the middle of the floor for their first dance as husband and wife, Arlene handing him off with a kiss to the cheek of her new daughter-in-law. All eyes followed them as they swayed together, their arms around each other and faces close as they spoke words meant for nobody else. And when Wyatt took his new wife —*his new wife*— by one hand, spun her, then pulled her back into his arms for another kiss, Ally's chest hollowed, as if all the air had left it. The image in front of her blurred. What she'd said to Harper was true. She sincerely was happy for them.

But some dreams were hard to let go.

Zane smiled as the limousine pulled away amidst cheers and waves from the wedding guests. The new Dr. and Mrs. McCowan were on their way to building a life together, and he couldn't be happier for them. Maybe he hadn't known them as long as most of the others, but working so closely together over the last seven months, albeit from two different states, had made them more like family.

Closest thing he had to one, anyway. Which was fine. He was used to it. He made family-friends every time he settled in a different place or in a new job. What did Harper call them? Framily. That was it. They were framily.

Over their time together, he'd heard all about Wyatt and Harper's story. How they'd been best friends as kids until a falling out in high school. They hadn't seen nor spoken to each other for over ten years before she showed up as a student in a psychology class he was subbing in at Dallas Heritage

University. They rekindled their friendship, which quickly blossomed into something more, and now they were husband and wife. Two years younger than his thirty-one and on their way through life together. As a unit. A partnership knit with strands of faith and trust, love and respect.

What must it be like to find the *one* who filled that space inside your heart shaped only for her?

Back in the much cooler ballroom, he bobbed his head along to the catchy country tune. Some of the remaining guests hit the dance floor while others clustered in small groups at tables to visit. At his chair, he pulled his phone from the pocket of his suit coat he'd left draped over a chair. He winced at the missed call notification that popped up on his screen. Considering it was an hour later in Atlanta, he should return it now rather than later.

With the music and dozens of voices talking and laughing all at once, he needed to find a quiet place to make the call. He threaded his way through the tables out to the terrace, disappointed when his friend's voicemail picked up.

"Hey, sorry I missed you." He turned back toward the ballroom. "I'm at the reception but give me a call when you get this."

He opened the French door to return to the cool inside and nearly collided with a woman on her way out. Her head popped up, and she stopped short. "Talk to you later, Phebes." He disconnected and looked at the young lady standing in the doorway. "Sorry 'bout that. I shouldn't walk and talk at the same time. Dangerous combination."

"No, I'm sorry." She stepped to the side. "I wasn't watching where I was going."

He tipped his head. "You're the one who caught the bouquet, right?"

Pink suffused her face. "Yes. Excuse me."

Her voice broke over the words, and her eyes filled before

she walked away, which told him her evening could only go up from here.

She stopped at the ornate, Italian-esque balustrade, her arms crossed tight over her middle as she stared out over the courtyard below. Something wasn't right, but he didn't know her from Eve. Best to let her be.

On his way through the door, he took another look over his shoulder. She was tall, thin but not skinny, with thick, honey-blonde hair falling to the middle of her back. When she sniffled and brushed a finger under her eye, he reached out, letting the door hit his open palm before it could close. Probably not the wisest idea to get involved in some emotional business that wasn't his, but now that he was aware of her, how could he just leave? He was a minister, after all. This was his calling, to help others.

He moved toward her and stopped several feet away so as not to startle her. "Excuse me. I know I'm overstepping, but is there anything you need?"

She swiped at her face but didn't turn. "Um, no. I ... I just wanted to get some air."

A tear rolled its way down her cheek, and he questioned again the pull that had brought him over here. He wasn't all that great with tears, seminary degree or not.

He pulled a handkerchief from his back pocket and held it in front of her. Dad was right. One never knew when a hankie might come in handy.

She hesitated a moment before accepting it. "Thank you." She patted her cheeks, then glanced over at him. Something was definitely up. Or the girl really didn't like weddings.

"Can I get you a glass of punch? Or water? I think champagne is the only thing stronger they're offering, but I can grab you one. Or three."

That elicited a small chuckle. "No, I'm fine." She looked at him again. "Thank you, though."

"No problem." When he didn't move, she held out his handkerchief. "Keep it."

She nodded and turned away again.

Should he go away? Leave her to her thoughts? Her rigid posture screamed that's exactly what she wanted. But he couldn't make himself walk away.

The crickets and the muffled strains of a country tune blended in the air around them as he debated what to do next. *Lord, a little wisdom here, please. Do I leave her alone? Do I stick around? What would You do?*

The answer came as quickly as his plea. Jesus had never left someone in need.

"They say I'm a pretty good listener, if you need an ear. Or two. Which I have."

Another chuckle escaped. Good. If he could get her laughing, she might even decide to go back in and join the fun. He'd noticed her earlier, line dancing and laughing it up with her friends. What could have happened since then?

He took a step closer to lean against the balustrade, stuck his hands in his pockets, and grinned at her. "You know, I've been to a lot of weddings, and I've seen women practically tackle each other to catch the bouquet. But I don't think I've ever seen someone try so hard to *not* catch it."

Even in the dim light, he noticed the blush that tinged her pretty features. She looked down at her hands, twisting the handkerchief around her fingers.

"I figured you had a flower allergy or rose phobia or something." He gestured toward her with his head. "Clearly, it's an allergy."

A smile pulled at her lips when she raised her eyes to him. "Yes. Exactly. That's what this is. Allergies."

Her willingness to banter encouraged him to keep her talking. "So, honestly. What's the story with your aversion to bridal bouquets?"

She shook her head. "It was a little … awkward, I guess you could say."

"Not from what I saw. Maybe you didn't want to, but your catch was spot on. Like a third baseman fielding a line drive without thinking about it."

This time her smile revealed straight, even teeth set behind full lips with only a hint of added color. She didn't need it, in his opinion. But then, he preferred the natural look.

"Didn't want to take it in the face, or duck and let it hit Shannon, who was hiding behind me." She rolled her eyes. "Chicken."

Progress. He'd take a smile any day over tears. And she apparently had a sense of humor.

A breeze lifted a lock of her hair, and she brushed it behind her ear. Her hand moved to the pendants hanging around her neck to slide them back and forth along the delicate chain. He'd never seen someone wear more than one on a chain at the same time, but these delicate charms suited her.

Peals of laughter, the hum of conversation, and the strains of a power rock ballad made their way to the veranda when the door opened and a couple stepped outside. Would she want to dance if he asked? Or was there another guy in the picture? Perhaps the reason she was out here crying instead of partying with the other guests?

When she offered nothing more about whatever had brought her out here for *some air*, he cleared his throat. "Um, I was wondering, would—"

His phone vibrated, and he reached back to pull it from his pocket. He checked the screen and swept his finger from one side to the other. "Hey, Phoebe. Just a sec." He took the phone away from his ear. "I'm sorry. I need to take this call. A work thing. But, listen, I'd love to talk some more. Would you save me a dance?"

Her face blanched, and she let go of her necklace to wave him off. "It's fine. Don't worry about it."

8

"No, I mean it. I'll look for you in a few minutes."

She only nodded before he turned and put the phone to his ear. "Hey, thanks for calling me back."

Ten minutes later, he returned to where he'd left the pretty lady in the light floral dress. When she wasn't there, he went inside, where the reception was still going strong. He walked around the ballroom, even watched the hallway that led to the restrooms for a few minutes, but she never appeared.

Ashlen, Harper's three-year-old niece who'd acted as the flower girl, skipped by carrying the bouquet her aunt had tossed earlier. "Hey, Ash."

She turned around, and her little face lit up. "Mr. Zane! Horsey ride!"

"Sure thing." He knelt down and helped her climb up onto his back again, the bouquet still clutched in her hand now dangling below his chin. The scent of roses wafted around him. "Where did you get your pretty flowers?"

"Miss Kay gived 'em to me."

Kay. He at least had a name, although it was clear that dance wouldn't be happening. Guess his mystery lady would have to remain just that.

CHAPTER TWO

$\mathcal{O}$n time and with five minutes to spare.

Ally let herself in the front door of Wyatt and Harper's house just before seven after getting caught late at the hospital. She'd barely had time to change out of her scrubs into shorts and a light blouse to make it to the Monday ConnectUP planning meeting. The cool air in the foyer offered a welcome respite from the late August heat as she followed the cacophony of voices and laughter down the entry hall to the family room where the other eleven team members gathered.

"Ally!" Harper scurried around the expansive kitchen island to envelop her in a tight hug. Honestly, Harper gave the best hugs. One never walked away from a Harper hug without knowing they were cared for.

Ally pulled back and smiled at her beaming hostess. "Wow, married life looks good on you."

"You're very kind. And look amazing, as usual. Let's plan a day here soon to catch up."

"Absolutely. As long as it involves shopping."

"But of course! We'll get Rhonda, Shannon, and Yolanda, and make a girls' day out of it."

Wyatt walked up and drew her in for a side hug. "Great to see you. It's been too long."

Five weeks, to be exact. The newlyweds had been on their Hawaiian honeymoon for ten days, and, since taking more administrative duties with ConnectUP, they'd given up their leadership of the Arlington club to move around all four. This would be their first time back with their original team since the wedding.

And the first time Ally had seen them since they left their reception to begin a new life together. But instead of the heaviness of heart from that night, she now sent up a silent prayer of gratitude that she no longer experienced a sense of loss around Wyatt. In its place was peace in accepting that, although her first love, he was never meant to be her forever love.

"Good to see you too."

When Reed, Wyatt's older brother and new captain of the Arlington club, called for everybody to find a seat, Ally planted herself on the short side of the sectional between Shannon and Jenny, Reed's wife and her long-time friend.

Jenny grabbed her hand. "Oh, good, you're here!"

Ally laughed. "Where else would I be on a Monday night?"

"I wanted to make sure you didn't miss the new guy from Becker. Came in Saturday and we met him yesterday at Sunday dinner. He's staying here with Wyatt and Harper until he finds a place. I thought you might've seen him at church."

"I had a shift at Memorial, so I went to the early service."

Another temp job she wouldn't be making permanent, like the other three offers she'd turned down. Being back in the States and volunteering again with ConnectUP was a joy. The job front, not so much. If only she could find something here that brought the same satisfaction as working with the people in Central America last year.

"Great guy." Jenny continued. "Very handsome. *Very* single."

Ah. That's what Jenny was up to. "Then I hope he finds himself a nice Texas girl."

"You're a nice Texas girl."

Ally shook her head. "Jen, honestly, I'm in a really good place right now and not looking for a guy." Her fingers went to the pendants around her neck. "If God wants to bring a man into my life, great. If not, I'm content to plant my roots right here on my own." In her someday house, with her someday little dog and a flower garden, with Jesus in the middle of it all.

With a self-satisfied grin, Jenny gave her hand a squeeze. "I love hearing that. But when you're truly content, that's usually when you find someone. Trust me. I've had outstanding success putting folks together. I even got Steve and Yolanda together, as you know, after they'd been circling each other for months."

Ally shrugged. "I have to admit, that was a good one. But if I lose my roommate, Jen, I may have to move in with you."

Roommate, best friend. The sister of her heart. Although Yolanda was dark-haired with the soft, brown skin of her Guatemalan heritage, while Ally's ancestors were decidedly Scottish.

"We could do a lot worse than having a live-in pediatric nurse with our three hooligans."

Ally grinned as Reed called for everyone's attention. But she found it difficult to focus when cute-guy-with-no-wedding-ring popped into her mind. And not for the first time in the past five weeks. What a rotten time to meet someone whose dimpled grin made her kind of squirmy-in-a-good-way inside.

But that night had also knocked some sense into her. The mortification she carried around for days after the poor guy found her in the throes of her own pity party had her chastising herself for continuing to wallow in the pit of broken dreams. It was past time to pick herself up, dust herself off, and recommit to being everything the Father already said she was. Loved, redeemed, treasured, forgiven. Everything they worked to instill in their CU kids. Now she had to practice what she preached.

Twenty minutes into their meeting, Reed smiled at someone behind her. "Zane. Welcome. We'll be finished here in a minute, and then we'll introduce you to everybody."

"No hurry," the voice behind her said. "Happy to listen in."

Tingles cascaded over her skin, from her scalp down to her toes. That voice. It couldn't be. She must be remembering it wrong. She'd only spoken to cute-guy-with-no-wedding-ring for a few minutes. No way could she know his voice so well, no matter how many times she'd heard it in her daydreams. Jenny smiled and waved at the man behind them over her shoulder, but Ally didn't have the nerve to look.

Once they'd finished their topic prep for Wednesday's conversation circles, Wyatt took his brother's place in front of the fireplace. "As y'all know, without Becker Ministries coming alongside to sponsor ConnectUP, we wouldn't be anywhere near where we are right now, with three new clubs launched in the past six months. But because things are happening so quickly, the Becker board decided we should have a representative here in Texas. Which brings me to Zane Carpenter."

He looked over and smiled at the man still standing somewhere behind her.

Please, God. Let me be wrong.

"Harper and I met Zane last December at Becker Ministries' headquarters in Atlanta, and over the last several months, he's become a brother we've grown to love and respect. He's picked up his life in Georgia to follow God's leading, and we're beyond blessed to have him."

He held out his hand. "Zane, why don't you come say a few words. Y'all, let's give him a big Texas welcome."

The leaders clapped and whooped as if George Strait himself had paid them a visit. *Please, God, don't let it be—*

Ally's heart dropped to her stomach and hands halted mid-clap as the man rounded the end of the sectional and stopped beside Wyatt.

Oh. No.

Shannon looked at her with a bright smile and eyes open wide. "That's cute-guy-with-no-wedding-ring!" she whispered.

He most certainly was.

Jenny leaned in on her other side as the clapping died down. "Told you he was handsome."

Yep, already aware. Up close and personal. Way too personal. He'd seen her at her most vulnerable. Yet she knew nothing else about him, other than he was apparently in the habit of carrying a handkerchief.

"Thanks, everybody, for that astounding welcome." The same voice that had asked her if she needed anything on the veranda spilled out into the room. His eyes passed her and darted back again, zeroing in and bringing a heated flush to her face.

Or maybe she picked up a bug working the pediatrics floor at the hospital.

His smile grew as he stared at her for another few seconds. A few seconds listening to her heart beat against her eardrums.

"I recognize a few familiar faces here." He looked away, and she began to breathe again. Passing out would definitely bring attention she didn't want. "I'm excited to jump in and see what we can accomplish together. We've been working on some strategies for new launches, fundraising, and volunteer recruitment, but I'm looking forward to seeing you all in action."

His eyes strayed to her again, and she wished the couch would swallow her whole. What must he be thinking, seeing her here oh so comfortable in Wyatt and Harper's home after finding her crying—*crying!*—at their wedding reception only weeks ago?

He offered a few more words she barely heard, turned the

floor over to Reed to finish up the meeting, then joined Harper at the breakfast bar.

Jenny angled her head toward Ally. "He totally noticed you."

Shannon leaned in from her other side. "You should've asked him to dance at the wedding."

Ally's face heated up another alarming notch. Yes, he'd noticed her, but for all the wrong reasons, she was sure.

Keeping her focus throughout the event planning portion of the meeting proved a futile endeavor. They had the back-to-school barbecue and swim party to organize, as well as the annual Labor Day trip to Six Flags with all the other clubs. But her scattered thoughts had other priorities. Mostly trying to formulate a plan of escape.

Okay, seriously? Hadn't she learned anything in all the time she'd spent in the Word the last few weeks and talking to God about how she desired to be authentic in the way she lived her life? To be broken and shaped and strengthened in her spirit to become all He wanted her to be, do all He wanted her to do?

And all she could think about doing in this moment was run. Which really hadn't gotten her anywhere. Ever.

No, she would have to stick it out and put on a brave face if they should cross paths. At least they wouldn't have to work together, since he was there to open the ministry office and launch new clubs, and she was firmly ensconced with the Arlington team. She might see him once a month. Twice at most.

Reed closed the notebook he'd been scribbling in. "Okay, that should wrap things up. Let's pray and then get some food."

Following his prayer, Ally took her time putting her Bible and electronic tablet back in her bag while the others hurried over to the kitchen.

Wyatt sat on the coffee table in front of her. "Hey, Al, have a minute?"

She sat up and looked over when Reed perched on the arm of the sofa, then back to his brother. "Sure."

Her mind scrambled. What could they possibly want with her that had them looking so serious? At least being cornered by the McCowan boys meant she wouldn't have to face cute-guy-with-no-wedding-ring-she-now-knew-as-Zane quite yet. A quick look around the room yielded no sight of the man, so perhaps he was as reluctant to meet up with her again as she was with him.

Shouldn't she feel better about that?

Wyatt cleared his throat. "Reed, Mason, and I were talking yesterday with Zane."

Yesterday. Right. Jenny said they'd met Zane at Sunday dinner. Mason and his wife Rhonda were Wyatt and Harper's best friends and always considered family. It made sense they would've been here for dinner, as well.

"He asked if there was anybody from the leadership team who could go with him when he visits the other clubs, introduce him to folks, keep him organized, generally be his right hand. And we all three said you with no hesitation, if you can work it around your job, that is. We don't want to pile more stuff on you."

Her heart skipped a beat. Maybe half a dozen. She couldn't be sure, but she was suddenly light-headed. Work alongside the man who must think her a pouty drama queen? That kind of awkward was right up there with catching the bouquet at her ex's wedding. She rarely let down her guard with anyone, except maybe Yolanda. It wasn't comfortable laying all of her personal baggage onto someone else. Even a supposedly safe stranger.

Thankfully, she hadn't told him what had sent her out onto the terrace that night. Finding her falling apart was embarrassing enough, not to mention his offer of a pity dance.

A sweet thought, but she hadn't been *that* desperate. So she ran.

A heap load of good that did.

Wyatt continued, clearly unaware of the hubbub going on inside her. "You were with us at the beginning and know everything about CU from the ground up. Would you be willing to step away from the Arlington club to help him out?"

Her mind whirled. "Ummm ..."

"Don't worry about us," Reed said, thankfully misinterpreting her hesitation. "Shannon's more than ready for her own circle, and we have three more volunteers who've just completed their training."

"Um ..." Words. Use. Words. "Sure." She swallowed when the answer barely made it past her throat. "Whatever you need."

CHAPTER THREE

"*T*hanks, Ally. I knew we could depend on you."

Wyatt's reply ricocheted around in her head.

Depend. One little word. But for Ally, her personal kryptonite. It went against everything she was to bow out of something others needed her to do. No matter the cost.

At the tender and baffling age of thirteen, back on the mission field with her father … without Mom … thousands of miles from her brother Michael … she'd discovered her strength and purpose in taking care of others. First, taking care of her widowed father, then stepping in wherever she could at the mission. Which, in turn, led to her chosen profession. One where employers and patients alike relied on her to show up, to have the answers, to *care*. It's what she did. It's who she *was*. And she'd always found satisfaction and peace in her purpose.

Until maybe just now. Because of her love for, and commitment to, ConnectUP, the ministry heads could *depend* on her to work with Zane. Count on her to follow through. No pressure at all. If only she could convince her roiling nerves of that.

Wyatt stood and looked around. "Hmm. I don't see Zane.

I'll go find him so I can introduce you. Then you guys can make a plan on when to meet."

She simply nodded instead of correcting his assumption they had never met, because how could she possibly explain *that?*

Oh, Zane and I go way back, from the night he found me melting down at your wedding.

Yeah, no. Definitely wouldn't be offering that information.

Rising, she followed Wyatt to the kitchen.

"Harper," he called out to his wife working at the opposite counter. "You know where Zane went?"

"His room," she answered over her shoulder. "To return a call."

Okay, that was good. Maybe it would be a long one, affording Ally the time she needed to organize her jumbled thoughts. When her phone pinged with an incoming text, she stepped away from the group helping themselves to the food covering the kitchen island. She pulled the device out of the back pocket of her red shorts and brought up the message from her brother.

Have you talked to Dad today?

Odd question. Michael knew she talked to their father every other Tuesday night, because Michael's calls were the other Tuesday nights.

Not today. Why?

Her head still down waiting for Michael's reply, she walked back to the family room. When a pair of strong hands took her by the arms, her head snapped up, and her stomach relocated to a different part of her anatomy.

"Oh, I'm sorry." She stared into the deep brown eyes of their new Becker ministry coordinator and held up her phone. "My brother. In Colorado. Texted me." She blinked. Where had all those years of education gone? She could decipher medical jargon in an instant, but she suddenly couldn't string more than two words of English together.

"No problem. Good thing I wasn't a wall, though, or you could have a concussion now." He released her, and extended his hand with a grin that sent her insides into a jitterbug. "We've never been properly introduced. Zane Carpenter."

"Allyson Kincaid." She slipped her hand into his, and her skin tingled all the way up to her shoulder. She really needed to get her act together. Sure, the guy was nice-looking, although not in a movie star or magazine cover model kind of way. His was more that all-American, rugged, guy-next-door brand of handsomeness. Dark hair, eyes to match, and just enough stubble on the face to be casual but not unkempt.

His smile left and forehead scrunched as he stared at her. "I thought it was Kay."

She cocked her head. "Where'd you get that?"

"Ashlen. At the reception. Had your flowers. She said *Miss Kay* gave them to her."

"Ohhh." She smiled. "I help out in children's ministry at church on Sundays when they need extra hands, and I've been in Ashlen's class a few times. The kids call me Miss K, for Kincaid. She stopped me on my way out to tell me how pretty my flowers were, so I gave them to her."

There was that grin again, with those twin dimples. "I think that little beauty could talk a miser into giving her his last penny."

"Right?"

"Allyson, then. Not Kay."

"Not Kay. And most everybody calls me Ally."

His eyes widened. "Oh, *you're* Ally. My new Phoebe."

Phoebe. The girl who'd called him that night on the terrace? "Excuse me?"

"Phoebe's my co-worker in Atlanta. Kept me in line. Guess that's supposed to be your job now. If you're up for the challenge, that is."

Oh, wow. It *had* been a business call. "A-And you'd be okay with that?"

He turned his head slightly and narrowed his eyes at her. "Some reason I shouldn't be?"

A loud burst of laughter from the kitchen made her jump. She'd been so focused on the man in front of her, she'd forgotten anybody else was in the room.

Zane glanced past her to the others before looking back at her again. "Have you had anything to eat yet?"

She shook her head. "Not yet." And now she wasn't sure she could, no matter how hungry she was.

The phone in her hand vibrated with an incoming call. She'd turned the sound off for the meeting, but the caller ID told her it was Michael, which upped her worry meter a notch or two. He'd never called her on CU planning night before. "I'm sorry. My brother. If he's calling now, it must be important."

"Absolutely. Take it. We'll catch up later."

She nodded and pressed the green button on her phone. *"Miguelito.* Hey."

"Hey, *'manita.* I know you're busy, but can you take a minute?"

She stepped out the back door to the covered deck with its hanging strings of lights. "Sure. We're done with our meeting. What's going on?"

"Hopefully nothing." With the door closed behind her, the sound of crickets and cicadas replaced the voices and music from inside. "I got a voicemail from Dad asking if I might be able to get on your video call tomorrow, but he didn't say why. Just wondered if you knew anything."

Her stomach rumbled with a mixture of worry and hunger. The three of them had a regular video call every second Sunday of the month, so the last was only two weeks ago.

"No, I haven't heard from him today. But it's odd he'd ask

us to be on one so soon." Her mind halted at one possibility. "Unless ..."

"He's coming home." Her brother finished the thought for her when she paused.

"You mean *leaving* home." Mercy, had she said that out loud?

"Al ..."

Yep. She had. "Sorry. But you have to agree, he's never thought of the States as home. Even with you and me here." Even with their mother buried here.

His sigh carried through the line. "I know, '*manita*. I get it. But the concern is why he needs to talk to us both right now."

She bowed her head. So selfish of her to not think of that. "You're right. I hope he isn't sick or something."

"Let's not assume anything yet. I just wanted to see if you'd talked with him. Guess we'll find out tomorrow."

"Yeah, I guess."

"Anything yet on the job front?"

She grimaced. "I've had some offers, but nothing's felt right."

"What are you looking for?"

Good question. Fulfillment, purpose, challenge. Making a difference, doing something meaningful. "Not sure. I just know none of these gigs the temp agency has sent me on is something I'd like to do full time. I'm not ... I don't know."

"Zealous about it. Not like when you were in Central America working with those kids. You were all in."

"All in," she echoed under her breath, her thoughts meandering back to that year, working side by side with her physician father in his remote clinic. Treating illness, disease, injuries, the likes of which one rarely saw in the modern doctor's offices and hospitals here in the US.

"These other jobs can't be as challenging as what you had to deal with at the clinic. I kind of thought that's why you went back to Arlington, that maybe it was too much."

"Working at the mission clinic was only supposed to be for a few months, remember? I never intended to stay as long as I did." When her dad had mentioned their head nurse had to leave unexpectedly, it seemed like perfect timing to go help until the replacement got there. Things had just ended with Wyatt, and she'd needed some time away.

Somewhere to run. Where she wouldn't have to see him at church or ConnectUP. Somewhere she could focus on other people's troubles and forget her own. Which had worked a little too well, leaving her unprepared to find Wyatt was more than over her when she returned. He was in love with someone else.

"But when the new nurse arrived, we were in the thick of a Zika outbreak. I couldn't leave with so many sick, and before I knew it, I'd been there a year."

"Everybody knows they can depend on you to get the job done. Dad was really hoping you'd stay."

And there it was. That word again. *Depend.* Not a bad word, but sometimes she wondered about her compulsion to never say *no.* To always be the one people knew they could turn to.

"Oh, trust me. He asked me often enough. But it was never my intent to go into full-time foreign missions."

"I understand. I'll pray you find something soon that fulfills you as much as the work there did."

"*Gracias, Miguel.*"

"Are you seeing anybody?"

"I see lots of people."

His laugh carried through the line and made her smile. "I'll take that as a no."

"I'm not looking for anybody. I'm working on being me and finding my place here. I don't need a man mucking up the works." *Not even a charming, dark-haired guy who carries a handkerchief.*

Good night, where had *that* come from? Sure, cute-guy-with-no-wedding-ring might have entered her thoughts a time

24

or two, or a few dozen, over the past month. But that was when he was the fantasy guy from the terrace she'd never see again. He was *safe*.

Her brother's chuckle brought her back to the present. "I hear you. Just don't be afraid to get back out there, *hermanita*. No doubt there's a great guy out there for you."

"*Gracias*." It was natural for them to sprinkle Spanish into their conversation when they talked. Having been born and raised on mission fields in Central America, Spanish was practically their first language. They spoke it more growing up than they did their native English. She and Yolanda still had complete conversations in Spanish, years after leaving Guatemala. "I'll keep my eyes open."

"And your heart?"

She stared at the moonlight's reflection dancing on the surface of the pool. Was her heart ready to let someone else in who could fracture it all over again? It had been almost two years since the break-up, and so much had changed. Wyatt was married now, and she hadn't even been on a date since that last one with him.

But maybe it was time to test the waters. Take all she'd learned over the past twenty-three months, about herself, life, God, what she wanted versus what was best, and step out in faith into uncomfortable territory.

"Working on it." Just not with cute-guy-Zane, who probably wasn't interested anyway after witnessing her at her humiliating worst.

"That's all I can ask."

"So, when are you and Paige going to be making an announcement?"

"Hopefully soon. I already have the ring."

"No, seriously? Oh, I'm so excited! You'd better tell me the second she says *yes*."

"Maybe not the very second, but you'll be the first person I call. *Te amo Allyson. Vaya con Dios.*" *I love you. Go with God.* The way he always ended their calls.

"I love you, too, *Miguel. Dios te bendiga y te guarde.*" *God bless you and keep you.*

She disconnected and sighed. How she loved her brother. Three years her senior, he'd been her best friend, confidant, and protector in a world where nobody had looked like them, with their blond hair and light skin. Their brown eyes were the only physical characteristics they'd shared with the other children. Yet it hadn't mattered as they'd run barefoot through the village, played soccer in the dirt streets, ate tropical fruit right off the trees.

She swept her hand across her forehead. Although night had settled in, the heat was palpable. Time to face cute-guy-Zane. Or just Zane, as she should probably start referring to him. She'd need to keep her wits about her if she was going to work with the guy.

Assuming he hadn't changed his mind. He'd appeared non-plussed about the pathetic figure she cut the night of the wedding. But now that he'd had a few minutes to think about it, maybe he would decide he needed someone more stable to help him out with something so important. Nothing she could do but go in and face the music, despite her bone-deep embarrassment.

But inside the house, all she found were the ladies gathered around the kitchen island.

"Did y'all kick the menfolk out?"

Harper shook her head. "The college guys challenged the old guys to a game of hoops, so they're headed down to the park around the corner."

Ally grabbed a paper plate and eyed the food. "Works for me." On so many levels. "I'm starving."

CHAPTER FOUR

*Z*ane walked into the house behind Wyatt, then waited for Reed before closing the door. "You all right there, bro?"

Reed shook his head. "I'm definitely going to be feeling that tomorrow."

Chuckling, Zane clapped Wyatt's brother on the shoulder as they sauntered slowly down the entry hall. "We gave them a run, though. Thirty to twenty-six isn't bad, considering."

"Thanks to you. You've got some skills, my man."

Zane shrugged. "High school hoops. Some rec league in Atlanta."

In the kitchen, they grabbed bottles of water from a large, metal bucket of ice, and Reed joined his brother at the table, sagging into a chair as though it took the last ounce of his energy. Although they'd been on the same team, the McCowan brothers had ribbed each other mercilessly during their game, but it was clear they were the best of friends.

A familiar stab of grief threatened to open the old wound. Would he and Emma still be close? As the oldest, he'd been fiercely protective of his sister. Walked with her to and from school, watched after her when they went to the lake with their friends to fish or swim, made sure she was safe when they played outside.

Except when it had mattered.

He shook himself out of his past and took a long pull from the water bottle, scanning the folks standing around the kitchen. A petite blonde who'd introduced herself as Shannon sat at the breakfast bar with Jenny and one of the younger volunteers talking to Harper. Reed and Wyatt slouched in their chairs at the table, gulping their water, while the college guys stood at the island helping themselves to more food. Turning, he did a quick check of the family room. Empty.

So she was gone. Again. Hopefully, the phone call from her brother hadn't been bad news. Either that, or he had the distinct impression the girl was avoiding him. First blowing off his invitation to dance, now leaving before they could connect about working together. And when his eyes had found hers during his introduction, the scrunch in her forehead didn't exactly broadcast she was overjoyed to see him.

Half an hour later, as the others trickled out, he threw his empty bottle into the recycle container in the pantry and started clearing the island. His hostess had refused his offer of help after his welcome-to-Texas dinner Saturday and again yesterday, when Wyatt's family had come over after church. Tonight, he wasn't taking *no* for an answer. It was time to earn his keep.

Wyatt returned to the kitchen after locking the front door behind their guests and pulled down plasticware from a cabinet to store the leftover food the college guys hadn't taken with them. "How'd the office hunt go today?"

"Slowly." Zane rinsed a bowl and stuck it in the dishwasher. "The DFW Metroplex is crazy. Lost track of how many exits I missed and had to backtrack, even with my GPS app. I also checked a couple of apartment complexes I scouted out online but wasn't thrilled about the rent rate. May have to look into a roommate situation."

"No rush on that. You have a place here as long as you like."

"You're newlyweds, dude, and don't need me all up in your space. I'll be out of your hair as soon as I lock down a lease."

Harper sprayed cleaner across the island. "No hurry, Zane. Seriously."

The McCowans' generosity and five-star hospitality made him want to stick around as long as possible. At least until he knew more about what the next few months would hold for him. The call he'd returned earlier could pose an issue if he was bound to a year-long lease.

Not that he was eager to leave now that he was in Texas, finally able to work with the ConnectUP team side-by-side. The proposals and plans and charts and statistics on CU that he, Wyatt, and Mason had been discussing since January sat right now in a three-ring notebook in his room. It was important work. Work with a purpose. A purpose he embraced and enjoyed. But work that needed more than the six months remaining of his post-seminary commitment to Becker.

Regardless of how long his tenure in the Lone Star State might or might not be, however, he couldn't stay here, in Casa McCowan. These two had enough on their plates without adding him to the mix. Harper, full-time student, cheer coach at a local high school, and part-time employee with ConnectUP. And Wyatt, an adolescent psychologist with a thriving practice, adjunct professor at DHU, and Director of ConnectUP Student Ministries. Not to mention, newly married.

Which meant Zane really needed to get into his own place soon. Something that wouldn't break his wallet if he had to break a lease.

Wyatt put several containers of leftovers in the refrigerator. "I saw you speaking with Ally earlier. Did you set a time to meet?"

Zane dried his hands on a towel. "Her brother called before we had a chance. Then she was gone when we got back."

Wyatt's brow furrowed. "Mike called on a Monday? I hope everything's okay." He turned to his wife. "Did she leave right after her call?"

"No, she left maybe twenty minutes ago. Seemed fine to me." She stopped wiping down the stove and looked at Zane. "I can give you her number. Or send her yours."

He folded the towel in half and laid it on the counter. "I'm not sure how thrilled she'd be about that, since this is twice now she's disappeared on me."

The crease in Wyatt's forehead deepened. "Twice? In one night?"

Zane winced, realizing too late what he let slip. "Actually, we kind of met at your wedding."

"Kind of met."

"Yeah, we sort of never got around to exchanging names. We were talking out on the terrace, then I had to take a call. I asked her to save me a dance, but she was gone when I got back. Just like tonight."

Harper leaned against the island and crossed her arms. "Maybe she had an early shift the morning after the wedding. I know she does tomorrow."

"Shift?"

"Pediatric nurse. Gifted. And willing to help out any hour of the day or night if someone asks." She looked over at her husband. "Remember when Ashlen choked on some watermelon at our Fourth of July party? Ally was over there in an instant, before anybody else knew what was happening."

"I do remember that. Ash stuck with her the rest of the day, like a little shadow." Wyatt grinned over at Zane. "Guess jobs was something else you *sort of* didn't get around to?"

He shook his head. "I didn't mention I was with Becker, but then I wasn't aware she was with ConnectUP. She was a little … emotional, I guess you could say."

Wyatt's expression sobered, and he looked at Harper. "I thought she was doing okay. She was involved in all the things and seemed as on board as anybody else."

Her expression mirrored her husband's. "I thought so too."

Zane looked from Harper to Wyatt. "All the things?"

"Pre-wedding things," his friend answered. "Our engagement party, Harper's shower, the bachelorette weekend get-away."

Harper nodded. "And at the reception, she was out there dancing with all of us and the CU kids. She felt weird about catching the bouquet, but I really thought she was all right."

"It's about a guy, then?" Zane asked. "Recent break-up or something?"

Wyatt exchanged another glance with his wife. "You could say that, although not all that recent." He sighed. "Ally and I used to date. In fact, she was the last girl I was serious about before Harper. She told me at the time we broke up she agreed it was best, but later I found out that wasn't exactly the case."

Wait. *Wyatt and Ally?* He figured it was about a guy, but her being hung up on *the groom* had never entered his mind. No wonder she'd tried so hard to *not* catch the bouquet.

"She didn't tell me any of that."

Though it explained a lot. Wyatt might have moved on, but she clearly hadn't.

Harper put the cleaner back under the sink. "I'm not surprised she didn't tell you. Ally doesn't talk about herself much."

"Much." Wyatt chuckled under his breath. "Try never. Maybe with Yolanda, but then they've been best friends since they were kids. That was the big issue in our relationship. I listen to people for a living, but it was difficult getting her to open up with me. It left a certain distance there we could never close. I cared about her a lot, though. She's a great girl."

"She is. I love her to bits and feel awful she was having a hard time at the wedding."

Zane crossed his arms over his middle. "She seemed fine tonight, here with you both. Not awkward at all. Now, with me …" He shrugged. "That appears to be a different story."

Harper flipped her hand toward him. "Just be your normal, charming self. Ally's super sweet, and I'm sure she'd be delighted to help you out. She'll be at club Wednesday night. Maybe you can touch base then." She stifled a yawn. "I need to hit the hay, guys. Cheer practice at six-thirty. Those girls are determined to repeat as state champions this year."

Wyatt gave her a quick kiss. "Right behind you. Early workout tomorrow." He turned back to Zane as Harper disappeared around the corner to the master suite. "Mason and I work out every Tuesday and Thursday morning in the university fitness center. You're welcome to join us any time."

"I'll do that. Thanks."

Wyatt scratched his temple and dropped his hand. "Listen, about Ally. She really is terrific, and I know you'll work well together. She's an organizational genius and sharp as a tack. My right hand when I was getting CU up and running. She'll be a huge asset to you. Like Harper said, just be you and she'll loosen up."

Zane hitched one shoulder in a shrug. "Don't know who else to be. I is what I is."

"Wouldn't have it any other way. See you in the morning. We'll leave around six-fifteen."

Back in his room, the blinking light on the cell phone he'd left on the bureau caught his attention. He picked it up, saw the number for a missed call from California, and dialed into his voicemail.

"Zane, Jerry Lassiter here, Global Reach Missions. I apologize for calling so late your time, but I was in meetings earlier when you called. We've reviewed your application, references, and resume, and are very impressed with your current work at Becker Ministries and your educational qualifications. We have a spot sooner than expected at one of our Honduran missions, so be thinking about that and we'll be in

touch with more information. Looking forward to possibly working with you."

His pulse raced. This was it. What he'd been hoping and praying for. A foreign mission assignment.

He paced the room. Traveling the globe was not only his dream, but his goal. His father's voice still echoed in his mind, expressing in vivid detail his longing to see the world beyond the fifty miles stretching between their little town and the thriving metropolis of Indianapolis.

Someday, son, we're going to stand in front of that old Sphynx, you just wait.

Can you imagine what it'll be like to see the empty tomb in Israel, son?

I can't wait until we can walk along the Great Wall, son. You'll see.

Dad died in the same bed he'd slept in as long as Zane could remember, in the same modest house he brought his young bride to, in the same small Indiana town he'd been in all his life. Without ever having seen Mount Rushmore or the Grand Canyon, much less exotic places such as Egypt or China.

The same would not be true of Zane.

Two days before Dad passed, Zane promised he would see the world as they'd always dreamed. And he would make it happen. Someday. And the prospect of doing so while sharing the gospel only made him more determined to carry out what his father hadn't lived long enough to do.

With his father gone, and Mom only God knew where, Zane had left little Gallagher, Indiana, at eighteen and never looked back. The apartment he'd rented in Atlanta the past three years had been the longest he'd landed anywhere since. Yet it hadn't taken him much time to pack up what mattered and sell or give away the rest, as he always did when he moved. It was easier to start over than lug stuff around from one place to the next.

The only possession he would never part with, though, was

his beloved '76 Ford Bronco, produced before *sport utility vehicle* was even a thing. As a boy, they'd gone camping in that car, lugged hunting and fishing gear in the back for weekends in the woods. He learned to drive in that Bronco, just him and his dad along the back roads where he couldn't run into anything. Followed by root beer floats at the old-fashioned soda fountain on the town square.

No, he didn't need a lot, never desired to hold on to *things*, but that Bronco he cherished. As if carrying his dad with him wherever he went.

But to actually go to a foreign country, live out his father's most fervent desire, that would be the ultimate way to honor the man who'd raised him.

His pacing stilled as his gaze fell on the three-inch binder with the ConnectUP logo.

Would he be able to walk away from Wyatt's dream to fulfill his own?

CHAPTER FIVE

"*M*ercy me." Ally swiped her hand across her forehead, out of breath after a fast-paced line dance with several of the ConnectUP girls in the community center gym. "I'm clearly not getting enough exercise."

Shannon shot her a look, her chest heaving, which made Ally feel better for some reason. "Hardly. We're just not sixteen." She pointed back and forth between them. "We look awesome for our age."

Ally smiled and threw her arm around her friend. "I love you, Shan."

"Love you too. Up for another one?"

The rousing strains of "Footloose" blasted from the speakers, and the girls jumped in, their feet, hips, and arms moving in sync. Amazing how that song transcended time.

"Wish I had a tenth of their energy. I'm going to go help set out the snacks. And catch my breath. You have fun."

Shannon nodded and stepped in line between two of the girls. Dressed in modest shorts and ConnectUP T-shirt, with her hair in twin braids hanging over her shoulders, Shannon at twenty-four looked more like one of their teen charges than a leader. But she was a fantastic leader. Strong in her faith and mature beyond her years. If Ally needed to turn her group over to anyone so she could help launch more clubs, she'd have no problem entrusting her girls to Shannon.

If Zane even still wanted to work with her. She hadn't heard anything from him since their interrupted conversation Monday night. And if he'd wanted to speak with her tonight, there had been plenty of opportunities. Yet all they'd exchanged when he arrived earlier was a friendly, if brief, *hello* before he turned his attention to helping Reed and another volunteer set up chairs for conversation circles. And for the last twenty minutes, he'd been engrossed in a hotly contested game of hoops.

Had he changed his mind about her being his *new Phoebe?* Not that she could blame him. First impressions were important, and hers had been abysmal at best.

Meandering through the vast space where the Arlington flagship club met, she let her gaze roam over all the activity. Wednesday night club was by far her favorite part of the week, spending the evening with high schoolers of different ethnicities, socio-economic classes, and peer groups. Sharing the love of Jesus with not just her words, but her hands, arms, feet. Any way she could serve these kids, she was up for it. And every Wednesday, without fail, she left this place uplifted and ministered to as much as any of their kids.

As she neared the kitchen at the far end of the gym, her eyes caught and settled on the dark-haired man mixing it up on the basketball court with Wyatt and some of the boys. Zane must have been a star at some point, by the looks of the skills he exhibited. And he clearly kept himself fit, which she could see even though his Atlanta Falcons T-shirt and long gray shorts hung loosely on his frame. He took a shot at the hoop, and the ball sank through the net.

When he glanced her way, she quickly turned, her face heating from more than the dancing. Last thing she wanted was for him to think she was a creeper on top of whatever it was he already assumed about her.

In the stark commercial kitchen, she found Jenny, Harper, and one of the college-age team members organizing the evening's refreshments. "Can I help with anything?"

Harper gave her a smile. "Absolutely. Here. Put out your arms." Ally did as instructed, and Harper set two platters of cookies on her forearms, picked up two herself, and they walked out together to the refreshment table. "Have you and Zane gotten together yet?"

The platters tilted slightly on Ally's arms before she righted them. "T-together?"

"To work out a schedule." Harper set her platters down and relieved Ally of hers, which she placed at the other end of the table. "He's still officially on vacation time until Monday, but you'd never know it. He's already scouted out several office spaces and met last night with Wyatt and Mason about drafting curriculum. It's like his mind spins constantly."

"Oh. No, we haven't … gotten together."

Harper's gaze swept the table with its array of dessert and finger food offerings. "He's probably waiting for a good time to talk to you when it's not so crazy in here."

Yeah, maybe. But when they called everybody over for refreshments ten minutes later, he still didn't make the effort to talk to her. She caught herself staring again when she found him standing with several of the high school boys, his small paper plate piled high with chips and sweets. What she wouldn't give for a man-sized metabolism.

A burst of laughter from the group tipped up the corners of her mouth. He was a natural with the kids, his eyes alight and attention genuine.

Choosing to do something constructive rather than continue to stare at the guy she *wasn't* creeping on, she consolidated the left-over cookies onto one platter. It really was unfortunate they'd met during her uncharacteristic weepy moment. That love-sick, self-pitying woman wasn't who she was. She was a working professional, a dependable friend, a woman of faith, and a CU leader who loved teenagers. If only *that's* who he could've met instead of the sniveling fool she'd been that night.

But maybe it wasn't too late. If he wasn't going to broach the subject, then perhaps she should. The CU leadership was depending on her, after all. She should at least make an effort to follow through. And then leave it up to Zane to decide if he needed her help or not.

After stacking the empty platters and setting them aside, she turned and nearly collided with a body behind her. Her hand came up to cover the red and black bird on his shirt as her eyes looked up into a pair of dancing brown ones. "Zane. Hi."

"Hey. Fancy running into you. Literally." He grinned that grin that made her feel squishy inside. Which was plain silly. She was a grown woman, for crying out loud.

She realized her hand still rested against his chest and quickly pulled it back. Another smashing impression she was making. "I—I was just coming to talk to you."

His eyes widened. "Really?"

"Um, yeah."

He clearly found that surprising. But then, could she blame him? Not only had she not ever sought him out on her own, she'd purposely evaded him the last two times they met instead of sticking around to finish their conversation.

After grabbing two more cookies from the table, he straightened and faced her again. "So, what's up?" He popped an entire snickerdoodle in his mouth.

"Up?"

He swallowed his cookie and brushed a knuckle across his mouth. "You said you wanted to talk to me?"

"Oh. Uh, right." She gave herself a mental kick. "I wanted

to see—check if you, you know. See if you still needed any help. With your ... stuff."

Really, Al? This guy would never believe she had a master's degree and spoke two languages. Not when she could barely string a sentence together around him. "Unless you found somebody else."

The pall of disappointment knotting her insides confused her. On Monday night, that was exactly how she would have preferred it. But Reed and Wyatt had asked her to help, so she at least needed to make herself available. If Zane could just get past his horrid first—and second and third—impression of her, that is.

He shook his head. "No. Yes. I mean, no, I haven't found somebody else, and yes, my stuff and I could most certainly use your help. I hear you're an organizational wizard, and I'm kind of all over the place."

Her cheeks warmed with her grin. "I don't know about wizard, but I'd be up for seeing how I can help. And I also wanted to ap—"

"Hey, Zane." Reed walked up and stood with them. "Can you stick around for a few minutes after club? We'd like to have you meet with a few of our student leaders. Great kids who would be delighted to give you their thoughts about club."

Zane nodded. "Sure thing. I'd love to pick their brains."

Reed looked at Ally. "You, too, if you can. We've asked some of the older guys to stay, so can you see if a couple of your girls can stick around to meet Zane?"

"Happy to," she answered. "I'm pretty sure Tonya and Finn came together, anyway."

"Perfect. Let's get circles started."

She looked up at Zane as Reed walked away. "We can talk another time."

He stared at her a moment. "Can you meet me after the meeting-after-the-meeting?"

"You mean, a meeting after the meeting-after-the-meeting?"

He chuckled. "See? You get me already."

Smiling, she looked away at the kids moving to their circles. This was the guy she remembered from the terrace. The one who'd chased her tears away that night now easing her discomfiture at having been seen at her worst. Maybe this could work.

She turned her eyes back to him. "I can probably stay for a bit, but I have an early morning tomorrow."

"Not a problem. It'll just take a minute. Or maybe three. I have some groveling to do, but I'm an expert so it really shouldn't take me long."

She somehow kept her jaw from dropping. Groveling? *Him?* If anybody had groveling to do, it was her. Then he could decide if he still wanted to work with her, or if he would feel more confident in somebody else.

Two days ago, that's exactly what she wanted. But now ...

Now she just needed to convince him she was capable and focused and committed to the work.

Whatever it would take.

CHAPTER SIX

*Z*ane watched Ally leave the community center from across the room.

At least this time she wasn't ditching him on purpose. On her way out the door behind one of her girls who'd spent most of the evening in tears, she turned and mouthed *I'm sorry*. He gave her a nod and said a quick prayer for them both. He could wait. She was needed elsewhere.

He pulled his attention back to the group he stood with—the McCowan brothers and their wives, and several of their senior students—and listened as a boy named Finn shared his story. A tight end on the football team and star baseball player, he'd met Wyatt last year while on in-school suspension.

"Yeah, if Dr. Mac here hadn't shown up that day, I doubt I'd be standing here right now." He took the hand of the girl at his side—Tonya, according to the name badge on the lanyard she wore identifying her as a student leader. They exchanged a tender smile before he looked back at Zane. "I was so angry, you know? I wasn't even sure why and had no idea how to change it.

"Then Dr. Mac had me come over to his house to meet these buffoons." He jerked a thumb to indicate the two boys standing on the other side of him—Carlos with the big grin and the tall blond kid who'd introduced himself as *Tyler-but-call-me-Ty.*

"Got involved here, found God, and now everything's changed. My grades are comin' up, things are better with my mom and stepdad. They even go to church now. Some of my old friends don't get it. Keep asking me to hang out and party, but that's not me anymore. Not even who I wanna be. I invite them here all the time, and a few have come. It's been really cool to group up with the Christian guys before football practice and pray and stuff."

Zane's smile widened as his heart nearly burst. *This* was why he was in ministry. For kids like Finn, and all the rest who had been there that night. "That's very cool. Thank you for sharing that with me. What a fantastic testimony."

A blush crept up Finn's neck to his face as he turned to Wyatt. "Yeah, well, I've said it a hundred times, Doc, but thanks."

Moisture pooled in Wyatt's eyes, and the sheer love and pride in Harper's countenance as she gazed up at her husband tightened Zane's insides. Nobody had ever looked at him that way, and he wondered what it must be like to find that kind of love.

Wyatt swiped a finger under his eye. "You being here and being *you*, exactly how God designed you to be, is all the thanks I need, sport."

The rest of the teens chimed in with their stories and thoughts on how the ministry could reach more kids, and Zane left the building after clean-up with an even greater fire in his gut. He'd been living, breathing, and talking ConnectUP for the last eight months, all of it through video chats, email, and phone calls. But being here, witnessing how an actual club worked, was eye-opening. Heart-lifting. Soul-filling.

He reached the Bronco, sparkling under the parking lot lights since he'd spent Sunday afternoon scrubbing her down after his two-day road trip. Not that it took that long to get to Arlington, Texas, from Atlanta. He simply preferred driving along the county highways and farm-to-market roads rather than taking the much faster interstate. He saw and learned things passing through the smaller towns he never would by going around them.

Several minutes later, he pulled into the driveway and parked behind Wyatt's gray Toyota Sequoia sitting in the garage. Inside the house, Harper stood at the kitchen island, pulling her laptop and a textbook out of the backpack she carried for school.

"Hey, Harper, quick question for you."

She met his eyes across the expanse of the granite. "What's up?"

"You offered the other night to give me Ally's number. We talked before circles and planned to meet up after club, but it looked like she had a distraught girl she needed to tend to."

"Oh, right. Blair." Her brow wrinkled. "She's only been coming to club a few months but a really sweet girl." She flipped her hand in the air. "Ally's fantastic with her girls, though. She'll make sure Blair's okay."

"I thought I'd give her a call, since I don't know when I'll see her next. You think she'd be all right with that?"

"Absolutely. I'll text you her number."

"Appreciate it." A grin spread across his face. "You guys certainly didn't exaggerate about club night. It was incredible."

"Isn't it?" She climbed up on a barstool and opened her laptop. "I felt that same way my first time. Seriously, it changed my life. Like I'd finally found my place."

Wyatt walked into the kitchen. "Until I almost chased her away. Thank goodness she listened to Rhonda and not me."

"I never blamed you for that, honey. Not once. I totally understood." She grabbed her phone and tapped on the screen. "There's her number."

"Thanks." Zane glanced at the text she sent him, then back across the island. "You still have homework to do?"

"About an hour's worth I didn't get finished before club."

"And cheer practice at six-thirty again?" He shook his head. "I honestly don't know where you get your energy."

She threw him a wink. "Coffee and clean livin', my friend."

After talking with Wyatt for a minute, Zane went to his room, deciding to text Ally instead of calling in case she was still with the girl. He hit send, then changed into swim shorts. Maybe a few laps would help him relax and come down a bit from the excitement of the evening.

His phone rang as he started out of the bedroom, and he walked over to retrieve it from the dresser. Not Ally, unfortunately, but he recognized the California area code.

"Zane Carpenter."

"Zane. Jerry Lassiter here. Global Reach. Sorry to be calling so late again. I know you're a couple of hours ahead of us there."

"Not a problem, Mr. Lassiter. How are you?"

"First, call me Jerry. And if you can tell me you can be here by the end of October, that would make my day. We've had some developments in our Honduran mission and would love to have you out there by January. But that means training needs to start by no later than November first. You also need that time to get your funding completed."

Zane's pulse raced, and he sat down on the edge of the bed. First of November? That was only two months away, and he had six months left with Becker. The position had come with a full-ride to seminary if he agreed to a four-year commitment to the ministry. He made it through school in two years with his Master's in Christian Leadership and had been putting it to work ever since.

But although he loved working with kids, his heart had always sought to serve on a foreign mission field, and Becker only sponsored domestic ministries. So, he'd put out some feelers to see what other opportunities there might be for next spring. He never expected something to come up this quickly.

And what about ConnectUP? He'd just arrived in Arlington and was excited about their progress. Even more so after spending one evening with the kids.

He'd been praying for God to lead him to a position in foreign missions, but he thought it would be obvious when He did. This was like swimming in a swamp, with no clear view to open water. Go one way and live out his dream? Or stay and do the work he had committed to? If he passed on this opportunity, would they even consider him for another?

"Zane?"

"Yes. I'm here." He released a sigh and closed his eyes, bowing his head for a moment before looking back up. "I wish I could tell you I can be there by then, but … well, I have a contract with Becker through February. I'm sorry, but I need to see that through."

Although the right way to go—he'd given his word and signed his name to it, which meant something to him— disappointment sat heavy in his chest. He could only hope another opportunity would present itself. If not with Global Reach, then another mission. Hopefully, Jerry would understand his conviction to be true to his obligations.

"I can respect that. But let's still pray on it, and in the meantime, I'll email you the information packet. If we can work things out by September thirtieth, we'll be in good shape to get your training scheduled. Otherwise, we'll have to see what else might come down the pike. I don't have anything else right now, but you never know."

End of September. Five weeks. Perhaps if he talked with Maggie Watson, Becker's Vice President of Operations, she would agree to let him finish out his contract remotely until he met his commitment. There was no way he would shortchange Becker after all they'd done for him.

"Thanks, Jerry. I'll definitely be praying about it. And I appreciate the offer. Really. I'm honored."

"We'd be honored to have you if it works out. Don't hesitate to get in touch with any questions."

"Yes, sir. I'll do that."

He disconnected and stared down at the floor, his mind running a thousand miles an hour. Finally, thirteen years after leaving home with a head full of dreams of seeing the world, it was nearly in his grasp.

Yet still just out of reach.

CHAPTER SEVEN

*F*ather, please give me the wisdom and the words to guide this precious girl through the pain of rejection to Your unconditional acceptance.

Seated with Blair at the frozen yogurt shop near the community center, Ally had heard Blair's recounting of being dumped after dating a whole seven weeks and three days. Via text. Which had only rubbed salt into an already gaping wound.

"It's like I never really mattered to him." Blair stirred her raspberry-watermelon concoction, sending colorful little gummy bears swirling around in a pink whirlpool. "Like all he wanted was the … you know. Physical stuff." Her head snapped up. "Not that I ever gave in. I didn't. And that's why he dumped me—because he found someone who would." A lone tear spilled down her cheek. "I guess I should be grateful he broke up with me instead of cheating on me behind my back."

How Ally hurt for this sweet girl. Wyatt might have broken her heart once, but he'd been tender about it and had never treated her with disrespect. During or after their relationship.

Blair deserved the same, if only Ally could convince her of that.

"Oh, sweetie, I know that's hard. But please don't measure your worth based on somebody else's expectations. Especially expectations that go against what you know is God's best for you. You do matter. Not only to God, but to a lot of people, and for the right reasons."

"You're right." Blair let out a shaky exhale. "You've been right all the other times when you told me I deserved better. I wish I'd listened."

Ally reached over and covered her hand. "That's in the past. Today's almost gone, and tomorrow is a clean slate. Will it hurt when you wake up? Of course it will. And you're entitled to your emotions. But here's what I want you to do. Promise me you'll try this for at least a week."

Blair's eyes widened. "Okay. I promise."

"Every night, leave your Bible next to your bed open to Psalm 139. Or have it on your phone, however you want to read it. And every single morning for the next seven days, before your feet hit the floor, read that chapter. It's all about how God made you intricately special and how utterly precious you are. You don't need a guy or a title or any group telling you who you are. Your Maker knows exactly who He made you to be, so look to Him alone for your identity."

A genuine smile brightened the teenager's face for the first time all evening. "I can do that."

"And call or text if you need some encouragement. If I don't answer right away, it's because I'm at work, but I'll respond as soon as I can." She looked at her watch and winced. "It's almost ten-thirty. Your parents won't be worried, will they?"

Blair shook her head. "I texted my mom when we got here. She's cool."

Blair's mom might be cool with the teen getting home late on a school night, but Ally would definitely be feeling it when she had to get up at five-thirty to be on the pediatric floor by seven. Even so, she sent a silent thanks to the Lord that, although devastated by the afternoon's events, Blair had decided to still come to club.

But this was what CU was all about, providing a safe place for teens who needed support, encouragement, a shoulder, or a listening ear. That ConnectUP now met in four different parts of the DFW Metroplex brought Ally a joy she felt in every part of her. And with Zane Carpenter here from Becker, spearheading their efforts to launch even more clubs, reach even more kids, she couldn't think of anything she'd rather do than help him achieve the goals the leadership had set out for the coming months and years.

At the community center, she pulled up beside Blair's Mustang, the only car remaining in the lot, and walked around to meet her between the two vehicles. She hugged the now-composed girl, prayed over her, then watched her drive away before getting back in her little Honda.

She hadn't intended to skip out on Zane yet again, but this time it couldn't be helped. Hopefully, he would understand and they could touch base soon. Except he didn't have her number, and she didn't have his. She could probably get it from Harper and made a mental note to call during her lunch break tomorrow. Harper should be done with her morning classes by then.

In the car, she checked the phone she'd left in the console, since she hadn't wanted any distractions while talking to Blair, and found a text from an unfamiliar number. When she opened it, her breath lodged in her chest as she read the message.

> Hey Ally, it's Zane. Got your # from Harper.
> Call when you have a chance.
> Don't care how late. Thx!

She looked at the clock on the dash and winced. Ten forty-five. He said he didn't care how late, but it would be beyond embarrassing if he was already asleep. Was he an early-to-bed kind of guy, or did he sit up and read a bit before calling it a night? Or perhaps he watched the late-night talk shows.

The message had come in an hour before. Maybe he would still be up. She took a deep breath and pressed the phone icon above his text, listening to it ring four times before voicemail picked up.

"Hey, you've reached Zane Carpenter. If you're a friend, leave a message. If you're selling something, I'm a poor minister, so I'm probably not your target customer. If you're my boss, I'm working really hard, I promise, and will get back to you right away. Vaya con Dios!"

Grinning, she pulled the device from her ear and stared at it for a second. Zane ended his message exactly as her brother did—*Go with God*. When she heard the beep, she put the phone back to her ear.

"Hi, Zane." She cleared her throat. "Um, this is Ally. I have nothing to sell, and I'm certainly not your boss, so I guess that leaves friend. I'm heading home now. If you get this before eleven fifteen, feel free to call back."

She disconnected and pulled out of the parking spot. Ten minutes later, as she let herself in through the door from the garage, her cell rang, and Zane's number popped up on her screen.

Fumbling with her keys, bag, and phone all at once, she clicked to answer and promptly dropped the device onto the kitchen's ceramic tile floor. With a groan, she shut the door, flung her bag and keys onto a barstool, and retrieved her phone.

"Hey, Zane." Oh, mercy. She sounded like a breathless schoolgirl. She inhaled quickly and let it out. "Sorry about that. I was juggling too much."

"Glad that's all it was. And I should get hearing back in that ear in a day or two."

Laughing, she climbed up onto the other stool at the

breakfast bar. Yolanda was probably still at Steve's, since her car hadn't been in the other garage spot when Ally pulled in. Most evenings, if Yo wasn't over there, he was at their place. Good thing he was a great guy, a godly man she deemed deserving of her best friend. Even if it meant she had to share her.

"At least you have a spare."

The laughter was his this time, and she couldn't help joining in. "Very true. Hey, everything all right with your girl?"

She released a sigh. "It will be. Dealing with a bit of a broken heart, so I needed to spend some time with her. Sorry I couldn't meet with you after club."

"No worries. What you were doing was more important. I won't keep you because I know you said you had an early day tomorrow. I just wanted to see if we could set up a time to go over schedules, turn over some ideas. And I owe you a good groveling."

She shook her head. "I have no idea why, but it could be interesting."

His low-throated chuckle caused a warm tingle to cascade from her ear to her neck and down her arms. "Would you be able to meet tomorrow night? What time are you off work?"

"I'm off at six, and I don't have any other plans."

"You'll probably be hungry. How about we go for dinner somewhere. My treat, since I'm hoping to entice you to help me out."

She ran her fingers along a gray vein in the otherwise white quartz countertop. "I thought you were a poor minister."

"I think I can afford a couple of burgers. Maybe even some onion rings. Or does something else sound good?"

"I love hamburgers. And onion rings."

"Great! Tell me the best burger place in Arlington, and I'll meet you there. And not fast food. Real food."

She rattled off some of her favorite places, and they agreed on one between her house and the McCowans'.

"Seven? Seven-thirty?" he asked.

"Let's make it seven-thirty. I never know if I'll need a shower when I get home, depending on what ends up on me."

"I think there's a story there I'd like to hear."

"Probably not over dinner. Trust me."

He laughed again. That seemed to come easily for him. "See you tomorrow."

After disconnecting the call, she sat there a few minutes while her thoughts spun. She'd done a complete one-eighty since wanting to flee once she realized who he was Monday night. Now anticipation coursed through her at the prospect of being instrumental in the growth of ConnectUP.

That's all it was. It wasn't about *him*. She wasn't ready for a *him*. Even a him whose laughter caused her skin to warm. A him whose dark eyes danced when he smiled. A him who loved God, was great with kids, and excited about ministry.

A *him* who could break her heart all over again if she let herself fall.

CHAPTER EIGHT

*Z*ane waited to put his name in at the hostess counter at The Blazin' Grill. He'd been encouraged as the day ticked by with no call from Ally citing some reason she couldn't make it. Not that last night could be helped. It was much more important for her to be there for one of her girls than to meet with him. But disappearing at the wedding and again Monday night? Jury was still out on that.

After putting his name on the wait list, he walked back outside to stand in the shade of the awning. The sign in front identified this place as *Home of the Best Burgers in Texas*. A pretty big claim and, hopefully, it wouldn't disappoint. The sandwich he'd downed around eleven at the McCowans' was a distant memory here at 7:20. As hungry as he was, though, even a mediocre burger would taste like the best thing ever.

He stood with his hands in the pockets of the long navy shorts he wore with a striped, collared shirt and a pair of white Vans. He hadn't wanted to overdo it because this wasn't an actual date. But showing up in baggy shorts, a T-shirt, and flip-flops probably wouldn't make the best impression. The three times he'd seen Ally, she looked well put-together, even dressed casually in shorts and a ConnectUP shirt last night.

His gaze caught sight of her walking through the parking lot toward the restaurant, the rays from the setting sun turning her hair to burnished gold. Yep, good call on the clothes. Tonight, she wore a pair of those jeans that hugged her legs and stopped with a cuff above the ankles, white, with a flowery blouse in pinks and yellows. She looked comfortable, fresh … pretty.

He started toward her. When her eyes met his, she smiled and pushed the strap of her pink handbag higher on her shoulder.

"Am I late?"

He returned her smile and shook his head. "No, I'm early. I'm still finding my way around and never know if I can count on the time my GPS tells me it'll take. So I always give myself extra."

"Good thinking."

"You look nice. Not like you came home with any unspeakables on you."

Her smile widened. "Yes, I got through my day relatively unscathed."

"I put my name in already. Shouldn't be too much longer, but let's go in out of this heat."

He held the door, and she preceded him inside, leaving the light scent of her perfume wafting behind her. It reminded him of the orchids Maggie—his boss, mentor, and friend—grew in the greenhouse behind her lavish home. She always had a blooming orchid plant, or five, in her office.

He followed Ally to a bench, mesmerized by the way her hair moved against her back. Straight but not flat, and she had a lot of it. With this heat, it was no wonder she'd had it up in a ponytail when he saw her Monday and in some kind of clip last night, keeping it up off her neck. He liked it down, though, as he had on the terrace that night.

She stopped along the wall of the waiting area. "Is this okay? Means we stand, but it's out of the way of the door."

Nodding, he backed up to the wall at an angle to her to let an older couple take the last two seats on the bench. "Perfect. I've been doing too much sitting today, anyway." His eyes widened. "But you're a nurse, right? I bet you've been on your feet all day. They can probably make a spot for you."

"No, I'm good. I do a fair amount of sitting during a shift, updating charts and admin stuff." She tilted her head. "Did I tell you I was a nurse?"

"Harper mentioned it. Said you were a pediatric nurse. Gifted, I believe is how she put it."

Her face brightened. "That was nice of her to say. I do enjoy it. I'm freelancing at the moment, waiting for the right position to come along. My current assignment ends Wednesday, so I'm looking at some others, trying to decide where to go next."

"You prefer working in a hospital or a doctor's office?"

She shrugged. "They both have their pros and cons. More variety in hospital work, but better hours in an office. I think at this point, I prefer the better hours. Easier to make plans and commit to other things."

"Makes sense." His gaze roamed around the restaurant, taking in the full-on Texas theme. A huge metal star hung above the hostess desk, a Texas flag mural adorned one entire wall with the skyline of Dallas on another. Chairs with cutouts of a lone star in the middle of the back surrounded rustic oak tables set out on the brownish-red, stained concrete floor. All the wait staff wore jeans and red shirts with *BEST BURGERS IN TEXAS* arching over a logo of a grill with flames shooting from it on the back. "I like this place."

"Wait till you try their hamburgers."

He matched her smile. "Best burgers in Texas?"

Light flickered in her eyes when she laughed. "That's what they say. And so far, in my case, true. Not that I've been to that many places outside of Dallas."

"How long have you lived here?"

"About ten years. I came out for college and stayed, except for the year I was in Central America."

His ears perked up. She liked to travel? "When were you in Central America?"

"Last year. Returned to Texas last November."

"What took you down there?"

Her gaze flitted away. "My dad lives there. He's a … doctor."

Hmm. Her dad lived in another country, but what about her mother? Had something happened to her? Was that why Ally had been there a year? There had to be a story there, but he barely knew the girl. Certainly not enough to pry that deeply. Yet.

She looked back up at him. "Listen, about the wedding—"

"Zane." A female voice called out from the hostess stand. "Table ready for Zane."

"That's us." He gestured for Ally to go ahead and followed her through waiting patrons and tables of folks eating and talking while country music poured from overhead speakers. Thankfully, their table was in a corner where it was a bit quieter.

The list of offerings on the menu was exhaustive, but after pondering between three, he narrowed it down to the bacon double cheeseburger. Simple, but his stomach rumbled just thinking about it.

Ally ordered the Greenhouse Burger that had some healthy, leafy stuff on it, and they decided to split one order of fries and another of onion rings between them. She had a great figure, but he appreciated her appetite for burgers and fried vegetables instead of ordering one of the few salads the place offered.

When the young waiter left, Zane looked across the table at his pretty dinner companion. Not that it mattered, but she was definitely easy to look at. Skin like cream, a generous mouth, and wide smile. And eyes the color of a mocha latte.

Not dark brown, but not hazel either. Somewhere in between.

He cleared his throat. Again, not that it mattered. "Tell me more about your work. Do you find it to be a demanding job?"

"It can be. Although I've found it to be a bit less so here in the States. I'm not in emergency medicine here, but in Guatemala, I saw everything."

"You worked with your dad there?"

"He's at a mission clinic there, in a small town about two hours from Guatemala City."

He sat up at attention. "Mission? Like a foreign mission? Your dad's a missionary?"

She nodded, then picked up her glass and took a long swallow of water.

"Does that mean you spent some time in the field too? Other than last year?"

"Yes. Growing up."

"Wow, that's awesome." She'd actually lived on a foreign mission field. Amazing. "It must be fulfilling work."

A shadow passed over her face. "He enjoys it."

Zane studied her for a moment. Wyatt was right. She certainly didn't share much about herself. Maybe he shouldn't push, although his curiosity was punching him in the gut. Her father was a *missionary?* He had a million and one questions.

"Have you seen your dad since you came back?"

"Only on Zoom. Oh, but he's coming here the first week of October, I found out during our call on Tuesday. Surprised my brother and me, actually, because he's not on furlough for another year. He absolutely assured us it isn't bad news, so we think he might be coming to tell us he's retiring. Or relocating for a new assignment. That wouldn't surprise me, either."

Her dad was coming here? If he could meet the man, boy, could he bend his ear. He'd love to talk to someone with firsthand experience in foreign missions. "That's great that he'll be here."

"I can't wait. Especially since Michael's flying out too. I'll get them both at the same time."

His chest clenched. What he wouldn't give to see his father again. To see Emma again. If they could go back to the day before everything came apart, alter the following twenty-four hours and stay together and be normal and ...

He bowed his head. Desperate, useless dream. Emma and Dad were forever gone, and Mom —

"Zane? You okay?"

His head snapped up as he came back to the present. "I'm sorry. Didn't mean to space on you."

"No problem. I hope I didn't say anything —"

"No. No, nothing like that. You were talking about having your dad and brother together, and it made me think —" He shook his head. "Never mind. Not important. That's very cool. I'm glad for you."

"Yeah." The crease in her forehead remained as she studied him. "It'll be nice."

He leaned forward again and crossed his arms on the table. "I appreciate you coming this evening, especially when I was starting to get the impression you weren't too keen on working with me. At first, anyway."

Mirroring his posture, she looked down for a moment before bringing her eyes back to his. "May I be honest?"

"I'd rather you straight-up lie, but honesty's fine if you're determined." He sent her a grin and a wink.

Her mouth quirked in a quick smile at his teasing, then she tucked her bottom lip between her teeth and stared at the salt and pepper shakers in the middle of their table. Was she about to give him a polite *thanks, but no thanks*? He hoped not, because he'd welcome the opportunity to get to know her better, especially after finding out she'd been on the foreign mission field.

"After we talked at the wedding, I was so ... embarrassed. The only consolation I had was that I'd likely never see you again." She lifted her eyes to his. "Then there you were on Monday, and, well … when I came in after talking to my brother and you guys were gone, I was kind of relieved, to tell you the truth. I stayed for a while, but I had an early shift so I needed to go. Or so I told myself. I think I just needed some time to think about what to say to you."

Hmm. That was interesting. He thought they'd genuinely connected on that terrace, until she took off. "Why were you embarrassed?"

She tilted her head toward him. "Really? Having a meltdown at a wedding? Totally embarrassing."

"You call that a meltdown? Most dignified meltdown I've ever seen."

"I was mortified and decided to leave before you could claim your pity dance."

He pulled his head back. "Pity dance? That's not what I intended at all."

Her eyes rounded. "You didn't?"

"Not even close. I really wanted to talk some more. And this is where my groveling begins. When I came back and couldn't find you, I felt terrible. Like I'd let you down."

Her jaw fell slack. "Let me down? How could you let me down when you didn't even know me? You were a nice guy checking on a weepy girl when you should've been inside having a good time."

"I *was* having a good time. Talking to you. I know it was beyond rude to take that call, but I needed some information from Phoebe that couldn't wait. I'm truly sorry for leaving without asking your name or anything."

"Seriously, Zane. No apology necessary. It's on me. All I could think to do was leave so you wouldn't feel obligated to follow through on your offer."

"An offer I very much wanted to follow through on."

"You did?" She straightened in her chair. "Really?"

"Did. Really." He pointed at her. "And you missed out on a great dance partner, if I do say so myself."

They shared a laugh before he took a long drink from his water and set the glass down.

"I figured you might be ducking me. Especially when you disappeared Monday. Which is why I didn't bring it up last night at club. I didn't want you to feel pressured just because the guys had volunteered you. I'm glad you said something."

"Me too. I'm really excited about doing more to grow the ministry. It's very close to my heart. And I really am sorry for ducking out on you. I have a tendency to run from uncomfortable situations. God and I are working on that." She shrugged. "We must be making some progress because here I am, not in another country."

Not in another country. Had something sent her fleeing to Central America? Perhaps a broken heart? How close to the break-up with Wyatt was her excursion to Guatemala?

Their burgers came, and after he prayed over their meal, the discussion turned to ConnectUP, her experience being with the ministry from its inception, and his ideas for launching new clubs, curriculum, and marketing. He was surprised when she pulled an electronic tablet from her bag and took notes while they ate and talked. Guess that's why she was an organizational wizard, and he was ... well, not.

He polished off the last bite of his burger and chased it with a hearty swallow of soda. "Man, that was good." He looked at her plate, with a third of her burger still sitting on it. "Was yours okay?"

"Delicious." She patted the corners of her mouth with her napkin and set it on the table. "I'm stuffed. I never can eat the entire thing."

For his part, he'd had no trouble with that, even with downing more than his half of the onion rings and fries. "Great choice for dinner tonight."

"Glad you liked it. Next time we have a work dinner, I'll

treat you to our famous Tex-Mex. Yolanda and I have a favorite spot we go to at least once a week."

"I'm in." Especially for the *next time* part. Of course, they would be seeing each other a lot over the foreseeable future, based on the schedule they'd put together. Yet he wondered if she might enjoy dinner without the work.

Which sounded an awful lot like a date.

Except this probably wasn't the best time to contemplate anything more than a working relationship. Was she still nursing a broken heart? If so, she hid it well. She and Harper were tight—that much he'd witnessed Monday at the leadership meeting and again last night at club. With Wyatt, too, she appeared comfortable and friendly.

Even if she was ready to move on, though, he wasn't sure he was the right guy. Not when there was the very real possibility he would be taking a foreign mission assignment when one opened up. Perhaps sooner rather than later.

Yes, definitely better to keep things professional. No matter how much he already looked forward to *next time*.

CHAPTER NINE

*A*t the sound of the doorbell, Ally grabbed her large handbag that included her day planner, electronic notepad, and folder containing printouts on commercial properties for lease. With her hand on the knob, she took a deep breath, let it out, and opened the door to Zane standing on her porch. And, yes, he was as down-to-earth-didn't-even-have-to-try handsome as she'd thought him from the moment she laid eyes on him all those weeks ago. And every time since.

Seeing him Monday might have been a shock, and speaking with him Wednesday about helping him left her hopeful. But dinner Thursday had been … eye-opening. Not only had she found herself relaxed and not at all self-conscious, but ended the evening with a new friend.

Biggest lesson of the night? She really needed to get over herself. His *groveling* because he thought he'd let her down humbled her. She might have been embarrassed, but running off after he'd been so gracious was selfish and cowardly. She truly was fortunate he still wanted to have anything to do with her, much less be willing to work so closely.

"Happy Saturday morning." He grinned that dimpled grin and there went her pulse again, tripping over itself. What *was* that? She barely knew the man, even if they had enjoyed a nearly three-hour conversation over hamburgers, then ice cream at a small shop they'd walked to from the restaurant. And last night they'd spent a couple of hours here at her place organizing his presentation for the all-area leadership meeting coming up on Monday.

But the bulk of their time together so far had centered on ConnectUP, not anything personal. It made no sense to get all swoony whenever he smiled.

"Good morning." She stepped out onto the porch and locked the deadbolt behind her. "I have all the stops mapped out based on location. And I've scheduled walk-throughs with agents or the property managers at all but one, and he gave me the code to the lockbox to let ourselves in."

"And what did you do in all your spare time?"

She couldn't help but grin at his teasing. "You said you wanted organization."

"Yes. Yes, I did. And I can already see Wyatt's description of your organizational genius was in no way overstated."

She looked over at him as they sauntered down the walkway toward the curbside guest parking spots. "Wyatt said I was an organizational genius?"

"Uh, yeah." His gaze darted away. "When we were talking about you helping me out."

"That was nice of him to say."

He cleared his throat and thrust his hands into the pockets of the light blue shorts he wore with a navy *V*-necked tee and tennis shoes. "According to him, you were a big part of getting the ministry up and running. His ideas, your planning."

"It was more than just Wyatt and me, for sure. Reed, Jenny, and Mason played a huge role, as well. But Jenny was busy with a toddler and a baby, and I didn't have classes since it was summer, so I was happy to take on the bulk of the administrative stuff."

"Speaking of Reed and Jenny, you're coming to the back-to-school barbecue tonight, right? For the Arlington club?"

"Wouldn't miss it."

"Great. That'll give me a chance to show off my meat-smoking skills. I put Wyatt and Harper's new outdoor kitchen to good use and popped a couple of briskets in the smoker last night."

"*Oo.* Can't wait. We Texans love our bris—" She stopped, halting him with the back of her hand across his chest as she stared straight ahead, her mouth agape. "Is that your Bronco?"

"It is. Why?"

She turned her widened eyes to him. "What is that? A '76? '77?"

The furrow in his brow deepened. "A '76. How'd you—"

"My uncle." She dropped her hand and started toward the vehicle shining under the mid-morning sun, Zane catching up beside her. "His business is restoring vintage automobiles. I fell in love with those old cars and trucks and would go hang out at his shop whenever I could. Asked him a million questions, even worked on a few with him."

"You're kidding." She caught his surprised smile out of the corner of her eye. "You like vintage cars?"

She nodded as she walked a circle around the Bronco. It was gorgeous. Lovingly restored. Shiny, moss green paint, white roof and trim on the windows, large tires perfect for off-roading, custom rims. Had Zane bought it finished, or had he actually done the work? "I saw it on my way into the restaurant the other night but didn't notice the Georgia license plates." She turned to look at him, lifting her hand to shield her eyes from the sun. "How did I not see it at the leadership meeting on Monday? Wouldn't it have been in the driveway if you're staying there?"

"I got there late, remember? Had to park around the block. I moved it to the driveway after everybody left."

"Oh, that's right. Well, it's a beautiful piece of machinery."

"She's my baby."

He held the passenger door open and took her hand to help her up into the seat. When her pulse did that hitchy thing again, she turned her attention to the inside of the vehicle instead of looking into those dancing brown eyes that always seemed to render her incapable of proper grammar.

She let her gaze roam the interior while he walked around the front. Again, an immense amount of love had gone into the restoration of the dash, the dark gray upholstered seats, matching carpet on the floorboard, and white headliner. A soothing scent of rich leather wafted from an air freshener clipped to one of the vents, and sun poured through the spotless windshield and windows. He certainly spoiled his *baby*, if the immaculate interior, not to mention glistening exterior, were any indication.

After pulling away from the curb, he looked over at her. "You're navigating."

"Oh. Right." She pulled her attention from admiring the SUV to the map on her phone, where she'd input all the addresses in the order they would see them. "Take a left at the stop sign."

Little more than four hours later, after five showings and Thai off a food truck for lunch, they left the last office space, looked at each other, and shook their heads.

Back in the Bronco, Zane turned the air conditioning to high against the afternoon heat and nodded to the file folder open on her lap. "Did we get them all?"

"For today." She released a sigh. "I can't believe none of them are right. These were my top contenders. There are a few more from the listings Harper gave you we can go see. I work Monday through Wednesday next week, but I can make some appointments for Thursday, if you're free."

"I'm totally flexible. Just let me know when you need me to be available around your schedule."

"My last day at the hospital is Wednesday, so no more

weekends or twelve-hour shifts. They asked me to stay on, but after you and I talked at dinner, I decided to take a part-time gig that came up at a pediatrician's office. Mondays, Wednesdays, and Fridays, seven thirty to two. That'll give me more time to throw at ConnectUP."

His eyes lit up. "That's great. As long as it doesn't mess with your income."

"I'm good. I have a decent nest egg, and I'll still make enough to cover rent and the basics. I know you had a full-time staff member working with you in Atlanta, so I didn't want to only give you a few days here and there. We have a lot to get done."

"I appreciate it. Really."

"No problem." She shifted her gaze out the windshield to the building in front of them. "Now if we can find an office, that would be a huge check off the list."

He shrugged, put the car in reverse, and backed out of the parking space. "We'll find it. God knows already where we're supposed to be."

"You're right. I just wish He'd use one of those beacons to show us. The way we're growing, and with all the ideas you have for expanding CU's reach, we're going to need space sooner rather than later."

"We'll get there." He glanced at his watch. "And speaking of sooner rather than later, it's almost three. What time are the kids supposed to be at the McCowans' for the barbecue?"

With a gasp, she looked at her Fitbit. "Oh, no. Is it that late? The party starts at four, and I told Harper I'd be there to help her set up. I'll never get there to be any good to her now, not with you having to take me all the way back home."

"Why don't you come with me, then? Or did you need to pick up anything at your house?"

Hmm. She'd baked cookies last night while they worked on his presentation, but they could pick some up at a bakery on the way, and she would keep hers for their visit to the Grand

Prairie club on Wednesday. The swimsuit and towel stuffed into the tote waiting by the door were no big deal, since she wasn't sure if she'd even care to swim. And the yellow shorts she wore with a daisy-print blouse and white sandals for this office-hunting expedition in the August heat would work fine for the party.

"If we can make a quick stop to pick up some cookies, then I won't need to go home. But I'll have to find a ride later." If only Yolanda were still with the Arlington club.

A gap opened up in traffic, and he pulled out onto the road. "Rumor has it the new guy drives a cool vintage Bronco. Maybe he'd give you a ride in it. If you ask real nice."

Laughing, she shook her head. "Except he lives there. I really don't want to inconvenience him to take me home."

"Doubt it will be a problem. I hear he's a super nice guy. Very charming, extremely handsome, makes a mean brisket. And a very safe driver."

Her jaw dropped. "He makes a mean brisket? Count me in."

He sent her a mock glare. "You completely missed the charming and handsome part."

"No, I didn't. They're just not as important as brisket. And a good driving record. Both very impressive qualities in a man."

His side-long grin accompanied by a quick wink sent prickles along her skin. "I'll keep that in mind."

Oh, mercy. Was he flirting with her? Or was she imagining things that weren't there? Her stomach rolled into a ball. Of course, that could be the Pad Thai she'd devoured at lunch.

Or maybe it wasn't.

CHAPTER TEN

$\mathcal{A}$fter Zane finished cleaning the McCowans' smoker, he closed it up and looked over at Ally. She'd been walking around the pool with a large trash bag, picking up discarded cups, plates, and napkins, but now stood staring up into the night sky.

"You okay, Al?"

She looked over in surprise, her smile big and eyes alight. "I just saw a shooting star!"

He walked over to join her and followed her gaze skyward. A gentle breeze mellowed the warm evening air, and a tendril of hair that had escaped her ponytail tickled his upper arm.

"Yolanda and I used to lie on our backs on the porch of my house in Guatemala and watch the stars." Her soft voice floated into the air. "They were so thick because there wasn't any light pollution. We'd pick out the constellations, count how many shooting stars we would see in a week." She sighed. "Such carefree days back then. Just two giggly girls pinning their wishes on streaks of light."

He turned his head and watched her gaze search the heavens, lost in her memories. If she had any idea how beautiful she was, she gave no hint. In the hours they'd spent together over the past three days, he'd never seen her primp, or worry about her hair, or if her make-up was melting in the heat. In fact, when he arrived at her house last night, she answered the door in loose-fitting shorts and a T-shirt, her thick tresses pulled up into what she'd called a *messy bun*, both her face and feet bare.

And she'd been stunning.

Tearing his eyes from her, he cleared his throat and perused the pool area. "I'm done with the smoker. Anything I can help you with?"

"Oh. Uh, I was going to wipe down the counter next."

"On it." He walked back over to the outdoor kitchen and picked up the bottle of cleanser, giving the granite surface a good spray. "Fantastic party."

"It was." She threw more cups into the bag and moved a chaise away from the edge of the pool. "I missed last year's since I was out of the country, but the back-to-school bash has always been one of my favorite events. This and the Christmas party."

"Is that here or somewhere else?"

"It was here last year. Wyatt's only had this house a little over a year. Before that, we would reserve the clubhouse at the apartment complex where he and Mason lived."

"They go back a ways, huh?"

She laughed. "Joined at the hip, those two. Since Wyatt was a freshman and Mason a sophomore at DHU." Her face sobered. "Wyatt said Mason is who helped him get through the grief of his best friend's suicide. That pretty much cemented their relationship." She walked over with her trash bag, and he threw the soiled paper towels into it.

He stuck his hands on his hips and watched her tie the top of the bag. Over the last couple of days, she'd thrown out tidbits about Wyatt and Mason, Wyatt and Harper, Wyatt and ConnectUP. But she'd never once mentioned how she and

Wyatt met, had never shared they'd once been an item. Did she even know he was aware of their history? Seemed like it was something she should. He hated thinking he was keeping something from her, something that might embarrass her if she found out some other way.

"Hey, Ally?"

She looked up at him. "Yeah?"

"I feel like I need to tell you something."

Her eyes rounded as she straightened, the bag falling over onto its side at her feet. "That sounds ominous."

Chuckling, he grabbed the trash. "Not at all. Let me toss this and then let's sit."

After he put the bag in the bin at the side of the house, he joined her at the patio table. The kids had left, Wyatt and Harper were cleaning up the kitchen, and the Arlington team was gathered in the living room conducting their weekly planning meeting—doing it tonight meant they wouldn't need to meet after the all-area leadership gathering Monday night. Ally would normally be in there with them, but now she'd float with him between all the clubs.

He had to say, after her supposed hesitation on Monday, she'd jumped in with both feet. And last evening, she was an absolute God-send, creating slides and graphics of timelines, maps, and goal-setting. All the stuff buzzing around in his head or jotted down on various papers in his binder now sat neatly organized and labeled on her laptop.

She crossed one leg over the other and swung her foot back and forth, her hands clasped in her lap. "You're not firing me already, are you?"

"Are you kidding? I'd be lost without you."

She blinked, and he realized his words, although true, could be misconstrued.

"Literally," he added. "Without your spot-on navigating, I'd probably still be driving around the Metroplex."

One of her bubbling giggles spilled out. "Doubtful. You do have your own phone."

"Yeah, but it's nice being with someone who actually knows where they're going and plays tour guide along the way. We covered a lot of ground today, and I can't wait to present our plans on Monday. Especially with the way you've fixed it all up and made it look so cool. We make a good team."

"I agree." She tilted her head. "So, what did you want to tell me?"

He leaned forward with his elbows braced on his thighs. "Um, about the night we met —"

"Wait." Her eyes widened. "You mean, that first night, when we really didn't meet since we didn't exchange names? Or this past Monday at the planning meeting?"

"I mean the wedding. I thought you should know I, uh ... I mentioned to Wyatt and Harper that you and I met at the reception. I had no idea ... well, that you and he —"

"Used to date." A pink tint colored her cheeks, and her gaze flicked away as one hand went to the pendants on her necklace. The same ones he'd noticed while talking on the terrace and that she'd been wearing every time he'd seen her since.

The silence stretched. Maybe he shouldn't have brought it up. The break-up was still clearly painful territory for her, no matter how at ease she appeared with the newlyweds.

"We met in the library at Dallas Heritage in grad school." When she brought her eyes back to his, he expected to see hurt and maybe even tears. But to his surprise, she was composed. Collected. Not emotional like that first night.

"Were you together long?"

"A couple of years."

He let out a soft whistle. "Two years is pretty long. Like, serious long." He'd dated a girl for a little while in college, which ended in disaster. Then there was Lisa in Kansas City, who he was with about a year. But a couple of years? He couldn't imagine being with someone that long.

Story of his adult life. Never landed anywhere for an extended period of time, never kept anybody very close. The former didn't bother him. It was exciting discovering new places and experiences. But the latter ... after being here only a week, watching Wyatt and Harper, witnessing how tight the ConnectUP folks were, the first spark of yearning flickered to life inside of him. For something more. Something deeper. A deeper connection. Friends. Companions. Perhaps even some*one*.

"Pretty serious." Her voice pulled him back to the conversation. "We'd never really talked about marriage, but the night he broke up with me, I actually thought he was going to propose."

He grimaced as he sat up in the chair. "Ouch."

"To put it mildly. I mean, I had my dress picked out, knew who I would ask to stand with me." She sighed and released the pendants she'd been sliding back and forth along the chain. "I didn't want to fall apart in front of him, so I told him I agreed breaking up was the best thing, and that was that."

"Except it wasn't."

"Not so much."

"Is that when you ran?"

Her brow crinkled. "Ran?"

"You said at dinner the other night you have a tendency to run when things get uncomfortable. And something about being in another country."

"Oh. Yeah. My dad needed some help, and I thought some time away would help me get some perspective. But when I returned last November, I realized I hadn't dealt with it at all while Wyatt had already moved on."

She gave her head a shake. "Of course, it had been fourteen months since we'd broken up. Coming back with the hope we might be able to make another go of it only ended up making me look pitiful."

"It's not pitiful, Ally. You were hurt."

"I was, but I was a big girl. I shouldn't have still been licking my wounds." She looked down for a moment before returning her gaze to his. "As for what happened at the wedding ... what you saw ... I don't want you to think I'm still pining after Wyatt. I've been past it for a while now, even before the wedding. The closer Harper and I got, the easier it was to let him go, because it's impossible not to see how perfect they are for each other."

Definitely a true statement. He'd never seen two people more suited to each other.

And he was happy for Ally, to see how far she'd come from a broken heart to being able to share her story of healing and victory. Which he considered a win, since he'd been told she didn't open up easily.

"You do seem like you're good friends. With both of them."

"Oh, one hundred percent. Harper's a kindred spirit, and what I feel for Wyatt now is how I feel for any other guy friend."

She turned to stare out over the pool, the light from the ripples of the water reflecting over her face, the thwack-thwack-thwack of the ceiling fan overhead blending with the crickets. "That night on the terrace, it was ... well ..." She looked back at him. "In a nutshell, it was more about the loss of the dream than the guy. I don't know if that makes sense."

He moved his head from side to side. "I think so. You'd dreamed of your wedding day and somebody else was getting it."

"No, it wasn't about the wedding, really. It was the idea." Her fingers found her necklace again, as if of their own volition. "Putting down roots, building a stable life together. Wyatt's a great guy, but part of the appeal was he was born and raised right here in Arlington, went to college here, has his practice and started his ministry here. His roots go deep. *That's* what I was having a hard time letting go of the night you and I met. I'm not sure it was even about Wyatt, but what he represented."

"I can see that." Stability. That's what she'd seen in Wyatt. Because Wyatt *stuck*. He hadn't moved over half a dozen times in thirteen years, chasing after that elusive prize called *purpose*. He'd known his since college, to hear him tell it. And while Zane loved his work and enjoyed the sense of accomplishment at having completed his seminary degree, he still couldn't claim he'd found his life's calling.

His gaze went to the pendants in her fingers and back to her face. "Your necklace. I've noticed you wear it every day. Special significance?"

She looked down at the pendants between her fingers. "Oh. Um, yes. I call them my dream charms." With the fingers of her other hand, she separated each of them. "State of Texas. Obvious. Where I live and plan to live the rest of my life. A house because I hope to buy a house within the next couple of years. I've been keeping my eye on listings. And, of course, if I have a house, I need a dog. Right?"

"Absolutely. Do you have a favorite breed?"

"Just a rescue dog. I'll know him or her when I see them." She showed him the next one, a bouquet of flowers. "I also would love to have a garden. A real one. I have pots, as you've seen, since I'm renting. But I want a true, in-the-ground garden with flowers and vegetables."

A memory stirred his heart. Something he hadn't thought about in years. Or hadn't allowed himself to. "My mom had a garden. I remember her cooking with fresh vegetables, and there were always flowers around our house during spring and summer, straight from her garden." Until there weren't.

"That's exactly what I want." She looked down and separated out the last one. "This one's my favorite. The cross.

To remind me it's okay to have dreams, as long as I keep Jesus in the middle of them."

"That's really cool. I write my goals down, but I don't think I've ever worn them. Guess I could get them tattooed on me somewhere."

She laughed and crossed her arms over her middle. "They used to be on a bracelet, but it broke so I stuck them on a chain. Anyway, they're what Wyatt represented to me. A life right here in Arlington. That's what I was emotional about that night, and why I was so mortified when I realized who you were. How pathetic I must seem to you."

He pulled his head back. "I don't see you as pathetic at all. What I see is someone who put aside her own feelings to come out and celebrate her friends' new life together. Who could've let heartbreak make her bitter and angry but instead decided she'd take the high road and *showed* up. I don't pity you, Ally. I respect you."

Another moment stretched as she stared at him, her lips parted as if in surprise. "Thanks, Zane."

"It's true. And I'm glad you shared that with me. Wyatt didn't give me any details, just that you and he had dated and that you were really great. And it was clear they both consider you a valued friend."

Her smile seemed to brighten the already well-lit patio. "I feel the same about them."

His attention moved to the back door. "Good thing, because I think they're about to crash our little party."

Wyatt stuck his head outside. "Is this a private meeting, or can we join?"

"Come on." Zane pulled his chair around next to Ally as the other couple took the seats opposite them. "Excellent barbecue tonight, you guys."

"And amazing brisket. Let me know what we owe you."

Zane shook his head. "No way. Consider it a small thank you for letting me bunk here."

Harper laughed. "It's been all of seven days, and you've been gone more than here, anyway. It certainly hasn't been a problem."

"Still. I appreciate it." He winced. "And after researching more apartments, it looks like I may be here a bit longer than I'd planned. Until I can find a studio apartment or a roommate."

Harper looked at Ally. "Didn't Yolanda say something about Steve needing a housemate?"

Ally's face brightened. "That's right!" She looked over at Zane. "Steve just bought a house but has been looking to rent to someone to help him with the mortgage. It would be a lot less than an apartment."

His pulse quickened. "Is it close?"

"East Arlington. About ten minutes from Yolanda and me, fifteen from here."

"I'd love to talk to him about it. I'll give him a call tomorrow."

"It may not be a long-term arrangement, though. He and Yo are already batting the word *marriage* around, so it wouldn't surprise me if they're engaged by Christmas."

"Oooo!" Harper clapped her hands together. "That's so exciting!" Her smile left and hands dropped. "Wait. If they get married, it would be here, right? Or would they go to Guatemala?"

"Definitely here. She would probably want to do a traditional ceremony in Pamoca sometime later, but when she does get married, it'll be here."

A potentially short-term arrangement. That could work in his favor.

He'd met Steve but had only seen Yolanda from afar as one of Harper's bridesmaids, the brown-skinned girl with black hair nearly to her waist. Another nurse who loved her work, considered it a calling, just as Ally did. Just as Harper and Wyatt did with CU.

The spark inside him grew to a flame. That desire to commit, to stick. If only he could find that one thing he was meant to do. But for all his seeking and asking and moving from one opportunity to the next, he still had no clear picture. Only a dream. A dream he might finally be on the cusp of realizing.

A dream that would mean leaving ... again.

CHAPTER ELEVEN

"*O*kay, we have him back." Ally studied the numbers on the monitor and counted the beeps now indicating the little heart was once again beating. She handed an empty syringe to a co-worker for disposal and checked the boy's oxygen level. "Stop bagging."

The nurse at the head of the bed removed the oxygen bag used to push air into the boy's lungs. Silence permeated the space that had been hectic and intense only seconds before as every eye studied the blips and digits on the screen.

Ally let her shoulders relax. "Breathing on his own. Blood pressure coming up."

The doctor's sharp gaze snapped to her. "Good work, Allyson. Let's get him intubated to protect his airway and up to ICU, stat. I'll need you to assist."

"Yes, Doctor."

She glanced at her Fitbit. She was supposed to have clocked out twelve minutes ago, but the sudden emergency on the peds floor took priority over schedules. Nobody expected little Brent Hudson to go into cardiac arrest following his relatively minor surgical procedure done the day before. Thankfully, Dr. Franklin had been on the floor to check on a patient when she called the Code Blue. She already had the boy flat on his back and had started chest compressions by the time the rest of the team arrived.

Once h'd been prepped for transfer, the boy's shell-shocked parents followed closely behind as orderlies wheeled him down the corridor. Ally stopped in the hall next to the doctor, tossing her latex gloves after his into the designated container.

Dr. Franklin crossed his arms over his chest. "I hear we're losing you today."

"Yes, this was my last shift. In fact, I'm late meeting Ms. Amblin to turn in my badge."

"Nothing we can do to change your mind?"

"I was very appreciative of their offer, but I have another opportunity I need to throw more time and energy at. Just not the right time."

Or the right job, really. What had transpired over the last fifteen minutes was satisfying and fulfilling—saving the life of a child. But since returning from Guatemala, she often found herself restless in her vocation. Somewhat … discontent. Her spirit cringed at the negativity of that word. Still, at times it shouldered its way into her psyche, as if prodding her to do more, be more.

But more what? She was in the field she'd been called to. She loved nursing. Loved the children. Loved helping them get better. What more was she to do?

Maybe working with Zane to increase the reach of ConnectUP would answer that question. The past week had been exciting and fun, going over ideas and planning events and researching fundraising campaigns. It must be the Spirit's prodding. It *must* be. Because outside of nursing and CU, she didn't know what else she would do.

"It's a shame to lose such a gifted nurse." Dr. Franklin's voice brought her out of her thoughts. "I appreciated how well you kept your cool in there when that other nurse got flustered. We had enough going on without me having to rein in a panicked newbie."

She hitched a shoulder. "Ben's only been on the floor a week. This was his first code. He'll come around."

"One can hope." The doctor held out his hand. "Good luck to you, Allyson. We'll miss both you and your superior skills."

She shook his hand, her face warming at his words. It wasn't often one of the physicians gave a compliment to a nurse, and while nice to hear, it still made her self-conscious. "Thank you, Doctor. It's been a pleasure."

Dawn, a floor nurse who had become a friend, joined her as she turned to walk down the hall. "He's not wrong. If half of the temps they sent us were as good as you, we'd be ecstatic. Why don't you have a permanent position yet?"

"I've had some offers. Just nothing that's ... fit."

They stopped in front of the nurses' station, and Dawn rested her elbow on the counter. "Perhaps because you should be in emergency medicine or in the ICU. Something that tests you more than taking blood pressure and administering meds."

"You do a lot more than that. You're a sensational nurse. If I were to take a permanent job, it probably would've been this one. I've really enjoyed working with all of you."

Dawn shrugged, the ends of her light brown hair brushing her shoulder. "We've enjoyed having you, but maybe the mission work you mentioned a while back is more your thing. I love my profession, but I'm not sure I could handle the conditions you had to work in."

Ally looked past her co-worker at nothing, really, but could see the small, rustic clinic her father ran in Guatemala. Efficient, tidy, and organized, yes. Well-equipped and staffed? Not even close. They'd had to MacGyver their way through more procedures and treatments than she could count. But the lives they'd saved, the lives they'd touched ... made every hardship, every challenge, worth all of the extra effort and energy.

She brought her gaze to her friend. "It's fulfilling work, but you have to have a clear calling to it. Not for the faint of heart. If you're not prepared, it can be overwhelming. I'm used to it because I was raised with it. But it's not my calling."

Dawn shrugged again as she straightened. "I don't know about that. Seems like it's exactly what you were made for." She reached out and pulled Ally in for a hug. "Take care of yourself. And if you ever want to come back, we'd be delighted to have you."

"Thanks, Dawn."

The other nurses, even newbie Ben, came over to say their goodbyes before she walked down to the locker room to gather her things. Sitting in front of the open locker, she stared into its emptiness.

Seems like it's exactly what you were made for.

If that were true, why did she find it so difficult to think about going back? That accidental year she'd spent there eight years after moving to the US for college had been just that—an accident. Unintended. If circumstances at the clinic had been different, she would've been back in Texas after her initial three-month commitment. But she couldn't leave her dad even more short-handed than he already was. With a brand-new head nurse who, although well-experienced with a thirty-year nursing career, had never served on a foreign mission field. Over the next several months, however, Nora had proven herself more than capable of handling the less-than-ideal conditions, so Ally had complete confidence leaving her in charge and returning to the States.

Of course, at the time, she'd been anxious to see if Wyatt might have reconsidered the status of their relationship in her absence. But even after it was more than clear that door had closed, she hadn't once considered returning to Guatemala.

She stood and shut the locker. No, this was where she belonged. Here, in the US, in Dallas. Putting down roots.

Finding a stable career. And maybe there would be a special someone in her future to share her life with. Make a home with. Grow old with.

Her phone pinged with an incoming text, and she smiled when she read it.

> Hope your day went well.
> My treat for dessert after club tonight.
> Pick you up at 6?

She grabbed her purse and typed in her reply as she walked out of the women's locker room.

> Hey Z, sounds great. Found new
> fundraiser idea I want to run by you. See
> you at 6.

After Zane texted back his thumbs up, she grinned all the way to the nursing manager's office. She really enjoyed the friendship they were building. Since their dinner Thursday, they'd spent part of everyday together, including lunch Sunday after church followed by a drive around the Dallas/Fort Worth Metroplex to help him get a lay of the land. After the all-area meeting on Monday, they met Steve and Yo for pie at a nearby diner. Last night he'd been back at her house to brainstorm their social media strategy over a large pizza, and she still looked forward to going with him to the Grand Prairie club tonight.

For someone usually guarded with how much of herself she shared with others, it surprised her how comfortable she already felt with him. The only other guy she'd ever experienced that with was Wyatt. And while it had at first appeared that didn't turn out so great, she believed now it worked out exactly as it was meant to. He'd found his soulmate, and she'd found herself.

In Ms. Amblin's office, she turned in her badge and again

declined their offer of a permanent position. It was nice to be wanted, but she was at peace with her decision. This wasn't where she was supposed to be.

CHAPTER TWELVE

"Zane ..."

At the sound of wonder in Ally's voice, he turned and watched her amble around the large conference room in the office they'd been touring. Her hand with its pink polished nails glided along the built-in bookshelves, and when she looked over at him, the delight in her eyes and open smile made his heart clutch.

"This is it. Don't you think?"

He nodded, swallowing as his pulse accelerated. It had to be the excitement of finally finding a space that could work. Not because of the way Ally was looking at him, the brightness of her amber-hued eyes, the joyful glow on her face.

Their Thursday morning had begun early, both of them in denim shorts and white tees with the ConnectUP logo printed in blue on the front. When he picked her up, they had a good laugh at how they'd inadvertently dressed alike, but he was delighted she hadn't insisted on changing.

So here they stood, in their would-be CU uniform, at the third listing they'd viewed so far that day. One that finally looked like a winner.

"Uh ... yes." He had to tear his gaze away to look around

the room. "I love it. Excellent layout with space to grow as we add staff." He let his eyes venture to where she now stood at the window. The two-story building had been constructed around a sizable courtyard comprised of benches, walking paths, and tables with chairs under pergolas to be shared by all the building's tenants.

Her chuckle reached him across the room. "I can tell you right now, Harper will be out there working more than in here when the weather's nice. She'll love this outdoor space. It would also be a great place to meet with kids."

Hands in his pockets, he sauntered over to join her. Her light orchid-like fragrance wafted toward him as he stood behind her taking in the view. He didn't know if it was her perfume or maybe her shampoo, but it suited her perfectly. This was actually the first time he'd seen her not wearing something with flowers on it. Even her home spoke of her love for all things floral, from the upholstered chairs to the kitchen decor and art on the walls.

"What's the lease rate on this one again?"

She glanced at the printout and winced. "A little outside of our budget." She turned and looked at him. "But it's been on the market over a month already. Maybe they'll come down."

"Worth a try. Let's call Wyatt and see what he says." He reached around to his back pocket but came up empty. "Oh. I left my phone in Phyllis."

Her eyes narrowed. "Phyllis?"

"My car."

Her lips quirked up at the edges. "You call that souped up, uber-macho machine *Phyllis*?"

"What?" He cocked his head. "You don't think she looks like a Phyllis?"

"More like a Hank or a Bubba, but okay. Phyllis. The Bronco." She pulled her cell out of her pocket. "I got it." She clicked on the number and put it on speaker.

Wyatt picked up after one ring. "Hey, Al, what's up?"

"Hey, there. I'm here with Zane, and we have news."

"Let me guess. You ran off and eloped."

Zane laughed at his joke. "Not yet, my friend. That's on next week's agenda."

Her cheeks pinkened in the most charming way as she rolled her eyes. "You guys are a riot. Do you want to hear about this amazing office space we found or not?"

"Yes," came Wyatt's answer from the other end of the line. "I most definitely want to hear about this amazing office space you found."

Zane gave him the run-down before spilling the bad news. "It's a bit over budget, though."

"Define *a bit*."

"About two-fifty."

"Hmm."

Silence stretched until Ally cleared her throat. "But it's been on the market a while. I suggest we come in with an offer of four hundred below and see what they counter with."

A couple more seconds ticked by. "Okay, do that. If you can get it to no more than a hundred-fifty over per month, we can swing it."

Zane stepped forward. "You don't want to tour it before we put in the offer?"

"I trust your judgment, so go ahead and put it in. You think Harper and I can stop by late this afternoon to see it? If we all agree and the price is right, we can submit the application by end of business tomorrow."

"Can't see how that would be a problem. I'll arrange it with the landlord and text you to confirm."

"Sounds good. Great work, both of you. I know you've looked at a lot of spaces."

They had, but although it would be nice to finally have an official office, he'd miss these hunting expeditions with Ally. He couldn't even enlist her help to look for an apartment, since he was moving in with Steve over the weekend. Maybe she'd be willing to go with him to shop for some bedroom furniture and a desk.

"If they don't come down, we have a few more to view. We already have two appointments set for this afternoon. We'll keep those in case we need a back-up." When he looked at Ally, she nodded. Good. They could grab lunch and spend some more time together today.

Why that was important, he didn't know. But he couldn't imagine anything he'd rather be doing at the moment. Or anybody he'd rather be with.

Which was new. And a little confusing. Even when they weren't together, Ally had been taking up a large amount of his awake hours, like first thing in the morning, in the middle of his day when she was at work, and when he lay in bed at night. It'd been a while since a woman took up so much space in his cranium, and never after knowing her less than two weeks.

"Good plan." Wyatt's voice through the tiny speaker brought him back to the matter at hand. "I'm leaving the university now and have a couple of counseling appointments. See if we can stop by around five."

"You got it."

Ally disconnected and stuck her phone in the pocket of her shorts. "So ... next week. Monday is the CU Labor Day trip to Six Flags, Tuesday night is my Zoom call with my dad, I work Wednesday and Friday at the new job, so if we elope, it'll have to be Thursday."

"Thursday, it is."

CHAPTER THIRTEEN

*A*lly followed Zane out of the office they'd returned to a few minutes ago as Wyatt pulled his Sequoia into the space next to Phyllis. She still giggled a little inside every time she thought of the Bronco named Phyllis.

"Hope they like this place as much as we do." She came to a stop beside him and waited for their friends.

He braced his hands on his hips. "Especially since neither of the others we saw today would work."

Wyatt opened the door for Harper, and the couple walked over hand-in-hand. "Hey, you two." He stopped, stared at them for a moment, then grinned at his wife. "I think we missed something."

Harper laughed out loud. "Do you always dress in matching outfits?"

"Of course." Zane threw Ally a wink. "Remind me about tomorrow? Leather pants, right?"

She nodded, but it took some effort to keep her expression as straight at his. "Black, with green Crocs and Hawaiian shirt."

"Right. You and your flowers." He turned back to the

others. "I suggested black tanks, but she wouldn't hear of it. Had to be flowers."

Ally's cheeks warmed. He'd noticed her love of flowers? Somehow, that made her feel ... special. As if he'd been paying attention.

Wyatt's gaze roamed from Zane to Ally and back again. "Right. Ally and her flowers."

Harper's eyes danced with unconcealed mirth as they zeroed in on Zane. "I would pay big money to see you in leather pants and a Hawaiian shirt."

"And I would pay big money to *not* see that," Wyatt said, and Ally could no longer keep the grin off her face at their bantering.

Zane's jaw dropped in mock offense. "I can totally rock a pair of leather pants, dude."

"I wouldn't spread that around if I were you."

Harper threaded her arm through Ally's. "Come on. Show us this amazing space. Especially the courtyard you texted me about."

After touring the office suite, they met with the building owner, who had agreed to lower the rent, and Wyatt completed the application on the spot. When the owner left them to look around again, they stood in a circle inside their potential new office to pray over it. Her hand clasped in Zane's on one side and the other in Harper's, Ally's soul filled with equal parts peace and excitement. Getting this office would be a huge step in growing ConnectUP's reach and message.

Wyatt finished his prayer, and after their joint *Amen*, Zane gave her hand a squeeze. She looked over and returned his smile. When he let go and followed the others out into the hall, she took a deep breath and gazed around the space again. She'd miss these office hunting excursions with Zane, but what a blessing they'd found this ideal space in the perfect location.

After one last turn, she sighed and sent up another prayer of gratitude.

Back outside, Zane turned to Wyatt. "You guys want to grab some dinner?"

Wyatt looked at Harper.

"I wish we could," she said. "But I have a ton of homework tonight. Let's do something another time, the four of us."

"Definitely," Zane answered.

Ally did a double-take at Zane. What? The four of them? Like a ... date? She turned to the other couple. Certainly, they didn't think she and Zane —

"Great," Wyatt said with a smile. "This weekend's pretty full, but let's plan something soon."

"Sure thing. We'll get with you on that later and compare calendars."

Oh, mercy. That sounded like a *we* we. Like the kind of *we* that would go out on a date. And they weren't that kind of *we*. Were they?

Before she could formulate a response, Harper pulled her in for a hug. "Thank you for all your hard work finding us this spectacular office. I can't wait to get moved in."

"Yeah. It was fun."

Fun looking up properties on the Internet, fun organizing all the showings ... fun being with Zane. Had it really only been a week since their first meeting over hamburgers? It seemed like she'd known him much longer, probably because they'd seen each other every day and had spent hours touring offices, planning new launches, creating training processes for new leaders. And there was still a lot of work to do to make ConnectUP a viable ministry for national distribution. Which meant they'd continue to be together quite a bit, although much of their time would also be with other leaders.

Back in the Bronco, Zane blasted up the air conditioner. "I hope that wasn't presumptuous of me. I should've asked you first before saying we'd get back to them."

"No problem. Sounds like fun."

His grin lit up his face. "Awesome. So, what about right

now? You've been stuck with me all day, but how about dinner? On me."

She gave her head another shake. "Nope. Tonight's on me. Remember I told you about Yolanda's and my favorite Tex-Mex place? Does that sound good?"

"I'm in. Just tell me where to go."

Twenty minutes later, they were seated in a booth in the small, hole-in-the-wall restaurant, ordered their dinners, then Ally took a long pull of water through her straw. Zane swept a chip through one of the bowls of salsa and popped the whole thing into his mouth.

She pulled her lips from the straw. "Hope you like spicy because that one's—"

His eyes widened as he grabbed his glass of water, forgoing the straw to gulp down the contents.

"—hot. Yep. That one's hot, the chunky one's mild."

Sweat beaded on his forehead and his face reddened. "You might've mentioned that sooner," he said with gravel in his voice. Waving his hand in the air, he motioned for the waiter.

Ally looked up at the college-aged boy as he refilled Zane's water. "A glass of milk for my friend, please." The kid laughed and left the pitcher at the table, for backup, apparently.

Zane gulped down more water until the young man returned with a tall glass of milk. "Thank you," he rasped.

Ally couldn't help giggling as she dipped a chip into the spicy sauce. "Sorry. I forget you're not from around here."

He set the half-empty glass of milk down on the table. "Wow. I'm going to be feeling that for a while." He watched her eat the chip with a crease in his brow. "You like spicy, I take it?"

"Kind of grew up on it."

"I see. Well, this Indiana boy clearly needs to toughen up. Your eyes didn't even water."

Their dinners arrived on piping hot plates, Zane blessed their meal, then picked up his fork. "Tell me more about hanging with your uncle who restored vintage automobiles. That wasn't in Central America, was it?"

She shook her head. "Denver, when I was in middle school."

"Was your family on furlough?"

She looked down at her combo plate as her chest filled with the familiar ache that had taken up residence there sixteen years before. Over time, it had settled into the recesses of her heart, only reappearing when she let herself meander through her memories. "Something like that."

Silence stretched between them. "I see," he said when she offered nothing more.

When she brought her gaze back to him, the crinkle between his eyes asked the question he hadn't voiced and that she wouldn't answer. She hadn't talked about that time in her life with anybody but Yolanda. That terrible, painful time. Dealing with a loss she'd never imagined. A loss difficult for most to understand.

Apparently picking up on her reluctance to elaborate, he didn't pursue it and took a hefty bite of his chicken enchilada. "Wow, you weren't kidding. This is fantastic. I can see why this is your favorite place."

She took a couple of bites of her own enchilada while he finished off the first of three on his plate. "Speaking of vintage cars, how long have you had ... Phyllis?"

He brushed his napkin across his mouth and returned her grin. She had to admit, the name was growing on her. "All my life. My dad bought it when he was seventeen. His first car. Then my first car. My only car."

"Really? That's so cool. Did you do the work on it or have it done?"

"My dad and I did most of it. Got it up and drivable by my sixteenth birthday. Then I finished it over the next few years."

"On your own?"

His eyes clouded. "My dad died from pancreatic cancer

when I was eighteen. He was determined to watch me walk across the stage at my high school graduation. And he did." He swallowed, his gaze directed at his plate. "It was the last time he left our house. Hospice came in two days later."

Tightness clamped around her throat. He *did* understand. None of her friends had lost a parent, so she'd never felt comfortable confiding. Not even to Wyatt when they were together, even though he was a well-respected psychologist. He was aware her mother had died, but she'd never shared her deepest feelings about it—the grief that still swamped her at times like a rogue wave.

But Zane, he'd been there. He got it. The man who smiled easily and laughed often, now sat with grief etched across his features.

"Zane. I am so sorry." More than she could articulate, and her inability to put words together this time wasn't about his eyes. Which at the moment weren't dancing but held a pain she understood all too well. A pain he hadn't hesitated to share with her. Could she be as brave in sharing her deepest wound as he'd been? Would it be a comfort to know she empathized with him from her own experience? Could they find that with each other?

"Yeah, me too." The gravel in his voice now had nothing to do with salsa.

"You were close, you and your dad?" Yes, better to focus on him than share her own history.

"He was my best friend. A good man. A great man. A few weeks before he passed, he sat me down and told me he'd prepared everything for me. Had sold the hardware store his father had owned before him. Said he didn't want me saddled to it, to go on to college as we'd planned. He'd also arranged for the house to be sold along with any of the contents I didn't want and the money put into trust for me to collect at twenty-five."

He ran his finger back and forth across the crease in his

chin, something she'd witnessed him do a few times when deep in thought. "There wasn't anything I really wanted from the house. A few photos, gifts he'd given me. I just wanted the Bronco. Most of my trust money is still sitting there. Figured I'd use it for a house someday. Or to travel like my dad always dreamed of doing. He talked all the time about traveling the world but never got farther than Indianapolis, about an hour from Gallagher, where I grew up. I'd love to do and see the things he never had the chance to."

Travel the world? Is that what Zane truly desired to do?

Not wanting to dwell on why that made her stomach coil, she cleared her throat. "What about your mother?"

The muscle in his jaw clenched before he spoke. "Mom's been out of the picture since I was thirteen. She didn't come for the funeral, and to be honest, I'm not sure what I would've done if she had."

Out of the picture. By choice? How did a mother leave their child? "You haven't had any contact with her since you were thirteen?"

"She'd send birthday and Christmas cards sometimes. I sent her cards for a few years, but then they started coming back as undeliverable." He shrugged as if it were no big deal. But the haunted cloudiness in his eyes told a different story. This hurt went deep. "I stopped trying around my sophomore year of high school. Figured if she moved and didn't tell me where, she wasn't interested in hearing from me."

He started in on his second enchilada while her appetite had disappeared. Her heart broke for the boy whose mother, for all intents and purposes, had cut him out of her life. Yet the man seated across from her was funny, charming, confident. A man of faith. She detected no bitterness, no self-pity, in his words or demeanor. Only regret for what he'd lost, first his mother, then his dad. One was still alive, but she was as nonexistent as if she too had died.

Did he have no siblings? He hadn't mentioned a brother or a sister, so did that mean he was alone in the world?

"I'm so sorry, Zane." Such feeble, insufficient words. Grief over a passing she understood. But abandonment? The utter aloneness of having no other family? She and Michael had always had each other and even now spoke or texted at least once a day. And her father, while miles away, was always *there*. If she needed him, he was only a phone or video call away. But Zane ... who did he have? "I can't imagine a mother being able to do that. Disappear completely."

He placed his fork on the plate and rested his forearms on either side of it. "She has a sister, my aunt Gina. Dad asked a friend of his from church to send word to Aunt Gina after he passed. I think he held onto the hope Mom would show up so I wouldn't be on my own."

He paused and stared down at the table before looking back up at her. "I wasn't in a great place then. Spiritually, psychologically. I was angry and wanted nothing to do with her. Like I said, I honestly don't know what I would've done if she'd shown up at the funeral. Was actually relieved she didn't. That sounds awful, but I ..." His sigh conveyed what his words hadn't.

She reached over to cover his hand. "I can understand that. Who wouldn't be angry and hurt in that situation?" She looked at their hands, quickly withdrew hers, and picked up her fork. "Um, so you don't know where she is?"

He shook his head. "No idea. And I haven't looked. She's made it abundantly clear she doesn't want a relationship with me, but I still make sure Aunt Gina knows how to contact me in case anything happens to her. Other than that, I don't expect her to ever be in my life."

A cold tingle grew from the base of her skull and traveled down her spine. No wonder he longed to travel the globe. He had no ties. Nobody to answer to, that he was responsible for.

And he had his trust money. He could do whatever he wanted, wherever he wanted, whenever he wanted.

He nodded toward her plate. "I hope I didn't ruin your dinner by dumping my sad family history on you."

"Not at all. Thank you for sharing that with me." Her eyes locked on his. He'd been so honest, so transparent, in telling her his story. Could she do the same? Could she trust him with it? Confide that she understood to the deepest part of her how he felt in losing his father?

The decision was made for her when her phone sounded from inside her purse. She pulled her gaze from him and glanced at the screen. "It's Yolanda."

He gestured with his hand. "Absolutely. Take it."

She put the phone to her ear. "Hey, Yo."

Her friend's heavy sigh carried through the line. "Hi, Al. I'm at the store, and the Vee-Dub won't start. I think it's the battery. Can you come and bring your cables with you? I'd call Steve, but he's out of town for work."

Her eyes met Zane's across the table as he finished off the last of his rice and beans. The man must have liked her favorite place because he ate every bit of his dinner. His brow creased as he put down his fork. "What?"

"Hold on a sec, Yo." She took the phone from her ear. "Yolanda's stuck with a dead battery at the grocery store, and Steve's out of town. Do you have anything you need to get to right away? If you do, it's no problem to take me home to get my car."

"I can definitely go with you."

"Really? You don't mind?"

"Of course not. I insist."

"That's great. Thanks." She put her phone back to her ear. "Hang tight and we'll be there in about ten."

She hung up as the waiter brought their bill to the table. When Zane pulled out his wallet and asked the young man for a to-go-box for her half-eaten dinner, she put out her hand.

"Huh-uh. My treat, remember? You've paid for every meal we've eaten together. It's my turn."

He pulled a playful scowl as he put his wallet back in his pocket. "I'm not used to letting a lady pay for dinner."

"Welcome to the modern world, Z."

He grinned then, and there went that hitch in her pulse again. "I'm an old-fashioned guy. It's how I was raised."

"And your dad did a good job. Just saying it's okay to let a friend treat you now and then."

His smile softened. "I'm glad we're friends, Allyson Kincaid."

Warmth spread through her chest. "Me too."

But for how long? He could get the itch at any time to go live out his father's dream. Travel the world and leave all of this behind. Could their fledgling friendship withstand the distance? Or maybe having no ties was exactly what he wanted.

CHAPTER FOURTEEN

*Z*ane couldn't think of a better way to experience Six Flags Over Texas than with teenagers.

As they exited one of the roller coasters, Ty shoulder-bumped his friend Carlos. "Man, you screamed more than my little sister."

"Yeah, Carlos." Dwight grinned at the other kid. "My ears are still ringing."

With his ever-present, high-wattage smile in place, Carlos shook his head. "Only when we were upside-down. Finn was yellin' pretty good too."

Finn raised his hand. "Hey, now. Don't go rattin' me out to Tonya. She thinks I'm a stud."

"Stud or dud?"

Zane's laughter joined the boys' as they walked away from the coaster. Witnessing the camaraderie between the Arlington guys he'd been hanging with the last hour or so, his thoughts meandered back to his own high school days and the buddies he'd considered brothers. From mischievous little boys in Vacation Bible School to teammates on and off the basketball court, he thought then they'd be neighbors and best friends forever.

Before the news that sent his life in a new direction. One without his father, his anchor. One that put him on a downward spiral until God finally got his attention again, thanks to a couple of college roommates who refused to give up on him.

That seed planted toward the end of his junior year grew into a passion for student ministry. It was important that these kids knew they had people to encourage them through the hard things, celebrate with them through the good things.

Today's excursion to the amusement park had been all about celebrating the good. He'd made the rounds throughout the day, tagging along with different groups as they crossed paths. And although he and Ally had passed each other a few times, they hadn't spent more than a few minutes together yet.

Evening had descended, and the park would be closing in a couple of hours. Maybe they could still take on a couple of rides before then. He should shoot her a text to see if she wanted to meet up somewhere.

As they rounded a corner, Ty backhanded Finn's arm and pointed. "What's that about?"

Zane followed the direction he indicated and found a group of other ConnectUP kids—easily identifiable in their matching CU shirts—gathered in a circle, nobody smiling or talking. Concerned, he jogged over with the others trailing behind and nudged his way to the center, where he found Ally kneeling next to a young girl with her leg stretched out on a bench.

Tears flowed down the teen's face as Ally gently probed the area around her ankle. The girl—Lydia, Olivia, something like that, if he remembered correctly—let out a yelp and an agonized sob.

"Sorry, Livi." Ally laid a reassuring hand on her leg. "I'm not trying to hurt you. I just need to get a feel for what we're looking at here. All right?"

Livi nodded, and Ally then ran her fingers along the other side and behind her foot. Thankfully, that didn't bring out any new cries of pain. "Okay, sweetie, there doesn't appear to be a break, which is the good news. But I do think we need to take you in to have it looked at."

"Yes, m-ma'am."

Zane walked over and put his hand on her shoulder. "Hey, what happened?"

She looked up in surprise. "Hi." She stood and turned to him. "A couple of the girls were running to meet their friends when Olivia took a bad step and twisted her ankle pretty badly."

"Good thing you were here. What can I do?"

Tonya kneeled beside Livi while Jill, a petite blonde who was one of Harper's cheerleaders, ran up with a bag of ice she'd apparently picked up at a nearby concession stand.

"Can you text Harper and tell her Olivia from the Arlington club hurt her ankle and I'm with her, please? She'll want to alert Jenny, and she may want to put in a report with the park."

"On it." He sent the text, waited for Harper's response, then looked over at Ally, now on the phone with the girl's mother. She must be amazing with her patients and their parents. She'd calmed Livi down with her confident assurances and was now doing the same with the mom. Olivia leaned into her while Ally stood beside her stroking her hair, as if her touch alone brought the comfort she needed.

Ally disconnected and turned to him. "Her mom asked if we could take her to Memorial and she'll meet us there. I really hate to ask, but I came with Shannon and don't have my car."

"Absolutely. Not a problem. Definitely more room for Livi to stretch out in the back seat of the Bronco than Shannon's Mini. I'll go bring it up front." He waved over Finn and Dwight, both football players every bit as big as, and probably stronger than, he was. "Hey guys, can you help Livi here to the gate? Very carefully, please, and slowly. Let her rest when she needs to and listen to Ally."

"Yes, sir," the boys said as they stepped up to wait for instructions.

He reached out and squeezed her hand. "I'll text you when I pull up."

"Thanks, Z. I appreciate it." The smile she gave him did that fluttery thing to his stomach before he let go of her hand to jog toward the exit and the vast parking lot beyond.

Looked like they wouldn't be going on any of the rides together, but at least now he'd get to spend some time with her when he took her home later. Because, truth was, he missed her. He hadn't seen her for any length of time since Saturday, when he moved his few belongings into Steve's house. Afterward, she'd gone with him to buy bedding, towels, and a few other items he needed, then stayed for dinner with him, Steve, and Yolanda.

Yesterday after church, he and Steve spent the afternoon at the Texas Rangers game with some boys from the Irving club. And today, in an effort to spend time with different kids from the various clubs, he'd only seen her in passing.

It surprised him, really, how much a part of his everyday life she'd become in such a short time. His friendship with Wyatt and Harper had grown tight over the past eight months. But in the two weeks he'd known Ally, she was fast becoming his closest friend.

Okay, so maybe it was more than that. He'd had several close friends of the female persuasion over the last several years. Yet he'd never taken notice of how the light reflected in their eyes like he did Ally's dark irises with their amber-hued spots around the pupils. Had never wondered how it would feel to slide his fingers through their hair like he did Ally's thick tresses. Had never noticed how they fit against him when he hugged them. Not the way Ally's willowy frame did.

He hadn't fallen asleep thinking about them, or counted the hours until he would see them again. Not like he did with Ally.

When she reached across the table the other night and

covered his hand with hers in a gesture she meant to comfort, he couldn't help wondering what it would be like to walk with her hand-in-hand, how her fingers would feel against his cheek …

He gave himself a mental shake. Better to keep his head here, since he had no idea if she felt remotely the same. Less than two months ago, she'd been nursing a broken heart at the wedding. She'd told him it was more about the lost dream than it was the man, but was she truly past it? Would she even be ready to move into something new with someone new?

And if so, would he be the best someone for her? Knowing how she longed for roots right here in Texas? A guy who hadn't known a true home since leaving his at eighteen without so much as a glance in his rear-view mirror?

At the Bronco, and a bit winded from the long jog in the still warm evening air, he climbed in, turned the AC on high, and drove through the lot toward the front gate. He couldn't help the grin spreading on his face. Witnessing Ally in nurse mode had been cool. Harper had called her gifted. He might have only seen a glimpse tonight, but he didn't find it surprising. Not when he knew firsthand how easy she was to talk to, confide in. How giving and showing care came so naturally to her.

He pulled up to the curb and picked up his phone to shoot her a text.

At the gate

A few seconds later, her response popped up.

Almost there

No rush

He stuck the phone back in the cupholder and hopped out of the car to run over to the guard by the gate. "Excuse me."

The man walked over to peer at him through the bars. "What can I do for you?"

"I'm here with a group of kids, and one of our girls was injured. We have a couple of the boys helping her out here, but I wanted to make sure they would be able to get back in."

"Not a problem. Sorry to hear about your girl. Do you want to file a report?"

"We let our admin know about it, so she may be contacting the park to file a report. We don't think it's anything serious. Hopefully just a sprain."

"We'll keep a good thought." He looked down at Zane's T-shirt, where two arrows made a cross for the *T* in *ConnectUP*— a horizontal arrow with points at both ends and the other pointing straight up. "You're a Christian group, you and your kids?"

"Yes, sir. ConnectUP is a student ministry to high schoolers. Our objective is to provide a safe place for connection with kids from all walks of life and ultimately with God."

The guard smiled and nodded. "Very good. We just moved here from Arizona. I have a boy who's a sophomore here in Arlington. Doesn't know anybody. I'll tell him about your group."

Zane grabbed his wallet and handed the man a business card. "We'd love to have him. He can check out our website there for more information, but the Arlington club meets every Wednesday at seven at the community center."

"Thanks. I'll tell him."

He looked past the guard and spotted Olivia, her face pale and drawn, being carried between the two football players, with Ally walking in front. "Here they come. Thank you for your help."

"Any time."

Zane jogged back over to the car to open the back door while Ally spoke to the park official at the exit. The guard nodded and opened the gate for them. The grimace on Olivia's tear-streaked face pulled at Zane's chest. Not a great way to end a fun day.

Finn peered into the vehicle once they had Livi situated with her leg spread out on the seat. "Hey, Liv, we'll be praying. Text Tonya later to let us know how you are, okay?"

She nodded. "Thanks, you guys. I appreciate Tonya and Jill letting me borrow you."

"No worries," Dwight assured her. "Hope your foot's okay."

The boys walked back through the gate held open by the security guard as Zane pulled away from the curb.

"Okay, navigator. Tell me where I'm going."

She threw him another smile, and his pulse did a little jig. So much for keeping his head.

CHAPTER FIFTEEN

"*Y*ou were certainly the hero of the day."

Ally rolled her eyes at Zane as they walked side-by-side through the emergency room waiting area. "Hardly. Just at the right place at the right time."

"I don't know. You in nurse mode is pretty impressive."

Heat suffused her face at his compliment. "Then I believe you must be easily impressed."

With a low chuckle, he put his hand to the small of her back as the exit doors opened with a *whoosh*, and they walked out into the night three hours after arriving with Olivia. The sticky air foretold of coming rain, but it was the warmth of his palm she was most aware of. Until he removed it to fall into step beside her. Their hands brushed against each other's a couple of times, and she wondered if his fingers might wrap around hers to walk hand-in-hand out to the car.

A quick mental shake chased the thought away. She and Zane were friends, co-workers in ministry. And it had only been two weeks to the day since she'd set eyes on him again five weeks after that night on a moonlit terrace. She certainly shouldn't be thinking about him so much. Regardless of how well they'd clicked from the beginning. How easy he was to talk to, or how much he made her laugh, even when they were up to their eyeballs in spreadsheets and budgets and curriculum.

The last man who'd captured her attention so wholly had broken her heart. In hindsight, she could see they'd held onto the relationship longer than they should have. Wyatt was never meant to be hers, and she was never meant to be his. And he'd been the wise one to finally call it. Her heart was in one, solid, content piece now, and she'd promised herself she would handle it with more care in the future.

Which meant these daydreams about the handsome man beside her really had to stop.

Once at the Bronco, he helped her up into the passenger seat as he always did, holding her hand until she was seated inside. Tonight, though, did he hold on a little longer? Was that a little squeeze he gave her along with that knee-melting, dimpled grin before he let go and closed the door?

"Stop it, Allyson." She watched him walk around the front of … Phyllis, making sure he didn't catch her chastising herself out loud. "He was just being his sweet, chivalrous self."

He slipped behind the wheel, started up the powerful engine along with the air conditioning, and looked over at her. "I'm a bit turned around. Which way to your house?"

"Go left out of the parking lot, take the first right, then a left onto I-30."

"Okay, I can probably figure my way from there."

"No doubt."

She covered a yawn with her hand. Good thing tomorrow —er, today—wasn't a workday. Her new temp job started Wednesday, and now that they'd found the office space, they hadn't made any plans to meet for ConnectUP business before that night's visit to the Irving club. Her Tuesday was hers to do whatever she wanted.

Except what she wanted was to spend the day with Zane.

"What do you have going on tomorrow?"

She looked back over at him. The man had many talents, but mind-reading couldn't be one of them. Could it? "Nothing, really. Thought I'd work on the leadership training material."

"I was thinking the same thing. Wanna work on it together, or will you get more done without me?"

"Sure, you can come over. Any time is fine."

"Sounds like a plan. I'll come after my one o'clock Zoom with Wyatt and Maggie."

Now that her Tuesday was looking up, she put her head back against the headrest, closed her eyes, and let the music from the radio lull her into semi-consciousness.

"When did you decide to go into nursing?"

His question pulled her out of her fog, and she raised her head to stare ahead at the road. Traffic had thinned, and light from the streetlamps reflected in neatly spaced pools on the pavement. "I can't remember ever really wanting to do anything else."

"Because of your dad being a doctor?"

She turned to the passenger window. "My mom, actually."

"She's a nurse?"

A familiar but unwelcome fist squeezed that place inside her chest where all her grief resided. "Emergency room nurse." She swallowed against the lump in her throat and looked over at Zane. "She met my dad when he was a resident at the hospital where she worked in Denver. When they started dating, they realized they'd both been called to missions and went immediately into the field after they were married. Their first assignment was in Costa Rica, and there were five more after that. My brother was born there, and I was born in Nicaragua."

"Wow, six foreign mission assignments." He took the correct exit without asking. Looked like he really was learning his way around. "I bet they have some exciting stories."

She didn't answer right away. Hearing her parents' stories growing up, that's exactly how they described it.

Exciting, thrilling, challenging. They'd loved it. Her father still did.

"It was their life. My mother radiated joy. All the time. And the people adored her wherever we were."

Silence stretched for a moment as he turned onto the street that led to her house. "What happened?" he asked quietly. "With your mom, I mean. You told me you were in Guatemala last year with your dad. But you've never mentioned her before now."

Her hands clasped in her lap drew her attention as emotion clutched at her throat. How was the pain still this raw after all these years? When he shared with her about his father's passing, she'd decided it wasn't the right time to tell her story. Was it really that she hadn't had the courage to open up about her own loss?

She took a shuddering breath. "My mom ... passed away."

He glanced at her and back at the road. "Oh, wow, Ally. I'm so sorry. How long ago?"

"I was twelve." She brushed aside a tear and looked at him. "I'm sorry I misled you when you asked the other day if we were in Colorado on furlough. I've just never ... it's not easy—"

"To talk about. I get it. But I also know how much it helps to let others in to help you carry the hard things. The heavy things. Especially if they've been through it themselves."

He pulled up to her townhome and turned off the ignition. "I hope you know you can talk to me about this, if it will help. Whenever you're ready."

She stared at him for a long moment. Was she? Ready to share the grief she'd kept buried inside since she was a girl? To trust him with this burden they had in common?

He'd been brave enough to recount his deepest sorrow with her. Certainly, she could muster up the same courage from the same Source. *Father, please give me the strength ... the words ...*

She took another deep breath in an effort to steady her

voice. "My parents were serving in a remote area of Honduras when Mom collapsed." Her breath hitched, and she turned to the windshield as if she could see that rustic clinic in front of her, with the cracked concrete floor where her mother took her last breath.

"I remember watching Daddy do CPR ... it took so long ... I was hysterical. Michael was shaking all over but held onto me to keep me out of the way. Looking back, and knowing what I do now, Dad had to have known it was too late. We were just too far away from the resources that could have saved her. But, still, he tried."

"Ally ..." He reached for her hand and covered it in a firm grasp. "I'm sorry that happened to you when you were so young."

Her gaze roamed the well-lit courtyard in front of the Bronco as she fought back the emotion that threatened to overwhelm her. Zane didn't fill the silent space between them, simply gave her the time to find her voice. "The autopsy showed she had an undiagnosed congenital defect that caused her heart to stop." She met his eyes again and found compassion swimming in their depths. "We came to the US to bury her in Colorado, where my parents were raised. She was only forty years old."

Her voice broke, and she shook her head. "I never wanted to go to another mission after that."

Seconds passed before he spoke. "But your dad?"

"After we'd been stateside almost a year, I began to think we would stay. Get our own house, I could stay at the school I'd been attending with my cousins, grow up in an American neighborhood where there were medical facilities close by, emergency services. That if anything were to happen to Daddy or Michael, at least we could get them help. I wouldn't lose somebody else I love because we didn't have adequate resources."

She inhaled and let it out slowly. "Then the ministry

LORI DEJONG

organization my dad works for called. They had an opening for a director at an already established medical mission in Guatemala if he wanted it."

A tear escaped, and she brushed it away. "He didn't even talk to Michael and me about it. Just told us we were returning to Central America. I lost it. Couldn't believe he would consider taking us back to a place like the one I blamed for killing my mom. I know now that's not true, as an adult and a medical professional myself. But at the time, that's all I had. All I knew. I was mad at a *place*, if that makes any sense."

His thumb stroked hers in a slow circle, the gentle sensation calming, reassuring. "Makes perfect sense. I blamed everybody and everything when Dad passed away. Even God. Spent most of those first three years in complete rebellion. And I was practically grown, not twelve years old."

Her heart hurt for a young Zane, all alone in the world, angry at God, looking for someone, anyone, to care. To value him. To comfort him. She'd had her family, friends, a counselor, all helping her cope. But he'd had no one.

Turning her hand over, she held his palm-to-palm, hoping to comfort him as he had her. "It's understandable that you'd look to other things to help you get through it. Especially since your mom wasn't there for you. Maybe I didn't want to go back to the field, but Daddy was at least present for my brother and me. I don't know how you did it."

"Not well, that's for sure." He studied her for a moment. "How'd you move through it? At such a young age?"

"My dad had us both in grief counseling here in the States. Of course, back on the field there were no counselors, but he did his best to help me adjust. Still, I kept mostly to myself when we first got to Pamoca. Until school started, anyway. Then I was pretty much forced to interact with the other kids."

"You weren't homeschooled?"

"Not in Guatemala. I attended an accredited private school

there. Daddy told me later the school was part of the appeal of that particular mission, so I could go to college. It was the only place we were ever assigned that was already established. In the past, it was my parents who started the clinic, literally from the ground up."

"Is that where you met Yolanda, at school?"

"I didn't meet Yolanda. God *gave* me Yolanda. She was as extroverted in eighth grade as she is now. Determined to draw me out of my shell from that first day of school. We bonded immediately and became more like sisters than friends. She practically lived at my house since there were five other kids at hers, and it was only me at mine."

He cocked his head. "Just you? Michael stayed in the States?"

She nodded, the memory of saying goodbye to the brother she adored, her first best friend, turning her belly to stone. "He was a junior in high school and already planned to attend a small Christian college in Colorado. So, he stayed with my aunt and uncle while Dad and I went on to Guatemala. It was awful, being there without Mom and Michael. Like I'd lost them both."

When her eyes filled, Zane let go of her hand to pull something from his back pocket. She smiled despite her tears when she saw another white handkerchief.

She took it and patted her cheeks. "I've never known a young man to carry a handkerchief. And this is twice you've come to my rescue with one."

He shrugged and grinned. "My dad always carried one. They're handy for lots of things."

"I washed the other one, but I keep forgetting to give it to you. I'll wash this and get them both back to you."

"So not worried about a couple of hankies, Ally." His smile softened. "Thank you. For sharing your experience with me. It means a lot that you would."

Her cheeks warmed, and something fluttered in her

midsection. Wyatt had tried a few times to help her open up about her life after her mother died, but she never had.

Yet in less than two weeks, Zane had her spilling all of that history she kept pent up inside, because certainly nobody could understand, right? How abandoned she felt? How lost she'd been? It took a while for her to be on speaking terms with God again, but the night she fell to her knees in the dark, empty mission chapel, she found Him there, waiting, listening, caring. Loving her as He always had.

But Zane understood. He'd gone through his own version of rebellion against the God he blamed for his deepest hurt. And he also returned. The Lord had taken the broken parts of them both and made them stronger.

Everything inside her began to unravel. The stone in her stomach dissolved, the fist clenched around her heart loosened its grip. The taut muscles in her shoulders relaxed, and the vice around her throat opened.

Lighter in spirit than she'd been in a while, she smiled. "No, thank *you*. Yolanda's the only other one I've shared any of this with, and it was because she was actually there. Walked me through a lot of the grief to find Jesus was still with me. Always with me."

"And always will be." He gave her hand a quick squeeze. "Stay put."

He got out of the car and came around to her door. But after helping her out, he pulled her close for a hug. They'd hugged plenty of times over the past couple of weeks. A hello hug when he'd come over to work or when they saw each other at an event or at church. A goodbye hug when he left.

But this felt different. Closer. Warmer. With her cheek to his shoulder, her forehead pressed to his neck, her arms wrapped around him. The muscles under his shirt flexed beneath her hands and she closed her eyes, breathing in the heady, earthy scent of his skin, taking in the warmth of his body.

After a moment, his hands traveled up her back to her arms, and he pulled away. Just the slightest bit. He brushed a strand of hair from her cheek and stared down into her eyes. Powerless to look away, her breathing shallowed as her gaze locked onto his. His face angled over hers, and his breath fanned across her mouth before he closed the distance between them.

Darkness descended as her eyes drifted shut. She was aware of only him. The feel of him, the scent of him, the taste of him. Her lips conformed to his of their own volition as his arms moved around her again. Pulled her closer. Her heart pounded. Or maybe that was his. Her hands came to his chest—

A car drove by, the sound yanking her back to reality. Her eyes sprang open, and she pulled out of his embrace.

"Al—"

"I can't do this, Zane. Not now. It's too … I'm not … I mean—"

"It's too soon." His hand reached for hers, but she took a step back and he let it drop. "I understand. I'm sorry. I didn't mean to rush anything."

"No, it's not you. I just …"

How could she explain? That she didn't trust her own judgment? Because she'd done this before and had finally found herself again?

"Ally, it's okay. We're okay."

But were they? She needed some distance. Some perspective. They'd become too close too fast. A false intimacy. It had to be.

Because she couldn't be falling for him. Not already. She'd tumbled head over heels for Wyatt the night they met and ended up with a shattered heart two years later. Older and wiser now, she needed to keep her wits about her.

Before she lost herself all over again.

CHAPTER SIXTEEN

I'm sorry, Zane, not able to meet today.
Will send you what I get done this
morning. Apologies for the late notice.

*Z*ane sighed and shook his head. "She's doing it again."

By her own admission, she'd ducked him at the wedding, then again that night after the CU Arlington team meeting. And now, for the third time this week, she'd come up with an excuse to not see him. At least, not alone.

"I have a tendency to run from uncomfortable situations."

Ally's words from that evening they'd spent talking over *the best burgers in Texas,* reverberated in his head. When she canceled on him Tuesday afternoon, the day after that heart-stopping, albeit ill-conceived, kiss, she'd at least been honest about it.

"I just need a little space, Z. To clear my head. I hope you understand."

Well, yeah, sort of. He understood he'd crossed a line Monday night. That he'd given in to the pull to kiss her after wondering about it so many times. He understood she wasn't ready to move into something more than they already were. And all of that was fine. He could handle it.

Yesterday, when he'd texted her to see how her first day at the new temp job had gone, though, she sent back a simple and much too formal, *It went well. Thank you for asking.* Followed two hours later by a text letting him know she would meet him at the Irving club's Wednesday night meeting instead of going together like they had last week to Grand Prairie. No reason why. And once there, she made sure they were never alone, stuck close to Yolanda, and left while he was talking to a couple of the boys.

Now this. They were supposed to get together this afternoon, since Thursday wasn't a regular workday for her, to finish up the details for the new leadership on-boarding training videos. Though, apparently, she'd started without him and would be sending him her progress.

But no explanation as to why they couldn't work in person like they'd been doing from the start? Yep, the girl was clearly running.

Which wasn't getting either of them anywhere. ConnectUP was fine. The work was getting done. But the friendship they'd built was crumbling around their feet.

> I understand. Can we touch base tonight?

He waited a long two minutes before his phone pinged.

> I'm sorry. Meeting w/shannon and one of the arlington girls.

"Seriously?"

> Ok. Tomorrow night? We need to start on budget for the office.

And he needed to see her. To get this awkwardness of his own making out of the way. To let her know she was safe with him. That he would never expect anything of her she wasn't ready to give.

> Started a preliminary one yesterday. Will send you what I have. Feel free to change anything. I could do a zoom after work if you want. 3pm?

A Zoom call. They'd only worked through video call a couple of times, both of which were ideas one or the other of them had come up with after they'd already been working together—in person—and parted for the night. Was that going to be the new normal now?

> Would rather get together but can make it work. See you at 3 tom. Have a good day, Al.

He wanted to tell her he missed her. That he was sorry he'd stepped out of line. That she was too important to him to just walk away.

Maybe he should show up on her doorstep unannounced, make her talk it out with him, so they could get past this awful silence.

Except he preferred she be on board. Blindsiding her wasn't the way to handle this. He would have to pray, keep things on a more professional level with her—since that's obviously what she wanted—and give her the space she'd asked for. No matter how much he wanted to go after her.

What he couldn't make sense of, though, was why she was trying so hard to keep him at arm's length. Was it to discourage his feelings, or protect herself from her own? Because one thing he knew without a doubt. She'd been as much a participant in that brief but incredible kiss as he had.

Deciding food would improve his mood, he walked into the kitchen to put together a sandwich. He pulled turkey, ham, provolone, lettuce, tomato, and mayo out of the fridge, then a loaf of whole wheat bread from the pantry. Sandwich made, he plopped it on a paper plate with some potato chips, grabbed a soda, and took his lunch over to the couch.

As he settled in to eat, his gaze caught on the open Bible he'd left there after his morning quiet time. A time in which he'd asked for some guidance, not only in his work with ConnectUP, but his relationship with Ally. So he could grow both of them into whatever God would have them to be. Because, if truth be told, the ministry, as well as Ally, had come to hold a significant place in his life.

So much so that if a foreign mission assignment didn't come up for a while, he wouldn't have a problem sticking it out with ConnectUP. This ministry, the leaders, and the students had burrowed their way into his heart, and he could easily see himself a part of it for the foreseeable future.

He took a bite and chewed, his thoughts churning. For the first time, the idea of staying put in one place, having close, long-term, maybe life-long friends, living somewhere familiar instead of learning to navigate a new city every few years … finding someone to share life with … sounded pretty good. He'd wondered if that person might be Ally, seeing how they gelled from the get-go. How easily they'd fallen into a working rhythm. How fun it was to banter back and forth.

There was no denying his feelings went beyond the friend zone, and he'd thought perhaps hers did too. He'd been told, by her ex-boyfriend, nonetheless, she didn't confide easily. Yet she'd opened up to him about aforementioned ex-boyfriend that night after the barbecue, then her mom on Monday. Clearly, she'd felt safe with him. Close enough to share her deepest regrets and heartaches.

Before that kiss that sent it all sideways.

After finishing up his lunch, he threw the paper plate away and took a seat in front of the laptop on the kitchen table. He'd just pulled up his email to retrieve the documents Ally said she'd send when his phone chimed with an incoming video call.

He smiled as he answered. "Maggie. Good to see you. Did we set up a meeting during our call Tuesday that I forgot to write down?"

Ever since Becker Ministries came on board to sponsor ConnectUP back in January, he and Wyatt had met with Maggie via video call every Tuesday afternoon. But he'd been so unfocused two days ago, he honestly couldn't remember if they'd discussed getting together today.

"No, we didn't set up anything." Maggie's face shone as usual with her natural effervescence. "But I needed to talk to you. Is this a good time?"

"Uh-oh. What'd I do now?"

"You went and grew up on us, my boy," she said with a laugh. "And while my mama bear feelings for you may not be ready to let you go, my mentor instincts tell me it might be time."

His smile vanished as he sat up at attention, his belly tightening. "Let me go? You're letting me go?" His mind whirled back through the last few weeks. He'd been joking, but had he actually done something that didn't meet with their approval? Had someone not been happy with the work he was doing?

"No, no. I'm sorry. That came out wrong."

"Whew." With a sigh, he relaxed into the chair again. "You scared me there for a second. So, what's going on?"

"I got an interesting call last week but didn't want to mention anything until I'd prayed over it and checked things out with the board."

"A call? About me?"

"Jerry Lassiter from Global Reach Missions."

Heat flooded his face and prickles cascaded over his skin. He should have told Maggie about Jerry's offer. It never occurred to him the man would call her himself.

"He and I go back a ways," she continued. "What with both of us running major ministry organizations. He said he reached out about an opportunity they have in Central America, but you turned him down."

"I was just putting out feelers, Maggie, I promise. I wasn't trying to get out of my commitment to Becker. I'm beyond grateful for everything you've done for me and am more than happy to stay through—"

"Relax, sweetie. I know you're happy here, and while your work has been impeccable, I also know your heart has long been set on foreign missions. And, unfortunately, that's something we're just not able to offer yet.

"But never would we stand in the way of God calling one of our own into another area of ministry. We have to have policies in place to run with any efficiency. But our business, if you want to call it that, also has a spiritual component we have to keep at the forefront of everything we do. We have to be amenable to God's will over-riding our policies from time to time. And this may be one of those times."

The prickles intensified. Was she serious? They would actually release him from his contract to go work for another ministry?

"Maggie ... I don't know what to say. I absolutely told Jerry I had to complete my commitment. There's been no question on my part about that. Ever."

He had much yet to do here, for one thing. He and Ally had accomplished so much the past couple of weeks, and he and Wyatt had put in hours upon hours of planning and strategizing and researching over the last nine months. Could he leave them in the middle of it?

And hadn't he, mere minutes ago, been content to stay if that's how it played out? Maggie's news tossed that out the window pretty quickly.

"I know, Zane. If you'd wanted to talk about an early release, you would have reached out to me. But I know you too well. You're a man of integrity, and your word is golden.

However, we would never hold you back if you felt called elsewhere."

She sighed, then offered him a small smile. "Which is why I'm getting in touch now. If you had no barriers to moving on, would you? Do you believe Global Reach is where you should be? We'll be happy to work with you to bring somebody from Becker up to speed on ConnectUP so you have peace you're leaving them in good hands, if that should be your decision."

He nodded, but no words came. Leave Becker. Leave ConnectUP. Leave Wyatt, Harper, their leadership team, the kids. Leave Ally. He'd been dreaming about and praying for an opportunity like this. But now that he was faced with it, was he ready? Could he leave everything behind again? Start over in yet another new place?

He'd never had an issue with that before, moving on to something new every couple of years or so. Following God's call that eventually led him to Becker. But even after almost four years with the highly-esteemed ministry organization, the itch to move on to *what's next* hadn't hit him yet. At least, until this conversation. Now he wondered what it all meant.

Was God calling him to go ... or to stay?

He swallowed hard. "Any certain time frame you need my answer by?"

She shook her head. "No. Can't put a deadline on God, now, can we?" She laughed, then leaned forward on her arms crossed on her desk. "I have no doubt that whatever you decide, Zane, you're going to do amazing things for the Lord. You already have. Rest assured you will always have my unwavering support. Not only as your boss but as your friend."

Nodding, he cleared his throat of the knot growing there. "That means more than you know, Maggie. Really. I'll give Jerry a call to see where things stand."

What was it the man had said the last time they talked? They would need to know his decision by the end of September so they could onboard him in November.

Three weeks. And perhaps in California in two months. Although he wasn't happy about the distance growing between him and Ally, maybe it really was best to let things lie. Keep the relationship professional and do the work in front of them.

If he could just convince his heart of that. Because one thing he knew for sure. Ally would be the hardest to leave behind.

CHAPTER SEVENTEEN

A kaleidoscope of brightly colored spots played across the ceiling as Ally skated off the rink and plopped onto a bench next to Yolanda. "Only two spills in the last hour. Think I'm making progress on these inline things."

Yolanda laughed and gave her a one-armed hug. "You could've gotten the old-fashioned quads if you wanted."

"And look uncool in front of the kids? No way."

This Saturday night's skating party was a joint venture between Grand Prairie and Irving, and she and Zane had been invited along. On one hand, she'd been surprised he didn't ask during their Zoom yesterday afternoon if she wanted to ride together. But then, since Monday night's startling and confusing ending, she'd been pretty adamant about keeping her distance. Looked like he was doing exactly as she'd asked —giving her some space.

Not that it had helped much. She missed him like crazy. More than she should for someone she *wasn't* falling for.

So, she'd driven here on her own, since Yo came with Steve and she was weary of being their chaperone. And although friendly whenever their paths had crossed, Zane hadn't made a point to spend any one-on-one time together. Which was probably best.

Even if it didn't feel like it.

Ally looked around as Taylor Swift belted out her latest tune through the speakers planted at each corner. "Where's Steve?"

"Concessions. One of his boys asked if he could talk to him. Figured I'd take a few minutes to catch my breath."

"Same. These kids are skating circles around me. Literally."

Her gaze roamed the rink and stopped, again, on Zane. Last time she saw him, he'd been with a group from the Grand Prairie club. Inline skating posed no challenge for him, as evidenced in his relaxed posture and ease with which he moved. He could actually skate and talk at the same time, a feat she had yet to master.

But now he skated alongside one of the new Grand Prairie volunteers. Nicole. The perky kindergarten teacher with long blonde hair and stunning blue eyes. He didn't even have to slow down to accommodate her. She glided along beside him without even a falter, gesturing with her hands, her face lit up with a wide smile. Zane laughed at whatever she'd said, and Ally's heart dropped. They were actually pretty cute together.

Yolanda nudged her shoulder. "He doesn't look at her the way he looks at you."

Ally's head swiveled to her friend. "What? No. Zane and I are just … friends. Co-workers. Well, he's a worker, I'm a volunteer, but you know what I mean."

One eyebrow hitched up on Yolanda's forehead.. "Honey, when he looks at you, that isn't a *just friends* look. Hasn't been since the first time I met him, when we went for pie after the all-area team lead meeting. And you'd only known each other, what? A week at that time?"

"Sort of. We met at the Arlington team meeting the week before, then started working together that Thursday. No way could the man develop any kind of *look* in so short a time."

"Sure he could, *amiga*. And so did you. Chemistry is a powerful thing. And with God in the middle of it, anything is possible." She glanced over her shoulder and Ally followed her line of sight to Steve, seated in the snack bar across from a teenage boy with something very heavy on his mind, by all appearances. "I'm going to marry that man. And I knew it after our first date, even if we weren't aware it was a date at the time, thanks to Jenny. He walked me out to my car after the dinner she'd tricked us into going to, holding my hand, didn't even kiss me. Just hugged me good night. And yet I knew. This was the guy."

"I couldn't agree more. You're perfect."

"No. We're not. We work at it. We talk and we pray and we keep God front and center. But my point is, time doesn't matter. I think with some people, they know after years. Look at Wyatt and Harper. They knew each other how long? Since they were kids? But then there are people who know after a couple of weeks. Maybe you're *that* people."

Ally's chest constricted as she gave her head a small shake, watching Zane and his new friend make another circle on the floor. "I did that before, Yo. And when it came apart, I didn't know who I was by myself."

"That's true. When you were with Wyatt, it was all about Wyatt. I think he knew that too and wanted it to be more about you. He just didn't know how to do that."

Her eyes searched Yolanda's. "He said that?"

"Not to me. Probably not to anybody. But, sweetie, even I know how hard it can be to get close to you when you don't want to open up. Thankfully, my thirteen-year-old self didn't know when to back off, or we might not be the sisters we are now. But look what happened when you finally shared with me all that pain you brought with you to Pamoca. And everything we've walked through together over the years. We're bonded for life, you and me. Because you trusted me with it."

Yolanda took her hand. "You've grown so much since the

break-up. You definitely know who you are all by yourself, as you put it. Maybe now you should trust Zane with some of the things you hold so close. Let him in and see what happens."

Except Ally knew what could happen. What already had. She'd confided in him, left herself vulnerable. And she'd kissed him. Given in to all of those squiggly feelings she'd been mulling over … well, really since that night on the terrace. Allowing herself to daydream about the mystery man she'd never see again.

Until she did. And it turned out he was even better than the fantasy guy in her head.

Could she trust her feelings, though? Everything in her told her Zane was a good man. A man who matched up with most, if not all, of the points on her list of traits she'd imagined in a future husband. Strong faith, trustworthy, kind, great sense of humor, easy to talk to. Yes, he was all of that and so much more.

If only she could take the time to figure it all out. Which was difficult when they needed to communicate so often about ConnectUP. She couldn't keep him at a distance like she had this week if they were going to be any good for the ministry.

Her gaze searched the skating rink. Nicole had joined a group of girls from her club, the five of them side-by-side singing along with a popular new song. Their hips and feet moved in sync, and Ally couldn't help being jealous for a whole new reason—that Nicole was so sure on her inline skates while Ally looked like one of those tube-like air dancers outside the car dealership she passed so often on her way home, wriggling around in the wind.

Not that she had reason at all to be jealous of Nicole for any *other* reason. Of course not.

But where was Zane? Finding him nowhere on the floor, she craned her neck to look around the seating area. The bench gave a little on the other side of her, and when she turned to see why, her breath halted.

"Oh. Hey there."

"Hey back." Zane gave her that grin he had to know threw female hearts all a-twitter. Then again, he probably had no clue, based on the recklessness with which he used it.

Yolanda leaned over to return his smile. "Hi, Zane. Having fun?"

"Tons. I haven't been on my inlines in a while. Forgot how much of a workout it can be, though."

Ally chuckled. "Ditto that."

Especially flopping all over the place. If not for Steve and Yo flanking her, she would have spent the first half-hour on her backside. Once they let go, though, she'd contorted herself in ways she didn't know she could just to stay upright.

His gaze moved back to her . "Looked like you were getting the hang of it pretty good there. Wanna give it a go?"

She looked out onto the floor, then back at the man next to her. "Uh ... now?"

"I thought next week. But if you want to go now, that works."

His wink caused an alarming flutter in her chest. They'd been working together for over two weeks. Had spent hours in each other's company. She really should be immune to the man's charms by now.

Except that now, not only did his dimples and that mischievous wink melt her insides, she couldn't look at him without remembering that kiss, the way his arms held her so close, the warmth of his body pressed to hers ...

Yolanda gave her a nudge. "Go. As soon as Steve's done, we'll join you."

Ally nodded and looked back at Zane. "Okay. Let's see how much more I can humiliate myself tonight."

He stood and held out his hand. She stared at it a moment before bringing her eyes up to his. But instead of the playful humor that had been there a second ago, she saw question mixed with what she could only describe as a plea.

Her need for distance over the past few days had been unfair to him. In her effort to regain some of her emotional equilibrium, she'd sent his even more off-kilter with her silence. If only she could figure out how to fix it, how to go back to what they'd been.

She slipped her hand in his and let him pull her up onto her skates. It took a second to balance, but then he guided her onto the rink.

Once out on the floor, he let go of her hand to slip it around his arm. "I've got you."

She kept her eyes pinned to the polished concrete passing under her, pushing one foot back, then the other. "Okay, yeah. It's easier this time."

"You're doing great."

Halfway around the circle, she realized she held his arm in a death grip. "Oh. Sorry." She loosened her grasp. "Hope you still have feeling below the elbow."

"Does tingling count?"

She laughed and was surprised it didn't cause her to wobble. Maybe she really was catching on.

"Have you never skated inline before?"

She shook her head. "I've skated, but the wheels were better positioned for balance than these things. I was determined to overcome, though."

"And you have. Good job."

She slipped her hand from his arm to test her balance. So far, so good.

Other skaters rolled past them, but Zane stayed beside her as if he had nothing better to do.

"Are we gonna be okay, Al?" he asked as the song changed to something slower. "Should we ... talk about it?"

Her gaze slid to him and back to the floor. "To be honest, I don't know what to say. I'm sorry I've been so distant this week, but I don't think I'm ready to talk about it. Whatever *it* is."

"Then maybe that's where we need to start. Define whatever *it* is and go from there."

A couple of boys whizzed by, knocking her off-balance. Her skates skittered and arms flailed wildly until Zane caught her around the waist before she could go down.

"You all right?"

She nodded once her feet were in alignment again. "Yeah. All good."

He let her go but pulled her hand through his arm again. "Just so you don't have any more close calls," he said, probably anticipating resistance on her part.

And she should. Resist, that is. Because not only did she need to learn to balance on her own two feet, this physical closeness reminded her how far over the line they'd gone. But at the moment, holding onto him afforded her a security she hadn't had going it alone.

Silence stretched between them before he cleared his throat. "Do you still want to work with me?"

His quiet question tore at her heart. "Yes. I like what we're doing and the plans we have in the works. But maybe we should keep things more about the ministry and less ... I don't know. I just ... I think we've blurred the line a little with all this time we've spent together *not* working on CU business."

His gaze moved around the rink before coming back to her, but she was unprepared for the cloud of hurt in his eyes. Did he believe she was abandoning him, just as his mother had? That she'd somehow found him lacking? Because nothing could be further from the truth.

"Okay," he said before she could let him know it wasn't his fault in any way. Her doubt was in herself, not in him. "I don't want to put you in an awkward position. I have to admit, I don't think of you in a strictly business sense. You're probably the best friend I have here. And if I've messed that up, I'm truly sorry. But I'll do or be whatever you need so you feel comfortable with me again."

His best friend. And she'd blown that for him. By making herself so emotionally vulnerable, she'd made herself physically vulnerable, as well. Allowing herself to be swept up in a moment of weakness.

And now their friendship, one forged from a kinship she'd only experienced with Yolanda, hung in the balance.

CHAPTER EIGHTEEN

S trictly business wasn't working for him.

Zane looked across the kitchen table at Ally.

Not. At. All.

Her fingers moved at lightning speed on her laptop. They'd spent the past couple of hours on this Thursday afternoon going over their social media strategy and how to build up their email list to garner interest across the country. They'd scheduled all their posts for the next month and were now putting together their monthly electronic newsletter.

For his part, he'd been creating graphics to go along with her post captions and newsletter verbiage. If he could only keep his eyes from straying across the table.

He turned his laptop around. "What do you think of this for the leadership training post?"

Pulling her focus from her work, she leaned in to study his screen. "That's great. Perfect." Her typing resumed, and he turned the screen back around to face him.

"Excellent. Moving on to the next one."

Today was his first day back at her house since the night everything came apart. At least she hadn't changed their plans at the last minute to meet by Zoom or a neutral location, as they had Tuesday when they'd worked on drafting the renovation budget for the new office for nearly three hours at her favorite coffee shop. It was much easier to work together, in person, and not be distracted by other things going on around them.

Of course, she still wouldn't get in a car with him. Ever since that night, she'd met him everywhere they'd gone. Last week's visit to the Irving club, skating Saturday night, Monday's leadership meeting with the Dallas team. At least her excuse for declining his offer of a ride to last night's Dallas CU club had been a legitimate one.

"Thanks, Zane, but I'll be coming from Shannon's. There's an issue with one of the Arlington girls I used to lead, and we've been meeting with her over the last week to help her navigate."

Maybe the same girl from last week, when she canceled their Thursday work plans? Which was fine by him, if that was the case. That was exactly what they were there for, to guide and direct kids through these sometimes-treacherous teenage years. If she had to give him a reason, that was a good one.

Still, the distance between them was killing him. If nothing more came of their relationship, he'd be happy to simply get back to what they'd been. Until he knew where he'd be in the near future, it was probably better that way. He just missed his friend and the easy camaraderie they'd once had.

"Okay." She stopped typing, but her eyes never left her screen. "I'll insert your graphic for the CU statement of faith, then put in the link to the montage video, and this should be good to publish as the first auto-response in our welcome sequence." She finally looked over at him. "Your graphics are amazing, by the way. Do you have an inner artist I'm not aware of?"

He laughed and shook his head. "Can't draw to save my life, but I do enjoy graphic arts."

"You're good at it."

"I keep telling you we're a great team. You're good at

writing and organizing, I'm good at throwing out a million ideas for you to make sense of, and I guess graphic art."

That garnered one of her smiles he'd missed over the past nine days. Oh, he'd seen it often enough—at the two clubs they'd visited, the leadership meeting on Monday, skating last Saturday—but never directed solely at him. Not like before. So, although not back to the *old* normal he preferred, things appeared to have thawed a bit since their abbreviated talk at the skating rink.

When his phone beeped with an incoming text, he picked it up, glanced over at Ally, once again concentrating on her screen, then sent a quick reply. This could be interesting. Two weeks ago, he'd have been pretty sure of her response. But now? Nothing to do but ask.

"Um, that was Wyatt." He waited for her to look up. "He and Harper were wondering if we were free for dinner on Saturday. There's a new restaurant they've been wanting to try over by the mall."

Her eyes rounded, and he could practically see the wheels turning for an excuse to decline.

"Not a date," he amended quickly. "I mentioned to Wyatt last night that we'd like to get with them sometime to go over the office budget and all the other work we've been doing. I guess they thought it would be fun to go somewhere and do it over dinner."

Her throat moved up and down. "So … just a business meeting? To bring them up to speed?"

"Exactly. A … business meeting." That would look an awful lot like a date. Except if he ever did get to ask her out, it certainly wouldn't be for a double date with her ex-boyfriend and his wife.

"Uh, well. Okay. That should work. Just let me know where to meet you."

"I can pick you up."

She flipped her hand in the air. "If it's by the mall, that's the other direction from your house. Easier to just meet."

"Okay." He shrugged. What more could he say? Knowing her love for vintage automobiles, if he offered to let her drive Phyllis, would she be tempted enough to actually get in a car with him? He'd have to keep that in mind if this went on much longer. "Let me know if you reconsider. It's not that far out of the way."

"I appreciate it. But I may be with Shannon again Saturday afternoon and will leave from there." Her eyes clouded as she looked back at her screen, but her gaze was a million miles away.

He scooted his laptop back and crossed his arms on the table. "Is this still the thing with the Arlington girl?"

A small nod of the head was her answer before those amber eyes, brimming with tears, met his again across the table.

His gut twisted. "Uh-oh. It's bad?"

"Very bad."

He watched the emotions play across her face. "Do you want to talk about it, or is it something you can't share?"

"I can share within the confines of CU leadership. Wyatt's aware because we got his counseling practice involved."

Oh, wow. It *was* bad. And she'd been carrying this around since last week? If he hadn't messed things up between them, she probably would've confided in him days ago.

She swallowed hard. "Remember that first club you came to, when we were supposed to meet afterward but I had to talk with one of my girls?"

"I do. Blair, was it?"

"That's right. The boy she'd been seeing only a few weeks dumped her by text, but she was heartbroken. So hard to convince these girls they're worth so much more than that kind of treatment. He'd treated her badly all along, but she was crazy about him, for some reason.

"After our talk, I thought she was on her way to getting

past it, to see she deserved better. But then you and I started working together, Shannon took over my circle, and even though I checked in with Blair a couple of times, she never alluded to anything being wrong. Said she was doing fine." She shook her head. "I really thought she was doing fine."

Silence stretched for several long seconds while she stared at empty air. He cleared his throat. "Did she ... harm herself?"

Her eyes came back to him. "No." She sat back in her chair, crossed her arms over her middle, and released a tremulous sigh. "Labor Day, she was supposed to come to Six Flags but didn't show. Turned out this boy had asked her to meet him to talk things out. She thought it was all great, that he'd missed her and wanted to get back together. That maybe he'd even changed his spots.

"They went to a movie then back to his house. I guess his parents were gone. He gave her a soda, and later she started feeling weird. He took her back to his room, and ..." She brushed a finger under her eye. "He took something that wasn't his to take. She said she tried to resist, but it was like her body wouldn't work."

Zane's skin crawled. "That kid drugged her to ... take advantage of her?" A gross understatement. But he couldn't bring himself to utter the word it truly was.

"According to Blair. And she's so devastated, there's no way it was consensual. I've seen regret, and I've seen victims. This is a victim. He had her drink a lot of water afterward and, once she was somewhat steady, made her walk home. It was all some kind of game to him, teaching her a lesson for not giving him what he wanted while they were dating."

"That's ... terrible. I'm so sorry."

"Her mom had no idea what happened, just that Blair hadn't spoken or eaten since she got home Monday night, refused to go to school Tuesday. She didn't know what to do, so she called Shannon. We both went over right away, and that's when Blair finally confided. Completely dissolved.

"We took her to the hospital with her mom that afternoon to have blood work done, a rape kit done. Hoping there might be some residual evidence of a drug in her system or biological evidence on her body."

"Did they find anything?"

"Physically, some bruising compatible with forcible rape. And he did leave something behind. She'd already showered twice since it happened, so it's a miracle it was still there, although we won't know for a while if it has evidentiary value. Nothing left of the drug. All the water, then walking home, metabolized it faster, which makes us think he knew that, like he's done this before."

"That's alarming."

"Very. They got an attorney, and they've also pressed charges. Blair's mom is going to homeschool her for now but plans to put her in a private school once she's recovered a bit more psychologically. Talking to the police was grueling for her. And, of course, the online bullying has started, blaming her for getting this kid arrested."

Heaviness settled in his chest. "Her life is forever changed."

"Forever a statistic. Because of this kid's ego. Breaks my heart."

Forever a statistic. He understood that all too well, how a horrible decision made by someone else could mark you forever.

He shook off the weighty memory. "You said something about Wyatt's counseling practice?"

She nodded. "Harper had Wyatt connect Blair to one of his female partners, and Blair's gone about three times so far for counseling. Shannon, Harper, and I have been spending a lot of time with her, too, reminding her this wasn't her fault, praying with her, sitting with her. Whatever she needs. And her mother. A single mom who feels like she let her daughter down. So much healing needs to happen for them both."

"I'll add them to my prayer list. And you, Shannon, and Harper, of course. This can't be easy."

"Hardest thing I've done since I started with ConnectUP. But this is exactly what makes this ministry so vital. To help kids not only find their value in who God says they are, but to help heal these kinds of wounds. These deep, life-altering wounds. I'm encouraged that Blair appears to be digging into her faith."

"You're setting a good example for her."

And he was blessed to serve side-by-side with these fellow soldiers fighting the good fight for kids with too many voices pulling at them to go one way or another. Building this ministry to help them find the One Voice that would never lead them astray.

But he also had a choice to make. A big one. A life-changing one. Just that morning, the information packet from Global Reach had arrived with a pretty clear message that if he wanted the position in Honduras, it was his for the taking. As long as he could be in California by November first. A mere month-and-a-half from now.

If only he had a clear leading in one direction or the other.

After wrapping up their work for the day, ending with prayer as they always did, he made his way home. He would have rather stayed to cook dinner with Ally, as they had on other occasions, but didn't want to press his luck. That she'd agreed to go on Saturday night was encouraging, so he certainly didn't want to do anything to set them back.

Once at home, he finished off the tacos he'd picked up on his way before heading to his room. He slipped off his tennis shoes and settled back into the pillows piled against the headboard to read over Jerry's letter for the third time.

Dear Zane,

*Greetings from sunny California! We're delighted to welcome
you to Global Reach Missions and know you'll be an excellent
addition to the team. Please read over the enclosed information
and fill out the forms as instructed. We'll need the completed
and signed documents returned to us by no later than October
15 to begin the onboarding process November 1.*

*Our goal is to have you report to the Nueva Esperanza Mission
in Honduras by January 15, fully funded and trained. We
anticipate and look forward to sharing a long and meaningful
career of service to our Lord and Savior with you.*

*Please contact me at the number below to confirm your
intentions by no later than September 24.*

> *In His Service,*
> *Jerry Lassiter*
> *Central American Missions Director*

September 24. Exactly one week to make the biggest decision
of his life. So far.

He set the letter down and laid his head back against the
pillows, staring at the ceiling fan whirring above him. North
Texas temperatures had finally fallen south of triple digits, but
not far. The fan's gentle air wafting down on him was a
welcome accompaniment to the air conditioning.

"To go or not to go, that is the question."

His whisper drifted away, but his thoughts whirled around
in his head faster than the blades above him.

Stay and keep growing ConnectUP, with the possibility of
doing so with Ally by his side?

Or leave to do the Lord's work on foreign soil, knowing all

hope for something deeper with her would die a little more with each mile he put between them.

He sat up and threw his legs over the side of the bed. With his elbows braced on his thighs, he held his head in his hands.

Why would God bring him to this fork in the road, this muddy, foggy intersection, when before now, he'd never had a doubt where he wanted to go? Had he missed a sign somewhere along the way? A road he should have turned on before he got to this place?

Or was he exactly where he was supposed to be?

CHAPTER NINETEEN

*A*lly pulled yet another blouse over her head and threw it onto the growing collection on her bed.

"What time are you supposed to meet them at the restaurant?" Yolanda's voice preceded her into the room, where she stopped and looked over the pile of clothes on the bed. "If this is just a meeting, what's with all the fashion angst?"

Good point. Of course, what Yolanda didn't know was this wasn't the first time Ally had tried on half a dozen outfits before other *non-date* outings with Zane. Even last Saturday, it had taken her nearly half an hour to finally decide on a pair of yellow capris and a V-necked T-shirt emblazoned with a giant sunflower for the skating party, just knowing she would see him in person for the first time all week. Super cute with her sunflower-festooned Keds, forgetting she wouldn't be in her festive tennis shoes for the bulk of the evening.

Yolanda's eyes widened. "So … is this a date? You didn't mention it being a date, but if so, that's super exciting! Your first date in two years."

Two years, one week, and four days, to be exact. Her last date with Wyatt and she hadn't been on another since.

"It's not a date. Zane wants to update them on everything we've done, and I guess they decided it would be fun to do it over dinner."

"Hmm. And that's what he said when he asked you? *Would you like to go to dinner with Wyatt and Harper?* Because, I don't know about you, but that sounds like a date to me."

As she perused the contents of her closet, the churning in her stomach increased—from either hunger or nerves, she couldn't be sure. "Not a date."

Yolanda shrugged and sat down on the side of the bed. "Guess not if you're driving yourself. Didn't Zane offer to pick you up?"

"He did. But it's out of his way when the restaurant is the other direction from Steve's. And I thought I might be with Shannon and Blair today and would be coming from there. But Blair and her mom went down to Galveston to stay with her grandparents for a while."

"That sounds like a good idea."

"It is. They're strong Christians and Blair's very close to them. I think it'll do her some good to get away from everything here, and she can still meet with her counselor over video call."

"That's great." Yolanda cocked her head. "So, Zane asked you to go to dinner with Wyatt and Harper, offered to pick you up, and it isn't a date?"

"Not a date," Ally repeated, her voice muffled as she pulled a filmy white blouse printed with purple violets over her head, then stared into the full-length mirror with her mouth scrunched to one side. Hmm. Not too bad with her white slacks.

"What do *you* want this to be?"

Heat rushed to her face, which her friend must have seen in her reflection because she dissolved into giggles.

"So, you like him. I know you, *amiga*."

"Of course I like him. I just ..." She studied the girl looking back at her in the mirror, the one with the deep *V* in her brow, the frown on her face, the uncertainty written in her eyes. "This outfit doesn't work either."

"Uh-uh." Yolanda patted the space next to her on the bed. "Sit down here and tell me what's up. We didn't get to finish our conversation last Saturday at the skating rink, but I've been waiting all week for you to tell me if there was anything to tell. Not waiting anymore. Tell."

With a heavy sigh, Ally joined her friend on the bed and criss-crossed her legs in front of her. She stared at her hands clutched in her lap before looking up. "He kissed me."

Yolanda's eyes sparked, then narrowed. "You say that like it's a bad thing. Doesn't sound like a bad thing. Especially if it was a good one."

"It was a good *kiss*. I'm just not sure it was a good *thing*."

"I've never heard of a good kiss not being a good thing. I think that's impossible."

"It's all just ... too fast. How could we feel that way about each other so quickly?"

"Maybe because you spent every single day together. And look at what you just said. You didn't say it was too quick for *him* to feel that way. You said *we*, as in both of you."

Ally's mouth snapped shut. That had to have been a slip. She had no idea what she felt.

She gave her head a shake. "Yes, but because I was so focused on Zane, I missed the problem with Blair. Maybe if I'd been more available ..."

Tears sprang to her eyes recalling the day after Labor Day when Shannon called with the news. The whole thing was a nightmare. And Ally had questioned her decision to leave the Arlington club, and her girls, a dozen times since then. Maybe if she'd stayed instead of leaving to help Zane ... maybe if she'd been more in touch ...

Yolanda scooted closer and took her hand. "Honey, that didn't happen because you weren't there. You told Blair that even though you wouldn't be leading her circle anymore, she could call or reach out to you at any time. She chose not to tell you or Shannon that she was going to meet him because she knew you would disapprove. It's not her fault what happened to her. But neither is it yours.

"And don't turn this around into something it's not because you're afraid of your feelings. You haven't missed anything because you've been focused on *Zane*. You've been focused on everything you should be, working to grow the ministry. That you met a really great guy in the process is a bonus."

Ally blinked, her jaw falling slack. "Afraid of my feelings," she repeated quietly as a cold sensation snaked its way down her spine.

"You're telling yourself you've been wrong to spend so much time on all the work you've done for CU because all of that time has been spent with a man who makes you feel things you're not sure you're ready for."

"But I thought being more cautious and intentional would help me make a better decision. Yes, I'm past the break-up. I'm at peace with where I am in my life. But I don't want to make that mistake again, falling for somebody so quickly."

"Oh, *amiga*, Wyatt wasn't a mistake. Yes, you fell for him hard and fast, but he was a good boyfriend. Your first love. A godly man who treated you with respect and dignity. Even when things ended, he cared about your feelings. If anything, that should give you confidence to move into something new with another good, godly man, not make you afraid of how it will end. And if Zane's the guy, he would be that kind of man. One who trusts God and will take care of your heart. Just like Wyatt did."

Ally's mind whirled. Yolanda was right. Wyatt had been a good boyfriend. Taught her about the kind of man she'd want to be with the rest of her life. That it hadn't been him didn't matter. He'd shown her how a godly partner behaves, how he speaks, how he treats the special woman in his life.

Like Zane. The man who had only ever treated her with respect. He'd given her the space she'd asked for, kept things on a professional level, hadn't pushed her to talk about it when she told him she wasn't ready.

Because she hadn't been able to make sense of it, to put a name to it. Was it simply attraction? Two young, single, red-blooded adults looking for companionship? Or something deeper? Even now, twelve days later, she didn't know.

"... maybe that's where we need to start. Define whatever it is and go from there."

She hadn't had the words last week when he'd made his plea. Maybe she still didn't. But could she find the courage to begin the conversation?

CHAPTER TWENTY

Zane sipped from his sweet tea as Ally's fingers tapped away on her ever-present tablet, recording notes from their conversation now centered on the new office space. They'd finished their meals at the new steakhouse Wyatt had been wanting to try, and the verdict was thumbs up from all four of them. While not a five-star place, it was nicer than most establishments Zane made a habit of patronizing, and he was glad he'd dressed in slacks with a nice shirt instead of his usual casual duds.

Especially when Ally walked into the waiting area wearing that flowery pink dress that brought out all the warm coloring of her sun-kissed skin. It took him a moment to find his words, and he was relieved Harper had embraced her in a hug when she joined them so he could catch his breath.

His eyes came to rest on her again, sitting between him and Harper in the *U*-shaped, padded booth. Tonight, she'd pulled the sides of her hair into a clip at the back of her head, and his fingers itched to unclasp the barrette and watch the lush strands fall around her shoulders.

Frankly, he itched for any physical contact at all. A touch on the hand, a brush of shoulders. Their brief hello hug before they were shown to their table wasn't nearly as satisfying as one of her normal hugs. But he told himself before ever setting foot out the door to not have such high expectations of the evening. He wasn't crazy about all of this carefulness, but he'd told her exactly a week ago he'd do or be anything she needed so she would feel comfortable with him again.

If only he could go back to the night he flubbed it all up. He'd walk her to her door, hug her good night, and watch her go inside, knowing he'd see her the next day and the next and that nothing would be changed between them.

Her fingers halted. "All right, so Zane will be in the first office on the right, Wyatt gets the big office with the corner windows, and Harper gets the office with the door to the courtyard." She looked at Harper and grinned. "I had that pegged, by the way. The day we saw it." She turned to him, her eyes shining with her smile. "Didn't I, Z? That Harper would be working from the courtyard more than the office when the weather's nice."

His pulse tripped. Had she just called him *Z*? She hadn't been that relaxed around him in twelve days. He returned her grin and nodded. "Yep. You did."

Harper nudged her with her shoulder. "You know me so well."

Wyatt looked at him, then Ally. "Why doesn't Zane get the big office? He's our coordinator."

Zane shook his head. "But you're the director."

"The CEO," Ally added.

"Head honcho."

"The Big Kahuna."

"*El Presidente.*"

"Boss man."

Laughing, Wyatt put his hands out. "Okay, okay, you guys. I get it. But, Zane, if you can make use of that larger office, that's fine with me. I'll still have my office at the practice for a while."

"Nope. It's yours."

Harper stared at them with her mouth agape. "That was completely adorable, that thing you just did."

No, *that* was completely fun. He'd missed their banter, the way they played into each other's sense of humor so effortlessly. Although a bit subdued when she'd first arrived, over the course of the evening she began to laugh more, share more. Became more animated and less guarded. Perhaps they would make their way back to ... whatever they'd been. Before.

The ladies threw around ideas for decorating the office — paint colors, furniture, fabric for chairs, stuff to hang on the walls — all things he hadn't given a thought to, though they'd apparently given plenty. He chuckled at Wyatt's yawn but couldn't keep his gaze from periodically wandering back to the woman at his side.

As usual when they were around the McCowans, he watched the way she interacted with them. But it was as if that night on the terrace had been an anomaly. Or perhaps simply the last bit of grief she had to get out of her system over the lost relationship. Because, from all appearances, she truly was over it.

But did that mean she was ready for someone new? And if so, would he stand a chance of being that someone?

If you had no barriers to moving on, would you?

Maggie's question had replayed in his head a hundred or so times since her surprising call last week. Barriers? Was ConnectUP a barrier? Was Ally?

The work at CU excited him. They'd made so many plans over the last several months that were finally being put into action. He didn't know how he could read in someone new and catch them up when the ball seemed to be constantly rolling.

Not to mention the fact that, while Becker was willing to release him from his contract, he had signed his name. They'd held up their end by providing him his seminary degree. How could he fall down on his? It went against everything he was, everything his father had taught him about the strength and value of a man's word. Of keeping a promise. Following through.

Then there was Ally. He'd never experienced such a strong connection with a woman before. It went beyond attraction. She was outwardly lovely, no question, but even more so inside.

And he couldn't get her out of his head.

Was that of a divine nature, or were they simply kindred spirits with good chemistry?

"Zane? You with us, bro?"

Wyatt's voice pulled him out of the whirlpool of his thoughts. "Sorry. What?"

"You said you wanted to run an idea by us?"

"Oh, right. Well, after that first club, the Arlington one, when I met with your leadership kids, the wheels have been turning. I—" He looked at Ally and back again. "*We* did the same with the kids at the three other clubs and came away with the same thought."

"Which is?"

"Task force," he and Ally said together.

The couple looked back and forth between them, Harper with a grin and her husband with a raised brow.

Ally gestured to Zane. "You go."

"No, you're fine."

"Your idea. You tell them."

"You were the first to call it task force."

"But you came up with the concept."

Harper laughed out loud. "One of you tell us already. You're killing us here."

Ally looked back at Zane with a smile. "Seriously. You go. I'll take notes."

"Okay, but we share equal credit."

"I'll take it. Now, go."

"Yes'm." He shot her a wink, and she returned it with a smile. So, he hadn't imagined it. Hadn't wished for it so hard, he was seeing things that weren't there. She had definitely loosened up in the past couple of hours.

He looked back at Wyatt. "Meeting your student leaders was eye-opening, my friend. The stories I've heard have brought me to my rhetorical knees. And they all credit CU with changing their lives. Really powerful stuff."

Harper put a hand on her husband's shoulder. "That's so true. It's staggering to think what would have happened to a lot of these kids had you kept all of that pain from Glen's death inside instead of letting God do something good with it."

"She's absolutely right," Ally said. "I've thought that from the beginning, when you first came up with the idea, that it would change the world for a lot of kids. It's so exciting to see where it's going now."

"Well, thank you all for the encouragement." A pink flush tinted Wyatt's face. The man was nothing if not humble, one of the things Zane respected most about him. "And I appreciate you right back. CU wouldn't exist without all of us." He waved his hand in front of him. "Tell us about this idea."

A smile crept across Zane's face. "What do you think about putting together a task force, so to speak, of kids from the different clubs, to get them involved in ministry development?"

Ally looked up from her tablet. "From how to reach kids not involved in church—"

"—all the way to curriculum, events, retreats, summer camps. Just let them loose with their ideas and see what we can use. Tap into them for planning and executing events—"

"—discipling other kids, leading Bible studies or accountability groups. It'll take some of the burden off the adult volunteers—"

"—and give the student leaders some ownership." Zane put his hand out. "And it'll not only look good on their college applications but—"

"—prepare them for leadership roles as they move into adulthood. Maybe even with ConnectUP or missions."

Zane cocked his head toward her. "What she said."

Harper looked back and forth between them again, her head shaking. "Do you two use the same brain or something? How do you do that?"

He and Ally looked at each other and shrugged. He hadn't really given it any thought, other than how much he enjoyed how well they clicked, even from that first night over burgers. And he'd missed it. What made tonight different from the last twelve days?

Wyatt crossed his arms on the table. "Regardless of whose brain is doing what—although that was impressive—I think that's an epic idea. Get actual club kids involved in growing the ministry firsthand. Giving them some investment and experience in leadership."

Zane's pulse raced, as if he'd downed five cups of black coffee. "You should've heard some of the things they were throwing out just in a twenty-minute conversation. They're so ready to step up and take on some responsibility."

Ally nodded. "We thought we could start out meeting once a month. Use the new office as a central location."

"Yeah, let's go with that," Wyatt answered. "Get the kids together, ply them with free food, and let them go with minimal input from us. Just see what they come up with. Leaders from the different clubs can take turns hosting each month."

Harper's face beamed. "I love it. Especially letting them lead Bible studies." She looked at Ally. "Can we talk more about that here soon?"

"Absolutely. Would love to get you involved in that, if you have the time."

"I'll make the time."

Out of what, Zane had no idea. How Harper already did all she was doing was a mystery to him.

Wyatt fist-bumped Zane across the table. "Great work, you

two. You've accomplished a lot in only three weeks." He looked over at Ally. "We knew you were the perfect person to keep this guy focused. He has great ideas—"

"But I'm terrible at the administrative stuff." Zane laughed, but his pulse skipped when her gaze snagged on his and held. "You've been a huge factor in everything we've accomplished, not just keeping me in order. All of your ideas and the skills you bring to the table are priceless."

Ally's face reddened. "Like you said the other day, we make a great team." Another moment passed, but she didn't look away. "So ... are we getting dessert?"

The others laughed at her obvious discomfort, but he took the opportunity to reach over and give her hand a quick squeeze under the table. Compliments always seemed to fluster her, but she deserved more credit than she took. "Get two, since tonight's on Becker's dime."

Her grin turned shy. "Don't tempt me."

Their gazes held, as if by some magnetic pull, and everything around him faded into the background. Something was going on. With her. Maybe she thought they hadn't known each other long, but he knew her well enough to see something —maybe Some*one*—working behind those amber-hued irises.

Harper grabbed her attention to peruse the dessert menu, but he couldn't concentrate on the selections in front of him. If she should decide to let him in, maybe even back on the track he believed they'd been on before his impulsive act derailed them, where did that leave his decision about Honduras? Would she be a consideration? *Should* she be a consideration?

Six days. That's how long he had to make the decision that would determine the trajectory of the rest of his life.

CHAPTER TWENTY-ONE

"*H*ow did I not notice how big this place was when we originally toured it?" With her back to the wall, Ally slid down to sit on the floor, her arms resting on her bent knees. She really needed to get back to a regular workout, if two hours on her feet, bending and reaching, could make her this tired.

With a shake of his head, Zane joined her, his long legs spread out in front of him and crossed at the ankles. "Because we weren't measuring every square inch. This was a bigger job than I thought it would be."

"Much bigger."

He looked over at her. "Thanks for doing this with me today. Four hands make it much easier with the measuring tape. Steve's leaving for a work trip down to Waco later this afternoon, so he wanted to spend some time with Yo."

"It's been fun. I like this kind of thing, so I'm glad you asked." Her gaze roamed over the empty room that would be the foyer, lobby, waiting room—whatever they decided it would be—her thoughts going back over the last couple of hours. The afternoon really had been fun, being with Zane. Just like last night's dinner, once she let her guard down to be the friend she'd been before. The friend she should've been all along.

Lying in bed last night, looking back over the last two weeks in her mind, she finally saw her actions for what they were—running away. And just when she thought she'd come so far in her spiritual growth. What would have been more appropriate is what Zane had wanted to do from the beginning —talk it out. Give it a definition and deal with whatever it was between them that had drawn them together in an intimate moment.

She'd prayed for wisdom and guidance in how to reconnect with him, to get past the awkwardness and reclaim some of the ground they'd lost. So, when he'd sought her out after church to ask if she'd like to meet him at the office to determine how to implement the plans they'd hammered out over dinner the night before, she took it as a sign. Maybe the Lord was already answering her prayer for an opportunity to fix things with him, to figure out together where to go from here.

If he hadn't decided a more level-headed, kindergarten-teacher-type who could hold her own on inline skates was more to his liking.

She looked over at him. "I had an idea last night after I got home." Tossing and turning, unable to sleep, thinking of him but needing a distraction. "About how we might be able to outfit this place and not spend a ton of money."

"Do tell."

"Donations. Sponsors. We could put it out on social media and through our email list that we need furniture, equipment, and supplies. Kind of like a bridal registry, only for office stuff."

His face lit up. "I like it! We could even set up a donation page for people who'd rather give money."

"Great idea. And maybe we could find some companies or organizations to donate supplies or services. We'll put them on our T-shirts, on our website and social media, and on banners at our events as official sponsors."

He grinned at her. "You're brilliant."

Her cheeks warmed. "I don't know about that. I'm just piggybacking onto what we discussed last night. Becker's been beyond generous with their support, but we need to use that funding wisely. If we could get some of what we need donated, that would be huge. Let God provide what we need by blessing others with the opportunity to give to a ministry devoted to saving the lives of teens."

Silence stretched between them as he studied her with a grin.

"What? Do I have something on my face?"

He nodded, and that dimpled grin grew into one of his heart-melting smiles. "Jesus. I see Jesus in you every day. You inspire me to be a better man."

Her lips parted as warmth spread through her core. Nobody had ever given her such a compliment. She'd been called beautiful, smart, good at her job. *Dependable.* But nobody had ever said they saw Jesus in her. That meant more than anything.

Especially from this man. The man she'd done her level best to push away because she'd let fear replace faith. Let doubt crowd out assurance. Yet he still saw something admirable in her? Something Christ-like?

"I don't know how you could be a better man."

His dark, shining eyes bored into hers as his face turned serious. "Good enough for you?"

The air filled with something electric. Something that scurried along her skin and raced through her bones. "Probably too good."

"Not a chance." He reached over to take her hand. "I care about you, Ally. And I know what happened between us confused you. Maybe scared you. I can't apologize enough for

159

that, but I hope you know I never meant to hurt you or put you in an awkward position."

"No," she said with a shake of her head. "It wasn't your fault. I kissed you back, so it's as much on me. I think *that's* what scared me."

"Can you tell me about it?"

Several seconds ticked by as she gathered her thoughts, prayed for wisdom and the words to explain so he would understand she in no way held him at fault for that moment between them. That her distance wasn't because she blamed him but because she'd been startled by her own reaction.

She took a steadying breath. "When I met Wyatt, the attraction was instantaneous. He came over to the table I was at in the library, and we started talking. Closed the place down, then went to an all-night diner where we sat and talked until two in the morning. And I was completely smitten by the time I got home. We were inseparable for almost two years. Until we weren't. And losing him turned my life upside-down."

"I see." His throat worked up and down. "So, you're still not over it, the break-up."

Her head snapped back. "What? No. No, that's not it at all. I'm totally over it. Seriously, he and Harper are two of my best friends. What I mean is I've only ever dated one man, and I fell for him literally overnight. I haven't dated anybody since, haven't really wanted to, because I didn't trust my judgment.

"Then there you were, on the terrace that night, and the same thing happened. Instant awareness. Only you were that mystery guy I'd never see again, so I let myself crush on you a little. When you showed up that night at the leadership meeting, I couldn't believe it. The guy of my fantasies right there in living color." She pointed her finger at him. "Innocent fantasies, mind you."

"Good to know," he said with a chuckle.

"But then we started working together, I got to know you, and you were even better than the fantasy guy in my head.

Godly, smart, loves to cook, great sense of humor. I have abs for the first time ever because we laugh so much. Seriously, I burn more calories spending a day with you than I do on a two-mile walk around the lake."

When he laughed, she couldn't help joining in, as usual. And it was as if the last few bricks she'd erected between them disintegrated into dust.

He looked at her again, and the light she noticed that first night sparked in his dark eyes. "I feel the same way. I've had the best time with you. And just so you know, I thought about you a lot after the wedding. I was back in Atlanta but knew I'd be relocating to Arlington, so I wondered if I might run into *'Miss Kay'* again. It was a very pleasant surprise to see you sitting there that night at Wyatt and Harper's. And it only got better the more time I spent with you. Until I crossed a line I shouldn't have."

"You mean until I messed it up by running away. By not facing you and instead let it sit there between us. I'm so sorry, Z. Really. You wanted to talk about it, and I shut you down. I hope you can forgive me for that."

"No worries on that front. We're talking now, and that's all that matters. I wanted to understand how you felt and how I could help. But until you were ready to talk, all I could do was pray for you and let you know I was here when, or if, you ever were."

Her belly did that squirmy thing. How could she have turned her back on a man this patient? This kind? Who could have simply let her walk away and leave it at that. Instead, he prayed for her. He waited for her. Gave her the space she needed to work it out. The space to let God work on her.

He really was too good for her.

His gaze turned down to their joined hands. "So, what now, Ally?" He linked their fingers together and looked back at her, his smile gone, his eyes intense. "What do you expect now? Of me? Of this? If there even is a *this*. No pressure here. I have no expectations."

She gave his question some thought. Not that she needed to. She knew where she hoped things would go, as long as they could take their time. Her heart told her she was ready to move forward, but her head warned her not to jump too far.

"I care about you too. I've enjoyed our friendship a lot, but I'm open to seeing where it might go. If there's a *this*, like you said. All I know is I'm comfortable with you, even that night when I had no idea who you were. I trust you and am thankful for the honesty between us. I've missed that with you the past couple of weeks, but I know that was my fault for pulling away. But if we can get back to what we were, maybe we can see what we could be. Down the road."

He looked away. "Honesty."

His voice was little more than a whisper, but it was the wrinkle in his brow and downturned lips that put a clench in her midsection. Clearly, something weighed on his mind. Something he needed to tell her? Something he didn't want to?

With a heavy sigh, he let go of her hand and swiped his fingers through his hair. It had grown since he'd arrived in Arlington, but he could pull off slightly shaggy as well as short and neat. If only his perpetually laughing eyes didn't look so troubled.

"What's ... going on?" Her question cut through the heavy quiet, the first-time silence between them felt uncomfortable. Made her want to fill it in. "I'm okay if we only grow as friends, Z. I don't have any expectations, either."

He shook his head. "That's not it." He looked over at her. "I would love to take you out for our first true date, to start down that road to see where we could go. What we could be."

"But ..." Because she'd never heard an unspoken *but* scream so loud.

He took a deep breath and let it out. "I have an opportunity to take a foreign mission assignment. Starting in November."

A chill rippled down her body. "F-foreign mission? I didn't know you were looking into foreign missions."

"It's been a long-time dream of mine. I've always wanted to travel, like my dad dreamed of but never got the chance to. I can't imagine a better way to do that than to spread the gospel at the same time."

Her breathing turned shallow as her throat tightened. So, after all of this, all of the praying and finally being ready to venture forward into whatever had led them to such a spontaneous act, he was leaving, anyway. It didn't matter how she felt. How *they* felt. They'd never have the chance to discover what it meant.

She crossed her arms over her stomach and looked down at the floor. "So, you leave in November?"

"If I take it, I have to be in Sacramento by the first."

Her head sprang up. "*If* you take it?"

"I haven't come to a decision yet. Still weighing my options, praying about it. I love working with ConnectUP, and we have a lot of plans that will be put in motion over the next several months. And beyond. Becker can assign another ministry coordinator, but I have a certain ownership here that will be hard to let go of."

His gaze held hers. "And then there's you."

Over the past two weeks, she'd insisted on space. Now she wished with everything she was that what he'd said was true. That somehow she truly was in the mix of this decision.

She sat up and crossed her legs in front of her, staring at her hands clasped in her lap while she measured her response. "No." Looking back up at him, she shook her head. "There's no *me*. This is between you and God and what He's calling you to do." And in a few weeks, months maybe, her heart would get over it. "I would never want to get in the way of what God wants to do in your life."

He scooted around until he sat directly in front of her. "Yet I can't deny I have feelings for you, Al. Feelings that go beyond friends. I've never had such an instant connection with anybody before. That has to mean something. Right?"

Her sigh filled the space between them. "Where's the mission?"

"Honduras."

Goosebumps sprang up on her skin. "That's where ... my mother—"

"I know." He took her hands in his. "I know that's where you lost her. I'm so sorry if this brings up pain for you. I never meant for it to."

"When were you going to tell me?"

"When I'd made my decision. If I don't go, there's nothing to tell. If I do decide to take it, I was going to talk to you then. But you mentioned how honest our relationship has been, and I realized maybe I hadn't been. That you needed to know what I was considering before you could decide where you want this to go."

"I see." She pondered his face as the seconds ticked by before turning her focus to their joined hands. "Does anybody else know?"

"No. But after this conversation, I think I need to have a sit-down with Wyatt, just to read him in. I don't want to drop this on anybody out of the blue."

"That's a good idea. He'll support you, whichever way you go. We all will." She cleared her throat and looked back at him. "I don't want to be in the way here, Z. This decision has to be made without me in the mix. And I don't think I can do a long-distance thing. Especially knowing we don't share the same calling."

Like she thought they had until five minutes ago. Working in ministry to teens. Right here in Arlington, Texas. Right here at home.

"Al—"

"I will always be your friend. And I will support you one hundred percent if you take this mission. I'll work with whoever Becker sends, and the ministry will be fine. Would we like for you to stay and see all of your ideas and plans come to fruition? Absolutely. But maybe you've done what God intended you to do here."

He nodded. "Yeah. Maybe."

"When do you have to let them know?"

"By Friday."

Five days.

Remorse coursed through her. She'd wasted the last two weeks putting distance between them because she didn't trust her feelings. And while she should've protected their friendship instead of pulling away, maybe she'd been right to doubt. Even if she was ready to explore whatever was happening in her heart for this man, if he left to follow God's plan, then she clearly got ahead of the Lord. It would've been wrong to venture down another road if he was truly meant to be somewhere else. Somewhere she couldn't go.

No matter how much of her heart he already owned.

CHAPTER TWENTY-TWO

*T*oday was the day.

Zane had never been one to linger over a decision, usually clear about where he wanted to go and always eager for the next thing. But this one …

He read over the cover letter again before setting the large envelope and its contents on the coffee table. He should've called Jerry with his decision about Global Reach as soon as Becker released him from his contract.

Except he hadn't made his decision. Not then. Not even over the last week since receiving the info packet, although Jerry needed to know his intentions by September 24.

Today.

He stared at the packet lying in front of him, containing all of the information on Global Reach, the mission they hoped to send him to, a training schedule, and information on how to procure funding.

Everything he'd hoped for and dreamed of for years lay right there in front of him. All he had to do was call Jerry, accept their offer, put in his notice to Becker, and make all the arrangements to move himself and his few belongings to Sacramento. A month would give him and the ConnectUP leadership team plenty of time to on-board a new ministry coordinator to take his place.

Everything appeared to be in order for him to move on. To another temporary home in California followed by yet another in Honduras. Then on to wherever Global Reach needed him next. He could finally see the world, just like he'd promised his dad.

Then why wasn't he jumping on it? Picking up his phone, thanking Jerry for sending the package to him, and expressing his excitement about joining the team at Global Reach? He'd been praying about it ever since he received the formal letter from Becker releasing him from his four-year commitment. Waiting for some flash of wisdom or a sign from God about which way he should go. But there had been no clear message from above about whether he should stay or go. No writing on the wall. No burning bush. No talking donkey. Although that would be totally cool to see.

His gaze roamed the room, taking in the masculine homeyness of Steve's house. Like Wyatt and Harper's house, Mason and Rhonda's house, and the homes of other CU leaders, Steve used his as another ministry tool to help teenagers looking for a place to belong. To *connect*.

This was a good place. Not just the house itself, but the entire Metroplex. Plans were already in motion to launch another Arlington club, a second Dallas club, and their first club in Fort Worth. The work excited him. Humbled him. Inspired him.

With a heavy sigh, he slouched back on the couch, resting his head on the back cushion and staring up at the ceiling. "Lord, I want to do the right thing here. And I know You can bring good out of whichever ministry I choose to do. I just want to be a faithful servant and go where You tell me to go."

His gaze remained fixed to the white-painted ceiling. "Or stay where You want me to stay. I really like it here, and

ConnectUP is exploding. I love the people and the kids and being a part of it all. And Ally ..."

Closing his eyes, he let his thoughts meander back through the week. By the end of the evening Saturday, he and Ally seemed to have broken through that wall of awkwardness between them. On his way home, he'd decided to ask her after church the next day if she wanted to meet up at the office to work through some of the ideas they'd tossed around over dinner. The conversation that afternoon had finally—*finally!*—closed up that distance between them. She was ready to see what could come of whatever this was.

Until his bombshell.

He could see it on her face the second he said the words *foreign mission*. The shock, followed by guardedness.

And he knew then he'd lost whatever momentum they'd gained over the previous few minutes.

At least she'd let him pick her up for the Arlington team leadership meeting the next night. The delight in her eyes when he handed her the keys to Phyllis had him longing to do anything that would make it stay. But it hadn't. The quiet ride back to her house was broken only once he'd parked. Neither had moved to exit the vehicle, sitting in silence before she turned to look at him, her eyes shimmering like glass.

"I'm praying for you, Z." Her quiet voice in the confines of the car pierced his chest. *"That you'll have clarity for your decision. Please don't let ... this ... sway you. Do what you're being led to do. I've no doubt you'll be as amazing on the field as you have been here."*

Before he could respond or even reach for his door handle, she'd let herself out of the car and was halfway up the walkway.

This. They still hadn't put a word to what *this* was, but there was no denying there was one. He felt a big *this* for Ally. But a permanent *this*? How could he decide that in the next few minutes?

With a grunt, he sat up and rested his forearms on his legs, head bowed and eyes closed, the only sound being the cool air blowing through the living room vents. With Steve at work on this Friday morning, he had some time to spend in quiet meditation.

Show me, Lord.

Silence surrounded him, helping him rein in his scattered thoughts.

Use me, Lord.

In the stillness, peace came to rest on him. That peace *which transcends all understanding* that Paul spoke of in Philippians.

A verse their pastor had shared from the pulpit Sunday morning ran through his mind. *Commit to the Lord whatever you do, and he will establish your plans.* From the sixteenth chapter of Proverbs. *Commit ... whatever you do ...*

Whatever you do ...

Commit it to the Lord, and He would see it through.

Whatever you do ...

He opened his eyes and looked at the packet. Maybe he hadn't received a clear leading one direction or the other because he could work within the will of God no matter which way he went.

But where could he be the most useful?

His phone pinged with an incoming text, and he picked it up. From Wyatt.

> Hey brother, I know today's decision day.
> Praying for you. We'll always have your
> back no matter what. Love ya, bro.

> Thanks, buddy. Means more than I can
> say. Haven't made the call yet. Definitely
> need those prayers.

> Count on it.

Smiling, he returned the phone to the coffee table. In the almost ten months he'd known Wyatt, he'd grown to love him like a brother. As close as Keller, his college roommate who'd turned him back to the Lord and eventually brought him to Becker. When he'd gone over to the McCowans' Sunday evening, Wyatt directed him to his study where they could talk alone. He didn't even blink when Zane shared his news. The consummate psychologist, his friend had done more listening than talking and simply let Zane know they would support him one hundred percent whichever way he chose to go.

Just as Ally had said he would.

Ally. It always came back to Ally, even though she'd told him more than once she couldn't be in this equation. But he didn't know how to leave her out. He'd never experienced this before and wasn't sure what to make of it. How could he have fallen so far in so short a time? So far that he'd actually been wondering what a house here might cost and how he'd love to get a dog since Scout passed away a year before Dad. Something Ally had mentioned a few times as well, her wish to get a dog once she bought a house of her own. Moving as much as he did, though, made having a pet difficult.

But if he stayed …

The ringing of his phone startled him, so lost was he in his daydreams of a more settled life. He didn't recognize the number but answered anyway. A stalling tactic, perhaps?

"Zane Carpenter."

"Mr. Carpenter." The male voice on the other end was unfamiliar, and Zane hoped he hadn't answered a spam call. "This is Brian Foster. I'm the security guard you met at Six Flags the day your group had an injured girl. You gave me your card?"

"Oh, yes, sir. I remember. What can I do for you?"

There was a pause, a sniffle, and the man cleared his throat. Zane's smile vanished. Hopefully, this wasn't bad news.

"Mr. Foster?"

Another pause and the clearing of his throat. "Yes. Sorry. I didn't think I would get this emotional. It's just that … well, meeting you that day was an answer to a years' long prayer. Remember I mentioned we had just moved here, and my son was going to high school in Arlington?"

"Yes, sir."

"He was having a really hard time. Very angry. Didn't want to move here, but the reason we relocated was to get him away from a bad group he'd gotten involved with in Arizona. Raised our boys in church from Day One, and both of them were doing great. Until Craig got pulled in by one of the neighbor kids going down a bad path. It started with some attitude problems, then truancy and staying out past curfew. But when one of those kids he was hanging with was arrested for drug possession, that was it. We pulled him from school, put the house on the market, and were in Dallas within a month. The things we'll do to save our kids, you know?"

"I don't have kids of my own, Mr. Foster, but I can sure understand that. Do you have family here?"

"A cousin. Moved a couple of blocks over from them. Craig's at Conway High. I talked to those two boys who helped your girl out to the car that day, and they said they were at Conway. You know those boys actually sought out Craig the next day at school and invited him to your club night? Two days after meeting you, my kid was sitting in a Bible study. I'm telling you, Mr. Carpenter, that little part-time second job of mine that put me in the right spot to meet you may have saved my son's life."

The man's voice broke, and Zane's throat tightened. Being in the right place at the right time. All by divine intervention. God didn't cause Olivia's injury, but He sure used it for good.

"Please call me Zane. And I'm so glad you let me know this. May I ask what you do for a living, Mr. Foster?"

"Brian. I just got on as a sergeant with the Arlington Police Department. Served with Phoenix PD for sixteen years before we moved."

"Wow. Thank you for your service. Not an easy gig."

"No, but fulfilling. Most days. But what I see on the streets makes me perhaps a bit overzealous with wanting to keep my boys on the straight and narrow. I have a thirteen-year-old starting high school next year. My wife was on board, though. Left her real estate job and is working right now to get licensed here. Hence, me working two jobs until she gets up and running."

"If there's anything we can do for you, sir, we'd be happy to. ConnectUP is always ready to step up and help any of our families who might need a boost. No shame in that, considering why you pulled up stakes to move your family so quickly."

"That's nice of you, but right now, we're doing okay. Especially since my son told me yesterday that he committed his life to the Lord Wednesday night and prayed with one of those boys who helped your girl. Finn. Football player."

A grin spread on Zane's face. That had to be at least the fourth kid Zane was aware of Finn had led to the Lord since his own conversion earlier in the year. "That's Finn. Very on fire for the Lord."

"No kidding. I know he has practice every day and games on Fridays, but he's been over here at least four times in the last two weeks, just spending time with Craig, playing video games, watching college football on Saturday, talking to him about God when appropriate but not shoving anything down his throat. A senior putting that much time into a sophomore. It's been eye-opening. He's been a great influence on my younger son too."

"So excited to hear about Craig. I was there on Wednesday night and remember seeing Finn praying with another boy afterward. I didn't realize that was your son." A true full circle moment, from meeting Brian at the gate at Six Flags, learning he had a son in high school who was at loose ends, handing Brian his card, and now one of their CU kids had taken the boy the rest of the way.

That's exactly what missions was about. Serving where you

could bring the gospel to those who needed it most and introduce them to an all-knowing, all-powerful, faithful, loving God. Everything Zane had dreamed of doing since he came back to his faith in college.

"I won't keep you." Brian's voice pulled him back. "I still had your card and wanted to share what a difference that two-minute conversation we had at the gate made. Truly. A life saved. The whole reason we moved here."

"That's what ConnectUP's all about. Saving kids. I'm thrilled to have Craig on board. And we'll look forward to his brother joining us next summer."

"He's already talking about it."

After they ended their call, he held the phone in his hand and stared at it. With a nod, he brought up the number with the Sacramento area code. Time to call Jerry.

CHAPTER TWENTY-THREE

"*Y*ou were such a good girl today." Ally picked up the grinning baby from the exam table. "Didn't even cry when I gave you your shots." After handing the little one back to her mother, she grabbed the electronic tablet from the counter to type in her notes. "She's doing great. Has met all of her markers, her weight is good, growth right where she should be. You have a very healthy and beautiful little girl."

Relief flooded the young mother's face. "That's so good to hear. It was a difficult delivery, and we were told there could be some delays."

"She's doing exactly what any nine-month-old should be doing. Nothing at all delayed about this little one."

Thanks in large part to modern medicine and top-notch care. Something the people she'd worked with in Guatemala had never seen, and probably never would. Her first few weeks working with her father two years ago had been challenging. She'd had to adapt quickly, learn how to provide care and come up with solutions without the instruments, pharmaceuticals, diagnostic equipment, and facilities she'd had available during her education and subsequent nursing career.

Yet any frustrations from being underequipped and understaffed were far outweighed by the satisfaction and sense of accomplishment when a man with a family that depended on him walked on a leg that in years past would have been removed, if he lived through the injury at all. When a child woke from a fever-induced coma with no brain damage. When a young woman took home a healthy baby after a traumatic birth that might have ended both of their lives a decade before.

Ally loved working with her patients here in the States. She only wished they understood how blessed they were to have first-world medical care they probably never gave a thought to.

After walking mother and daughter to the check-out desk, she glanced at her watch. Five after two. End of her shift. Finally. She'd never been a clock-watcher. But today … well, today was the day.

She'd been praying for Zane all week, that he would have a clear path to whichever way he was to go. Although the idea of him leaving in only a few weeks filled her with dread, if that's where he was supposed to be, she would support him any way she could. Having been-there-done-that most of her life, she could definitely give him some tips for living on foreign soil with little to none of the luxuries they experienced stateside on a daily basis.

On her way to the nurses' station in the middle of the large office, she pulled her phone out of the pocket of her scrubs. There was a new text from Yolanda, but nothing from Zane. Of course, if he decided to take the assignment, he wouldn't tell her over a text. That was news he would deliver in person. It figured this was the first Friday they wouldn't be meeting. Not with everything she and Yo still needed to do to prepare for tonight's slumber party with the Irving girls. If she didn't hear from him by late afternoon, she'd have to wait until tomorrow.

And would already know in her heart what his answer had been.

She tried to ignore the sinking in the pit of her stomach as she read Yo's text.

> Can you run by the store on your way home since you get off before me?
> I'll send you a list. Pretty please?

> No problem. Send the list. See you around 5:30.

Yolanda worked full-time at a cardiac medicine practice where she'd been since they graduated from nursing school. Before leaving for Guatemala two years ago, Ally had a position at another pediatrician's office. They'd hoped to keep her position for her, but when it became clear she wouldn't be returning after her initial three-month stay in Guatemala, she gave it up. Freelancing had been fun, but she'd love to find a permanent position she found as satisfying as Yolanda did her job.

She'd just reached the nurses' station when her phone pinged with an incoming text. Not Zane, unfortunately, but Yo's heavy-on-the-junk-food grocery list.

"Have a great weekend, Ally." The nursing supervisor gave her a smile as she took the electronic tablet to store behind the counter.

"I'll do my best. Hosting about a dozen teenage girls for a sleepover tonight. Which means I may be sleeping all day tomorrow."

The older nurse laughed. "Better you than me. With my two girls out of the house, my overnighter days are over. Thankfully."

"Any tips?"

"No sugar."

Oh, if the other woman only saw what Yo had just sent, she'd know how unlikely *that* was. "Got it. I'll give you a full report on Monday."

One of the younger nurses walked up to the counter, her face alight. "There is a gorgeous specimen of maleness out in the waiting room with what has to be two dozen roses."

Ally looked at her. "He's probably the delivery guy."

"Sitting out there? No, he's definitely waiting for someone."

"Hmm. Quite the romantic gesture." Somebody's day was about to improve by about two dozen roses, reportedly. Maybe someday she'd get a surprise bouquet from a *gorgeous specimen of maleness*.

After grabbing her purse, she walked out to the waiting room ... and stopped dead in her tracks. Apparently, *someday* had arrived.

Zane stood and shot her his mega-watt smile from behind a stunning arrangement of her favorite flower. He wouldn't look like that if he was there to let her know he was leaving in a few weeks, would he?

Acutely aware of the eyes watching them in the waiting room, as well as from behind the glass partition at the front desk, she walked over to stand in front of him. Her heart beat a staccato rhythm behind her sternum, but she tried her best to appear calm and collected. Even if he was most definitely a gorgeous specimen of maleness.

"What are you doing he—"

"Asking you out on an official date."

Heat suffused her face when her gaze darted to the counter where several of her co-workers grinned from behind the glass. Definitely time to take this conversation outside. With her pulse still galloping along at an alarming rate—*he was staying!* —she wrapped her hand around his arm and led him out the front doors.

Once standing next to her car, she turned to face him. "Does this mean you came to a decision?"

He looked at the roses and back at her. "Oh. These are for you."

With a giggle, she took the large bouquet of white, red, and pink roses. The fragrance wafting in the air calmed her. "They're beautiful. Thank you."

"My pleasure. And, yes. I had a great morning of conversation with God, and a really incredible phone call I'll tell you about later. But whenever I thought about leaving right now, I wasn't settled in my spirit. There's so much going on here, so many things happening with the ministry, that I couldn't see myself leaving in the middle of it."

Her heart rate slowed. ... *leaving right now*. So ... still an option down the road?

He stepped closer and took one of her hands in his. "And this. I really do want to see this through with you. To see where we might go, what we might become. I'm ready for that if you are, but on your terms, in your timing. No hurry here, Ally."

Her gaze locked on his, and the earnestness in his eyes, the lack of uncertainty in his smile, had her returning the pressure of his fingers around hers. "You're sure of your choice, Z? I told you not to make it about me in any way. About us. Because there really wasn't an *us*. It had to be about you and God only."

"One hundred percent. And Jerry at Global Reach was very understanding when I told him I needed to stay with my current ministry because things were happening so quickly. Not to mention, I signed a contract with Becker Ministries and my commitment to them doesn't end until February. They were willing to let me out, but I signed my name to that, Al. *My name*. Their generosity allowed me to get my seminary degree. It never sat right with me to not hold up my part of the deal."

"Such a man of integrity." Her eyes misted over. "One of the things I respect most about you."

"I just want to be the kind of man that honors my dad. The man he taught me to be."

"No doubt he'd be very proud of who you've become."

He looked down and back up at her. "So, Allyson Kincaid.

Would you allow me the honor of escorting you to dinner tomorrow evening? Then I have a surprise in mind, if you trust me."

"As long as it's not inline skating."

His jaw dropped in mock indignation. "And here I thought that would be perfect because you'd have to hold on to me the whole time."

"Inline skating sounds awesome."

He threw his head back and laughed. "I'll file that away for the future. But for tomorrow, I have something else in mind. Something I know you'll love." He leaned in. "And you can still hold on to me if you want." He straightened and shrugged. "Your call."

The corners of his grin disappeared into those dimples that made her belly do that squirmy thing. Would she ever find herself immune to it?

She adjusted the flowers in her arms, releasing more of that intoxicating scent. "Yes, Zane Carpenter, I would be pleased to be in your company for dinner and … whatever … tomorrow evening." They shared another laugh. "I'll have to make sure I get a good nap in after the slumber party so I don't fall asleep on you. What a terrible date that would be."

"I can't imagine any time spent with you would be terrible. I'll pick you up at six. Steve gave me a line on a restaurant I thought we'd try."

"I'm up for anything."

"Then it's a date. Literally." He squeezed her hand and let go. "Enjoy your sleepover. I'm hanging with Steve and his guy leaders to take their boys bowling, then to laser tag."

"Have fun. I'll see you tomorrow."

"Tomorrow." He held her door open until she slid behind the wheel and placed her flowers carefully on the passenger seat. She waved on her way out of the parking spot and headed toward home, with a stop at the grocery store along the way.

At home, she curled up on the sofa for a quick nap before

the party, but found herself staring up at the ceiling a few minutes later. Apparently, no sleep for her, not when her head and heart were too busy defending their respective sides. Her heart told her Zane could be the one she'd been praying for, a godly man with whom she could build something.

If only her head would jump on the bandwagon instead of cautioning her he might not be around that long.

CHAPTER TWENTY-FOUR

*Z*ane scooped the rest of the cookies he and Ally had spent this rainy Tuesday evening baking into a plastic container while she put their dinner leftovers in her refrigerator—one for him, one for her. This was one of his favorite things—cooking with Ally. A great way to wind down after a day's work.

She turned, looked at the container of cookies, then him. "Don't you dare leave those here, or they may not make it to the Irving club tomorrow night."

Laughing, he put the container up on the breakfast bar, then leaned against the counter with his arms crossed over his chest. "In that case, I'll take them with me. Glad you liked them, though."

"Best cookies I've ever had. Where'd you get that recipe, and can I have it?"

"Sure thing. It was my grandmother's recipe. She passed away when we were really young, but her cookies were our favorite so we were always begging Mom to make them."

Her forehead furrowed. "*We?*"

His smile vanished and heart sank like a stone when he realized what he'd said. He'd never told Ally about Emma.

He'd never told her a lot of things, but had been thinking maybe it was time, four days into this new version of their relationship.

"Yeah. My sister and me. Emma."

Her eyes widened. "You have a sister? Why haven't you ever mentioned her?"

"Emma ... died." He swallowed the thickness in his throat. "When she was ten. Hit by a car."

Her jaw fell slack as her eyes pooled. "Oh, I'm so sorry. I had no idea."

"I know. And it's okay. I don't talk about it much. That's when our world kind of came apart." And the weight he'd carried from that day wasn't something he'd ever really shared. With anybody. The guilt. The grief that tore their family to shreds. The family that no longer existed.

He gave his head a shake and stood up straight. "Actually, I've been thinking over the past couple of days there are some things I need to tell you ... about me ... my past. You know, full disclosure and all that. In case you should decide to trade me in on a better deal."

In case she should decide he came with too much baggage. That his past would be too difficult for her to overcome. Because, even though he'd promised he'd go as slow as she needed, he couldn't seem to put the brakes on his own feelings. He fell for her more every day, which made it imperative that she know who he was, where he came from, what he'd done. If it was more than she'd bargained for, he needed to know now, before he let himself continue to imagine a future with her. Even if the past four days had been some of the best of his life.

Their first official date on Saturday had been a blast. Dinner at an Indian restaurant, sharing from each other's plates as they sampled various dishes. Then a concert at an area church featuring an up-and-coming Christian band she liked. Usually self-restrained, in-control Allyson Kincaid rockin' it out in full-on concert mode was a sight to behold. Best. Date. Ever.

A picnic after church on Sunday, the all-area leadership meeting last night followed by pizza with several of the other leaders, working together today on their beyond successful social media campaign to outfit the office, then fixing and eating dinner. They'd spent hours together, and he already couldn't wait to see her tomorrow.

Depending on the outcome of this conversation.

"A better deal?" Her quiet question brought his attention back to her. "I can't imagine that."

He shrugged. "Just so you can make an informed decision."

"About you?"

"About me. About us."

She stared at him for a moment. "Okay. Let's go sit."

Taking her by the hand, he led her to the sofa, back to the same spot they'd ended up in the past three evenings.

He brought his eyes to hers and studied her, drinking her in. If this was their last night together as a sort-of-couple, he wanted to remember everything. "I care for you a lot. And I really do want to see where we can go with this. It's just that I've been through some things you should be aware of. Things that could affect what direction this takes."

She sat up, bending one leg up on the sofa so she could face him, gripping his hand in both of hers. "You can talk to me about anything. I mean it. Because it's all part of what's made you *you*. I already know the man you are today, and that's all that matters."

That was certainly his hope. But he had to know for sure she could stick it out with him, warts and all.

He swallowed the knot in his throat. "I told you that after I lost my dad, I kind of went off the rails. Spiritually. It actually started before that. After he got sick, I asked him once why God would let all of this happen to us—losing Emma, Mom leaving, then him getting cancer. He told me that wasn't the right question. That we should be asking why *not* us and how can God use us through it all. But as he withered away and no miracle came, I got angrier. I wanted nothing to do with a God who could turn His back on someone who'd been so faithful."

A deep breath in helped him keep his emotions in check so he could continue. "After he passed and our house sold, I walked through one last time to take some things I wanted to keep before the estate sale. I saw Dad's Bible sitting on the nightstand next to his bed, so dog-eared and weathered. I started to leave it but turned around at the last minute and picked it up. Stuck it in a box and forgot about it."

He met her eyes again, and as usual, she was listening with her whole self. Leaning toward him, focused on his face, her hand holding tight to his. He'd never told another living soul about that Bible. Yet it had come so easily sitting here with Ally.

"I went to junior college in Indianapolis, moved in with a couple of guys from high school. They weren't Christians, and I went all in with their partying and drinking and ..."

He bowed his head and shook it. This was it. The truth he'd shared with only a couple of trusted souls on the planet. The truth that could pull her away. Because, if he were honest with himself, she deserved so much better.

His gaze met hers again. "Ally. There was a ... pregnancy. A girl I'd been seeing my sophomore year of college."

Her mouth dropped slightly, and some of the color left her face. "You have a child?"

Heaviness settled in his chest. "You know what's crazy is I was actually kind of excited, after the initial shock wore off. I figured I would quit school, get a full-time job, we could get married, and have this baby. And I'd have a family again."

"Oh, Zane," she whispered.

"Until she told me she'd taken care of it." His breath caught in his chest for a moment. A decision made by somebody else that had left behind a wound so deep, it still opened up when the memory would rub against it. "I was floored. She never even talked to me about it. About ... abortion.

"It gutted me, so I dove deeper into the party life. Seemed when I was drunk, I didn't hurt as bad. Wasn't as empty. How I kept it together to get through junior college with grades good enough to be accepted at Northwestern, I'll never know."

He stared into her eyes. Eyes the color of mocha with amber shards. Eyes that drew him in, gave him a window into her thoughts, her feelings.

A tear fell down her cheek. "I'm so sorry you lost your baby. But you know he or she is with Jesus, right? You'll see each other one day."

That heavy stone inside of him liquified. Of all the things he thought she might say, that wasn't it. He'd thought about that child many times over the years. What would have happened had it been born? Would they have made it as a family? Would he have settled down and settled in? Into marriage and fatherhood and more than likely a nowhere job?

A tendril of hair had escaped her ponytail, and he couldn't help reaching up to sweep it behind her ear. He loved the silkiness of her thick tresses, the softness of her skin under his fingers, her delicate orchid-laced scent that stayed with him sometimes after he left her for the evening.

"You're something else." His voice was ragged, and her face shimmered with the moisture pooling in his eyes. This woman who hadn't judged him, hadn't pulled away with his confession. This woman who had looked at him with caring in her eyes and expressed her sympathy for yet another loss he'd suffered.

This woman he was falling more in love with by the day.

"Tell me the rest," she said in a barely-there voice.

He took hold of her hand again and cleared his throat. "At Northwestern, I moved in with two guys who had put in for a third roommate on one of the school's social media sites. Turns out they were both strong Christians. To this day, I believe it was by God's hand that I ended up with them.

"Of course, I brought all my mess to Chicago with me, but they stuck by me instead of kicking me out like they had every right to do. The first time I walked home drunk in below freezing temps—even hammered I didn't want to chance wrecking Phyllis—they told me to call one of them in the future and they'd come get me. They made sure I had good meals, kept me accountable with my studies, asked me to play on their intramural basketball team. Invited me to church and to their Bible study constantly. I turned them down for months, although I started partying a lot less and hanging with them more.

"Then one of the guys—Keller—lost his father in a car accident. He was devastated, and I watched the way he handled that. About two weeks after his dad passed, I told him about losing mine. And you know what he did? He asked me all about my dad, about what we had done together, about the Bronco he'd passed down to me, how I felt when he was gone. Nobody had ever asked me about my feelings after I lost Dad. Just this guy whose own loss was only two weeks old. I went to their Bible study the next day."

Chuckling, he gave his head a shake. "It took a little while, but I eventually found my way back. And it was Keller who brought me to Becker Ministries a few years later."

A smile lit her face. "How'd that happen?"

"Oh, that's a long and winding road." He looked at his watch. "And it's almost ten. I don't want to keep you up too late since you have to work tomorrow."

"If you're okay sharing, I really want to hear about your long and winding road."

But did she really? Did he want to share with her all of the moving around, the instability of his life? The lack of *home*, which is all she wanted?

Yet she deserved to know all of it. If she chose to stay with him, it would have to be with *all* of him.

"Well, I graduated with a degree in mechanical engineering. Moved to Omaha to take a job and I hated it. My cubicle was claustrophobic, and the hours were unbelievable.

"But I found a great church there and started volunteering in the youth ministry. And that's where I found my calling. When Bruce, the student pastor, was offered a position at a large church in Kansas City, he asked me to come along as his associate youth minister."

"Mercy." Her eyes widened. "Indianapolis to Chicago, Chicago to Omaha, then Omaha to Kansas City? How'd you end up in Atlanta?"

"Keller called me after I'd been in KC about a year-and-a-half. He was working for a ministry organization that was planting a church in Athens, Georgia. Asked if I'd be interested in coming out there to start up their youth ministry. That was a hard decision because we were running on all cylinders at the KC church. But I couldn't ignore the pull to go help with this church plant, and Bruce encouraged me to spread my wings and go.

"So, I moved to Athens to join Keller at this new church. Turns out the organization he was with was Becker Ministries, and a little over two years in, I got a call from Maggie Watson."

"The Vice President at Becker."

"Right. They offered me a position there as a ministry start-up coordinator, and they'd pay for me to go to seminary. I was stunned. I'd been praying about my desire to go to seminary, then they offered to pay for it. Figured that was a clear answer, so I accepted the position. A couple years later, I came up with the concept of ReachOver, a student ministry to bridge social gaps in high school peer groups, and put it up on our website. That's how Harper found us."

"And now you're here." Her gaze tightened on his, as if

searching for something behind his eyes. "Did you like it in those other places? Or were you always itching to go somewhere new?"

He understood what she was asking. Would he grow bored here in Arlington? Get the itch to move on? Looking at the woman next to him now, he couldn't fathom not wanting to be right here. With her. For however long she wanted him.

But was it too early to tell her that? Would it be too much, too soon? The last thing he wanted to do was rush her and have her retreat again.

Looking down, he linked their fingers together before bringing his eyes back to hers. "I think after leaving Gallagher, I never felt truly at home anywhere. I was in Atlanta the longest, and even there, I never really settled in completely. Didn't even put anything up on my walls. But there's something about here that feels comfortable. Feels … good. The friends I've made here, our church, working with kids again." He tightened his hold on her hand. "And you. I didn't come here expecting to meet somebody, but I hear that's when it usually happens."

"When you least expect it."

"Exactly. I'm here, Al. With you. Ready to see where God takes us. What He has for us. I'm content here in Arlington and excited about the future. And I hope you're a part of that future."

Her nod was slow, her brow furrowed, for a long moment before her fingers found the pendants around her neck, and she looked away. He barely breathed, waiting for her to think through whatever was going on in her head, watching her thumb rub back and forth across the state of Texas. He'd laid a lot on her, but she needed to know. *He* needed to know she was on board even with all his baggage. His history. His journey to the here and now.

She looked back at him, and his lungs ceased to function while he waited to hear what she had to say. Her hand dropped back to her lap. "You know my dad and brother get here on Friday. Would you maybe … like to join us for dinner that night? Or for lunch on Saturday?"

Fireworks went off in his chest, and he couldn't keep back his smile. That certainly didn't sound like she was about to give him a polite *let's just be friends*. "I'd definitely like to. I was hoping I'd have the chance to meet them."

"They'll like you. No doubt."

She might not have a doubt, but that didn't squelch the question in his own mind. He didn't usually worry about meeting new people. He looked forward to it, stayed true to himself, to God, and whatever happened, happened.

But it was important he make a good impression on Ally's father and brother. Because nobody understood the importance of family more than someone who didn't have one.

CHAPTER TWENTY-FIVE

A man who cooks. Very attractive.

Grinning, Ally pulled her attention from Zane, who stood at the stove stirring a pot of sauce for the chicken parmesan that would be his contribution to tonight's dinner. With him in such close proximity, she had to dig deep to concentrate on building her lasagna in a large pan. They'd spent more waking hours together than apart over the last week, and at the end of every day, she found she'd fallen for him a little more.

Or a lot more. More than she'd thought she would after only a few days. Something she'd kept to herself, not even confiding in her friends until she understood what it all meant.

Which had taken some effort after the all-area leadership meeting Monday night when they'd arrived hand-in-hand to join several other leaders at a local pizza joint.

"I knew it!" Harper's wide smile and beaming face made Ally's cheeks burn after she and Shannon pulled her aside. *"I told Wyatt after dinner that night that you two were a thing. The way you guys finish each other's sentences and all. I just knew it!"*

"Well, in all honestly, we're only a sort-of-thing, and just for the last three days."

Shannon's forehead crinkled. *"What's a sort-of-thing?"*

"We're taking it a day at a time. Just to see where things go."

Harper clapped like a little girl. *"I see another ConnectUP wedding in our future!"*

"Hold up there, cowgirl. Let's wrangle those horses back into the corral, shall we?"

Although, Ally had to admit, she'd daydreamed about what a future with Zane might look like. Settling together here in Texas, getting a dog, buying a house where she could plant a garden and they could cook with vegetables from their own backyard.

She gave herself a mental shake and threw him another glance. When he'd donned Yolanda's *Kiss the Cook* apron, it had taken everything inside of her to not comply. But although they'd been together every day since his quick flower delivery to her office last Friday, he still hadn't kissed her. Again.

Which was probably a good thing, although a part of her wished he would. True to his word, he wasn't rushing her into anything. How, then, did she still feel swept off her feet?

She slid her pan of lasagna in the oven. "That sauce smells amazing." After closing the oven door, she set the timer. "Another recipe I'm going to have to get."

"I'll jot it down for you." He pointed to his temple. "It's all right up here."

"I don't know how you do that. I almost always have to go by a recipe."

He shrugged, laid the wooden spoon on a plate, and put the lid back on the pot. "I usually just wing it. Things don't always turn out the same every time, but that's why being in the kitchen with me is an adventure."

Laughing, she walked back to the counter to cut long baguettes into halves. She was of the mind that anything with Zane was an adventure, even their first official date on Saturday. She'd never had Indian food before but was now a big fan.

And after their picnic Sunday, he'd surprised her with inline skating along the bike path through the park. Had even taken it upon himself to borrow a pair of Rollerblades from Harper after finding out they wore the same size. Skating outside instead of around in circles was so much more fun and, yes, adventurous. She'd grown accustomed to the inlines much faster this time and didn't really need to hold onto him so much. Although her hand did find its way into his several times throughout the afternoon. Just to be safe.

With the bread spread with garlic butter and more parmesan cheese, she set it aside and walked to the window. For the third time in the last half hour. "Wish they'd get here."

"When did you last see your brother? In person, I mean."

She turned and crossed her arms over her stomach. "March. His girlfriend Paige had a surprise party for his thirtieth birthday, so I flew out there for that and stayed a few days."

"March? What day?"

"Sixteenth."

He plopped a chicken breast covered in flour into an egg wash, then rolled it in Italian breadcrumbs. "I'm a year and four days older than he is, then."

"Your birthday is March twelfth?"

"Since the day I was born."

Laughing, she pulled her phone from her back pocket. "It's going on my calendar."

The pan sizzled when he placed the breaded chicken into the hot oil. "And yours?"

"Nah, I don't need to put that on my calendar. I know when it is."

"Funny girl." He threw her a look she returned with a grin. "If I wanted to put it on *my* calendar, where would it go?"

"Ohhh. November fourteenth."

"Hmm. That's coming up. Gives me about six weeks to plan something."

"Nothing big. I'm good with dinner. Something simple. Don't even need a cake. Although I'd never turn away cake if it was forced on me."

More sizzling and an amazing aroma emanated from the pan when another piece of chicken hit the hot oil. "You do know who you're talking to, right? I don't do simple for important things."

She peered out the window again. "Dinner and un-simple cake."

"Dinner for fifty." He flipped the chicken breasts to cook on the other side. "No, a hundred. And a giant cake with twenty-seven candles? Twenty-eight candles? No! Sparklers! And a theme party. Like Roaring '20's. Wait, no. A 50's sock hop. Or Hawaiian luau. I wonder if Steve would let me dig a hole in his backyard to cook a whole pig." He looked over at her. "See? I have this thing halfway planned already."

A giggle bubbled out at his over-the-top ideas, but his thoughtfulness warmed her. "Dinner. Cake. Twenty-eight candles. You, me, Steve, Yo. No pig."

"We'll see." The wink he sent her warned her this discussion wasn't over.

With a shake of the head, a smile she couldn't keep back spread across her face as she returned to the kitchen. "Wish I had even the remotest clue what Dad's coming here to tell us."

"Maybe he's retiring, like you mentioned before."

"I considered that, but I honestly can't see it." With one hip propped against the counter, she crossed her arms over her stomach and watched him flip the chicken. "He's always said he'll die on the mission field, even if he's a hundred."

"Hmm." His brow creased as he moved the browned chicken from the skillet into a baking pan. "You're sure it's okay I'm here for this? Sounds like it might be a family thing."

"No worries. I told Dad about you and asked if it would be all right for you to come to dinner. He said it was perfectly fine, and he looked forward to meeting you."

He looked up from spooning sauce onto the chicken. "Told him about me, huh? That you'd met the most amazing man, who was handsome and smart and sophisticated and a stylish dresser?"

"My exact words." She sauntered back to the window. "Actually, I told him you were a strong man of faith, loved working with teenagers, had a great sense of humor, and drove a cool vintage Bronco." She shrugged as she glanced back at him. "And I might've mentioned smart."

The word *amazing* might have come up too, but she'd keep that to herself.

She peered through the blinds. "They're here!"

When she opened the front door, she launched herself into her father's arms before he'd even reached the porch. "Daddy!"

"Allyson." His voice broke. "It's so good to see you, my sweet baby girl."

She pulled back to look at him as tears fell down her face. "I've missed you so much. We've been apart much longer than this, and I've handled it better than I am tonight."

"Because we were together for a year. It makes the distance that much harder."

It did. More than he knew and more than she'd share. Her father's calling, his passion, was his mission. He loved his children, he loved his parents and brothers, but God was his first love. And he served Him well. She would never lay guilt on him for the distance between them. After all, it was more her choice than his, as he'd made it clear many times over the years he'd love for her to bring her nursing skills to work with him in the field.

She moved to her brother, who picked her up and spun her around.

"Hey, *hermanita*. You're more beautiful than ever."

When he set her down, she swatted his arm. "Stop. I'm not ten years old. You can't just throw me around like that."

A grin crossed his face as he winked at her. "Apparently I can."

Shaking her head, she stepped back and took Zane's hand. "Daddy, Michael, this is Zane Carpenter. Zane, this is my dad, Nathan Kincaid, and my brother, Michael."

Michael grinned at Zane and looked back at her. "Yes, we just met. While you were all weepy."

"Funny."

Zane held out his hand to her dad. "Dr. Kincaid. It's a pleasure."

"Pleasure's mine, my boy," Dad replied with a handshake and a pat to Zane's shoulder.

Ally herded the guys inside, and Zane pulled her up by the hand before she could follow. "Al. You catch up with your family. I'll finish up dinner."

"Are you sure you don't need any help?"

His jaw dropped. "You cast doubt on my culinary abilities?"

She couldn't help but giggle at his dramatic expression. "Not at all." She leaned in and placed a quick kiss on his cheek. "Thank you."

His eyes widened for a second, probably caught by surprise by her spontaneous gesture. "Not a problem. Go. Sit. I've got this."

Once back inside, Zane stuck the chicken breasts, covered with that incredible smelling sauce, in the oven while she filled glasses with sweet tea. She joined her father and brother in the living room, where they'd taken seats in the two floral armchairs. "Did you get checked in all right at the hotel?"

"No problems at all." Michael took the glass she held out to him. "Thanks."

Dad looked up when she handed him his tea. "Will Yolanda be joining us tonight?"

She shook her head and sat on the sofa. "No, she and Steve

will be with us tomorrow for dinner. They're having movie night with their club kids tonight."

Michael gulped from his tea and put the half-empty glass down on a coaster. "That reminds me. While I'm here, I'd like to have a sit down with you and Zane to talk about how to go about setting up some clubs in Colorado."

She sat up straight. "Seriously? You want to get involved with ConnectUP?"

"I'd love to. I've been interested since you guys started your first club. I knew Wyatt's goal was to start more groups locally, but now that you're here and working with Zane to cast a broader net, I thought why not see what I can do."

"We can totally do that!" came Zane's voice from the kitchen behind her.

Ally looked back and smiled at him where he stood chopping romaine for Caesar salad.

"Yes." She turned back to her brother. "We can totally do that. Zane's been working with the tech guys at Becker to make all of our training modules accessible online, so you don't necessarily have to be in Arlington to have what you need to launch a new club."

"Your sister came up with that, by the way," Zane said. "We'll have video training as well as manuals for launching a club, leading a club, PR for your club. Everything you need, right there from your laptop."

Ally rolled her eyes. "Concept was his, implementation was mine. He always gives me too much credit."

"No such thing."

"Anyway …" She threw a glance at Zane then looked back to her brother. "You can be our beta trainee and let us know if we've left any holes or questions unanswered, all of that."

"That's her official way of saying you'll be our guinea pig."

"Pretty much."

Michael looked back and forth between the two of them with a grin. "Sounds good to me. Looking forward to it."

Twenty minutes later, Zane called them to the table. Dad took his seat and looked at the spread. "Mercy, you two. This is quite the feast. Looks delicious."

After her father offered a prayer of thanksgiving, they dug into their Italian meal.

"My compliments to the chef," Michael said, looking at Zane. "I can cook, but not this well."

Zane shook his head. "Ally did most—"

"Nope." She put her hand on his shoulder. "I didn't. Zane did most of the cooking. I did lasagna and the bread, which was the easy part. The salad and chicken parm was all him. Even the from-scratch Caesar dressing."

Dad smiled at Zane, whose cheeks reddened for the first time she'd ever witnessed. She'd have to remember to compliment him more often. "Nicely done, young man. This chicken is so tender it melts in your mouth."

"Thank you. Got this recipe from a friend when I lived in Kansas City."

After several minutes of eating and catching up, Dad put his fork down and ran his napkin across his mouth. He put his arms on either side of his plate and looked at Ally, then Michael.

"Well, I'm sure you're wondering why I wanted to make the trip out here to see you two before my scheduled furlough."

Ally nodded. "Yes, definitely, but I didn't want to push."

"Same, Dad," Michael said.

Their father looked down at his plate, then back up to her, to Michael, and back again.

Prickles ran over her skin. "Daddy?"

"You know how I loved your mother." Emotion scraped his voice and moistened his eyes. "She was gone far sooner than I'd ever dreamed when she and I started our journey together. But I had you two and my work, and that kept me going. It was more than enough. It still is."

Their eyes held across the table. "Honey. Allyson. Having

you back in Pamoca was such a gift, and when you left ... well, that was the loneliest I'd been since we lost your mom."

"Oh, Daddy." Her heart clutched. She'd never considered that her father was lonely. He was always so happy working with the indigenous people of Guatemala alongside the other missionaries in Pamoca. "I'm so sorry."

"No. Don't be sorry. I fully support your life here and what you're building. And Nora fell into the work like she'd been born to it, although she'd never been on a mission field before.

"In those months after you left, she and I ... well, we spent quite a bit of time together, talking about our kids and our families. Our history. As you know, her husband suffered long and hard with cancer, and we lost your mom so quickly, with no hint of what was coming. Neither of us intended to marry again because of the pain we both suffered from our losses, so it's been a nice friendship to have."

"That's good. I'm happy God brought you two to the same place."

A shy grin spread on his still handsome face. At nearly sixty, he still kept fit and healthy, but that smile ... almost like a boy. "Well, about that. A couple of months ago, Nora and I realized our feelings had progressed ... for each other."

Tingling started at the top of her head and cascaded down. What was he—

"We've decided to marry."

"That's great, Dad!" Michael looked over at her. "Right, Al?"

"Uh ..." Words. Where were the words? "Yes. Yes, that's great. Married. You're getting married."

"We've spent the last couple of days in Nebraska, letting her kids know and introducing me to her extended family. She's flying here tomorrow morning because I wanted us both to have a little time with you."

"Her kids. Right. Two boys?"

"Yes. I met them previously when they came to the mission

a few months ago to spend some time with their mom. Really great young men. One in grad school, the other married and a physical therapist."

"And … when, exactly, is this happening?"

"We're thinking November, but it will depend on if you kids can get down to Guatemala or not. Maybe over Thanksgiving week."

"November. Thanksgiving."

Why couldn't she string more words together? Her thoughts skittered all over the place. Of course she was happy for him. He'd been alone for fifteen years. And Nora really was a wonderful, godly woman who loved working alongside him. Ally had just never imagined her father with anybody but—

"Sweetheart, I'm sorry this is such a shock. I'd hoped, with you knowing Nora from your work at the mission, that you'd be—"

"No, Daddy, it's okay. Really. And I am happy for you. Truly I am. I just wasn't expecting this."

Zane gave her a nudge. "Maybe I should head out. This is a family thing, so I should let you talk."

"Don't leave on my account, son," her dad said before looking at her. "Unless there are some things you need to discuss?"

She gave her head a small shake. "No, I'm fine." She looked at Zane. "Please stay."

He studied her and must have seen the plea in her eyes. "Of course. I'll even do the dishes. Just point me to the *Kiss the Dishwasher* apron."

CHAPTER TWENTY-SIX

"The boy's injuries were so severe, he would've never made it to Guatemala City."

Zane sat riveted to Dr. Kincaid as the man shared stories from his life on the mission field. Seated on the loveseat under the doctor's arm, Nora kept her hand on his leg, gazing up at him from time to time with love shining on her face. They were clearly besotted with one another and perfectly suited. Even Ally mentioned earlier that day how fun it was to see her father in love again.

"We operated on him right there in our clinic with no way to know if he'd ever see the light of another day. Over six hours. Dr. John, our other physician, had been a surgical resident when he was called to the mission field, so having him there was by divine appointment, I fervently believe. I would've been out of my element.

"Two weeks later, when his family saw that boy get up and walk, they all got saved. All twelve of them. Grandparents, parents, six kids. And now they work closely with us there in Pamoca to spread the gospel."

"Wow." Zane practically breathed the word. "That's amazing."

Gripping Ally's hand, he looked over at her sitting next to him on the sofa. "You were there for that?"

She nodded. "Front row seat to a miracle. One of many."

"Wow," he said again. "I'd love to hear some of your own stories sometime."

"Oh, I'm not nearly as good at storytelling as my dad."

She shared a grin with her father, who winked back at her, and Zane's heart lurched. He and his dad used to have that kind of connection. Would joke and laugh with each other. Could talk about anything.

It had been fun spending the day with Ally and her family, watching the way they interacted, the easy laughter and affection they had with each other. Even after Nora arrived that morning. And they'd included him in all of it.

Tonight, Steve and Yolanda had joined them for dinner at the girls' favorite Mexican restaurant. During the meal, Zane found himself looking around the table, taking it all in. Soaking up the love and respect and camaraderie between these people, although most of the conversation took place in Spanish. Good thing he and Steve both were pretty fluent in the language themselves.

It was all so new and warm and filled a space inside him he'd shuttered away following the death of his father. In some ways, it was easier not knowing what he'd been missing not having any people. Yet he wouldn't trade this evening for anything, being so unconditionally included in this kinship.

They'd returned to the townhouse for the pie he and Ally made last night after her father and brother left for the hotel. Now here they sat, in this cozy living room, listening as Dr. Kincaid regaled them with his tales of adventure, close calls, relationships built, lives saved, and souls brought into the kingdom over his thirty-plus years in the field. Tales Zane couldn't hear enough about.

"And you're with Gilead Medical Missions?" he asked, remembering Ally mentioning that early on.

"That's correct. Based on Jeremiah 8:22. *'Is there no balm in Gilead? Is there no physician there? Why then is there no healing for the wound of my people?'* Of course, Jeremiah is speaking of the Israelites in exile, but the wound is that of turning from God. And Gilead is referencing a region east of the Jordan that was known for its healing balsams. Our goal is to heal both the body and the soul. It's been very fulfilling work."

"I can imagine. Do they only send medical professionals, or do they also send administrative and pastoral missionaries?"

"Everybody. Our team has two physicians, a dentist, two to three nurses or nurse practitioners—like Ally, Yo, and Nora here—a mission administrator, and a pastor."

Zane looked over at Ally. "You're a nurse practitioner?"

She nodded.

"I didn't know that. That's impressive."

Pink tinged her cheeks before she looked down at her lap. The fact that she was highly educated came as no surprise, nor that she'd never mentioned it. She was humble and didn't like to talk about herself, but she deserved recognition for her hard work and the way she used her gifts. She always claimed he gave her too much credit, but he didn't think she received nearly enough.

He looked back over to Dr. Kincaid. "Your work is fascinating. I'd love to know more about Gilead, if you have the time while you're here."

"It would be my pleasure," Dr. Kincaid said, his smile much like that of his daughter.

Ally looked over at him with a deep crease in her brow. "Are you still interested in working in foreign missions?"

He met her gaze. While at peace about his decision to pass up the offer from Global Reach, he couldn't deny that part of him still hoped he might have another opportunity down the line. And if he and Ally were together, maybe she'd eventually come back to her love for the field. From the tidbits she'd added to the conversation throughout the evening, and her father's stories, it was clear she'd thrived there, with little to none of the modern conveniences she worked with in the States.

But the furrow in her brow and question in her eyes told him she wasn't anywhere near that yet. "I do find it interesting," he said with a squeeze to her hand. "But I'm not looking into it right now. Not with so much happening with ConnectUP."

She nodded, but that *V* remained etched into her forehead.

Later, after pie had been served, and the doctor, Nora, and Michael had said their goodbyes for the evening, it was just the four of them left at the house. Yolanda brought out a board game, and they teamed up, couple against couple, as the clock ticked toward midnight.

Steve looked over at him. "We should head out, dude. Church in the morning."

"Probably should." He looked at Ally next to him at the kitchen table. "This has been such a great day, spending it with your family. Thanks for including me."

"Absolutely." Her smile made his pulse lurch. "They really like you."

He swept the back of his hand across his forward. "Whew. That's a relief."

"As if you needed to worry."

She and Yolanda cleaned up their glasses and plates while he and Steve gathered up the pieces of the game the other couple had won two rounds to one.

Outside under the moonlight, standing next to Phyllis while Steve drove away and Yo went back into the house, Zane reached for Ally's hands and pulled her close.

He grinned and shook his head. "Family. You're blessed to have such a great one, Al."

"I am. I know I am. I just wished they lived closer, especially since it appears it'll be growing by two over the next year, with Dad getting married and Michael planning to propose to Paige."

"A stepmom and a new sister."

"Stepmom." She shook her head but with a smile. "That sounds so weird. Not that I'm unhappy about it. I liked Nora from the moment I met her when she came to Guatemala last year. Working with her for those months that saw so much disease and sickness proved what a blessing she would be to the mission. She's a gifted nurse. And to come to the field later in life took a lot of courage."

Hope sprouted in his spirit. "Sounds like you admire her."

"I do admire her. The work they do is hard, and she dove in like she'd been doing it for years."

"I guess that's what happens when you follow your calling. God gives you what you need when you need it."

"And my dad sure needed Nora. It makes my heart happy knowing he'll have someone to grow old with. My mom would approve of Nora. I have no doubt."

"Do you think you'll get down to Guatemala for the wedding?"

"Wouldn't miss it."

He nodded, staring down at her only inches away, and his heart constricted in his chest. She'd allowed him into her family, and they'd accepted him without question. If only he had someone to take her home to.

Her head tilted. "What is it? You just went away for a second."

"Just thinking how I wish I had someone to show you off to. A family who would take you in and include you like yours did me today." He swallowed the lump in his throat. "My dad. He would've been crazy about you. Would've told me in no uncertain terms to not let you get away before you realized how much better you could do."

She shook her head and tightened her hold on his hands. "I can't imagine a better man than you." Tears welled in her eyes.

"And you do have family. Maybe not by blood, but you have the ConnectUP family, and now mine. I hope you know how very much you're ... loved."

Loved. Did she love him? Could she possibly?

Because this thing, this feeling growing by the day inside him, had to be love. He couldn't put any other name to it.

"I do. The ConnectUP family has definitely taken me in, and I've enjoyed being here, working with everybody. Especially you. Since that first night and all those notes you took over hamburgers and fries. You've been my equal partner this whole way, Ally. I couldn't have done half of what we've accomplished without you."

And he didn't want to. No matter where God sent him, he hoped to see it through with this lady in front of him right now.

But for her part, would putting down roots on American soil trump the opportunity to work on the mission field with him?

Pulling her close, their arms went around each other, and he closed his eyes. He didn't know what God had planned for them in the future. But right now, he was right where he was meant to be.

CHAPTER TWENTY-SEVEN

"*H*arper, your Bible study is phenomenal." Ally looked up from the binder lying next to her plate at the small cafe where they'd met for lunch. The binder Harper handed her after last week's all-area leadership meeting with a quick *"Just a little something I wrote. Take a look and let me know what you think. Maybe we can do lunch next Tuesday after your dad and brother leave for the airport and talk about it?"*

Typical Harper. Michael, Dad, and Nora had left that morning, and Harper probably figured Ally would need a distraction with Zane otherwise occupied at a lunch meeting with several area youth pastors and Yolanda at work. Harper had an innate sense of anticipating another's need and filling it.

"Seriously." She reached across and laid her hand on top of Harper's. "This is perfect for launching our girls' Bible studies."

Her friend blushed and laid her fork on her plate. "You think it's good? Honestly?"

Ally pulled her hand back. "No. It's not good. It's beyond good. You have a gift, my friend. You need to look into getting this published."

"That's the hope. I pitched it to an acquisitions editor at the house that publishes Wyatt's books, and she asked me to send it to her. She works with authors of women's Bible studies and has been trying to find studies for teen girls, so this fits."

"It absolutely fits."

For a so-called *newbie Christian* only a year ago, Harper had certainly poured herself into getting to know the Lord and His Word. Over the past week, when not at work, with Zane, or her family, Ally had read through the entire thing, staying up way too late because she hadn't been able to put it down. She'd even shared some with Zane, who was equally impressed with Harper's talent and knowledge of the faith she'd embraced so whole-heartedly.

"I'm so glad you think so. You're the first person, other than Wyatt and my sister, who's seen it. They loved it, but I trust your opinion as someone who knows the Bible well. And who's, well, not related to me. I figured you could see if I'd missed the mark anywhere."

A warmth filled Ally's chest at Harper's kind words. She'd been raised steeped in the Word, but there were times she found she stored more in her head than her heart. While it appeared every new thing Harper encountered in the scriptures became part of her very life. "I didn't find anything that was off the mark. Even learned some things. Let's put together a beta group of girls between all of the clubs, and they can meet at the new office. Since we're already into October, let's shoot for them to start in January."

Harper picked up her fork and jabbed it into her salad. "That sounds great." She took a bite and swallowed. "Okay, enough shop talk. I want to know about Zane. Or more to the point, you and Zane."

And there it was. Ally smiled. She knew it was only a matter of time before Harper would ask. She shut the binder, put it into her bag, and looked back at her friend. "What about us?"

"How's it going? Are you still a *sort-of-thing* or an *all-out-thing*?"

Ally stirred her spoon in her chowder, the aroma of clams and potatoes that had basked in a pool of creamy broth all morning wafting up to her face. "Um, well, we're together. Exclusive, if you want to call it that."

"An all-out thing, then." Harper stared at her for a moment. "Or not? What's going on?"

"Nothing. I just … well …"

"You're not sure of him? About him? About what you want, or what he wants?"

"No, I know exactly what I want. I'm very sure about him." With a sigh, she laid her spoon down on the plate. "I guess I'm not sure he's sure about him."

Harper's eyes narrowed. "You lost me."

Ally picked up the spoon again and gave her chowder another stir. "Can I ask you a personal question?"

Harper glanced down before meeting Ally's eyes again, caution written in the crease of her brow. "Is it about my husband?"

"Sort of. But not because of … you know. Our history. It's about yours."

"Okay, shoot. Ask and I'll tell you if it's too personal."

"That's fair." She took another moment to choose her wording. She'd been thinking and praying ever since she went to bed Saturday night, asking the Lord to give her guidance. Maybe bringing her here, to this table with this particular friend, was His answer. "Last year when you two broke up — you know, when I made an absolute fool of myself?"

"Oh, sweetie, you didn't. I couldn't blame you for wanting him back. And I don't. You know that, right? No hard feelings at all."

"I know. And that means the world to me. *You* mean the world to me. That we could be such good friends after what I did. But you told me some time later that the reason you broke up was because you felt like God could be calling you to different things."

"Right. Yes. Hardest decision I ever made. But Wyatt was my Isaac. Like Abraham, I had to be willing to sacrifice that which meant the most to me to follow hard after God. But when we obey, He will always bless it. Whichever way it goes. It was agony being apart, but I was ready to walk away and move to Atlanta if that's what God wanted me to do."

"Until Wyatt came after you."

Harper smiled, and her emerald eyes lit up. "Yes, but until that very moment, I didn't know how God was going to work that out. If we'd ever be together again or if we'd just remain friends. Long distance, at that." She tilted her head. "Why? And how does this pertain to Zane not being sure ... of him? Or whatever you said."

Ally looked away for a moment, then back to her friend. If anybody would understand her dilemma, it would be Harper. "You know about the foreign mission opportunity he had, right?"

Harper nodded. "But he turned that down. Has he reconsidered?"

"No. But I'm not sure he shouldn't. Reconsider, that is."

"Wait. You want him to go?"

Ally's pulse jumped. "No! Not at all. Mercy, I'm messing this all up."

"Okay, start at the beginning. Like, when you and Zane first realized you were crushing on each other."

"Would your wedding be too soon?"

Harper's eyes widened. "Was it love at first sight? Zane mentioned he met you at our wedding, but leave it to a man to leave out the best part."

Ally laughed. "I wouldn't say love, but I was definitely crushing. Although, at the time, he was just a very handsome guy I met out on a moonlit terrace who I would never see again. I kind of let my imagination run with it, thinking it a harmless infatuation with a complete stranger."

With a dreamy smile, Harper let out a sigh, her gaze landing somewhere behind Ally. "So romantic. Two star-crossed strangers, a moonlit night, their eyes meeting, their hearts bonding, and then ... *poof*. They part, never knowing if they'll see each other again, but always wondering ... *what if* ..."

Ally glanced behind her and back again. "Um, hey, you with me here?"

Harper focused back in on her. "Oh. Yeah. Sorry."

"I think you've read a few too many romance novels."

"No such thing."

"Okay, well, back to regular programming. We met outside, had a two-minute conversation, then he got a phone call. I left, and that was that. Until that night he walked into the leadership meeting at your house. Then when we started working together, we meshed right away."

"Yeah, that was obvious to everybody." Harper picked up her fork. "Trust me, sister. Nobody's all that surprised you turned out to be a thing. All-out or otherwise."

"Well, *I* was surprised. I was in a season of focusing my energies toward growth in the Lord, being who He intended me to be, all by myself, just Him and me. Then this guy comes along and upends it all with his heart for God and love for ministering to teens. Not to mention his charm and humor. His smile and those dimples. And eyes the color of melted chocolate." She sighed. "I kind of have it bad, don't I?"

Harper let out a giggle. "You most certainly do. And I know he does too. So, what's the problem?"

Ally's mouth fell slack. "How do you know he does?"

"Oh, honey, let me count the ways. The way he looks at you, the way he speaks to you, the way he searches for you the second he walks into a room. The way he prays for you, considers you. Even the way he touches you, with so much respect. You're very blessed. And so is he."

A few days ago, Harper's summation would have made her all giddy inside, the way she felt whenever she met Zane's eyes from across a room, or whenever he took her hand. Or, frankly, every time the man took a breath. But today ... well, it just made her wonder even more if he—

"He said working in foreign missions had been a dream of his for a while. I don't want him to have regrets down the road. He didn't say he turned it down for me, just that he didn't want to leave ConnectUP right now because of everything we have in the works."

"But ..."

"But he showed up at my office the day he gave them his decision with a bouquet of flowers and asked me out for our —" She held her fingers in quotes around her face. "—*first official date.*"

"And that's bad because ..."

"Because it can't be about me, about us. It has to be because he's certain God wants him here. For the ministry. Or whatever else God has for him."

"And what if *whatever else God has for him* is you?"

Ally sat up at attention. "Does it work that way?"

Laughing, Harper nodded. "Why not? I have zero doubt God meant to bring Wyatt and me back together after not seeing each other for over a decade. At that exact time in our lives, when neither of us was looking but were focused on what God wanted us to do. I was just starting out in my faith and seeking His direction, and Wyatt was neck-deep into ConnectUP. We were both surprised at how quickly everything happened, but were pretty sure within a few weeks we would be together forever. Until the enemy tried to pull us apart by confusing what should have been clear, had we both been trusting wholly in God."

"Using your individual callings to split you up."

"Exactly. Wyatt had been carrying around a seed of unforgiveness that grew into a root of bitterness he didn't even know was there. Those were his words exactly, not mine. But his resolve to not make changes to ConnectUP had me questioning my conviction that we needed to extend our reach. It wasn't until I trusted God enough to follow those convictions to Atlanta, and Wyatt asked Him to show him if he was missing something, that we found our way back to each other. We have no doubt we're living in the center of God's will. *Together.* Ministering to teens, building a family. Doing His work. Why couldn't that be the same for you?"

Well ... hmm ... good question. Still ... "Zane and I aren't that invested in each other yet. He said he didn't do it for me, but I can't help wondering if maybe all of this between us played a part in it."

"Maybe it did. Doesn't mean it's wrong. If the man's falling in love with you, knowing Zane like we do, you know he didn't come to that without seeking God's input."

Falling in love with her? Ally's pulse hitched. Could he be falling in love with her? Already?

Her thoughts skidded to a stop. But wasn't she falling in love with him? Already?

She looked back at her friend, the knot in her throat making it hard to push the words out. The words that defined her true fear. "What if we give this a go and he's presented with another opportunity down the road he wants to accept? I'd have to let him go because I would never stand in the way of his dreams. Or his calling." *I'd have to let him go ...*

"Sweetie." Harper reached for her hand. "You know God is not a God of *what ifs*. He's a God of *what is*. And *what is* is a man who cares about you, who wants to build something with you. A godly man. A good man. A man I suspect you're already half-way in love with."

She wasn't wrong. About any of it. About God and Zane and ... all of it.

Harper gave her hand a squeeze. "Al, you won't know which way to go until you move. Until you step out in faith, one way or the other. I thought it was cute when you told us you were a *sort-of* thing. But you really can't sit on the fence and expect to get anywhere. You have to decide on a side and climb down into whatever is waiting for you there. You need to step all in, or step away. And the way you feel for Zane I think would make it difficult for you to step away."

"You're right. It would be very difficult."

"So why not go for it? You don't know if Zane will get a call to go somewhere else and serve. You don't know if *you* will. But today, if your relationship is based on godly things—mutual respect, a shared faith, serving others—why not give it everything you have and see what God does with it?"

Harper's gaze kept hold of Ally's. "If it's fear keeping you back, that's not of God. Step out in faith, and He'll meet you there. Trust me. Trust *Him.*"

Trust Him. With her heart, with her future.

A few years ago, she'd done just that, when she found a man she believed God had brought her to only to realize he hadn't been the one meant for her forever. Now here she was again, falling quickly for a man of strong integrity and faith in God. A man who cared about her and treated her well. Who made her laugh and who could get her to open up and talk about things she'd never been comfortable sharing before.

But as she'd learned with Wyatt, even if God had put Zane in her life now, that didn't mean it was a forever thing. Could she endure it again if she gave away her heart, only to watch him walk away with it?

CHAPTER TWENTY-EIGHT

*S*omething was definitely up.

Zane glanced at Ally sitting to his left at Steve's kitchen table. They'd spent that afternoon finalizing plans for two upcoming launches, before Steve and Yo brought in barbecue-to-go after finishing their work days. Now the four of them had been laughing and talking over dinner the last half hour.

At least, three of them had. Ally had been a bit quieter and less engaged, offering tidbits to the conversation and laughing with the rest of them, but always seeming to be a bit behind. As if distracted or far away. If only he knew what to do or say to help her.

Yolanda put down her glass of tea and looked at Ally. "How's the office coming along?"

Ally looked up from her plate. "Uh, good. It's almost done. The painting's finished, the vinyl wood plank flooring is in, bathrooms are renovated, and tech equipment installed. All completely donated. Didn't cost CU or Becker one cent."

Yolanda's jaw dropped. "That's incredible!"

"It's astonishing how much has come in. Oh, and we had an anonymous donor put up our first three months' rent." She

217

looked over at Zane. "You know, I have a sneaking suspicion the landlord is covering it for us. He's been so impressed with all the work we've done sprucing up that space he couldn't get rented."

"Wouldn't surprise me," he answered. "Super nice guy."

Yolanda's face lit up, and she practically bounced up and down in her chair. "We need to have a grand opening party! We can invite all of the people who donated time, money, resources. Club kids and families. The other businesses in the building."

A crease marred Ally's forehead. "That's a bunch of people. No way they'll all fit."

Zane picked up his pulled pork sandwich, or what remained of it, anyway. "We could use the outside space. String some lights, put out those citronella candles. Make it an open house, a come-and-go kind of thing."

A smile replaced the look of concern, and he felt an overblown sense of accomplishment. He'd do anything for that smile. "That's a good idea."

And with that, Ally and Yo got Shannon and Harper on speaker phone and planned a grand opening party at the office for two-and-a-half weeks out in about twenty minutes, complete with decorations, food, and how to get the word out. These ladies didn't mess around.

A couple of hours later, he took her hand and walked her out to her car. Yolanda had already left in hers, since she came over after she got off work, and he and Ally had given her and Steve a few minutes to say good night. When they stopped at the driver's door, he turned to face her. And for the second time that evening, he couldn't shake the feeling something was off. When planning the office party, she'd been engaged and alight. In her element. But once alone with him, she'd retreated back into her thoughts.

Replaying the past couple of days in his head—Sunday afternoon spent at the Fort Worth Zoo with her family,

Monday night's Dallas leadership meeting with Michael along to see how it worked—he finally had to admit her pensiveness hadn't started today upon the departure of her dad and brother. They'd had a great time, no question, but she'd clearly had something weighing on her the past few days.

If only he could draw her out, find out what happened between their amazing evening with everybody on Saturday night and Sunday's trip to the zoo.

She brought her gaze to his, studying him, as if she could see into his soul. Which was fine. There wasn't anything he didn't want her to know. Nothing he wouldn't trust her with.

"Just ask me, Al," he said in a quiet voice, not wanting to dispel the silence of the night around them. "Whatever it is, just ask."

The lines of her throat tightened before she swallowed. "How sure are you, Z?"

The tempest in her eyes tugged at his chest. Had he done something? Said something? Or perhaps he hadn't said *enough* in his effort to take things slow with her. "About …?"

"About not taking the mission assignment. How sure are you?"

Back to that? Confused about the direction of the conversation, he at least knew the answer to her query. "Very sure. No question."

She cocked her head. "Honestly?"

"Absolutely. I have complete peace about that decision. I told you that."

"I know you did. But then, Saturday night … with my dad. It just seemed like you were dialed in to everything he said."

"Of course I was. Your dad's work is fascinating."

"And you don't regret not taking the offer?"

"Zero regret. This is where I'm supposed to be. Working to grow CU. And hopefully building something with you. I'm exactly where I want to be."

Her eyes didn't leave his face, and he hoped, in the glow of the streetlamps, she could see the absolute truth of his words.

"Is this why you've been so quiet the past few days?"

Her mouth fell slack as she blinked. "I've been quiet?"

"A little. With me, anyway. I hoped you'd either talk to me about it or work through it. Or talk to me and we could work through it together. That's even better."

Her expression softened as her hand tightened around his. "I'm sorry, Z. I didn't mean to get quiet on you. That scheming devil knows right where to get to me. I'm not used to uncertainty. Have always been able to make decisions on my feet. Kind of a necessity in my work, but it's never been an issue with me even in my private life. So, when I get confused or unsure, I—"

"Retreat."

Her mouth snapped shut, and he hoped he hadn't offended her. But to grow, she needed to see the truth. By her own admission, and as he'd seen firsthand, she tended to run when things got uncomfortable. She needed to stop.

"Retreat," she repeated.

"Either physically, like you did at the wedding, or emotionally, like the past couple of days. Or both, like you did a few weeks ago."

Her head moved up and down as she thought about it. "You're right. I did it again. Why can't I stop doing that?"

He sent her a grin. "I'd say you're making progress. You didn't flee the country, ditch me, or refuse to get in a car alone with me."

When she giggled, the sound washed over him like a cool breeze on a warm day. "That's definitely progress."

"Definitely. But I'd love it if you would come to me when you have doubts. About anything. It doesn't even have to be about me. If you're uncertain about anything, let me be that safe place. I want to be that for you. So don't run from me in the future, physically or mentally. Run *to* me. With anything. Sound good?"

"Yes." With her smile, the knot in his midsection unwound. "That sounds good."

He looked down at their joined hands for a long moment before he looked back up at her, his smile gone. It was time he let her know exactly where he stood, how he felt, what he expected.

"There are going to be uncertain times, sweetheart. I won't be the perfect boyfriend, and I have no expectations that you'll be the perfect girlfriend. I wouldn't even want that. But I'm all in with you. I've never had this with anybody before, this instant ... thing. I couldn't stop thinking about you after that night at the wedding. And then to meet you again two days after I move here and it turns out you're the one the guys thought could work with me? What is that if it's not God?"

Her hands gripped his. "I felt it too. But like I told you before, it scared me how fast I was ... well, that I was falling for you. Then when I finally got to the place I thought I could explore that, you said you might be leaving. And it all came screeching to a halt."

He winced. "I should've been more up front with you about that. I honestly didn't even think about it."

"It's okay. I understand why you didn't. And, selfishly, I'm not disappointed you turned it down. Last week was so much fun, spending all that time with you, knowing we were headed down a new road. But then Saturday night, watching you listen to my dad, all I could think was that you'd passed on an opportunity to chase a dream and that you'd probably come to a point where you had to weigh whether staying here with me was worth not going to the field."

He gave his head a shake. "I have no regrets."

Which was absolutely true. Although, he still wondered what it would be like to work on a foreign mission field. To bring the gospel to people who otherwise wouldn't know. The fact that the Lord had brought him to Ally, who'd grown up on a mission on foreign soil, had him believing perhaps it was something they could explore together.

If she didn't appear so dead set against it.

"But neither of us knows today what God has in store for us in the future," he continued. "Not even tomorrow, really. Sometimes we have to live in the moment and trust that God has us well in hand. And in this moment, I really want to be with you. One hundred percent. But I need to know you want the same thing. That if you ever have questions or uncertainty, about my intentions or your own, you'll talk to me."

"I will. I promise, I will. I'm tired of running when it's better to stay and face it."

"That's all I ask." Still holding onto one of her hands, he put his other along her face, brushing his thumb across her cheek. "I can't get the first time I kissed you out of my head. And I say *first* because there's about to be a second. If you're on board with that."

"One hundred percent," came her whispered response.

He smiled, then leaned in close, stopping a mere breath from her face for a forever second before closing the distance. It was a chaste kiss. Soft, yet it reached down into his soul. A kiss he would never forget, just like the last time.

When she pressed into him, his arms went around her to pull her closer. They fit so perfectly together, as if two halves of a whole.

Before he lost himself completely, he ended the kiss and put his forehead to hers. "Ally ... I've been wanting to do that all week."

"I've been wanting you to."

He pulled back and smiled. "Seriously?"

"Don't wear a *Kiss the Cook* apron unless that's exactly what you want."

"I'll keep that in mind."

He swallowed her giggle in another kiss.

Yes, definitely no regrets staying here. With this woman, and in this place that already felt like home.

CHAPTER TWENTY-NINE

Zane let his gaze roam the courtyard outside the new office space. People stood under strands of white lights, mingling, laughing, enjoying this mild, late October evening celebrating the official opening of ConnectUP headquarters.

The new Arlington Two club had launched last week, Dallas Two would launch in a week-and-a-half, then they could put their energies toward Fort Worth with a Mansfield start-up right behind it. He'd also heard from two youth pastors from churches in nearby towns asking how they might get a CU club in their areas. Things were happening quickly.

And not just with CU. He and Ally had grown closer by the day, and he was head over heels in love with the girl. Even if he hadn't voiced as such to her yet, his mind had already played out different scenarios for their future together. Perhaps settling here in Arlington, getting a house—and a dog— planting a garden, raising a family, growing old.

Or if, over time, she could see herself returning to the mission field, they could make their home among the people and raise their children to experience different cultures. Just like she had as a child.

But that was a big *if*.

He gave his head a shake. Way too early to consider any of this, whichever direction their relationship took. He only knew that whatever his future held, he wanted her in it.

When his cell phone vibrated, he pulled it from his pocket. The same number had called him once yesterday and then this morning. Now here it was again. If it was a solicitor, they were certainly persistent. He clicked on the red phone icon to get rid of it. If it was something he needed to know, they could leave a message.

Shannon walked up, her beaming smile and sparkling blue eyes directed at him. "Hey, Zane, have a sec?"

"I have several. What can I do for you?"

"The Fort Worth club is launching in January, right?"

"That's the plan. Why?"

"Cuz I'm interested. I'd love to be part of a new launch."

His pulse sped up as it always did when something good was about to happen. "Seriously? Would you want to captain it or stay in your capacity as a group leader?"

Her brows pinched together. "I'll have to pray on that. My first impulse is to say, yeah, I'd love to captain it. But I'll also be starting my internship at Wyatt's counseling practice in January. And I'm in the accelerated master's program at DHU."

"A lot on your plate. I get it. Let's talk again as it gets closer, and we'll see where we are. Either way, consider yourself on the Fort Worth launch team."

Her face lit up. "Oh, I'm so excited! I'll miss the Arlington club, since that's where I started, and I love my girls. But to be part of a brand-new club would be amazing."

"We'll make it happen. Thanks for stepping up."

"I can't wait." She looked around before bringing her gaze back to him. "I picked you out, you know."

His eyes narrowed as his smile waned. "Picked me out?"

"For Ally. First time I saw you, I thought *that guy's perfect for Ally*. And, of course, that was just based on your looks. And the fact you liked little kids. Ashlen was pretty much attached to you the entire evening."

Grinning, he nodded. "The wedding."

"Yep. I told Ally she should ask you to dance. But she balked."

"Guess she wasn't as sure as you were that I was perfect for her."

She shrugged. "That was a weird night for her. But she's over it, and she's nuts about you. So it all worked out."

"Nuts about me, huh. You think?"

"I *know*. It's all over her face whenever she looks at or talks about you. Like it is with yours when you see her. She deserves that. Deserves a guy who gets how amazing she is. Take care of my friend, okay?"

"I'm on it."

His phone vibrated again, and he pulled it from his pocket, his stomach rolling when he saw the caller ID. He looked at Shannon. "I'm sorry. I need to take this."

"No worries. Talk to you later."

She walked away, and he turned to move to a quieter area to answer the call. "Aunt Gina?"

His mother's sister never called him. He only made sure she had his number in case anything ever happened to his mom. The last time he'd spoken to his aunt was two weeks before he left Atlanta, almost three months ago.

"No, honey." The voice on the other end of the line made his blood run cold. "It's ... Mom."

For someone who always seemed to have something to say, he couldn't think of a thing at the moment. The line sat silent and heavy between them.

"I've tried calling you the past couple of days from my number," she continued when he still said nothing, her voice timid and quiet. "But you didn't pick up, and I didn't want to leave a message out of the blue."

The ice in his veins turned white hot. "You mean since we haven't spoken in, how long has it been? Eighteen years?"

Since the day she left and never looked back. He went to school that morning, and she was gone when he got home. No letter. No *goodbye*. No *I love you*. But then he hadn't heard her say she loved him since the day Emma died. No, she blamed him. She hated him for it.

And he'd hated himself for years. Even after getting right with the Lord, the guilt still hung on him like a ball and chain.

Now it nearly choked him, simply hearing the voice of his accuser.

"It's unforgivable." Her whispered words increased the pressure in his chest, until he realized she wasn't responding to his thoughts but to his words. "The way I left. Staying away for so long. There were things … choices I made … that I regret."

"Why are you calling me, … Mom?" He swallowed the emotion scraping against his throat, his other hand balling into a fist at his side. He hadn't called anybody *Mom* in almost two decades. It sounded foreign even now. "Because you need something?"

He didn't want to be cruel, but the pain in hearing her voice was almost more than he could handle right now. In this place. On this night that had been so full of joy and fun and laughter. A night spent looking forward to a bright future reaching more at-risk kids for Christ. Not a night he wanted to look back at his darkest days.

She didn't answer for a moment. "I-I'd like to see you. I can come there. I know you're busy with your work. I don't want to take you away."

"Yeah, now wouldn't be a good time to leave."

The anger roiling through him shocked him. He hadn't

even realized it was there, living and breathing inside of him. While mad at everybody and everything after Dad died, he'd never been angry when Mom left. Just confused, hurt ... guilty. But it must have been simmering there, deep in his soul, now pouring out like a lava flow after a volcanic eruption. Because that's what this call felt like—like his world blowing up.

"I can hear you're busy right now." She cleared her throat. "Can we talk another time? Please, Zane? I'd really like to see you."

His throat tightened and eyes burned. "I don't know. I ... I need to think. Give me a couple of days?"

"Yes. If that's what you need, that's fine." Her voice cracked, and sympathy leaked through the dam he'd built in his heart between himself and the reservoir of pain this woman had dumped into his life.

"I'll call you." He disconnected before that sympathy could flow any further. He didn't want to feel for her. Didn't want to feel anything for her. Not this anger, not pity. Certainly not love. Not after she'd thrown him off like a dirty, tattered blanket she no longer had any use for.

A hand settled on the back of his shoulder, and he spun to find Ally looking at him with a crease in her brow.

Her eyes widened as she pulled her hand back. Could she see the unfamiliar rage coursing through him? After a moment, she put her hand on his arm. "Are you okay?"

He stared down at her, the hot current of emotion inside him slowing at her comforting touch. She'd left her hair loose, and strands of her honey-hued locks floated in the breeze. The pink and purple floral dress hugged her in all the right places, and her face shone as if with an inner light source. He'd watched her throughout the evening, greeting club kids with hugs and big smiles, introducing herself to parents or patrons who'd helped them outfit the office, laughing with the other leaders. And his heart skipped every time. How God had seen him fit for such a lovely creature was beyond him, but he was thankful every day for the gift she was.

Composed now just looking at her, he cupped her cheek with his hand. "You're beautiful, you know that?"

A shy smile crept across her face. "Thank you. But you're changing the subject. Why are you over here by yourself?"

He dropped his hand. "I just got a call. My mom. First time I've heard her voice in almost twenty years."

Her mouth fell open and eyes widened. "Is she—is everything all right?"

He shrugged. "I don't know, to be honest. I told her I couldn't talk right now. But she wants—" He swallowed hard. "She wants to come see me."

"Oh. Wow."

"Yeah. I'm not sure what to do with that."

"But you're going to see her, right? I mean … I know it's been a long time, but she reached out—"

"Can we not talk about this right now?" He smiled and waved at one of the kids across the courtyard before looking back down at her. "It's been a great night, and I don't want to think about it. Not now."

Her forehead furrowed as she studied him, and he looked away from the hint of disappointment he saw in her eyes. Or maybe it was confusion. Either way, he didn't like it. Didn't like disappointing her, didn't like that she couldn't understand his need to protect himself.

She took his hand in both of hers. "Hey." She waited for his eyes to meet hers again. "I'm here for whatever you need, Z. Whether you want to talk or not. And when or if you are ready, I'll still be here. Whatever you need."

Whatever he needed? Right now, he was looking at all he needed.

But could he be all *she* needed?

Hearing that voice from his past brought back all the pain,

all the heartbreak, from those awful, gut-wrenching days, weeks ... years, after his mother left him. Knowing he wasn't enough—not good enough, not valuable enough, not lovable enough—for his own mother to stay.

How could he expect to be enough for Ally?

CHAPTER THIRTY

*A*lly preceded Zane into his and Steve's house and flipped the switch to turn on the gas fireplace while he went to the kitchen to grab two bottles of water. They'd spent the evening at the Arlington One club, and, as usual, it left her heart full after catching up with the girls she used to lead.

Blair was back after spending the last five weeks with her grandparents, and it had been good to see her laugh and talk with the other kids, who had welcomed her with open arms. Three other girls had come forward with allegations after Blair had so courageously refused to keep her attack in the shadows, and most of the online bullying subsided when that came to light.

She would start at the private school second semester, and Ally couldn't be more proud of how the girl had handled the whole situation.

Ally sat down on the couch and pulled the light throw draped over the back around her. It was only four days before Halloween, yet there'd been a chill in the air tonight. Fall was upon them, and she loved the crispness of the season as it descended.

Zane plopped down next to her and put their water on the coffee table. "How are the wedding plans coming?"

Grinning, she snuggled into him and pulled her arm through his. "Nora called this afternoon about an idea she had. She was so excited. Giddy, like a bride should be. I know it's a second marriage for them both, but it's going to be a beautiful wedding."

"I'm glad you're happy about it."

"Oh, absolutely. It took me by surprise, but by the time she arrived here in Arlington, I was over-the-moon happy for them. My dad's been without someone for too long. And I adore Nora."

"I'm looking forward to the trip to Guatemala and spending some more time with your family. Good thing I already have my passport. It'll be my first stamp."

The popping of the flames in the fireplace filled the silence. *Family.* Zane had enjoyed meeting her father and brother back when he considered himself alone in the world, with no family to speak of. Now he had a chance to fix what was broken between him and his mother, but he hadn't so much as mentioned her or her phone call the past four days.

She looked up at him. "So, um, have you talked to your mom?"

When that smile she loved faded and he pulled away to stare down at his hands, she almost regretted asking. But he needed to deal with it. If only he'd open up to her.

"No." He swallowed hard. "Aunt Gina called me yesterday. I didn't answer because I thought it might be my mom again, but she left a message and I called her back."

"What'd she say?"

He let out a deep sigh and crossed his arms over his chest. "It was ... interesting. Explained some stuff about Mom."

"Anything you can share?"

He looked over at her. "This is just ... difficult. I'm having a hard time with the words to describe what's going on in my head."

"Okay. Why don't you tell me what you remember about your mom?"

He turned back to stare at the fire for a long, quiet moment. "She was ... amazing ... beautiful. Inside and out. Always moving, always doing something for us or for other people. Involved at church, teaching kids' Sunday School and leading a women's Bible study. Our house was where all our friends wanted to be because she was always baking something."

Ally's heart caught. Her mother had been much the same. Beautiful, joyful, loving, and kind. Everybody wanted to be around her. "She sounds wonderful."

"She was. Until ... that day."

"When your sister—"

"Yeah." His lips formed a hard line as his eyes narrowed. She knew he was looking back, to that day. That awful day. His Adam's apple rose and fell before he spoke. "She fell apart when Emma died. Completely turned from God. From Dad. From me. Aunt Gina said it was because she couldn't handle the guilt. That she didn't answer Emma when she asked if she could go with me because she was on the phone. It didn't dawn on her Emma had left until she heard the screeching of the tires."

"How awful. That it's her last memory of her daughter."

"It is awful. The whole thing is awful." He laid his head back against the couch with a sigh, his gaze directed to the ceiling. "I didn't know she blamed herself. I always thought she blamed—" He pulled his head up to stare again at the fireplace. "I wish she could've gotten help or something." He looked back at her. "To just give up? Harper wasn't even walking with the Lord when she lost her little girl and look at her now. I'd always thought my mom was a spiritual giant, like my dad.

They were perfect together, walking their faith, completely in love. Until that day."

Her heart cracked at the picture of this woman losing herself in the mire of grief. "In my line of work, I've seen every reaction you can think of following the death of a child. The one you thought would fall apart holds everybody else together. The one you thought would be the rock crumbles into pieces."

"Yeah. Aunt Gina said to live with it, Mom turned to drinking, pills, whatever would get her through the day. I had no idea she had a substance abuse problem. But how would I? I haven't seen her since that morning when I left for school and she didn't even turn from the kitchen sink when I told her I loved her."

"Zane …" Ally's chest constricted thinking of the boy who longed for his mother's love and acceptance. "I'm so sorry."

"I guess she didn't beat her demons until about a year ago. Back in rehab for the third time. She's been sober since then and decided it was time to make amends." He shook his head. "This whole thing has really thrown me. Even after all the praying I've done, I still don't know if I want to see her. Ever."

Her breath caught. "You honestly don't want to see her?"

His gaze snapped to her. "Why should I when she hasn't had anything to do with me most of my life? Just because she wants to say she's sorry? What's that going to do? Make her feel better? Make *me* feel better? Doubtful."

Ally tried not to respond to the words spoken from a place of hurt. But how could he not take advantage of the opportunity to reconnect with his mother? If only she had the chance —

She bit her lip. This wasn't about her, no matter how much her heart yearned for even five more minutes with her mother.

"Is she walking with the Lord?" she asked quietly.

He didn't answer right away. Just sat with his arms crossed tightly across his chest, staring straight ahead. "I guess so." His voice was ragged, pensive. "My aunt said Mom had been praying for months about contacting me. For the courage to reach out."

"It did take courage. She had to know you might simply hang up on her."

"Thought about it."

Ally flinched at the sharp edge to his voice. She'd never seen him like this, heard him like this. Zane was always up, always happy, always looking out for others before himself. But this …

"I'm such a hypocrite," he said in a torn whisper. And it hurt her even more to hear his derision turned onto himself.

"You're not, Z."

His chest rose and fell with a humorless chuckle. "But I am. Here we tell our CU kids to forgive, to pray for those who hurt them. And I haven't prayed for my mom in years. Not really. Maybe a mention from time to time. But I haven't asked Him to bring her back into my life since I was a teenager. I'm not sure I want her here. That's brutally honest even though I know it's not godly."

A piece of her heart tore open, that part that had been pierced all those years ago in a jungle village when her light, her anchor, had been ripped from her. That piece that still sat scarred and tender inside of her.

"I'd give anything in the world to have my mom back." Her words barely penetrated the quiet between them, so painful were they to speak. "If only for a day or just a moment. To hear her voice, see her face. Touch her."

Zane looked over at her but kept his arms held tight against him, as if protecting himself, guarding his heart. Probably as he'd been doing the past eighteen years.

She cleared her throat. "I know it's not the same. I'm not saying you should forget everything that happened, that it shouldn't still hurt. Of course it does. But if she really has found her way back to the Lord, this is a *gift*. You could

237

actually have your mom back in your life where I never will. I
just don't want you to miss it."

Silence stretched between them before he turned toward
the fireplace and the flames licking against the gas firelogs. The
hot-fudge-colored eyes that used to render her speechless with
their dancing sparkle now sat like hardened recesses in his
granite face. He didn't say anything for a minute, simply stared
as if searching for an answer that eluded him.

"I know what you're saying." He looked back to her. "I
wish you could have that time with your mom too. I do. But I
… this is really hard. I had no idea how deep it all went, and
I'm really struggling with what I should think, how I should
feel."

Turning to face him, she laid her hand on his arm. "You
know who's really struggling with this?"

His brow furrowed. "My mom?"

She shook her head. "That thirteen-year-old boy whose
mother walked out on him. He's the one who needs to deal
with this, to forgive, before the thirty-one-year-old man can."

"How do I do that?" His voice sounded as if he'd pulled it
across sandpaper, fighting hard against the emotion he didn't
want to give in to.

"You start with asking for help. And the person who can
help you the most through this is Wyatt."

"Wyatt? His family's perfect. How could he possibly
understand?"

"It's not about understanding. It's about listening and
guiding. As an adolescent psychologist, he can help that
teenage boy walk through his mother's abandonment. You're
stuck there, Z. You need to go back to that time, work through
the pain, then grow past it."

"Counseling. I've never considered counseling."

"It doesn't mean you don't have it together. It just helps you
navigate through some of the things that block your way to
moving forward in a specific area of your life. This one's about

your mom. You've never moved past the pain of her leaving because you've never been pressed. Now you are. Your mother wants back in your life. It's up to you if you allow that. But you need to heal, either way you choose."

"Either way I choose," he echoed quietly.

"Look at it this way. It's an upside-down version of the story of the prodigal son. In this scenario, your mother is the prodigal. What you have to decide is whether you're the father happy to welcome her home, or the older brother who grows bitter about her reappearance."

His eyes hardened again. "Wow, Al, don't pull your punches. Anything else you'd like to get off your chest?"

Shocked, she stared back at him. "I—I'm sorry. I didn't mean that to sound judgmental. It's your choice what happens next, but I don't want you to have regrets down the road. I guess I love you too much to *not* say the hard things."

She stood and folded up the blanket to place back on the couch. "If I've overstepped, I apologize. I didn't intend to hurt you or offend you. But I think we should probably put a cap on this conversation tonight before either of us says something we can't take back."

"Yeah, probably a good idea."

Prickles like pinpricks ran along the back of her neck, and tears sprang to her eyes. She turned and started toward the door so he wouldn't notice as he followed her out. He had enough on his shoulders right now without worrying about her.

Not that he was. He was too angry. And she'd never seen an angry Zane. It cut her to the bone that she was the one who had brought him out.

The ride back to her house was a long, silent one, although it only took the usual ten minutes. When he brought the Bronco to a stop, she put her hand to his when he reached to turn off the ignition. "Don't worry about seeing me to the door. I'm fine."

But when his eyes met hers, it wasn't anger she saw. It was hurt. Deep and raw. His words hadn't been delivered in anger but from a place of pain. And she'd caused that.

If it cut her deeply to know she'd made him angry, realizing she'd hurt him left her heart in pieces.

CHAPTER THIRTY-ONE

*T*en after one.

With a heavy sigh, Ally pulled her eyes from the bedside clock for at least the dozenth time in the past two hours and rolled onto her back with her hands splayed on her stomach. It had been a mistake to end their conversation when she had. Even if they didn't talk, they should've at least prayed over the situation, or ended the evening with a hug and gentle words.

"Don't let the sun go down while you're still angry," she whispered in the dark. The wisdom of those words from Ephesians had never rung so clear.

The vibration of the cell phone on her bedside table startled her. A call in the middle of the night rarely meant anything good. She grabbed the phone, and her breath caught.

She sat up and clicked the phone icon. "Zane?"

"I couldn't sleep."

"Me, either."

"Meet me outside?"

"When?"

"Now?"

She scrambled out of bed. "Wait, you're here?"

She held two slats of the blinds apart with her fingers and peered between them, her heart skipping when he raised a hand in a small wave from where he stood at the curb. "I'll be right down."

With shallow breaths, she yanked on a pair of sweatpants and a jacket over her sleep shirt, stepping quickly into a pair of Ugg knock-offs while she ran her hand through her tousled hair. Trying to be quiet so as not to wake Yolanda, she took the stairs down to the living room and clicked on a lamp on her way to the door. A deep breath in and a slow exhale didn't do much to calm her anxiety as she unlocked the door. A guy wouldn't show up in the middle of the night to break things off. Right?

Remorse washed through her like a flash flood through a dry desert creek. Not that she wouldn't deserve it. She'd been too hard on him. Expected too much of him out of her impossible wish to see her mother again this side of heaven.

The clomping of her boots on the concrete sounded even louder against the silent darkness as she made her way down the walk. Mercy, he looked good standing beside Phyllis in jeans and a brown leather jacket. And here she was, no make-up, with bed hair, marshmallow jacket, and baggy sweats tucked into her bulky boots.

"Hey, what's —"

"You love me too much?"

She stopped a few feet in front of him, her thoughts screeching to a halt. "What?"

"That's what you said. You *guess* you love me too much to not say the hard things. You guess, or you know? Do you love me, Ally?"

Taking a moment to gather her courage to give him an honest answer, she studied his face. The uncharacteristic uncertainty in his eyes, the furrow between his brows. As if he wasn't sure anybody could love him the way she did.

Her arms hugged her jacket closed as she stepped closer to

him. "I do love you. So much that I want to help you through this hard thing. I just should've chosen my words more carefully. It kills me that I hurt you."

He returned her scrutiny, but she refused to look away. If he needed to see it in her eyes to believe it, then she'd stand there and look at him all night. "I'm so sorry, Ally."

Her heart slumped against her sternum. Not what she'd expected him to say after declaring herself. "Sorry for ... what, exactly?"

"For letting anger dictate my words. Even if it wasn't really you I was angry with."

"Zane, you don't owe me an apo—"

"She blamed me."

Her face blanched. "What?"

He swallowed hard. "From as far back as I can remember, Emma wanted to be wherever I was, no matter what I was doing. One day I left to go fishing with a friend. Got on my bike and headed down the street. I was almost to the next block when I heard this horrible scream. I turned around and rode back to see what was going on." His voice broke and eyes filled. "It was my mom, in the middle of the street ... screaming, sobbing. And Emma ... she was all bent up ... broken, is the only way I can describe it. So much blood."

"Zane. I am so sorry."

"She rode out in front of a large SUV." He swallowed. "Probably trying to catch up to me. I dropped my bike and ran over to them. I was out of my mind, bawling, yelling at her to wake up. Then my mom—"

His breath hitched, and he put his head back to stare up at the dark sky. A lone tear fell down his temple into his hair. "I've never told anybody this."

Closing the distance between them, she took the front of his jacket in her hands. "I've got you."

He brought his gaze back to her, tears spilling onto his cheeks. "I'll never forget how she looked at me ... eyes blazing

... her face red as she screamed at me that it was my fault. That it wouldn't have happened if I'd have waited ... made sure Em was with me, that she was safe."

He ran his hand down his face, brushing away the tears. "And she was right."

"No—"

"Yes." His eyes snapped to her. "I should've known Em would follow me."

She tugged on his jacket. "Zane, listen to me. You were how old?"

"Twelve."

"Twelve years old. You were a *boy*, not a man. Your mother was speaking from a place of shock. She should've been protecting *you* in that moment, but instead she needed someone to blame. I'm so sorry you've carried that all these years."

How could a mother look at her young son, kneeling and sobbing in the street next to his broken and bleeding little sister, and lay that on him? A mother who then abandoned him and never looked back?

Loathing for someone she'd never met sprang to life inside of her, and she said a quick prayer to squash it. She didn't want to give any energy to that kind of anger, yet her desire to protect this man who'd once been a little boy desperately in need of comforting he didn't get was all-consuming.

"My mom as I'd known her disappeared that day. Rarely spoke to either of us. Didn't want to leave her room except to go to Emma's. She kept it the exact way Em left it that day and would go in there and sit in silence for hours."

A tear slipped down Ally's cheek. Her disdain for this woman she might never know melted into compassion. The pain must have been unbearable. Just like Harper had endured when her little Megan was taken from her. Did it matter that Harper had more time to say goodbye? Or was the jagged emptiness the same no matter how a child was lost?

"Dad ... he was the rock he'd always been. Made sure I

had his attention. Wouldn't let me escape into my own world but kept me in the sports I played, would take me to the store to help him stock shelves and serve customers. Our family had owned the hardware and feed store in Gallagher for three generations, and I always thought I'd take it over someday. I never dreamed in those days I'd leave Gallagher. But, you know ... I was still a kid when my dad died, and he didn't want me saddled with it. Told me to go on to college and reach for higher things."

"I love your dad, even though I never met him."

"He was a great man."

"Was he aware you blamed yourself for your sister's death?"

With a nod, he swept a hand across his cheek, the other still buried in the pocket of his jacket. "He told me many times it wasn't my fault. But he wasn't there that day."

She let go of his coat and grabbed his hand. "You need to listen to *his* voice, Z. Let it cancel out your mother's. Because she was wrong." Her gaze bored deep into his, willing him to understand. "And my guess is she knows that. You said your aunt told you your mom didn't know how to deal with the guilt. *Her* guilt. Not yours. She knows it's not your fault."

They stood looking at each other, a cold breeze wrapping itself around them. She watched as he worked to keep his emotions under control. "Ally." He cleared his throat. "Forgive me? For earlier? Please?"

"Of course. And please forgive me for not understanding. I wish I had before giving you my opinion. I had no idea you were carrying around that kind of burden. A burden that should've never been yours to begin with."

"So, we're good?"

"We are *so* good. In fact, I think we're better. We both kind of hurt each other tonight, but we faced it and talked it out before it festered. That makes us stronger."

He put his hands to her arms. "I don't know what I did to

deserve you, but I'm so blessed to have you in my life. You make me laugh. You make me think. You make me want to be a better man every day." He reached up and brushed her hair behind her ear. "And I'm crazy in love with you."

Everything inside of her puddled when he pulled her close. Resting her head against his shoulder, her hands slipped inside his jacket and over his back as they stood there, rocking back and forth while the world slept. The darkness, split only by the light of the streetlamps, became their momentary cocoon, where they were the only two people in existence.

He pulled his head back and gazed down at her. "You're beautiful even when I get you up in the middle of the night."

"I'm a mess."

He shook his head, then pressed his lips to hers in a tender kiss. Her heart pounded against her ribs when he took her face in his hands and angled his mouth over hers to deepen their contact. Mercy, the man could kiss. Or maybe they were just that good together.

As her lungs began to burn with the need to breathe, he pulled back and laid her head against his shoulder, his chest pushing against hers with each breath. Closing her eyes, she settled into him as he ran his hands up and down her back. Didn't matter how late it was or how cold it was, she wanted to stay here, tucked in tight against him where nothing could hurt her.

After a few minutes, he reached up to smooth a tendril of hair off her cheek. "You were right. About the prodigal thing. I don't like being angry. It doesn't feel good. I'm going to call Wyatt tomorrow. Or today, I guess I should say. I think I need to work some things out if I'm going to be able to see her face to face."

"And I'll be here every step of the way. For whatever you need."

"All I need is you. I don't deserve you, but I'll love you the best I know how."

CHAPTER THIRTY-TWO

*H*e could do this. He could. He had to.

Zane's heart thrummed like a bass drum as he paced between the escalator and baggage claim. He could do this. If he didn't pass out first.

He'd met with Wyatt four times over the past two weeks to talk about how to move past his mother's abandonment and decide if it was in his best interest to allow her back into his life. Ally's suggestion had been on target. His healing began with that first meeting, and in two weeks, he was surprised at how far he'd come in not only forgiving his broken mother, but himself. That weight he'd carried, blaming himself for his sister's death, had been loosened in one particularly emotional session.

So, four days ago, he'd finally issued the invitation for his mother to come for a weekend visit. She'd jumped on it, probably afraid he'd change his mind. And perhaps there was good reason for that. He'd had second, third, and fourth thoughts over the past few days, but everything was already in place for her to come. No backing out now.

When she texted him a recent photo yesterday, he'd stared at it for a long time. In his mind, she was still the thirty-something woman he'd last seen. The one smiling back at him from his screen was definitely older. Only in her early fifties now, but alcohol and pills had taken a toll. Not to mention grief and guilt. Her face appeared gaunt, her cheeks sunken with lines etched around her mouth. But those dark eyes held a hint of the light that had been extinguished the morning Emma died. Maybe she really had found her way back to her faith.

He came to a stop when his gaze settled on a woman coming down the escalator, her loose-fitting sweater with jeans tucked into boots right at home in this Texas airport. Her hair had grayed and lay in soft curls to her shoulders, and although thin, she didn't appear unhealthy. Her eyes roamed the area and passed over him before coming back again.

A flood of something warm he hadn't expected filled him inside, and his breath halted. Tears blurred his vision when she stopped in front of him, her own eyes welling with moisture.

Her hand came to his cheek. "Zane Alexander." Her smile wobbled as a tear slipped down her face. "My sweet boy."

The endearment undid him. At twelve, it had embarrassed him if she used it around his friends. But after that day, that awful, horrible day, he would've given anything to hear it again. Until she left, and he lost all hope.

He worked to loosen the knot holding back everything he wanted to say, and it took him a moment to find his voice. "Mom."

The dam that had sprung a leak in their first phone call finally collapsed, and the years of pain and torment washed away in a rush. Sobbing, he let her pull his forehead to her shoulder. She dropped her handbag at their feet and swept her other arm around him, rubbing her hand over his back.

"I'm so sorry." Her voice rasped as if pulled from a deep place. "I'm so sorry. Sweetheart, I'm so sorry."

He didn't know how long they stood there, other travelers and their greeters walking around them as they clung to each other. He didn't care. His mother holding him, comforting him, loving him, filled up that empty space she'd left all those years ago. He was suddenly twelve again and had his mom's attention, holding him tight to let him pour out the grief they shared.

So much for his plan to keep her at arm's length until he could be sure of her. In one look, one touch, the wall he'd erected around that Mom-shaped abyss in his heart had crumbled. She was back. And all he wanted was to stay here for a little while, soaking in all the love he'd been starving for the last eighteen years.

Again, Ally was right. That boy had needed to heal. He needed his mother.

Zane glanced at his mom sitting next to him in the Bronco. He'd never lost it like that. Not even when Dad died. Not since that day he knelt next to his little sister in the middle of the road and begged her to wake up.

The day he also lost his mom.

Maybe this was what full circle meant, what closure was.

"I know a great little sandwich shop in Arlington next to a park. We can grab something and find a bench, if that sounds good. It's really nice outside today."

"That sounds wonderful."

Forty minutes later, they had their sandwiches and drinks and walked a block to the park to claim a bench to enjoy the sunny day.

Mom looked around while she unwrapped her sandwich. "Much nicer weather than what I left in Michigan."

"No doubt. We had a cold snap here recently, but this week's been great."

They ate in silence for a moment, until he recalled something she mentioned in her first call to him. "You said on the phone you knew I was busy with work. Were you guessing, or do you know what I do?"

After placing her sandwich back on the wrapper, she looked over at him. "I've been following you for a while now on social media. I knew when you graduated from seminary, when you moved here. What you're doing with your ministry here. You're a busy young man but for all the right reasons. Your father would be so proud of who you've become, what you've accomplished."

Those blasted tears burned his throat again, so he took another swallow of tea to keep his composure. "I'd like to think so. Although there was a time I'm sure he would have been disappointed in me." He looked back at her. "You're not the only one who turned their back on God. When Dad died, I wanted nothing to do with God."

Her brown eyes clouded. "I can understand that. You really had nobody, because I wasn't there for you. Not like I should've been all along. Gina was stationed out of the country when everything happened, which was why she never saw you. She kept tabs on you through your father, but once he was gone, she was just happy to hear from you every now and then, even if it was only to update her on where you were moving next."

Zane nodded. He didn't know his mother's never-married sister very well, as she'd been serving with the Army throughout his childhood. He hadn't even known his father had been communicating with her until a few weeks before he passed, when he gave Zane her number with instructions to make sure Gina knew where he was in case his mother ever wanted to reach him.

At the time, Zane thought it a useless exercise. Looking at his mom now, he was grateful he'd followed his father's wishes.

"Gina didn't know how bad things had gotten with me until she retired and settled in Michigan. She had me come live with her about four years ago, and that's when she saw firsthand my addictions. Got me into rehab but I ran after about a week. The second time wasn't much better, but the third time … well, I guess I finally decided I wanted to live."

She released a tremulous sigh. "When things are simple and life is good, it's easy to be strong. I was so happy in Gallagher, with your father and you kids. We weren't rich, but we had each other, and we made the most out of every day. You and your sister were our joy and delight. Then I got distracted and …"

Her voice hitched, and she stared out over the park. "And everything changed. I was tried by fire and let it destroy me. Destroy our life together. I was so lost once my idyllic little world crumbled."

He watched the sunlight play across her face, reflecting in the tears gathered in her eyes. "I'm so sorry, Mom."

She turned to him and blinked away her tears. "You don't have anything to be sorry for. What happened to Emma was never your fault. Never. And it wasn't really mine. Emma knew to look. I don't know why on that day she didn't. But it was an accident. A brutal, heinous, tragic accident. And I turned on the child I had left out of my misconception that it was *my* fault. I couldn't live with that, so I put it on you. I failed you both that day and every day since."

She looked away again and shook her head. "I can hardly forgive myself for that. I don't know how I could ever expect you to."

"Because I'm forgiven."

She faced him again. "But I just told you there's nothing to forgive. You had no fault that day."

"Maybe not that day. But I'm forgiven all the same. For all of the other things I've done in my life that pulled me away from the Lord. Things I do now, even though I have a close walk with Him. If I can't forgive, then I'm a hypocrite of the worst kind. The one who takes what's freely offered by grace but refuses to offer it."

He reached over and took her hand. "I forgive you, Mom. And you need to forgive yourself."

Tears trickled down her face. "I do love you, son. Looking at you now, it's almost overwhelming how much so. I hope even with all of these years between us, we can build something together. I don't ever want there to be that distance between us again. But I'm leaving that to you. I've hurt nobody more than I have you by the choices I've made."

"Except yourself. But you're here now, and we're together. This is a good start."

She swiped at her face with her napkin. "It's a very good start. Thank you for letting me come."

"Thank you for reaching out. I apologize I was less than cordial at first. I was ... I never expected to hear from you, so it was a shock."

"I'm sure it was. And I completely understood why you were distant when we first talked. I was relieved you didn't hang up on me, that you actually did call me back like you said you would."

"You can thank Ally for that. She helped me see my way through all the stuff that came crashing down on me."

"I can't wait to meet your Ally."

His Ally. His heart swelled with the words. "You'll see her later today. She gets off work at two and will meet us later over at the McCowans. You'll love her, no doubt." Of course she would, because how could anybody *not* love Ally?

"It's so nice of your friends to offer to put me up, but I don't want to be an imposition."

"No worries about that. Hospitality is Harper's gift. She hosts people all the time. You'll swear you're in a bed and breakfast. Trust me. I stayed with them a couple of weeks when I first moved here. And she insisted on you staying with them when I mentioned letting you have my room at Steve's and taking the sofa. His third bedroom right now is a home gym, and Ally and Yo only have the two bedrooms at their place."

"And this Harper, her husband runs the ministry you work for?"

"He founded and directs ConnectUP. I'm a ministry coordinator with Becker Ministries, an umbrella group that sponsors smaller organizations. Becker thought it would be better for me to be here, locally, instead of trying to keep it all going from Atlanta."

"Do you like it here?"

He looked around the quiet park. With school in session, the playground sat empty, and nobody ran around the basketball court. There were a few people walking their dogs or jogging along a meandering sidewalk, and an elderly couple sat on another bench, holding hands and talking. All taking advantage of this beautiful fall day.

"I love it here." He looked back at his mom. "Best place I've been since Gallagher. I love the city. I love my church. I have fantastic friends. ConnectUP is exploding. And then there's Ally."

"So, you'll probably settle here, then."

Nodding, he looked away again. "Probably."

"Tell me about your fantastic friends."

"Oh, wow, how much time do we have?" He told her about moving in with Steve and how seamlessly that had worked out. He told her about Mason and Rhonda, Shannon, Reed and Jenny, and the other leaders he'd grown close to.

"And Harper and Wyatt. They're a pair. I'll let them tell you their story, but it's a whopper. From childhood friends to marriage. With a lot of twists and turns between."

"Sounds like a very interesting story."

"Oh, and the best part? They just announced they're expecting sometime next June."

"That's exciting."

"They're over the moon about it, although, according to

Wyatt, it's a little sooner than they'd planned." He stood and held out his hand for her empty sandwich wrapper and bag. "I should probably get you over there. Ally will be there in about an hour. She thinks dinner at their house is her birthday party. I can't wait to see her face Sunday night."

Despite her claim she only wanted dinner and maybe a cake, Ally's surprise birthday party was planned for Sunday evening at their favorite neighborhood Mexican restaurant. He'd compromised between her party of four and his of one hundred and made reservations for twenty-five. Probably not the best weekend for a visit from the mother he hadn't seen in nearly two decades, but he hadn't had the heart to put her off.

He tossed their bags in a trash bin. "Be prepared. Ally has a list of things she wants to take you to see around Dallas tomorrow and after church on Sunday. Hope you brought comfy shoes. Steve, Yo, and Shannon will take the cake and decorate the tables at the restaurant Sunday before we get there."

"You're sure I won't be in the way? I kind of invited myself."

"No, I invited you. I'm glad you'll be there, and she will be too."

"Okay, then. I'm looking forward to it."

When they returned to the Bronco, his mother ran her hand along the door. "You've done a beautiful job with this old car. Your father picked me up in it the day he bought it to go to the drive-in. We were seventeen. He was so proud of it, even though it needed a little work even then. He tinkered with it all the time."

"It was fun working on it with him. He didn't get to see it finished, though. I had the exterior paint done about five years ago."

"Do you still call her Phyllis?"

He smiled. "Of course."

She laughed then, and the sound was so joyous, he couldn't

help joining in. "I don't know where he came up with that name, but it somehow stuck. We always referred to the Bronco by name."

"I remember." He closed her door after she climbed in and went around to his side. "I've been thinking I may need to get a second vehicle sometime in the future to be my everyday car. I don't want anything to happen to her."

"You're a sensible man, Zane. I'm sure you had to grow up pretty fast."

He shrugged as he pulled away from the lot. "In some ways. In others, it took me a while."

"And you've never married?"

"No, ma'am."

"You think Ally's the one?"

If he had anything to say about it. "It's early on yet, but she's the first person I've ever been able to see myself settling down with."

And if that was right here in Arlington, he could probably be content with that, even though, if given a chance, he'd still love to see other parts of the world. And maybe Ally would someday want to go along. If not, then he'd have to trust God to change his heart.

Because at the end of every day, a little more of it belonged to Ally.

CHAPTER THIRTY-THREE

"*Surprise!*"

Gasping, Ally pulled up short and took a step backward, hand to her chest. Zane's laughter rumbled against her back as he grasped her waist.

Once she caught her breath, she looked over her shoulder and found that grin she loved. "Oh, you're pretty proud of yourself, aren't you?"

His brown eyes danced. "Kinda. Yeah."

With a smile and a shake of her head, she turned to her friends surging toward her. After accepting their hugs and birthday wishes, she let Zane lead her by the hand to a chair with so many balloons floating from it, she had no idea how it was still earthbound. Tables had been set up in a giant *U*, allowing her to see everybody, and Zane sat between her and his mother, who fairly glowed with joy after having spent the last two days with her boy.

While wait staff bustled about placing baskets of chips and bowls of salsa on the tables, she took a moment to let her heart rate settle. The weekend had been a whirlwind, starting with meeting Nancy, then dinner at Wyatt and Harper's Friday night with a much smaller group of their closest friends. She thought that was her birthday party and would've been delighted if that had been the extent of it. Harper had even baked a cake for her, so counting the gorgeous confection set up on a table to the side, she would have two.

Yesterday and this afternoon following church had been spent showing Nancy around Dallas and Fort Worth. It had been a joy watching the older woman smile and laugh with her son, walking with her arm pulled through Zane's as if afraid to let him go. Ally had been content to step back and let them have their time, but Zane always made sure to include her.

Tonight's agenda was to have been dinner with Steve and Yo. A nice, quiet celebration of her day. This, she never expected. And he'd clearly had help. The tables were dressed beautifully with floral centerpieces atop pink tablecloths, and the room festooned with balloons and streamers and a huge banner with *Happy Birthday, Ally* written across it. They'd been together all day, so her guess was Yolanda, Shannon, and Harper had worked their magic.

Once dinner had been served and devoured, Harper insisted on photos of Ally with her stunning three-tiered cake covered in roses. Before they cut it, Ally wanted a photo with Zane by the cake. Once she'd been sung to and the strawberry cake cut and served, a mariachi band waltzed into the private party room to entertain them.

When the band moved from one of their lively tunes to a slower ballad, Zane stood and held out his hand. "May I have this dance, milady?"

She looked around and back at him. "There's no dance floor."

"Who needs a floor?"

True that. Her feet hadn't touched ground since she'd walked into the room almost two hours ago.

Unable to resist the man and his sweet invitation, she placed her hand in his and stood. A few steps away from the table, he pulled her close to a collective *Ah* from their guests.

But everybody and everything faded into the background as she stared up into the eyes that used to send her smarts right out the door. Tonight, they seemed to sparkle even more. As if something had come to life inside of him.

Or perhaps back to life. Although he'd never voiced it, she knew he longed for family, a connection, a belonging. To someone tied to him by blood. And now he had it.

She pulled her arms tighter around his neck. "Thank you for this," she said for his ears only.

There went that grin again. Good thing he had such a good hold on her or her weakened knees might've sent her to the floor. "You're okay that I did this, then?"

"I'm just glad you didn't cook a pig in the ground. Or make me wear a poodle skirt."

He laughed before leaning in to give her a soft, lingering kiss, to the delight of their friends. "Next time."

"Okay, but be warned. I have four months to come up with something for yours. And I have Shannon. My secret weapon."

"I can't wait," he said, then gave her another kiss.

Others joined their impromptu dance as the musicians played on. Zane pulled her closer, and she put her head against his shoulder, her forehead pressed gently to his neck. She hadn't felt so special on her birthday since her twelfth, the last one with her mother. Mom had always made a big to-do of the day, with piñatas and games and lots of food for her and all of her Central American friends. Once her mother was gone, though, she hadn't let anybody throw her a party. Yolanda even knew better than to plan a surprise for her over the years, knowing she preferred a quieter celebration.

But Zane had put an end to that with tonight's amazing event. This evening spent laughing and conversing with friends over her favorite food had broken through that barrier, and once again, Zane had made it happen. In the little over two-and-a-half months since he walked into it, he'd changed her life in so many ways. Gave her room to open up and share the things she'd buried deep inside. Pushed her to stay and face her uncertainties instead of running. And shown her unconditional love in his patience and grace and kindness. Hopefully, she would spend many more birthdays with this spectacular man.

Much later than was probably wise, with tomorrow being a workday, they stood in the foyer at Wyatt and Harper's after dropping Nancy off for the night. She'd be leaving tomorrow, and Ally couldn't help wishing she could stay a little longer. When Wyatt asked Zane to look at something in the study, Nancy put her arm through Ally's and led her into the living room off the entry.

"With all the festivities tonight, I haven't had a chance to speak to you privately. I wanted to tell you how wonderful this weekend has been and how grateful I am for you."

"For—for me?"

Nancy's eyes shone as she nodded. "Zane told me how difficult it was for him to decide whether to let me come. Until you held his feet to the fire. His words, not mine. And he was pretty proud when he shared that with me. That you loved him enough and were strong enough to give him a push. You're good for my boy. And I'm so happy we had the chance to meet."

Held his feet to the fire? That hadn't been her intention, really, when she'd encouraged him to think about how to handle his mother coming back into his life. Zane was a godly man. He would've made the right choice even without her.

She smiled at the other woman. "I'm so glad you're here. And we can't wait until you can come back and stay a little longer."

"Yes, we'll have to talk about that, because I'd sure love to spend some more time with Zane. I know I don't deserve it—"

"He would disagree, and so do I. Every day is a new day. It's what we do with it that counts."

Nancy's mouth dropped open. "My husband ... Zane's

father used to say that all the time." Her eyes welled with tears as she reached out for Ally's hand. "You really are a kindred spirit. I'm so happy my Zane found you."

"I'm happy I found him. He's a good man, Nancy. A very good man."

"I'm seeing that. With everything that boy has been through, it's a testament to the power of God in a person's life."

Ally leaned toward her. "As are you. Don't ever doubt that."

"Hey, you two." Zane walked into the room. "You're not talking about me, are you?"

"But of course," Ally answered. "I was hoping to get more stories of you as a boy."

Nancy chuckled. "Next time I come, I'll bring photos. He was the cutest little boy. Everybody said so."

Zane's forehead wrinkled as he studied his mom. "You have photos?"

She nodded. "I have a couple of albums I've kept with me, even though I've moved around so much."

Ally glanced at Zane. Did he even realize how familiar that sounded?

"I almost left them behind that day," she continued. "But I threw them in at the last minute. I guess even then I knew I'd want to remember the good days at some point. I couldn't look at them until about a year ago, though. Once I got sober for longer than a couple of months. Now I look at them all the time, wishing they didn't stop when … well, wishing they didn't stop."

Zane looked down, then back at his mom. "I have the rest. From before, then after it was just Dad and me. He did a pretty good job keeping photos of everything. I kept them after the house sold. They're in storage with some other things I took. I—" He looked down again, and Ally stepped closer to wrap her hands around his arm. He looked at her with moisture building along his lower lashes before turning back to his mother. "I haven't ever looked at them. Not since I left the house. Our house."

Nancy took Zane's other hand in hers. "Maybe next time I come, we can pull them out? It's good to remember, son. We had a good life. A blessed life. I know I handled things poorly, crumbling like I did instead of standing strong in the Lord. But I can't continue to live there. We had many good years together as a family. We should remember."

He nodded but didn't say anything for a long moment. It had been a roller coaster for him the past two weeks, culminating in this visit.

"I would like that," he said in a tight voice. "I'd like that a lot. To share it with Ally."

Nancy swiped at her cheek and smiled at her. "I wouldn't have it any other way."

Zane leaned in to hug his mother. Nancy held on tight, her eyes closed as she held her son, and Ally's eyes filled. When Zane let his mother go with a kiss to her cheek, they said their goodbyes and left her for the night. He'd be back in the morning to take her to the airport.

Her hand held snug in his, Ally walked in silence beside Zane to the Bronco. Once at the passenger side door, he turned and drew her close. And like his mother had done only minutes before, she held on tight.

"Remember that night in front of your house?" His husky voice so close to her ear sent tingles cascading down her spine. He pulled back and put his hand along her face. "When I said I wished I had some family to show you off to?"

"I remember."

"I do now. I never let myself hope it would happen, wasn't even sure I wanted it to. But I have my mom back. And she loves you, as I know my dad would have." A lone tear slipped down his cheek. "Thank you. Thank you for making me face my anger and unforgiveness so that I could welcome her back into my life. Without you, I don't know if I could have done that."

"Yes, you could." She brought her hands to his chest. "You're such a good man, Zane. With a huge heart that beats for the Lord. You would have gotten there. But I'm so blessed to have witnessed it. To be a part of it."

"You're a huge part of it. And a huge part of my life. I can't believe how much in such a short time. But I love you and I want to have a future with you. I don't want to scare you, but I need you to know what my intentions are. What my hopes are."

Her heart beat hard against her ribs. That was everything she wanted too. To make a life and a future with this man. But would he be content to stay here, in Arlington? Go to work every day and home to her every night? Plant their roots here, build a family, and grow old together?

Or would he get restless and want to take her to a foreign land, as her parents had done? Move their children from one mission to another, pull them away from their friends and schools every few years. Could she live like that again?

She swallowed the knot in her throat and swiped at her cheek. "That's my hope, too, Z. That we can build something good together."

He looked deep into her eyes for a moment, as if searching for any hint of doubt. But when he kissed her, all her misgivings fled like shadows giving way to light. How she loved this man.

God had brought them together, of that she had no doubt. But where He would keep them was another matter for another day.

263

CHAPTER THIRTY-FOUR

*Z*ane had lived in a lot of places, but he'd never seen anything like this.

The van driven by the associate pastor of the mission church, one of several villagers who worked alongside the missionaries, continued its journey into the countryside. Lush vegetation flanked the winding road that had begun as paved but gave way to dirt the farther north they traveled from Guatemala City into the mountainous region. As they climbed, the trees and bushes encroached further onto the narrow road, and the van's shocks endured a more arduous workout.

Zane braced his hand on the armrest when the vehicle lurched from one side to the other, but his eyes never left the landscape. "I can't get over how green it all is."

Ally chuckled from beside him in the middle row. "And this is the dry season. Thankfully. All of the rain during the summer keeps everything green, but traveling here during that time can be a little dicier, with all of the mud."

"Yeah." Yolanda's voice came from the backseat where she sat with Steve, himself a newcomer to his girlfriend's homeland. "The mud, I don't miss."

Zane turned back to the window, unable to squelch the

anticipation of what was to come in the days ahead. He'd finally done it. He was in another country, just as his father had dreamed of doing all those years it was only the two of them. It had taken well over an hour to get out of the city, so dense was the traffic and sheer volume of humanity. But as they'd traveled through the suburbs, then out to the rural areas, the traffic lessened, the foliage thickened, and the roads became less maintained.

Zane drank it all in, from the packed streets of Guatemala City to the smaller villages they'd passed through, then into the green of the mountains as they neared Pamoca.

Dad, you would love this. I can just see your face ...

Tears threatened but he swallowed them back. He looked at Ally, smiled, and gave her hand a squeeze. If he couldn't be here with Dad, at least he was here with his favorite person, who had guided him expertly through the process of international travel. When the customs official asked for his passport, he'd had it at the ready, beyond excited to get his first stamp.

Another hairpin turn had Zane uttering a silent prayer of thanks he wasn't the sort to suffer motion sickness. It would take a healthy dose of Dramamine to travel very far from the city if one were prone. After another hour, the bumpy road began to smooth into a more hard-packed surface and humble homes sat closer together.

Ally squeezed his hand. "Welcome to Pamoca."

"We're here?"

"These are the outskirts, about ten minutes from the mission."

His insides clenched in anticipation. The town of Pamoca, Ally had told him, was home to approximately fifteen thousand souls. There were also several outlying villages close enough that the missionaries could travel there and back in a day, providing medical treatment and dental checks, all while sharing the gospel. He hoped they might get to go on one or two during their two weeks here. How cool to be able to see mission work in a foreign land firsthand.

The area became more congested, and the dirt road gave way again to pavement. In the town square, the marketplace teemed with people, including merchants selling everything from eggs to traditional clothing to woven goods and everything in between.

"Is there no central place to buy groceries?"

Ally shook her head. "You buy what you need from whatever merchant provides it. Meat from one, vegetables from another, beans from yet another, and so on. You'd be hard-pressed to find much dairy, though. Milk, butter, and processed cheese are a luxury. We'll have homemade cheese for the wedding dinner, but there's a good chance that's the only time we'll have it while we're here."

He peered out the window again. "So many kids. Why aren't they in school?"

Ally looked around at the people scurrying along the streets. "The school year is January through early November, so they're essentially on the equivalent of what a summer break would be back in the US. And, unfortunately, many of the kids don't go to school past third grade or so. They're needed to help at home, whether it's farm work, construction, brick-laying, weaving. Most traditional Guatemalans are of the opinion a higher education isn't as important as the help their children can provide at home."

"So true." Yolanda again spoke up from the back seat. "Thankfully, my parents were a little more open-minded. My oldest and youngest brothers and my two sisters left school after sixth grade. But Ernesto, the second oldest, and I continued. It helped that the mission school gave us scholarships to finish our education there. Being accredited meant we graduated from high school with qualifications to go on to college."

"That's because Yo and Ernie are gifted. The way Yo's mom

tells it, one of the teachers at the public school here attends the mission church. She saw what a shame it would be for either one of them to stop short of a college education and brought them to the mission school administrator."

"I wouldn't say *gifted*." Yolanda gave him a wink when he looked at her over his shoulder.

Ally leaned toward him. "Gifted. But, anyway, the administrator talked their parents into letting them come to the mission school on scholarship, and by the time Dad and I got here, the whole family had converted and were attending the mission church, Ernesto was a junior in high school, and Yo was in my grade."

"And we were kindred spirits from that first day of eighth grade."

Ally laughed. "Only because you saw this pathetic, sullen, little white girl and refused to let me wallow in my grief." She looked over the seat at Steve. "Seriously. If it wasn't for your girl here, I don't know what would've happened. I didn't want to be here and made sure Dad was aware of it as often as possible. He might've eventually shipped me back to the States."

"Then I wouldn't have come to Dallas Heritage or gotten involved with ConnectUP." Yolanda looked at Steve. "And I wouldn't have met you."

Steve shook his head. "That's a terrible thought. Glad you didn't let Ally wallow."

Zane glanced at Yo. "Where's Ernesto now? Did he go on to college?"

"Oh, yeah," she answered. "He went to med school in Mexico City and now practices there."

"A doctor and a nurse. Your parents must be very proud."

Yolanda smiled and turned her attention to her window.

Ally grabbed his arm as they turned onto a gravel drive that led to a gated arch. "Here we are. Mission *Cristo el Salvador*."

He smiled. "Christ the Savior."

"Yes. It was founded twenty-two years ago, and Dad's been here almost fifteen." They pulled through the gate into a round drive in the middle of a large, square compound. "It was quite a bit smaller back then, but the scope of the work they do here now is astounding. Which was another reason I stayed longer than I'd planned when I came out two years ago. They really needed the help."

"Still do," Yolanda said. "According to my *papá*, anyway." She looked at Zane as the van came to a stop. "He takes care of the facilities and grounds and has told me many times how badly they need more missionaries here."

Zane climbed out of the van and offered his hand to Ally. "Why can't they send more?"

Ally straightened with a sigh. "Money. Resources. People. You name it. It's hard to find people willing to come work out here, what with all the fundraising they have to do and the support they have to come up with. Plus, the facilities here are already bulging at the seams with the staff we have. We'd need more missionary housing before we could accept more personnel. Not to mention equipment and supplies."

We. It hadn't escaped Zane's notice that Ally referred to this place as if she still held some ownership of it. And it was clear she was fond of the work they did here, that she realized its importance in bringing the message to the Guatemalan people. Maybe they could come back in the future and work together. There was no telling what they could accomplish.

Yolanda's face beamed as she took in their surroundings. "My *papá* has done a really good job. This place looks wonderful."

It did. The grounds had been manicured to a fault, with green grass, tall trees, and the lush vegetation of the mountain region to which the mission catered. Some of the buildings he could identify right off—the church with its steeple and stained-glass window, and the clinic with the red cross on the sign and *Clinica Medica Cristo el Salvador* over the entrance. *Christ the Savior Medical Clinic.* And the school lay beyond, a humble two-story building with a small playground, benches, and a cross erected in front. The smaller buildings must be offices, or maybe dwellings for the missionaries who lived and worked here.

"This is fantastic. Seriously, the pictures don't adequately convey the breadth of this place. It's … heaven on earth."

With a smile and a light in her eyes, Ally looked around. "Mr. Morales and Yo's little brother Alejandro work together with a couple of other men from town who attend church here."

Dr. Kincaid and Nora came out of a side door to the clinic, walking quickly hand-in-hand to greet them.

"Welcome!" Nathan said. "Glad to see you all." He grabbed his daughter in a hug and shook Zane's hand before moving to Yolanda and Steve while Ally held onto Nora.

"Nora's boys got here yesterday, and your brother and Paige arrive tomorrow morning. And then the gang's all here. Can't tell you how excited we are."

Zane's attention was pulled from the doctor when several children sprinted toward them. *"Seño Allyson! Seño Allyson!"*

Ally turned toward the chorus of delighted voices, her face lighting up with her smile. *"Mis dulces bebes!"*

Zane stood back and watched the swarm of children envelop her, hugging her and jumping up and down in excitement. They all spoke at once, and he laughed when he picked up on the fact one of the boys took exception to her calling him a baby. But he was sure all of these children were Ally's *bebes*. He might even be able to figure out who was who over time, because Ally had shared many stories and pictures with him of the children of Pamoca.

Nora leaned toward him. "The kids started gathering about an hour ago, waiting for Ally to get here. They adore her."

"I can tell." He watched her interact with the children. She was a natural with the ConnectUP students and seeing her now with these little ones made his heart catch. Her face glowed as she hugged each one, kneeling to grab the smaller ones, who giggled and clasped her tight around the neck.

An older woman with two younger ones rushed in through the gate toward them, and Yolanda took off running their direction. From the happy squeals and tears, he gathered they had to be Yo's mother and two of her sisters. Steve followed at a slower pace and was immediately grabbed by the ladies to welcome him to their home.

On the drive here, Yolanda had practically vibrated with excitement, as it had been nearly four years since her last visit. She told Zane she loved the United States, and living in Texas, but she missed her family. And she couldn't wait to introduce them to Steve. Wouldn't surprise Zane one bit if Steve pulled Mr. Morales aside at some point during this two-week visit for a heart-to-heart about his daughter.

Nora patted Zane's arm. "Let's get you all settled."

The doctor gestured for the group to follow. Yolanda would stay with her family, in the newer home Ernesto had built for them a few years ago, and Steve and Zane would be with the missionary pastor and his family. Michael would room with his father, and Paige and Ally would bunk with Nora, until Nora left with Nathan for their honeymoon. The guys would move her things into the main house while they were gone, leaving Nora's bungalow available for other missionaries or visitors.

Today was Saturday, the wedding was scheduled for Wednesday, the Americans would enjoy a Thanksgiving meal with the US missionaries on Thursday, and the honeymooners were due back a week following the ceremony. That would give them a few days longer to visit before they all returned to the States on that Sunday, the fifth of December.

Zane had been reading up on everything he could get his hands on about Guatemala and even Gilead Medical Missions —the customs, the people, the culture, the work and ministry.

He'd already reached out to Pastor Ethan Sullivan, who had been with the mission going on three years now with his wife and two children, and Ethan had expressed his eagerness in showing Zane their work and welcoming his assistance.

Here now in-country, Zane was beyond excited to be on foreign soil for the first time in his life. So far, it was everything he'd dreamed it would be. Different climate, different landscape, different people and language and sounds and smells.

His soul felt full to overflowing, and they hadn't even unpacked yet.

CHAPTER THIRTY-FIVE

*A*lly laughed when Zane twirled her around, then pulled her back into his arms.

"You certainly didn't exaggerate your dancing prowess."

"Oh, yeah?" He spun her again, then dipped her before he brought her back up into his arms. "How about that?"

"Very dramatic."

Then he kissed her, tender and chaste due to their surroundings. Following the ceremony in the mission chapel, the wedding party and their guests had moved to the covered patio at the side of the church for a wedding feast of carnitas, tortillas, tamales, beans, and rice. After the cutting of the cake, the praise-band-turned-wedding-entertainment took their places, and tables were moved from the middle of the patio to make room for dancing.

Ally had stood by Nora during the ceremony, and the look on her father's face as he voiced his vows to his bride brought tears to her eyes. Yes, her mother would be happy he'd found love again.

Zane pulled back and looked down at her. "You look stunning tonight. Took my breath away when you started down the aisle."

Her face warmed with the compliment. "Thank you. When Nora told me she wanted us all to wear traditional Kachiquel dress, I thought it was an amazing idea. I brought a *corte* from home, but she had these made for us. I absolutely love it."

Nora had chosen vibrant hues of turquoise, magenta, and bright green for the skirts and blouses Ally and Lisa, Nora's daughter-in-law, wore as bridesmaids. Even Nora's wedding dress had been traditional and brightly colored. With all of the indigenous plants and flowers used for decorations, the wedding had been beautiful and festive.

She wrapped her arms around Zane's neck. "I've missed you. This is the most time we've spent together since the hike on Sunday."

Since then, their time had been hit or miss, with all his attention focused on working with Pastor Ethan. When she realized Monday he'd be with Ethan all day instead of hanging with her, she'd made herself useful at the always busy clinic. Yesterday and today had been much the same. Not at all what she'd expected to happen when they arrived here.

"I've missed you too. But the past three days with Ethan have been eye-opening. What they do here ... it's extraordinary."

The sparkle in his eyes usually delighted her. But tonight it only added to the knot of apprehension growing in her chest. They hadn't come here for him to work, yet that's all he'd wanted to do since they set foot on mission soil.

On the other hand, she couldn't argue with his summation. The work they did here *was* extraordinary. She had to admit she'd enjoyed working back at the clinic that served the people of Pamoca, even if she didn't have the latest equipment at her disposal like she did at the pediatric practice at home. Still, she hoped she and Zane could take some time for themselves over the next week, if she could get him away from the mission for a while.

"I'm glad you've enjoyed it here, but we haven't had any time alone since we arrived."

And she longed to be with him and only him with every breath. Just to hold each other and talk into the wee hours, like they did back home. To share sweet kisses without being under the watchful eye of her family and their friends.

Steve and Yo had found plenty of opportunities to be alone, but Steve was there on vacation for that very reason. To spend time with Yolanda. Zane was there ...

Well, it was supposed to have been vacation, but he'd thrown himself into the work at the mission right after church services on Sunday when Pastor Ethan invited him to sit in as he talked to a family newly converted to Christianity. Other than a group hike Sunday afternoon, game night on Monday, then the rehearsal dinner last night, she hadn't seen him at all. And none of that time had been spent alone, except for a few minutes at the end of each evening to say good night before retiring to their respective cottages.

This morning, he'd left early with the two pastors for home visits in a neighboring village, making it back in time to help set up for the wedding. They hadn't set eyes on each other all day, until she appeared at the end of the aisle and found him sitting on the groom's side of the church. Their gazes locked, and when he shot her that thousand-watt smile, her world righted itself again.

"I know we haven't." He brushed the tip of his nose across hers. "I was actually thinking about that when I first saw you tonight. About how busy we've been and how much we need some time alone."

"One hundred percent agree. Tomorrow's the Thanksgiving dinner, and Friday we're going to Jocotales, a village about fifteen miles from here. Let's take some time on Saturday. Just you and me. Do something fun."

"It's a date." He winced. "Although ..."

She nodded when the silence lingered, her spirits plummeting. "You already have something going on."

His countenance softened into a look of apology. "When Yo's brother found out I played guitar, he and the worship band invited me to play with them on Sunday. They rehearse Saturday morning at ten."

A smile crept across her face. How could she be upset about *that?* Knowing how much he loved to play? "I think that's great. I love listening to you."

He'd played for her a few times when they found themselves alone at his house, his talent evident in the easy way he worked the chords from the instrument. The first time she'd heard him was when he and Wyatt had taken out their guitars at the back-to-school barbecue and entertained the kids after the sun had set.

"I'm looking forward to it. Mason asked me last week if I wanted to join the CU worship team for the all-area meetings. So, I may get some other opportunities to play."

"I can't wait. And we can still do something Saturday afternoon, right?"

"Absolutely. I'm all yours."

Four days ago, she had no doubt that was true. Now, she wasn't so sure.

CHAPTER THIRTY-SIX

*T*he ear-splitting scream ripped the air in the peaceful village of Jocotales, and all heads turned toward the source.

Zane's breath caught when a woman stumbled into the street from the cooking area of a small home, barely visible through the fire quickly engulfing her. Before Zane could even move, Pastor Ethan took off toward the woman, tackled her, and rolled her onto the ground. Zane, with Steve right behind him, grabbed a blanket from the medical supplies and sprinted toward them, covering them both with the blanket, then his body to douse the fire while Steve patted them down.

When the flames had dissipated into acrid smoke, he rolled onto his back on the dirt road. The woman screeched in pain, but the pastor merely moaned.

Steve knelt next to Zane, placing his hand on his chest. "Zane. Buddy, you okay?"

"Zane!"

Ally's terrified voice rang out, and he opened his eyes to see her fall to her knees beside Steve, water bottles in both of her hands.

"I'm okay." His voice scraped against his singed throat.

Her wild eyes searched him head to toe. "Are you sure? Your neck is red."

"I'm sure. Take care ... of them." He laid his head to the hard-packed earth and focused on breathing. Adrenaline still surged through him, his heart beat fast and hard, and he was only now aware of the stinging pain from his neck.

"Steve." Ally's voice sounded from above him. "Can you go get more water bottles, please?"

"Sure thing, Al." He looked down at Zane. "You okay, buddy?"

"I'm fine. Go on."

With a light pat to Zane's shoulder, Steve stood and ran back to the medical tent erected in the center of the village where they'd come to offer medical services to the people. Zane stayed where he was until he could breathe normally again. The others from the mission team surrounded the group lying in the road while villagers gathered around, many of the women screaming and sobbing. As the doctor gave out orders, Ally's now controlled voice responded, again the consummate professional and not the worried girlfriend.

When he could, Zane sat up and watched the care the others gave to the writhing woman and the pastor lying still, his scorched shirt adhered to his blistered skin. Ethan's mouth moved as if in prayer, and Zane reached over to take his hand. "I'm here, man. You're going to be okay."

He looked up at Yolanda tending to the minister's wounds. *Right?* He mouthed the word.

Her nod was quick but succinct. Ethan had suffered severe burns, but nothing like the now sedated woman next to him. A breathing tube had been placed down her throat, and the dental assistant squeezed air into her lungs. Ally and Dr. John worked fast but methodically to treat her the best they could in the middle of a dirt street while Yolanda and the other nurse did the same for Ethan.

A frantic man ran down the road, two girls and a small boy

right behind him. Steve met him a few yards away to keep them from coming any closer. Thankfully, fluent in Spanish, Steve somehow calmed the man and walked him and the children over to a nearby bench.

Zane looked back at the two people being tended to. His stomach lurched at the pungent odor of seared flesh permeating the air but willed his breakfast to stay where it was. He wasn't leaving the minister.

After several more minutes, the medical team had Ethan and the woman loaded onto make-shift backboards of wood planks, ready to be taken to Guatemala City in one of two vans they'd brought that morning. Jose and Alec, the mission dentist, had unscrewed and removed the two back rows of seats so they could get the victims into the vehicle.

As they pulled away with the doctor and his two patients on board, Ally walked over to Zane and looked closely at his neck. "We need to get you cleaned up and bandaged."

She took his hand, walked him over to the tent they'd erected, and sat him in a chair. With deft but gentle gloved hands, she cleaned and medicated the tender spots on his neck and arms, then covered any skin that was blistered. The pain was immense, yet nothing like the woman or Ethan had endured.

He looked up at her standing over him. "It's going to take hours to get them to Guatemala City. Can she even live that long?"

A grimace crossed her features. "It's going to be close. She could die in the next five minutes, or hold on and recover. No way to know if her wounds are survivable until she gets to a burn unit. If we hadn't been here, though? She'd already be dead since her airway was so compromised. We're fortunate that we carry breathing tubes and bags with us now. Three years ago, we wouldn't have been prepared for a respiratory emergency."

"What about Ethan?"

Tears flooded her eyes. "Ethan's bad, Zane. I won't lie. He'll recover if they can keep infection from taking hold, but he'll have a long road. Probably in the hospital a month or so because I'm sure he'll need grafts. Only time will tell if he's able to stay with his post."

His throat tightened. Ethan was a good man. A gifted minister. And today, a hero.

Zane looked around the group trying their best to go about the business of making sure the other villagers received the care they needed, since they were only there every other month. Even Steve sat filling out paperwork as each patient came through the tent.

"Her family. Will they be able to be with her?"

"Steve spoke with the husband. He's going to arrange for his mother to watch their children and he'll go back with us. One of the staff will drive him to Guatemala City to see about his wife. And Alana too. Yo's sister can come stay with the kids while Alana's in the city. You and Steve can move over with Michael at Dad's for now."

"Yeah, no problem." In the hospital a month? And the woman even longer? That would cost a small fortune, much more than a humble missionary or farmer could afford. "How will they pay for their care? It could be tens of thousands of dollars. For each of them."

"The public hospital is free, except for medicine and supplies. With wounds that severe, it can get costly, so the mission will cover the woman's expenses. Cal's an amazing administrator. Wouldn't surprise me a bit if he's already on the phone and social media. As for Ethan, he'll be transferred to a private hospital, and insurance will cover his care."

Zane looked over his shoulder at the village. Small, unremarkable homes with corrugated metal roofs lined the dirt road, children in tattered clothing played in a field, and a group of tearful women stood in a huddle, comforting each other. He'd heard how often these types of accidents happened here, since almost all of the cooking was done over an open fire. But to witness it firsthand ...

He bowed his head. "How do you do this? I've never seen anything like that, and you were so calm and together and did the work." He looked up at her. "You amaze me all the time, but today ... your strength of spirit is beyond me."

Her hands came to his face as she looked down into his eyes. "You were the amazing one. If you hadn't grabbed that blanket, we might have lost two people today. But I wasn't calm at all when I saw you lying there. I was out of my mind."

"And the very next minute, the professional you are. I'm so proud of you."

She leaned in and gave him a tender kiss. "I love you."

"I love you back. Now, put me to work."

"I think you've done enough for today. Just rest."

He looked at the line that had formed once again at the tent and the few people there to do what was needed. Thankfully, Yolanda had come along so there were three medical providers still there, besides the dentist and his assistant. As nurse practitioners, Ally and Yo could render the more elevated treatments and give out prescription medications, while the registered nurse could take all the minor cases and administer vaccinations.

He might not be medically trained, but he could keep each station supplied, organize lines based on what treatment was needed, and generally be their gopher. He could watch children or pray with concerned villagers. There was much he could do without a medical degree.

As they worked through the afternoon, stopping only for a subdued meal of beans, rice, and tortillas, Zane wondered again how the mission accomplished as much as it did with so few hands. Two doctors, a nurse practitioner in Nora, two registered nurses, Alec the dentist and his assistant. Pastors Ethan and Jose headed up the ministerial needs while Cal, a missionary from Canada, handled the administrative side with Alec's wife assisting him.

The school was a separate entity run by another missions organization, but the mission itself could use another three or four workers, which would also mean they would need more housing, resources in the way of food, supplies, another vehicle, travel, and a host of other things. Which all required one thing—money.

They loaded up what supplies they hadn't used, gathered the injured woman's husband and his meager bag with what he would need for the time spent in the city, and made their way back along the bumpy road to Pamoca.

Zane's thoughts spun as he stared out his window, hardly noticing the beautiful foliage he'd admired on the way up. With Ethan, and probably Alana, out for the foreseeable future, could Pastor Jose keep up with the church and all its needs? Jose had a strong faith and unquestionable work ethic. But there was only so much he could do with his senior pastor out of commission.

Ally laid her hand on his leg. "You okay? Are you in pain?"

He was, but it wasn't as bad as earlier. "I'm fine. Just … thinking."

She nodded. "It's been a tough day. I know we'd hoped to spend some time together tomorrow, but we'll have to see how things go. Maybe we can at least get a walk in or something."

"Yeah. I thought I'd make myself available to Jose for anything he might need for Sunday and his home visits this next week."

"He'll appreciate that, I'm sure."

"Is anybody going to let your dad and Nora know what happened today?"

She shook her head. "I don't think so. They'll be back on Wednesday. If we tell them now, they'll head back right away, and they deserve this time away."

"Agreed. With all of us here, we can handle things. Let them have their time."

He gave her hand a squeeze and turned back to the window. There had to be something that could be done to help this mission he'd grown to love more every day he spent there. Like the Becker and ConnectUP folks, these were some of the finest people he'd ever worked beside. And if there was any way he could help to further their ministry, he'd do it.

If only he could figure out how to do that from two thousand miles away.

CHAPTER THIRTY-SEVEN

"*Y*ou're staying."

Ally's heart rate accelerated when Zane tightened his grip on her hands held in both of his.

He'd taken her out onto her father's patio on this night before they were to head back to Texas. Back home. But after he sat her down and pulled a chair up in front of her, she knew it wasn't about being together alone this last night. No, he had something to tell her. And by the somber look on his face, there was only one thing it could be.

Her breath sat trapped in her lungs, the skin of her face taut. "You're not coming back with us tomorrow. You're staying here."

He nodded. "Just until we know more about Ethan's status or if they're going to send a replacement."

Her stomach threatened to mutiny on her, the amazing dinner the church congregation had made for them to express their thanks now stirring violently inside her. *He was staying.* And she was leaving. Her worst fears coming to fruition.

A hard swallow did little to sweep away the foreboding tightening her throat. "This is what the meeting was about yesterday? With Gilead?"

"Yes."

"And my dad ... he's on board?"

Dad and Nora had returned to Pamoca on Wednesday, shocked to hear what had happened in their absence, but relieved, as they all were, to hear Ethan's prognosis for recovery was promising. He would need some skin grafts and would bear the scars of his heroic act on his chest and arms. But his life had been spared, while the woman still fought for hers in the ICU. As soon as his breathing tube had been removed two days after the incident, he'd told his wife he wanted to stay and return to his post.

"Ally." Zane scooted forward in his chair. "Your dad's on board, but this was my idea. Stepping in for Ethan last Sunday to preach, then working with Pastor Jose this week ... well, it seemed like I was here for such a time as this. I've been praying about it all week, so when Cal approached me with the idea of stepping in, I took that as a sign."

That's what he and the mission administrator must have been talking about that day she saw them sitting on one of the benches by the school. She should've known Cal would recruit Zane to help them. Cal loved this mission as much as her father did and always had its best interests at heart. Zane had fit right in from the first day, throwing himself into the work and garnering the notice of the other missionaries. It made complete sense Cal would pursue him to take over for Ethan, and then, hopefully, stay once the pastor returned.

Except Zane already had a job.

Her eyes sought his. "What about Becker and ConnectUP? Are you taking a leave? Resigning?"

"Right now, just taking a step back, although I can still be involved remotely. I had a video meeting with Wyatt and Maggie this morning, and we all agree that with the holidays coming up and with how well organized we are for the next quarter, we're in really good shape."

"And y'all didn't think I should be in on that call?"

He grimaced. "That was my fault. Wyatt suggested we pull you in, but I didn't want to say anything to you until I'd made a decision. I'm sorry if you feel left out of the loop. I was basically info-gathering at that point."

"This decision was just made today?"

"This morning's call was when the last pieces fell into place. But after speaking with the director at Gilead yesterday, if Wyatt and Maggie were supportive of the idea, then I'd pretty much decided to stay."

Still not appreciating being left out in the cold while all of this was decided, she instead chose to focus on the here and now. The decision had been made, so she would need to step up and take on Zane's CU responsibilities in the interim.

She cleared her throat. "What was decided on this call today?"

"None of us have any doubt you can take lead on ministry development. To be honest, you keep me on track when I'm flying in all directions, anyway. My mind spins constantly, but you're the genius at organization and implementation. And you'll have Wyatt, Harper, Steve—all the leadership behind you to step in where needed. I would not leave you abandoned."

Huh. Then why did she suddenly feel so alone? She took a deep breath in and slowly released it. "I understand." The words came out shakier and with less conviction than she'd hoped. But how did one say words they wanted to believe but couldn't yet wrap their head around? "So … how long do you think? Did they say?"

He shook his head and hitched one shoulder in a shrug. "It's coming up on Christmas, so the chances of getting a temporary replacement at this time aren't good. I'm already here, and the people know me. I've been working with Ethan and Jose, and I somehow preached last Sunday, even with only one day's notice—"

"And did an incredible job." She couldn't keep back the

smile that wobbled a bit. "I was really proud of you, stepping in like that and preaching in another language you hadn't used much until we got here."

"All God, Ally. It was all God. Which is what I think this is. I don't believe it was a coincidence we were here when this all went down. The Lord knew they would need someone to step in for Ethan. At least for a time."

Her eyes searched his. "And after Ethan comes back? What then?"

He didn't answer, but the battle she watched play across his face told her what he couldn't voice.

"Zane," she whispered as a cold sensation enveloped her from head to toe. "Are you thinking about ... *staying*? For good?"

"I don't know, sweetheart. Beyond today, this week, this month. I don't know what will happen after that. What God has for me, where He wants me to be. But I would never leave ConnectUP short-handed. If I need to be there to keep growing it, I will gladly do that."

His grasp tightened. "And there's still us, Ally. I'm not choosing this over you. I want to be in this together, like we've been in everything else."

"But I won't be here. And you won't be in Arlington."

The truth hit her like a strong gust of wind. She pulled her hands free and stared at this man she loved. Maybe she would have all of her CU friends to count on to keep things moving forward, but she wouldn't have *Zane*. The one she'd thought might be her true soulmate.

How had she messed that up again?

With a deep breath in to still her pounding heart, she bowed her head. *Lord, he's doing a good thing. Probably the right thing. Give me strength to handle this. To support him. To leave him here with You.*

Her breath hitched. *To leave him here ...*

She brought her head up, squared her shoulders, and

looked back at him. Her trembling hands clutched in her lap, she swallowed the knot in her throat. "It's okay, Z. It really is. If this is it, if this is what God has brought you to, then that's okay. I would never stand in the way."

"Al—"

"I've watched you here. Working with the people from that first day. Putting your life on the line for them. Stepping in where needed without hesitation. I don't know if you'd be content back ho—" Her voice caught. "Back in Arlington. Not when your heart is here."

"But what about you? Us? We've both said we believed God brought us together for a reason. What would that be if it isn't to be *together*? To grow together. Work together. We can't do that two-thousand miles apart."

A tear, followed by another, then yet another, slid down her cheeks. "Look around you. Look where you are. Would you be here if you weren't with me?"

His mouth fell slack for a moment. "You think God brought us together to lead me here? And then watch you leave?"

She shrugged. "He does work in mysterious ways." A tremulous sigh did nothing to ease the pain as she swiped at her face. "After Wyatt and Harper's wedding, I had a true come-to-Jesus moment when I realized my value comes only from God, just like we tell our CU kids. Not from who I'm with or who loves me. I wanted to have peace in that. And I did. By the time you came into my life, I was truly content with being who and doing what God pleased. Even if it meant by myself."

Ignoring the cracking and splintering of her heart, she leaned forward and took his hands again. "Harper once told me that when she and Wyatt broke up last year, she considered him her Isaac. That she had to be willing to sacrifice the most important thing in her life if it meant being in God's will. Yet it wasn't without pain. I think I truly understand what she meant now."

"That I'm your Isaac. Something you're willing to sacrifice for God." He bowed his head before bringing his tear-filled eyes back to hers. "But what if I don't want to be? I don't want to end this, Ally. There has to be a way for us."

"But this isn't my calling, Zane." Her eyes burned as she tried to speak through the tightness in her throat. "And I can't see you leaving this now, not after experiencing it firsthand. Gilead could definitely use you here, even after Ethan comes back."

"Are you sure, Al? That this isn't your calling?" His dark-eyed gaze speared her, pleading for something she couldn't give him. "You're so amazing with the people here. You're ... stunning. The way you work, the way you treat these incredible people. Watching you these past two weeks, seeing you in action, it's made me fall even more in love with you."

Her tears fell unheeded now. "These last few months with you have been the best of my life. But it's because of how much I love you that I think we need to step away. We could do a long-distance thing for a while, but if you did decide to stay at the end of this interim position, we would have to end it anyway."

"Ally—"

"And I don't want you coming back to Arlington because of me if God could be calling you elsewhere. That would never work."

She reached up to place her hand along his cheek. "I'm not running away. I'm letting you go." Her breath hitched with the acceptance. ... *letting him go.* "I need to take myself out of this equation so it's just you and God. So you can work for Him unimpeded and not be distracted by how I might or might not fit into His plan for your life. Just focus on what you need to do, where He's calling you to go. And if it's not back to ConnectUP, we've got it. We can handle it. Your ideas have turned into processes now that will take us to the next level. Maybe your work there is done."

He took her hand from his face and clutched it again in his. "We could do great things together, you and me. We already have. Imagine what we could do here. They need the help so badly, and you're so at home here. You honestly can't see yourself here? With me?"

"Zane." She raised her eyes to the night sky in an effort to compose herself. When she looked back at him, she shook her head. "Please don't expect things of me I can't give you. I can't leave CU. They're depending on me. And *this isn't my calling.* I can't make a home here. I never had a home here. Being on the field was never home after Mom—"

When a sob choked off her words, he stood and pulled her up into his arms. He held her tight, and she clung to him as she cried out her heartbreak of losing someone else she loved to the mission field. At least this time, it was only the death of a relationship, and she had no doubt Zane would go on to do great things in this place.

"I'm so sorry, Ally," he whispered against her hair. "I never meant to hurt you. Never." He pulled back with his hands on her arms, his own tears wetting his cheeks. "These last two weeks, being here, working with you and your dad and the others, it's been the most amazing experience of my life. Like this is what I was meant to do. I'd give anything if we could do it together, because I don't want to be without you. But if I were to go back now—"

"No." The strength of her voice surprised her, since everything inside her seemed to be disintegrating. "You need to stay. See it through. I would never ask you to choose. If this is where you believe God has placed you, then this is where you should be."

Taking half a step closer, she lifted her mouth to his for a last lingering kiss. She memorized the gentle pressure of his lips on hers, the warmth of his body pressed close, and that spicy woodsy scent that was so Zane.

When they parted, she put her forehead to his. "I love you.
I have no regrets about that."

"Ally ... please—"

"Good night, Zane." She pulled away and looked one last
time into his brown eyes, swimming with tears that fell down
the face she'd imagined one day waking up next to every
morning. "I'll be praying for you."

She turned and took the walkway that led to the bungalow
she would share with Paige, her future sister-in-law, one last
night. Her heart splintered into shreds with each step that
carried her farther away. Farther from Zane. Farther from her
dreams.

CHAPTER THIRTY-EIGHT

Zane shook Steve's outstretched hand. "Thanks for looking after Phyllis for me, bud. I appreciate you letting her stay. And I you enough rent to cover me through February."

"Yeah, no problem looking after your girl. I'll drive her around the block every few days so she doesn't just sit there. But, um, about the rent. You don't have to do that. At least, for the time you're gone." His brow furrowed. "You don't think you'll be gone that long, do you? I thought this was only a temporary thing, until Ethan's back."

Zane's gaze wandered behind Steve, where Ally, Paige, and Yolanda walked out the door of Nora's former cottage with their bags. The same cottage that would become his new temporary home. *Temporary.* Another home he couldn't truly call his own.

When Ally walked into church that morning she looked tired, her face drawn and eyes puffy, as if she'd slept about as well as he had. It was a total God thing that he was able to get up and preach today after tossing and turning all night, questioning if he'd made the right decision letting her go so he could stay somewhere he'd only been for two weeks. If he was her Isaac, he guessed that made her his—that one thing he loved more than any other he had to be willing to let go of to follow God's plan.

"Zane?"

His attention snapped back to Steve. "Oh, uh. No. I don't know. Right now, the plan is to cover for Ethan until he's back to full throttle. Last word was he's expected to be released in three weeks or so, but, obviously, won't be able to take the reins full on for some time yet. But no way am I leaving you without that rent payment. All of my stuff is still there, and when I come back, I'll need a place to stay."

If he came back. Yet even if he stayed with the mission, he would have to return to Arlington at some point to pack up his things and make arrangements to store Phyllis. Get a long-term visa. Go see Mom. Make sure his replacement was up to speed on ConnectUP. That would all take a few weeks. A few weeks of being in Arlington but not with Ally.

Steve's smile turned toward Yolanda, who now sported a sparkling diamond solitaire on her left hand. The proposal had happened a mere hour ago, over lunch so he could ask her in front of her family and friends. Zane had been right. Steve took Mr. Morales aside a week ago to ask for his blessing. When Steve dropped to one knee today, Yolanda was shocked but hadn't hesitated in her resounding *yes*.

Zane had choked up a bit himself as Ally and Yolanda embraced like the sisters of the heart they were, both with tears streaming down their faces. Until last night, he'd allowed himself to imagine a day like that for him and Ally. Now those dreams had all drifted away, like smoke in the wind.

Steve looked back at Zane. "Only if you're back before the end of May. After that, I'm kicking you out."

His jaw dropped. "May? You picked a date?"

"Nothing firm, but we're thinking Memorial Day weekend."

"Dude, that's fantastic! So happy for you."

He glanced behind Steve where Ally stood watching Pastor Jose load their luggage into the back of the van.

"Thanks, man." Steve took a step closer and leaned his head in. "So, it's true? You and Ally ... broke it off?"

Zane's heart slammed into his rib cage. "Last night. I didn't want to, but thinking and praying over it when I couldn't sleep last night, I see where she's coming from. She wants me to be sure of where God wants me without being any kind of influence."

Steve shook his head. "I really thought you two were the real deal. We all did."

"We were. And we may be. But doing this long-distance didn't sit right with her. I have to respect that."

"I see." Steve studied him. "You're considering staying on here, then? Indefinitely?"

"Considering, yes. Gilead needs the help, and I wouldn't necessarily have to go through the usual hoops right off to get my funding. I have my trust. I can use that while doing some work to drum up support from here. But that's only if I start with them full-time. That bridge hasn't been crossed yet. I haven't even come to it."

Steve reached out and gave his shoulder a squeeze. "We'll be praying for you, buddy. For both of you. And don't worry about CU. As Wyatt said yesterday, you and Al have done a stellar job getting everything in place for the next few months. We can take it from there, as long as Ally's on board heading it up."

"I appreciate it. And I believe she is. CU has her heart."

"As do you, my friend. I'm sure this has all been a little bit of a shock to her—you staying, her leaving. But we've got her. We'll take care of her."

Zane could only nod. Yes, Ally had good friends. They both did. If only that was enough to ease the pain in his chest at the thought of not seeing her, not being with her.

He and Steve walked over to the van to say their goodbyes. Yolanda reached out to give him a hug. "I hope you know what you're giving up," she whispered in his ear. "But I wish you only the best." She pulled back and looked at him with a sad smile. "I'll be praying for your work here. And you'd better be good or I'll hear about it from my *papá.*"

He tried his best to return her smile. "I'll be on my best behavior."

Steve took her hand and gave a last wave to Zane over his shoulder. Zane returned it, then walked over to Ally standing by the side of the van.

Her smile shook as tears welled in her eyes. "Well ... guess this is it."

Regret wrapped its fist around Zane's heart at the hurt written in her features. Regret that he'd caused it. Regret that he couldn't fix it. "Guess it is. But I'll still see you on the weekly Zoom calls. And you can always reach out with any questions or if you need anything with regard to ConnectUP. Or anything."

She nodded. "I think we can handle it. You'll have enough on your plate here."

They stood and stared at each other for a long, awkward moment. How he wished he could pull her close and kiss her until she was convinced her place was beside him. Wherever that would be. "Text me when you get home?"

Her brow furrowed.

"Just so I know you got there safely. I still care about you, Al. I always will."

Her nod was almost imperceptible. "I need to go. Please take care of yourself. I'll ... I'll be praying for you. For all of you."

"And I for you." He reached for her and she walked into his arms, her forehead pressed to his neck as they clung to one another.

"I love you, Allyson Kincaid." His voice came out a ragged whisper with the tears clogging his throat.

She nodded against his shoulder before pulling back and stepping away. "Goodbye, Z."

CHAPTER THIRTY-NINE

*A*nother great Christmas party.

If only Ally could conjure up the Christmas spirit that usually came so naturally. The kids didn't seem to notice anything amiss, and her heartache lessened as she focused on them throughout the evening's festivities. Helped her forget for a while that someone was missing. The one person she most wanted to spend this time of year with.

The one person she most wanted to spend any time of the year with.

With a trash bag held in one hand, she stacked several used cups left on the McCowans' coffee table with the other and tossed them in. Earlier in the evening, Harper and Wyatt's house had bulged at the seams with sixty-something kids and leaders from both Arlington clubs joining the holiday celebration. Good thing they had supportive neighbors who didn't mind the ruckus every now and then.

She tossed paper plates into the bag. Weird how much could happen in a year. It was at last year's party she picked up on the fact something was off between Wyatt and Harper, precipitating her humiliating attempt to win him back. Ironic that at the same time she'd been making a fool of herself with

Wyatt, Harper was in Atlanta meeting with Zane about a ministry concept he'd developed to bridge gaps between teenage peer groups.

It was Harper finding Becker Ministries online that had brought him and Wyatt together, and, eventually, Becker on board as ConnectUP's sponsor. But when Wyatt and Harper had returned from Atlanta, not only back together but engaged, Ally couldn't bear to show her face at CU after what she'd done.

Until the day Harper showed up at her door a few days after the New Year.

"If you'd rather not work with me, I totally get it," she'd said. *"I'll give you all the space you need. Work with a new club when the next one launches, or whatever will make you most comfortable. But, Ally, you were with Wyatt when he began this ministry. Helped him lay the foundation. You should be here to see what it can become. And we're bringing on this new coordinator from Becker. Zane Carpenter. He's amazing, has some fantastic ideas. I see some really great things coming, and you should be a part of it as much as, if not more than, any of us. Please. Think about it. Pray about it."*

She hadn't really needed to put all that much thought into it after that. And over the next few months, her friendship with Harper grew into the sisterhood it was now.

And then there was Zane. Her fantasy guy from the terrace.

The guy she'd fallen in love with and dreamed of a future with.

The guy now two thousand miles away, in the same place she'd run to the first time her heart had been broken.

Yes, funny what could happen in a year.

"Hey, girl!" Shannon grabbed her in a hug from behind.

"Hey." She laughed when Shannon let her go and came around to plop down on the sectional, pulling Ally down with her by the arm.

Shannon stuck her feet with her Santa socks on the now cleaned off coffee table. "Such a great party, don't you think?"

"The CU Christmas party always is." Ally set the trash bag on the floor and put her feet up next to her friend's.

Shannon pointed to Ally's red socks covered with Christmas trees. "From last year's party?"

"Yep. You?"

"Yep. Harper's wearing hers too."

In fact, Ally had at least three pairs of Christmas-themed socks as a result of these CU holiday parties. Because the socio-economic status of the kids ranged from trust fund to food stamps, instead of a gift exchange, they did a sock exchange, and nobody could pay more than ten dollars for a pair of socks. Tonight, Ally unwrapped a pair adorned with dogs of various breeds wearing Santa hats. She'd wear them to work on Monday, where her young patients would get a kick out of them.

Shannon laid her head on Ally's shoulder. "I'm so happy you came to our party this year. I thought you might go to Yo's club party."

"I wanted to be with my original club."

"And we always love having you back. I know I'm going to miss it when I leave."

"I hear ya. But you'll be fantastic as the new captain in Fort Worth."

Shannon lifted her head and turned her wide blue eyes to her. "You think so? Really? I'm a little nervous about it. That's a lot of responsibility."

"Girl, you'll be all over it. Zane and I prayed for you specifically after you told him you were interested in being a part of the new launch. We understood about having a lot going on, with school and your internship. But when you told us you decided you'd like to captain it, we couldn't have been more excited."

"That means a lot to me." Shannon's eyes narrowed.

"You're doing okay? Have you talked to him since you got back?"

Turning her focus to her feet, Ally shook her head. "Not one on one. Just a few texts back and forth, mostly about CU, and the last two Tuesday afternoon Zooms with Maggie and Wyatt. We're breaking for the holidays, so I don't know when I'll talk to him next."

Heaviness, like molten iron, seeped its way back into her chest. Tomorrow would mark two weeks since she'd left him there in Pamoca, and although she wasn't crying so much anymore, the pain she'd carried home hadn't lessened at all with the time and distance.

The seat cushion let out a *whoosh* when Harper joined them, sitting on Ally's other side and pulling her feet, with their reindeer-covered socks, up onto the table. "Whew. I love hosting these parties, but I'm done in."

Ally patted her leg. "I'm not surprised. You did most of the food, provided the house, finished up finals this week, and you're pregnant. That's a lot to ask of one body."

"Couldn't have done it if you hadn't spent the majority of your day over here helping me. Thank you so much for that."

"My pleasure. And we'll take care of the clean-up."

"Nah. Let's let the guys do that."

A hand reached over the couch behind them, and Ally looked up over her shoulder at Wyatt.

"We've got it," he said. "Hand me that bag and I'll finish up."

Ally reached down for the bag. "You're sure? I don't mind."

"You did plenty." He took the bag from her. "You guys relax and talk."

Ally gave Harper a nudge. "He's a keeper."

Her friend shrugged. "That's my plan." She looked at Ally with a crease in her brow. "Speaking of food, are you eating?"

"Of course."

"Honestly? You've only been back two weeks, but you look

skinnier. And I don't recall seeing you eat anything since you got here this afternoon. You don't need to lose any weight, girlfriend."

Chagrined, Ally moved her head from side to side. "I ate. But it's hard to eat much when you're sick to your stomach all the time."

"Tell me about it. But you have to try. Okay? If I have to come over every day of my winter break to have lunch with you, I'll do it."

"Me, too," Shannon chimed in. "Let me know whenever you want company, if Yo's out with Steve or something, and I'll be over in a flash."

Tears welled in Ally's eyes. "You guys are the best, but I'll be fine. This too shall pass, right?"

The three of them stared over their toes at the fire crackling in the fireplace, letting the silence linger with the men's voices and laughter in the background. Even knowing the futility of it, Ally's ears strained to hear the one voice that should've been there tonight. With a sigh, she looked down and swiped a finger under her eye.

Harper reached over and took her hand. "We all miss him. We support whatever he believes he needs to do, even if it means leaving CU, but it'll be weird for a while, not having him here. Even though he was only here a few months."

"A few months that changed my life." Ally's voice barely squeezed through the tightness of her throat. "Whether we're together or not, I'm forever different because of him. I won't ever regret it."

Shannon turned and tucked her feet under her with her elbow resting on the back of the couch. "Well, I, for one, think he's a complete dunce for letting you go. Sorry, but that's the truth. I love the guy. Respect his commitment to serving the Lord. But I also know how wild he is about you. How could he just let you walk away?"

Ally couldn't help the chuckle that bubbled up. Shannon

was nothing if not straightforward. "In his defense, he didn't *let* me. It was my choice. He all but begged me to stay with him there. To see what we could do together. But I … I don't know. I couldn't."

Shannon sat up straight. "Wait. He wanted you to stay? And you said you couldn't?"

"Pretty much."

"But why? Isn't that your home?"

Ally's gaze snapped to Shannon, taking in the authentic confusion in the way her brow furrowed . "*This* is my home. Arlington. This is where I've lived the past ten years, which is longer than I've ever lived anywhere."

"Yeah, but I mean you were there with your dad, right? Before you came here for college? Like it's your hometown. Where you came from. You didn't think you could stay there and work with Zane? Especially since your dad is there too?"

Ally turned back to the fireplace. Her hometown? Pamoca?

She'd told Zane the mission field hadn't felt like home since her mother passed away. Yet, in truth, before leaving for college, Pamoca had been the longest she'd been in one place since the day she was born. The first two years of her life were spent in southern Nicaragua, the next three in northeast Nicaragua, followed by three years in El Salvador, then the assignment in Honduras when she was ten. Where her mother died two years later.

A year in the States had her dreaming of settling there permanently, until her father moved them to Guatemala when she was thirteen. And there she lived until she left for college five years later.

But did that make it her hometown?

Her fingers came to the pendants at her throat, running them back and forth along the thin chain as her thumb rubbed over the little house. Was it her home because Dad still lived there and always had a place for her? Because every time she went back, she was welcomed with open arms and authentic love that never failed to fill up her heart?

She gave her head a quick shake and let go of the necklace. "I don't know, Shan. I was rebellious when we first moved there because I'd just lost my mom the year before on the mission field. The last place I wanted to be was on another one. Anywhere. I wanted to be with our family, with Michael. And it was only Dad and me in Pamoca."

"Wow, seriously? You *didn't* like it?"

"Hmm." Harper's voice had Ally turning to look at her. "You must have gotten over that eventually, because I've never heard you say one negative thing about Pamoca. Not one."

"Yeah, same." Shannon nodded when Ally looked back at her. "I know it's physically impossible, but you should see your face when you talk about being in Guatemala. The people there, the work they do there, the work you did there. The mission."

"You light up." When Harper spoke, Ally turned her head back to her again, like watching a conversational ping pong match. "And when they were visiting and you introduced Nora to us at church that Sunday, you were so proud to tell us about their work."

"I am proud. My dad's worked hard his entire career. He could be a rich man if he practiced here in the States, but his life's work is on the mission field. He'll get a good retirement from Gilead, but it won't be anything like he could do here. And I love that about him. He's not materialistic in any way. It's all about service. That's what makes him rich. The love he gets back from the people he serves."

"Just like Zane," Shannon said.

Ally looked back at Shannon, and goosebumps sprang up on her skin. *Just like Zane.*

Zane didn't care about money or things. Even a true home. He only wanted to serve.

"Which begs the question. If you love the place so much, why don't you think you could work there? With Zane?"

"It's not my calling." How many times would she have to repeat those words? "Maybe it's how I was raised, but that doesn't mean that's what God's called me to."

She looked back over at Harper. "And just like you had to do with Wyatt last year, it's better for us to be apart in order for him to get clarity on what it is God would have him do."

"Except I broke up with Wyatt because I was the one who needed clarity."

"Okay, hold up." Both of them looked at Shannon. A chiropractic adjustment might be in order if this conversation went on much longer. Shannon's wide eyes zeroed in on Harper. "You and Wyatt *broke up* last year? Was this when you went to Atlanta?"

A pink tinge spread on Harper's face. "We did. Except for losing Megan, those were the hardest fifteen days of my life. We loved each other, but we were arguing constantly about what direction the ministry should take. Neither one of us was wrong, we simply had different visions.

"But the bottom line was *he* was the director of the ministry. He had to stay true to his convictions about the best way to lead it. But I had my own convictions that I needed to see through." She nodded toward Ally. "That's how I found Zane and Becker Ministries."

Shannon threw her hands up in the air and let them fall again. "That explains Wyatt's quick trip to Atlanta. He was going after you."

"Not really coming after me. During the time we weren't together, God sent people and circumstances into both of our lives to show us the direction we should go. We both had to be willing to sacrifice anything in order to follow God's plan. I'm just so grateful He saw fit to bring us back together."

She looked at Ally, and her intense gaze made it impossible

to look away. "You know I love you and I only want what's best for you. So don't take this the wrong way."

Ally tensed, her eyes widening. Yeah, nothing good usually followed such a declaration.

"That night we talked after the Grand Prairie leaders' meeting, that first one you had to attend without Zane, I couldn't help but cry along with you because I understood the pain you were in. And I know you took the high road and let Zane go so he could be and do all God wanted him to be and do."

"Is there something wrong with that?"

"Nothing at all. But this isn't only about letting Zane go to follow his calling. Yes, that's a huge sacrifice on your part, but God values our obedience over sacrifice. You're doing incredible work for ConnectUP, and you were and are an amazing group leader. You're a natural. As if you were made for ministry. But what shape that takes is between you and the Lord. You have to be willing to dig deep. Have the courage to earnestly seek what it is He would have *you* do."

Ally tried to hold eye contact with her friend, but had to look away. *You're a natural. As if you were made for ministry.*

She'd heard that before, her last day at the hospital when she first started working with Zane, talking to her friend Dawn about the challenges of medical work on the mission field. *Seems like it's exactly what you were made for.*

Harper's hand tightened around hers, and Shannon hugged her other arm, sitting silent beside her.

Too much. Her head spun with too many thoughts, too many directions, too many words. Confusion wasn't of God. And right now, she was plenty confused. She did love the ministry of ConnectUP, working with girls who were getting to know who they were in Christ, finding their way in a world giving them all kinds of bad advice.

But on the professional front, she hadn't found any nursing jobs to be particularly fulfilling since she'd returned from her year in Guatemala. There simply didn't seem to be much out there that interested her.

With a sigh, she shook her head. "I don't know, you guys. I have too many things running through my head right now."

Harper nodded. "I'm sure you do. And I would encourage you to pray earnestly about it. Because whatever you decide, sister, you're going to rock it."

The smile she tried to give her friend didn't quite materialize before she directed her focus again to the hearth.

Have the courage to earnestly seek what it is God would have you do.

Her hand made its way to her necklace again, this time her index finger tracing the Gulf Coast of Texas. She'd already lost so much to the mission field. What more might He require of her?

CHAPTER FORTY

So much need. So much work. Everywhere he looked.
Zane strolled down the dirt path with Nathan and
Nora on this Wednesday after Christmas weekend. They'd left
the mission six hours earlier to visit some folks in the suburban
areas who had a difficult time getting to the clinic. Over the
last five-and-a-half weeks here, he'd become more
overwhelmed with each passing day by the scope of the work
that needed to be done and the lack of hands to do it all.

Peering up at the blue sky overhead, he blinked in the
sunlight. It would be dusk soon, and the mild daytime
temperatures that allowed them to work in light pants and T-
shirts would lower into the fifties after dark. Warmer than
Arlington. He'd been checking. Wondering if someone had
smoked some briskets and sausage for the Arlington club
Christmas party at the McCowans' in his absence, how Steve
and Yo's wedding plans were shaping up, if Ally had a nice
holiday.

If she missed him as fiercely as he missed her.

They passed another humble, ramshackle home no bigger
than an Airstream, where a mother with her three girls stood
around an open fire cooking their evening meal. Her husband

and two boys worked in a small garden to the side of the house. To his count, that totaled at least seven people who lived in this small home that looked as if it could fall around them if a strong gust of wind came up.

The woman looked at them, and her face lit up with her smile as she waved. "*Hola, doctor.*"

Nathan waved back to the beaming woman. "*Hola, Marta. Algo huele muy rico.*"

The doctor was right. The aroma made Zane's stomach growl, and Marta's smile grew brighter with the compliment to her cooking. Such a humble people, hard-working and kind. At every house they'd been to that day, Zane and the Kincaids had been offered food and drink, when it was clear some of the people didn't have much even for themselves.

Nora walked over to hug the woman and her young daughters, and he and the doctor stopped at the end of the path to wait at the edge of the road.

Zane let his gaze roam over the other homes along the dirt street. "How do you do it, Nathan?" He looked at the other man. "How do you see all of this need and not collapse under the weight of it?"

Nathan nodded, looking down at the ground in front of them with his ever-present smile. "One day at a time. One person at a time. One task at a time." He brought his gaze up to meet Zane's. "'*The harvest is great, but the workers are few.*'"

"From Matthew."

"And Luke. They both quote Jesus' words about the breadth of work to be done. He knew it better than anybody, yet He still met the people where they were, not just geographically but by their need. He fed them when they were hungry, healed them when sick. Gave them sight or hearing. One person at a time.

"Even though He was truly God, He was on earth as a man. A man who tired and hungered, laughed and cried. A man who had the ability as God to know every heart that needed Him, yet as a man could only do what was in front of Him to do."

Zane let that sink in for a second as Nora rejoined them. "I see what you mean. We can only do what's put in front of us at any given time. That's the ministry for that moment, that hour or day. To meet *that* need."

"Exactly."

Zane's thoughts meandered as they walked down the road. "But the verse then says, '*So pray to the Lord who is in charge of the harvest; ask him to send more workers into his fields.*' He had a burden for the needs of all and prayed for more help."

Nora chuckled. "We pray every day for more help. We know Gilead doesn't have the resources to send any additional full-time missionaries, and we'd also need more facilities for them here. We simply don't have room for more."

"What about short-term missions? Do you ever get folks here for days or a couple of weeks? Just to help with building or planting or running backyard Bible clubs? Anything like that?"

Nathan shrugged. "From time to time. We had a group out last July to dig some wells, and we had a college group come for their spring break to help at the school. And you saw the haul of Christmas boxes that came in for the children."

Zane grinned at the memory. The day they'd handed out all the shoe boxes filled with school supplies, socks, toys, coloring books and crayons, and other items to the area's children, had been one of the best days he'd had here in Pamoca.

"Where do you house the short-term teams when they come?"

"We all take in a few folks, and several of our parishioners look forward to having visitors come stay with them for a few days. If they have a sleeping bag and pillow, that's really all they need."

Zane's mind whirled for the rest of the evening and over the next two days. On Saturday, they celebrated Ethan's return with a meal prepared by the ladies of the church. He would need a lot of rest and physical therapy to continue his recovery, which could be done there at the mission clinic. But his smile never left his face.

After Sunday's service, the pastor clapped Zane on the shoulder and shook his hand. "Looks like I left my church in very good hands. I really enjoyed your sermon, and I've been hearing great things about the work you've been doing."

Ethan's words both pleased and humbled him. "Just picking up where you left off. This is your flock, but I'm here to help any way I can."

"I'm so thankful you were here when all of this happened." Ethan met his wife's eyes, standing beside him holding his hand, before looking back at Zane. "For so many reasons. If you hadn't been there that day, I wouldn't be standing here now. How does a man repay that debt?"

With a shake of his head, Zane waved his hand in front of him. "No debt to repay. God had everyone in place that day and every day since for a reason. We're all blessed to have you back. Just let me know how I can continue to help you. I'm sure you'll want to go easy for a bit."

"Yeah, that's kind of doctor's orders."

Alana looked up at Zane. "I'll need your help keeping him from doing too much. I know my husband, and he'll try to push himself too hard."

"I'm on it." He looked back at Ethan. "There are some things I'd like to run by you and Cal, with Dr. Kincaid there, too, if we can arrange it. Some ideas I've had running through my head to get you guys some more help out here."

The pastor's eyes lit up. "I'd be all over that. Yes, let's see when we can work up a meeting between the four of us in the next day or two."

Later that afternoon, Zane came through the mission gates after a mid-day stroll through town. His thoughts still ran rampant through his head, about how much needed to be done, not only at the mission but around the community and surrounding villages. Homes needed repairs and new ones built from the ground up. Crops needed tending to, clothing brought in or sewn. Food and supplies delivered, wells dug.

And none of that even touched on the medical aspect. If they could get visiting nurses, dentists, eye care professionals, to name a few, there was so much that could be done to take some of the burden off the clinic.

He walked to his favorite bench under a tree outside the church and took a seat. Looking around the compound, his heart rate eased. He truly loved this place. But he had to admit some of the luster had fallen away the second Ally was out of his sight. Four weeks without seeing her, hearing her, touching her. Taking in the soft floral fragrance she wore so well. Sure, he'd seen her twice since she'd left, but her image in a small box on his laptop screen was little consolation when he wanted her close. Here. Beside him.

"You must be thinking about my daughter again."

Zane looked to the side where Nathan approached. "What gave me away?"

"You're awake."

Zane laughed and gestured with his hand for the doctor to join him. "That's accurate."

Nathan sat down and stretched his arm across the back between them. "She spent Christmas with Michael up in Colorado. Just a few days, I guess, so she could get back to Arlington for work." He shook his head. "She's not happy in that job. She loves the kids. Loves being in medicine. But the work she's doing for ConnectUP is so much more fulfilling for her."

"She's good at it. But I loved watching her work here, with the people. She's fantastic with them, and they adore her."

"She is, and they do." He looked over at Zane. "She's doing well, though. Misses you, but she knows you need this time to work out your calling."

"Work out my calling. Yeah, I guess that's a good way to put it." He sighed. "I love this place. And you know I love the work. But when I see all the needs, my brain can't seem to stop trying to find ways to fix it."

"Ethan said you'd like to meet with him, Cal, and me this week. Want to give me a preview of that conversation?"

Zane looked down at his hands folded between his legs and took a moment to put his thoughts together. "I was thinking about what you said the other day about having short-term help every now and then, and I was wondering if there might be a way to manage that more efficiently. Get more help directed out here. And I couldn't help but think about ConnectUP."

Nathan's eyes narrowed. "ConnectUP?"

"Yeah. I've been thinking of ways we could tap into all that potential, all of those students who are just yearning to serve somewhere. If we could coordinate short-term missions through the ministry, we could help a lot of folks. Both in the States and abroad."

Nathan stared ahead and nodded. "An interesting concept. On the face of it, I like where you're going with that."

"I thought I might see if Wyatt and some of the other leadership would want to come out here and check it out. Just for a few days."

"Now, I *love* that idea. Why don't you go ahead and float that, then we can run this by Ethan and Cal once you hear back on whether Wyatt thinks this could work. I don't see why he wouldn't. Wyatt's always had a servant's heart."

"That's a fact."

"Now, back to my daughter."

Zane's pulse lurched. "Sir?"

"You're still struggling with the decision she made."

The statement was just that. Speaking the truth Zane couldn't deny. "I keep waiting for it to get easier, something to tell me it was the right thing letting her go. Or letting her let me go, however that went. Even knowing in my head it makes the most sense. That we couldn't keep things going long distance, especially if I do end up staying here for the long haul. But it's still hard to accept this is best when a part of me is missing."

The doctor studied him for a moment before nodding. "You know, back when Wyatt and Ally were dating, for a while there I wondered if he might be the one for her. But, son, I never saw her look at Wyatt the way she looks at you. Nor did they have the easy, natural way you have with each other, like you're two halves of a whole. Oh, she loved him, no doubt. But she's *in love* with you. Enough to walk away if that's what you needed to make this decision easier.

"Seeing you two together here was exactly what this father needed to know his little girl was in good hands. That she'd chosen well. And that hasn't changed. The decision she made to let you go to be who God's called you to be was a hard one but mature and wise. I'm proud of her for it."

The doctor rose and looked down at Zane. "But I haven't given up that you two might somehow make your way back to each other. If it's meant to be, God will make a way."

Zane watched Nathan walk back toward the home he now shared with his new bride. *If it's meant to be, God will make a way.*

The only way that could happen was if God showed one of them they were going the wrong direction. Because right now, he felt farther away from her every day.

CHAPTER FORTY-ONE

$\mathcal{T}$ he warmth of the coffee shop enveloped Ally like her favorite cozy blanket when she walked through the door. Delicious aromas of coffee and baked goods assailed her as she shook her dripping umbrella, then left it by the door with several others.

One last shiver shook her body as she looked around the bustling dining area, smiling when she spotted Harper at a corner table. She threw her friend a wave and made her way to the counter.

January had come in blustery and wet. In fact, two weeks into the new year and temps hadn't climbed above forty yet. The chill on this mid-morning Saturday almost had her longing for the seventies in Pamoca.

Her chest threatened to seize on her. That wasn't the only thing in Pamoca she longed for, as thoughts of the man she'd last seen on her computer screen on Tuesday erupted in her brain. It was the first time she'd seen him or heard his voice since their last Zoom two weeks before Christmas, and she hadn't been able to keep her eyes from straying to him during the call with Maggie and Wyatt. He looked tanned and happy, sitting there in a ConnectUP T-shirt, teasing them about the cold snap in Texas when things were mild and sunny in his part of the world.

Happy New Year, Ally, he'd sent in a private chat during their call.

Same to you, she'd answered. *Dad said Ethan's doing well but you still handle most of the speaking and heavy lifting.*

It's been a good experience. I've learned a lot.

Their private conversation lagged while the four of them discussed the opening of three new clubs, their first outside of the DFW Metroplex.

Great job, Al, he wrote a few minutes later while Wyatt and Maggie discussed some budget matters. *Three more club launches planned over the last month? That's fantastic!*

You laid the groundwork before you left. Still a team effort.

Several more minutes ticked by, then *I miss you* popped up on her screen.

With her pulse beating a staccato rhythm, it took her a few breaths to finally reply, *I miss you too.*

Maggie will probably mention it, but this is my last Zoom w/you guys. Lots going on here. Working on a new project and Maggie and Wyatt are really happy with everything you're doing.

Her breath had caught, and she'd almost missed a question Maggie directed to her. Even though it made her heart squeeze to see him on her screen and not in person, Ally couldn't imagine not seeing him *at all.*

After she somehow answered Maggie's question about the Tyler club launching in mid-February, she put her shaking hands to the keyboard.

I'm sorry I won't be seeing you, but I wish you the best with whatever you're working on.

His eyes moved across the screen. After a few seconds, he looked down for a moment before another message popped up.

I'm always here for you. Whatever you need. Just ask.

Moisture building in her eyes made it hard to see the screen. *I will. And same for you.*

And that was it. Maggie ended the meeting with the announcement Zane had warned her about, followed by a closing prayer. And Ally had heard nothing from him since.

She retrieved her caffè latte and banana nut muffin and joined Harper at the table, where her friend was already enjoying a coffee and scone.

"I hope that's decaf," she said in a mock reprimand as she took a seat.

Harper nodded. "All I'm drinking these days. Double whammy what with second trimester exhaustion and caffeine withdrawal."

"You're glowing, nonetheless."

"That's kind of you to say." Harper looked past her and waved at a young woman coming in the door. "There she is." She looked back at Ally while the woman walked across the dining area toward them. "Thank you for this, by the way. Melody asked me for some advice, and I knew as soon as she started she really needed to be talking to you."

"I hope I can help."

"I have no doubt." With a smile, Harper rose and greeted her friend with a hug. "Melody, so glad you could make it on this rainy day. You remember Allyson Kincaid, don't you? From Bible study last summer?"

"Oh, yes." Melody's smile didn't quite meet her eyes. "Good to see you again, Allyson."

Ally studied her for a moment. Something wasn't right, if Melody's troubled countenance and tense body language was any indication. When they'd been in Bible study together, she'd practically bounced with each step. Newly engaged to one of the junior pastors on their church staff, Melody couldn't wait until he graduated from seminary this May and took a full-time position. Being a pastor's wife was all she'd dreamed of being.

"You can call me Ally. All my friends do."

Harper put her hand on Melody's arm. "Do you want a coffee or something?"

Melody shook her head. "I don't think so. I didn't mean to keep you waiting."

"Not at all. Why don't you have a seat, tell Ally what you wanted to talk about, and I'll grab you something. Coffee? Hot chocolate? A muffin or something to eat?"

"Um, hot chocolate sounds good. Nothing to eat, though. I'm fine."

"One hot chocolate coming up. My treat."

Harper grabbed her wallet as Melody took the third chair at their little table. "So, um, Harper said you worked on the mission field. Is that right? A foreign mission?"

"I did. I was raised on the mission field, so I guess you could say I was a missionary by birth." She smiled, but Melody didn't return it. "Are you interested in working in the field?"

With a shaky sigh, Melody moved her hands to her lap. "Alan."

"Oh. Had you ever discussed this before?"

"Never. It came out of the blue, a couple of days after Christmas." She looked up when Harper set a fat, ceramic cup in front of her with whipped cream floating on top. "Thank you."

"My pleasure." Harper took her seat again. "Don't let me interrupt."

"So, Alan told you he's thinking about mission work ..." Ally prodded.

Melody took a small sip from her drink and set it back on its saucer. "We'd always talked about him eventually working full-time at Grace Covenant, and I would teach until we started our family and we'd work together in ministry. Right here. In Arlington. I've been at Grace since I was born, and he started coming when his family moved here when he was nine. It's where we met, where we grew up, fell in love, made plans for a future. It's our *home*."

A tingling sensation sprang up on the back of Ally's neck. "What did he say, exactly?"

"Just that he'd had a stirring in his spirit for a while, even before he proposed, but he'd pushed it down because becoming a pastor had always been the plan." She gulped and wrapped her hands around her cup. "He said over the past couple of months, though, he's felt a strong pull to the mission field—*foreign* mission field—and that he's considering putting in for a post with a missions organization he found through the seminary."

Her tear-filled eyes met Ally's across the table. "If God brought us together, why wouldn't both us feel this *calling*? I've honestly never given missions a thought. And now ... well, it's all I think about. And I'm terrified."

"Can you tell me more about that? About what scares you?"

Melody didn't say anything for a moment as her brow furrowed. She took another sip of her chocolate, then another before setting it back down. "Losing Alan?" A tear slipped down her face. "What if after all of this, we're not meant to be together?"

Boy, did Ally understand *that*. She reached out to put her hand on Melody's arm resting on the table. "Let's not go there quite yet, not before we dig a little deeper. When you say you've been thinking about missions but it terrifies you, *that's* what I want to know. What do you think about when you consider going out into the field with Alan?"

Melody swiped at her cheek. "Well ... I guess being so far from home. From what's familiar. Safety's a concern too. And children. You said you were raised on the mission field, but I can't imagine having children in a foreign country."

"Completely valid fear. So, let me tell you a little about living on the field." She sat up and took a deep breath. "I was born while my parents were serving in Nicaragua, and I didn't know anything except the mission field until I was twelve, when we moved to the States for a year after my mother passed away. My brother and I grew up speaking two languages, playing with kids who looked nothing like us, didn't sound like us, yet none of it mattered. They spent time with us in our home, and we spent time in their homes, learning the customs, traditions, and even trades of the people my parents served."

She smiled. "I remember the first rug I wove. It was a little thing, more the size of a welcome mat. But I thought it was beautiful, with all of the bright colors I chose. I was around nine, I think. I gave that little rug to my mom, and she went on and on like it was a true work of art. Actually hung it on the wall like a tapestry. That was in El Salvador, a year before we left for Honduras."

Melody's eyes widened. "You were in three different countries?"

"Three countries, four missions, actually, before my mother died. An undiagnosed heart condition unrelated to their work." She waited for the grief to wash through her, as it always did when she allowed herself to remember. But it failed to show, and in its place came a flood of warmth with the memories filing through her head. As if finally sharing all of that grief and sorrow she'd buried inside had swept it out of the way, leaving room for the joy of remembering her mother's wonderful life instead of only the pain of her passing.

Zane had given her that. Had given her the freedom to remember, to share her mother's life with others instead of letting the grief keep her buried in the dark recesses of Ally's heart.

Melody gave her hand a gentle squeeze. "I'm so sorry you lost your mother. Especially so young. I can't imagine."

"It was difficult. We spent a year in the States after that, then my dad was called by the organization he works for to replace a doctor at a mission in Guatemala. I lived there until I was eighteen and came here for college."

"Five missions." Melody swallowed hard. "By the time you were thirteen?"

"Yes, but not all mission assignments are like that. Before we lost my mom, my parents' principal function was to establish new medical missions in remote areas, then move on once they were up and running with new staff and facilities. When my father and I went to Guatemala, it was for a permanent position, for as long as he wants it.

"But I know missionaries who have been at the same mission their entire ministry. It really can be a wonderful upbringing for a child. And very safe, depending on where you go. My dad's served his entire career in Central America, and although there are regions that can be somewhat dicey, we've never had to be evacuated or moved for our safety."

"I see. And they train you, right? For the area you're being assigned to?"

"Yes, definitely. Training in culture, language, and for whatever type of mission you're being assigned to. As a teacher, your services would be in high demand, either to teach the children of other missionaries or the children where you might serve."

Melody's dark eyes stared at her for a long moment, as if drinking in every word. "But you had no other family there, right?"

"Not by blood, but you make family wherever you are. My best friend from Guatemala is my best friend to this very day. Although she's of the indigenous people there, we're like sisters and came out here together for college and still live together. Or will until she gets married in May."

Harper chuckled. "I'm going to be big as a blimp in that wedding. My due date is three weeks after."

Ally smiled at her. "You'll be beautiful as ever."

The corners of Melody's mouth barely lifted in a smile at Harper before she looked down to study her cup. This girl really was struggling, and Ally prayed she could help her make the best decision. If she truly didn't feel called to the mission field and Alan did, well, that didn't bode well for their future.

Ally knew the heartbreak of that all too well. At least she and Zane hadn't made plans for the future, not like Alan and Melody.

"You told me you and Alan had always planned to work together in ministry here, preferably at Grace. So, let me ask you. Have you been called to ministry? Do you have a passion for serving others, no matter what walk of life they come from, with the goal of bringing them to Christ?"

"Yes, absolutely. I'm a teacher, but my degree is in biblical studies because I've always wanted to be in ministry."

"That's wonderful. So, when you talk to the Lord about where He wants to use you, are you open to the idea He may want to use you elsewhere? You and Alan could no doubt do amazing things right here in Arlington, at the church where you grew up, where you're comfortable. But when you talk about working in ministry, are you accepting it as a true *calling*, or an occupation? Because there's a difference."

Melody's perfectly arched brows drew together as she studied Ally. "Hmm. Wow. That's a powerful question."

"I hope I haven't offended you. I'm not here to tell you where God wants you, or even if you're supposed to be with Alan. That's between you, Alan, and the Lord. All I can do is give you food for thought. Maybe challenge you to have an honest heart-to-heart with God. If He's truly calling you to ministry, that could be anywhere in the world. And if He sends you and Alan, as a family, a unit, to a foreign mission field, He's going to equip and use you powerfully for His kingdom because you're willing to go where He leads."

The dark eyes still looking back at her filled with tears. "No. I'm not offended. But I am convicted. And that's not from you, that's the Spirit."

She looked back down at the cup clutched between her hands. Ally met Harper's eyes across the table and caught her wink. Deciding to let Melody process whatever was happening in her head and heart, Ally picked a bite off her muffin with her fingers.

After a long pause, Melody looked back at her. "I know I've been called to ministry. But I believe what I've been doing is telling God what *I* want to do for Him rather than asking Him what *He* wants me to do for Him. I need to start there before I make any decisions about getting married or not. I'm madly in love with Alan, but I need to do what you said. Be honest before God, talk to Him about my uncertainties, my fears, but be willing to go. Just … go. And if that's the same direction as Alan, all the better."

Ally's throat tightened, and the bite of muffin she tried to swallow almost choked her. Her breathing turned shallow, and her thoughts spun as Melody's words ricocheted in her head. *I've been telling God what I want to do for Him rather than asking Him what He wants me to do …*

She tore her gaze from Melody to look over at Harper, who studied her with narrowed eyes. *I've been telling God what I want to do …*

The voices of the other diners, the music from the overhead speakers, the clanking of dishes, all faded to the background as her pulse thumped in her ears … *telling God …*

Harper turned to the other woman and reached for her hand. "That's a great place to start, Melody. Right there with God. He understands the things He sometimes requires of us are difficult. But that's because He wants us to rely on Him and Him alone. Not our intellect, not our training or knowledge, not our own strength. Just Him. Because He's the only one sure thing."

Melody's phone pinged with an incoming text, and she pulled the device from her purse. "Oh, it's Alan. We're meeting with a caterer in half an hour."

"Let's pray real quick before you leave." Harper reached across the small round table and took Ally's hand on one side while Melody slipped hers into her other.

Bowing her head, she tried to focus on Harper's words but could barely hear them over the sound of her own convictions.

Seems like it's exactly what you were made for. She could still hear Dawn's words from that last day on the pediatric floor.

You're a natural. As if you were made for ministry. Had it really only been a month since Harper had exhorted her to dig deep for the courage to ask God what He would have her do for Him?

After they prayed, she somehow stood on shaky legs to give Melody a hug before the other girl turned to leave.

She sank back down in her chair as Harper again took hers. Ally didn't look at her but she could sense her friend's eyes on her. Silence sat between them for several ticks of the clock while Ally ran her fingers over the charms around her neck. The state of Texas, the little house, the dog, the flowers. Then, finally, the cross, where they rested against its sharp lines.

Are you sure, Al? That this isn't your calling? You're so amazing with the people here.

Harper reached over and tapped on her hand, drawing her attention. "Something just happened, didn't it? What's going on, sweetie?"

I've been telling God ... "I ... I don't know. I just—I need ..." She stopped and swallowed. "I think I might've needed to hear what Melody had to say rather than the other way around."

CHAPTER FORTY-TWO

*A*t the sound of crunching gravel on the drive outside, Zane looked up from his laptop and peered out the window. "They're here."

Pastor Ethan, sitting on the other side of the desk he'd insisted Zane use since he still shouldered the bulk of the pastoral work, smiled and stood slowly to his feet. "I'm looking forward to meeting your friends."

Zane held the door for him. The minister had made great strides in his healing and mobility over the past month he'd been home. The woman he'd saved that day still had a long recovery ahead of her, but she'd sent notes of gratitude through her husband to both Ethan and Zane. Written simply, as she probably had no more than a third or fourth grade education, her words poured out her thankfulness. That although her life was forever changed, she would use her scars to tell the story of God's loving care.

Zane kept his note pinned to the bulletin board in his bedroom, along with others from their parishioners and pictures drawn by little hands that made his heart swell every time he looked at them. He loved these people. And if this weekend planning session worked as he hoped, they'd be able to do so much more for them.

After the van pulled to a stop on the circular drive, Jose jumped down from the driver's seat as Zane ran up to open the side door. He was smiling like an idiot, but he'd missed these friends of his so much in the last two-plus months since he first set foot in Pamoca.

Wyatt was the first to climb out, giving Zane a quick hug before opening the passenger door and leaning over his pregnant wife in the front seat. Mason and Rhonda followed, but Zane's attention was on Harper.

He moved beside Wyatt. "Is she okay?"

"Car sick, we think." Wyatt put his hand on her leg as she sat with her head down and arms crossed over her barely-there baby bump.

More people climbed out of the van behind him, but Zane still stared at Harper. "Oh, man. What can I do?"

"I've got her." The body that belonged to that voice he'd know anywhere, anytime, pushed between himself and Wyatt, her usual mane of honey-blonde hair pulled up into a ponytail.

Ally? Was here?

Unable as yet to come up with a proper greeting, he stared at her back as she knelt next to the van with a small cooler at her feet. She slid open the lid and grabbed—

"Soda?" He finally found his voice and that's all he could come up with?

Ally nodded but didn't turn. "Carbonation helps reduce the acid and alleviates nausea. Plus, I think her blood sugar is low, which doesn't help." She popped the top and held it up to Harper. "Small sips."

Harper's eyes widened. "But the caffeine—"

"You won't ingest near enough to be any risk to the baby."

Tears welled in Harper's eyes, and Ally rose to her feet to put her hand on her friend's shoulder. "Honey, what happened wasn't because of anything you did during your pregnancy.

She was born healthy. I promise you. I would never encourage you to do anything I thought would bring harm to this little one. But we need to get your blood sugar up, and this is the quickest way I know that will also help with the nausea."

Harper nodded and took the cola for a small sip, followed by another.

Zane met Wyatt's eyes over Ally's head, his own burning when he realized they'd been talking about the four-year-old daughter Harper had lost to cancer nearly six years ago. Of course Harper would be extra cautious. And once again, Ally had worked her magic on a terrified patient, just as she had an injured teenager in pain at an amusement park, and the patients he'd witnessed her serve here in Pamoca. She had a true gift for caring for people.

He knew, because he'd been one of them. His wound may not have been physical, but her tender care had walked him through the healing he'd needed in order to let his mom back into his life. She'd given him the gift of a love restored he doubted he would have known if not for her.

A hand came to his shoulder, and he somehow pulled his attention from Ally to find Steve behind him, along with Wyatt's brother Reed. He reached out to hug his good friend. "Hey, man. Great to see you."

Steve chuckled. "At least larger than a two-inch square on a computer screen."

Reed shook his hand. "It's been a while, Carpenter. You look good. Very tanned."

"The weather here is amazing," Zane replied, glancing back at Ally in time to see her look away. Was she as aware of him as he was of her? Every nerve sat on end simply from seeing her. So unexpected, but so welcome. He turned back to Reed and Steve. "At least until the rains come, I hear."

Once Harper was a bit steadier, she took Wyatt's hand and let him help her out of the van.

Zane pointed toward the bungalows a few yards away.

"Mine's the blue one. You, Mason, and Rhonda are bunking there. Two bedrooms but you'll have to share a bath. Go on in to get her settled and I'll grab your bags. If she needs food, I stocked up the fridge and pantry yesterday. Help yourself to anything. We won't be having dinner for another couple of hours, over on the patio by the church."

Ethan looked at Zane. "I'll walk them over, make sure she gets settled."

"Thank you." He scanned the group standing by the van. "Everybody, this is Ethan Sullivan. Ethan, these are my good friends, Reed McCowan, Mason and Rhonda Carlysle, and Wyatt and Harper McCowan. Wyatt's the Director of ConnectUP, and Harper's the neck that turns the head."

Wyatt laughed and shook Ethan's hand. "The man speaks the truth. Nice to meet you."

Harper gave them a sheepish grin, a little more color in her cheeks. "And I'm too tired to argue the point. Nice to finally meet you, Pastor. I look forward to seeing your wife tonight."

Ethan grinned. "She's anxious to meet all of you, as well. We all have been. Let's go let you lie down for a bit." He looked over at Reed. "I can also walk you over to Cal's."

Reed gave him a thumbs up. "Sounds great. Anxious to take a look around this beautiful facility."

The group started down the walkway, Harper between her husband and brother-in-law with the Carlysles following behind. "I was fine until about twenty minutes ago," she told Ethan. "These roads sure wind around."

Their voices trailed off as they made their way slowly toward the bungalow, Wyatt holding onto Harper, and Harper still carrying that soda. With the McCowans and Carlysles staying the weekend in Zane's bungalow, he'd planned to bunk in the spare room at the Kincaids. But their surprise guest would need that room, so Zane would have to find a couch somewhere. Which wouldn't be a problem. He'd be happy to sleep outside if it meant Ally was here.

He stole another look at her as she leaned into the van to retrieve her things. Had she lost weight? She sure hadn't needed to, but her jeans hung on her a bit. Hopefully, he hadn't been the cause of that.

Steve hooked a thumb over his shoulder, grabbing Zane's attention again. "Jose's going to take me over to the Morales' house to drop my things and say hello. Yolanda couldn't get away this time, but they offered to put me up."

Zane nodded. "Of course they did. You're family to them now, even if it's not official yet."

Steve's smile lit up his face. "It will be on May twenty-eighth. You'll be there, right?"

"Wouldn't miss it, my friend."

"Then would you do me the honor of being my best man?"

Zane's mouth fell slack. "Of course! The honor would be mine." And with Ally no doubt standing with Yolanda, they'd be paired up, which suited him right down to the ground. He held his hand out to Steve. "Thanks, man."

Steve pulled him in for another guy-hug before climbing back into the van with Pastor Jose.

When Zane turned to Ally, their gazes collided, like two cars headed full speed toward one another, and the impact was just as great. Whatever had been in his heart before she left him in Pamoca over two months ago was still there. Maybe even more intense than it had been before, if the rate of his pulse and the sheer will it took to not haul her into his arms was any clue. Good thing she had that cooler and a large tote gripped in her hands in front of her, or he just might.

Then she smiled, a small, uncertain smile. "Hi."

His lungs finally remembered how to function. "Hi. I didn't know you were coming." Yeah, that was smooth. "I mean, I'm really glad you did. I just wasn't aware."

She glanced down and back up again. "Kind of a last-minute decision, I guess you could say. My temp job ended Wednesday, and I haven't put in for a new one. Harper told me a couple of weeks ago they were coming down here, so I called her yesterday and invited myself along. Just lucky I could still get a seat on their flight." She tilted her head and narrowed her eyes. "I'm anxious to hear more about this new project of yours."

His cheeks burned. "I would've read you in, but I knew how busy you were with new launches and getting the student leader task force underway. Plus your job. This was a separate thing, so I've just been working with Wyatt, Mason, and Reed on it. And Maggie the last couple of weeks."

"That's okay. I hope you don't mind if I tag along and sit in for your discussions. I might have one or two things to offer." Her smile widened and the day turned brighter.

He chuckled. "No doubt you have more than that. You'd be a welcome addition." He stepped close and put his hand to her arm. "It's really good to see you."

Pink suffused her cheeks. "It's good to see you too."

His gaze fell to the necklace around her neck and the small silver cross lying against her flowered blouse. Where were her other pendants? Her dreams? He looked back up at her, and she must have seen the questions in his eyes.

"I was hoping we could find some time to talk," she said quietly. "I know you're busy—"

"Count on it. We're going to give everybody the tour this afternoon, but maybe after dinner?"

She nodded. "I'd like that. I'm going to grab my bag, go say hi to Dad and Nora—they didn't know I was coming, either—then go check on Harper. Her nausea came on really fast, so I think it's more about her blood sugar level and she'll bounce back pretty quickly."

He glanced behind him at the bungalow and back again. "That thing about Megan being born healthy but then getting sick—is Harper worried about this baby?"

Ally gave her head a small tilt. "We've talked about it a little. Losing a child ... that's unimaginable. So, although she's very excited about this baby, she has a little anxiety about what could happen, either during the pregnancy or once she's here. But Harper being who she is, she's using it as an opportunity to grow in her faith. Learning to leave it all in God's hands."

"That sounds like Harper. I'll be praying more specifically in that regard. I didn't know she was anxious about it, but it's easy to see why." A grin spread across his face. "*She?* It's a girl?"

Ally smiled back. "They found out last week. Wyatt's beside himself at the thought of being a girl-dad. He'd be happy either way, of course, but I think he was really hoping for a girl."

"He'll be a great dad, no doubt. And Harper's a natural mom. That's one blessed little girl."

"That she is." Their eyes locked and held for a long moment. "I'll join y'all on your tour after I check in on Harper."

"Absolutely."

At the back of the van, she picked up her bag while he grabbed Wyatt and Harper's and watched as she made her way to the clinic to see her dad and Nora.

His thoughts ran the gamut of possibilities of what *talk* could mean. Did she want to discuss the state of their relationship, whatever it was? Or was it merely some ConnectUP business and he was reading too much into it? She hadn't put in for a new temporary freelance position, and her pendants that represented her Lone Star dreams were gone. Could she be considering a move?

His pulse skipped. Was she thinking of coming back to Pamoca? If so, that could upend all the plans he'd already set in motion.

Plans he'd hoped would bring them closer together, not farther apart.

CHAPTER FORTY-THREE

"*I*'ll be right back."

Ally left Zane on the walkway in front of her dad and Nora's bungalow. She'd apologized earlier for taking his weekend quarters while the two married couples stayed in his bungalow, but he assured her he'd been invited to take the couch at Ethan and Alana's and that worked fine for him.

Night had fallen, along with the temperature, while the missionaries treated them to a feast of Guatemalan specialties —tamales wrapped in banana leaves, carne asada with meat grilled over an open flame, rice with spices and vegetables, and savory black beans, all served with homemade tortillas that rendered the store-bought variety almost unpalatable. Sitting next to Harper, who had clearly recovered from her motion sickness, as evidenced by the sheer amount of food that disappeared from her plate, Ally wondered if Zane might take the seat on the other side of her. Rhonda beat him to it, however, so she had to settle for stealing glances his way throughout the meal.

Seeing him again in person only confirmed what she already knew—her love for him had only grown in the two months they'd been apart. She had no way of knowing if his feelings for her had changed at all, except to come right out and ask.

In the small guest bedroom of the bungalow, she picked up the items she'd left on the dresser and put them carefully into the pocket of her jeans. Hopefully, she could explain their significance to Zane so he would understand the decision she'd come to over the last three weeks.

She took a deep breath and closed her eyes. "Father, give me the right words. And Your will be done for both of us, whichever way we're supposed to go."

Outside, she found him gazing up into the night sky. A canopy of stars hung over this little part of the world, made up of a million points of light. Knowing God called them each by name, just as He knew her and every living being on the face of the earth, brought her comfort when things were so uncertain. The peace that passes all understanding.

When she came to Zane's side, he gave her that grin that made her heart skip every time. Oh, how she'd missed it. "Ready for a walk?"

He nodded. "Definitely. I need it after that meal."

The others had retired to their respective homes for the night after a busy day, leaving the two of them alone to stroll along the walkway through the compound. He told her about the video calls he'd had with his mom over the past two months, she told him about the huge success of the Fort Worth club launch. He shared about the new converts they'd added to their number at the mission church, and she told him about the inaugural meeting of the student leader task force.

"Those kids are phenomenal. The ideas they were throwing around, the brainstorming. Our kids are going to change the world."

"No doubt. Wish I could've been there."

Silence stretched between them until she cleared her

throat. "Everybody misses you, but they understand why you need to be here. We all do."

"It's been an experience of a lifetime." He looked over at her. "Thank you for bringing me here. For ... well, for everything."

"I think God brought you here, but if I helped, then you're welcome." She looked down at the path in front of them. "That's kind of what I wanted to talk to you about."

"About God bringing me here?"

She stopped, and he turned to face her. "About Him bringing *me* here."

His eyes widened. "What? When? I mean, are you talking about right now, or when you moved here with your dad?"

"Either. Both." She shook her head. "The last few weeks have been a bit of a spiritual roller coaster for me. It started when Harper and I met with a young lady from church whose fiancé suddenly dropped on her that he feels called to the foreign mission field. Harper thought I might be able to help her understand a bit more about living and working in another country, and Melody said something before she left that day that literally took my breath away."

"What was that?"

"That she finally understood that all along, she'd been telling God what she wanted to do for Him instead of *asking* Him what He would have her do. And I saw myself immediately in that statement."

His hand reached for hers between them. "Al, I've seen your commitment to God and to ministry. Seems to me you've been very obedient to what He's called you to do. ConnectUP is where it is today largely because of the work you've done."

"And I've loved it. Every minute of it. It's exactly where I want to be. But you see, I never asked Him if that's where *He* wants me. I told Him that's where I wanted to be and I would be happy to serve there. Ever since I came to Texas for school, *that's* the only place I wanted to be. Where I wanted to live and grow roots and start a family and raise my kids someday. In one place.

"But when Melody confessed her spiritual short-sightedness, I was brought face-to-face with my own. And I knew I needed to be true to what I professed. That if I want to be one hundred percent on board with who God wants me to be, and be where He wants me to be, I have to be willing to go."

She reached into her pocket with one hand and turned his palm up with the other. "And I have to be willing to *let* go." She dropped the small silver Texas, house, flowers, and dog pendants into his hand. "I've worn these for years. To remind me of my dreams and what was important to me. But now all that matters is the cross. Everything has to be centered on Christ, or it doesn't work."

"Ally." He said her name on a breath. "Are you saying you want to come here? To stay?"

"I'm saying I want to be where He can use me the most. If that's here, then the answer's yes. If it's with another mission in another country, then the answer's yes. If it's with ConnectUP, then the answer's yes."

Her stomach turned over as she stared up into the face she loved and curled his fingers around the pendants with her hand. "But part of this decision depends on you. Before I left two months ago, you said you still believed God had put us together for a reason, a reason beyond me just bringing you here. That we could do great things here. Together."

She swallowed hard as his gaze stayed latched onto hers, giving her no indication of his thoughts. "Two months is a significant amount of time, and things may have changed for you. And if they have, I accept that. But if you still believe there's a future for us —"

"I do. I absolutely do. I love you more today than I did the day you left. But, Ally, there's so much I need to tell you."

The hope she'd been carrying exploded into joy she could feel in every heartbeat, every breath, and she couldn't keep back the smile that spread across her face. "Can you kiss me first, then tell me? Because I'm dy—"

With a tug on her hand, he pulled her close, molding his lips to hers in that familiar way, as if they'd shared their last kiss yesterday and not so many weeks ago. Their arms drew around each other into a clinging embrace. When he broke the kiss and laid his forehead to hers, only then was she aware of the tears on her face.

"I love you, Z."

"I love you too. So much." He pulled back and swept his thumb across her cheek. "But there really is so much I need to tell you. Why everybody's here this weekend."

"Your project you've been working on. That involves ConnectUP somehow. That's all I know. When I asked Wyatt about it on the way here, he said he'd rather you tell me."

His face lit up as he let her go to pocket the charms she'd given him. "Short-term missions. Bringing our CU kids here, initially, then eventually growing it into other countries, mission projects in the States, service projects in the communities where our clubs meet. It would be an entirely new branch of ConnectUP."

"That's genius. So many of our kids are itching to get out and serve. I can think of half a dozen right now who would sign up tomorrow to work a short-term mission."

"Exactly! We'd have to provide avenues of fundraising, walk them through getting passports, any vaccinations they would need, what to expect when they get to their chosen mission. It's going to be a lot of work. But as you know, Becker's provided the resources for CU to bring on two full-time salaried employees."

"That's amazing. So, you're thinking someone to run the missions arm of the ministry full-time?"

"And someone to work full-time on development.

Everything you're already doing, but you could get paid for it. Recruiting new leaders, reaching out to churches in other communities and cities to determine where to launch a new club. Training. All of that."

He took her hands in his. "Ally, I was coming home in a couple of weeks. Back to Arlington. Back to you, if you'd have me. The leadership came here to get a feel for what our kids could do here, the ways they could serve here and at other missions. But it's pretty much a done deal. I'm coming on staff with ConnectUP to develop and manage missions and service projects."

Her mouth opened, but she couldn't speak for a moment. "You—you were coming home?"

He shook his head. "No. I *am* coming home. To you. Sweetheart, we could do this."

"Together."

"Absolutely together. Home base in Arlington."

"With trips down here maybe three or four times a year with kids for short-term missions."

"Long weekends, holiday breaks."

"Maybe even month or summer-long trips." She gripped tighter to his hands. "Can you imagine what those kids could accomplish if they were here for a few weeks?"

"This place would never be the same."

"And neither would they."

They stared at each other while the crickets played their night music.

"Ally. We could do this. You and me. And build something together at the same time. Both of us called to mission work but managing it all from Arlington. From home. A home I didn't even know I was looking for until I found it. Found *you*."

"Except my home is where you are. A true home isn't a place or a building. It's where your heart is. And my heart's with you."

"Then let's go back to Texas. Give this whole you-and-me

thing a whirl, work together to give kids a chance to serve, and just see where God takes us."

Tears filled her eyes as she stepped into his arms and threw hers around his neck. "I'd go anywhere with you."

His eyes shone with that dimpled grin. "Then let's go home."

EPILOGUE

*Z*ane smiled at the group in front of him, trying not to get choked up. "Again, let me say how grateful I am for you and how proud I am of all you accomplished this week. Beyond my wildest imaginings. Can't wait until next time!"

Cheers and applause rang out around the covered patio of the mission church on this rainy Sunday night. The last night of the first ConnectUP missions trip, a resounding success in every way. Leaving this place five months ago had been difficult, knowing how great the need but few the hands.

But how right that decision had been. To go back to Arlington, pick up where he'd left off with Ally, and both of them coming on staff at CU. She'd decided on a part-time position so she could keep up her nursing skills, as well as her certification, by continuing to work freelance the other twenty hours a week. The other half of that salaried position had gone to Tonya, who only had a couple of classes the last semester of her senior year and could continue to work part-time after she started college at Dallas Heritage in the fall. Planning to pursue a career in ministry upon graduation, she'd proved to be a valued addition to the team.

Seeing the dozen kids on this patio tonight, mixed in with

the adults who'd come along on the trip, as well as the missionaries they'd served beside, gave him all the feels he couldn't find words for. As if his dreams, mixed with the time and energy they'd put into planning, and adding in the sheer amount of work these kids and leaders had accomplished over the past seven days, had culminated in the best experience he'd ever had.

Only one thing could make it better. Having already spoken with Nathan earlier in the week, he was ready and eager to move to the next step.

He looked at the woman walking toward him, her gaze roaming over the patio, the corners of her mouth turned up in a contented smile as she came to a stop beside him.

"You look happy."

"I am happy. More than happy." Ally swept her arm in front of her. "Look at this. And seeing what these kids did this week. My mind is blown." She nudged him with her shoulder. "I told you this was a genius idea when you told me about it in February. That we got this all planned in five months is a minor miracle."

"*We* being the operative word there."

"It's been an amazing week. So much more than I ever imagined."

A hand clapped him on the shoulder, and he looked over at Wyatt standing behind them with Steve and Yolanda. Zane had found an affordable apartment to rent close to Ally's townhouse after moving out of Steve's a week before the wedding almost two months ago, and a nursing friend of Ally's had moved in with her.

As for Wyatt, the new dad had only flown down a couple of days ago to spend some time with the kids on this inaugural mission trip, but Zane was sure he was anxious to get back to his girls.

Wyatt stifled a yawn. "I know it's only eight-thirty, but I'm headed to bed. This could be the last full night's sleep I'll have in a while."

Ally laughed. "Little Miss keeping you awake?"

"Just a little. Harper tells me I can sleep, but if she has to be up with her, I feel like I should be too. Although I think she was glad to be rid of me for a couple of days. Says I hover too much."

Zane shook his head. "That Baby Grace has you tied around her teeny finger already."

"True story."

"I can't blame you. She has her Uncle Zane pretty smitten too. Oh, and happy anniversary. Your first and you're spending it apart."

"We celebrated with a nice, quiet dinner out the night before I left while Harper's sister watched Gracie. It's all good."

Steve drew his arm around his wife. "We're headed back to the Morales' to spend some time with the family before we leave tomorrow."

"I'm sure they were happy to see you again so soon after the wedding."

Yolanda nodded. "They've actually been over the moon at how much they've seen me over the last few months. And they love this husband of mine as much as they do me."

Steve shrugged. "Maybe not as much, but close."

They laughed at Steve before Ally and Yolanda hugged each other good night while the men shook hands.

As their friends left, Zane took Ally's hand. "Sounds like the rain's let up. Walk with me?"

"Sure. I love how fresh everything smells after the rain."

He led her off the patio and onto the gravel walkway that meandered through the compound, in the middle of which stood two large tents that had been erected to house the kids and leaders for the week. Zane had wondered if the teens would complain about having to go into the other buildings to use the facilities, but not one of them had. Even when they were given a schedule so each kid would know whose residence they were assigned to for five-minute showers. It had all worked like a charm.

Zane smiled at the woman by his side. "You know you didn't have to sleep on a cot all week. You could've stayed with your dad and Nora."

She shook her head. "No way was I staying in a cushy house while everybody else bunked it out here. I came as a chaperone, so it was important to me to stay with the group. And, to be honest, it was fun. We'd get in our pajamas and sit in the middle of the floor with our pillows and blankets and talk by flashlight. About what they did that day, what they learned, who they got to know. A lot of really fantastic heart-to-hearts, girls really opening up to each other, even though they're from different clubs."

She pointed at him. "One thing I want to do, so don't let me forget, is get something for Tonya when we get home. A thank you gift. She's been an absolute god-send for translating. Some of the kids know rudimentary Spanish and could get by, some of the others don't know a lick of it, and Tonya was a huge help."

"Great idea. Having her and Finn along as mentors on this trip has been huge. Finn gets the boys up and rallied in the mornings. They'll both make excellent team leaders."

"And we're going to need them with all the new club launches coming up."

"Speaking of launches, how'd your brother's last one go? That's four now, right?"

"Yep. Went great. And he can't wait to take the position CU offered him to head up that region. Who knew we'd be outside of Texas within a year?"

He shrugged. "Just God. And it's sure been a fun ride. I only wish Wyatt would take a salary for all he does."

Ally laughed. "He won't do that until he's no longer

working at his counseling practice. How he keeps up with all of it is beyond me, but he loves counseling kids. He won't take a salary with ConnectUP when he'd rather see it go for another staff position."

"Speaking of staff, now that Finn's stepfather's company has provided a huge influx of funds, we need to start thinking about retreats and camps. That'll be another whole division. Wyatt mentioned to me today he'd like to see our first official ConnectUP camp launch next summer."

"Lots of exciting stuff."

He stopped and turned to take both of her hands in his, grinning down at her. "You know what today is, don't you?"

Her brow wrinkled. "Sunday ... the seventeenth ... Wyatt and Harper's anniver—" Her eyes lit up with her smile. "The night we met. A year ago today."

"Almost to the hour. My life changed that night, and I didn't even know it yet. Now I can't imagine not being here. And I don't mean in Guatemala or Texas or with ConnectUP. I mean *here*. With you. Anywhere with you. You're the miracle God brought into my life to make me finally whole."

Her hands tightened on his. "You're going to make me cry. But I feel the same. That you're that missing part of me I wasn't even aware I needed."

All of the things he felt for her filled his chest and tightened his throat. He looked down at their joined hands for a moment before bringing his moisture-filled eyes back to her. "Ally, you really are my everything. First thing I think of when I wake up, the one I can't wait to see every day, the last thing I think about at night. The one who prays with me, and laughs with me, and keeps me on point when my scattered thoughts threaten to take me off on another tangent. You've given me so much of yourself, so I want to give you something back."

As he reached into his pocket, he brought her hand up with his other. "Your dreams." He clasped a silver charm bracelet around her wrist. "I want to give you your dreams and make even more with you. Like this one."

His fingers found the charm he'd added to the others she'd handed him five months before, and she covered her mouth when she saw the tiny bride and groom hanging from the chain. He reached into his other pocket, and tears fell down her cheeks when he knelt to one knee and held up a sparkling diamond ring.

"Allyson Marie Kincaid, you're the one who made me want to stop moving and be still long enough to find a true home. And I want that home to be with you. Ally. Will you marry me, dream some more dreams with me, make a home with me?"

More tears fell as she nodded. "Yes. Yes to all of it."

After sliding the ring onto her finger—a perfect fit thanks to intel from Yolanda—he stood and pulled her close for a soul-binding kiss as the group gathered on the edge of the patio several yards away erupted in cheers. They pulled apart, laughing as they cried, having no idea they'd had an audience.

He looked down into her beaming face. "I can't wait to make a home with you, Ally Kincaid."

Her arms tightened around his neck. "With a dog, our own garden. And Jesus in the middle of it all."

ACKNOWLEDGMENTS

Have you ever had one of those encounters you absolutely knew was of divine origin? Well, I had one of those the first day of the 2022 ACFW National Conference, when I met Natalie Arauco on the way to the Finalists Reception. We got acquainted as we walked through the maze of hallways at the Hyatt and realized we were from cities near each other in Texas. But what she told me next stopped me in my tracks.

When I started the first draft of "Love's True Home", I knew Ally had been raised on the mission field, but I wasn't sure where. Somehow, I landed on Guatemala and started my research.

Enter Natalie. A TRUE BLUE MISSIONARY IN GUATEMALA, Y'ALL!! I couldn't believe it when she told me she was currently serving as a teacher in the Guatemalan village of Chivoc. Talk about a God moment. Over the next several months, we had Zoom calls and exchanged emails. She graciously answered my myriad questions, sent me dozens of photos and videos of the area where she serves, gave me ideas for plot points, and brainstormed with me for world-building and scene ideas. That's how the city of Pamoca was born.

I've gotten to know Natalie during this venture, and for that alone, I am grateful. She's a true servant of God, and I pray for her and her ministry regularly. If you'd like to know more about Natalie and her work, follow her at https://natalieinguatemala.com/. I am so thankful for her willingness to share her experience. It brought Guatemala to life for me, which I hope translated onto the page.

This book would not exist without my writer posse. Thank you from the bottom of my heart to Kristi Woods and Wendy Klopfenstein, my sisters from our KWL Crit Group. When I was pressed up against my deadline, they read multiple chapters in a week's time and gave me exceptional feedback. Many thanks also to Lori Altebaumer, brainstorm and critique partner extraordinaire. Thank you for helping this book get born (terrible grammar, I know) and for all of the amazing encouragement and advice along the way.

I'm so grateful for my writer groups that encourage, support, educate, and inspire me to keep going. ACFW National, ACFW Dallas/Ft. Worth, CenTex Writers Group, Faith, Hope, and Love Christian Writers and my FHL South Central ladies, Novel Academy, and 540 Community.

I love being a part of the Scrivenings Press family, and so appreciate my editors, Heidi Glick and Amy Anguish. Thank you for putting the polish on a diamond in the rough.

The day I turned in this manuscript, my dad had been in the hospital for eight days. I'd go sit with him and work while he slept. It wasn't the ideal setting for inspiration, but I'm so grateful I had that time with him. I was at his bedside holding his hand when he passed peacefully into the arms of Jesus thirteen days later. He's rejoicing in heaven while we miss him terribly here in this life. It warms my heart that he lived to see my dream of being a published author come true and he was so encouraging as I wrote this next book in the series.

Thank you also to my mom, my husband, Eric, and my daughter, Michaela, for traveling along with me on this journey. I wouldn't be able to continue if not for them and their unending love and support. I love you with all my heart.

Finally, all the praise, honor and glory go to my Heavenly Father, the ultimate author of all that is good and lovely and worthy of praise. My most fervent hope is that the words on the pages of this book reflect the light of His love to a dark world.

ABOUT THE AUTHOR

Hey there, y'all! I find writing about my fictional characters much more fun and exciting than writing about myself, but here goes.

First of all, I love Jesus and the Bible and writing stories full of grace and the redemptive power of God's love that inspire others to get to know Him better. I couldn't ask for any more than that from the words I put to paper. Nothing else matters.

I was born and raised in Phoenix, Arizona, but arrived in Texas in 2005 and dug those roots right in. I do love me some Texas, especially here in beautiful Georgetown, where my husband and I live in our empty nest (except for our two fur babies, Buddy and Lily). We have one daughter, Michaela, who is living and thriving in the Dallas area and is the absolute joy of my life.

I love to write about love and romance and all that fun stuff, with a firm foundation of faith. Clean but sassy, sparkly, and even goose-bumpy romance is a *thing*, y'all! With God in the middle, and with characters seeking and learning and changing, nothing could be more heartwarming or spine-tingly.

My debut novel, *Love's True Calling*, was the 2020 winner of the Scrivenings Press Novel Starts Contest, the 2022 winner of the ACFW Genesis Award for Romance, and a double finalist in the 2024 Selah Awards. It was published by Scrivenings Press in June 2023, *Love's True Home* is Book Two of the series, and *Love's True Measure* will release in 2025.

ALSO BY LORI DEJONG

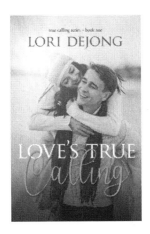

Love's True Calling
by Lori DeJong

After years of jumping through other people's hoops to be all they thought she should be, and enduring a tragedy no mother should, self-described "newbie" Christian, Harper Townsend, has finally found her true calling ... and her true love. Until it appears that to follow one may mean leaving the other behind.

Adolescent Psychologist, Wyatt McCowan, is beyond delighted to have *the-girl-who-got-away* back in his life—and his heart. But even as they fall more in love, he realizes that being obedient to God's calling on each of their lives may pull them apart. She rejected him once in favor of another, which left him hurt and angry. But this time, he can't fault her for following hard after the God she loves with all her heart, even if it means leaving him once again.

Get your copy here:

https://scrivenings.link/lovestruecalling

~

Scrivenings
PRESS
Quench your thirst for story.
www.ScriveningsPress.com

Stay up-to-date on your favorite books and authors with our free e-newsletters.

ScriveningsPress.com